About the Authors

Liz Fielding was born with itchy feet. She made it to Zambia before her twenty-first birthday and, gathering her own special hero and a couple of children on the way, lived in Botswana, Kenya and Bahrain—with pauses for sightseeing pretty much everywhere in between. She finally came to a full stop in a tiny Welsh village cradled by misty hills, and these days mostly leaves her pen to do the traveling.

For news of upcoming books—and to sign up for her occasional newsletter—visit Liz's website, www.lizfielding.com

Meredith Webber lives on the sunny Gold Coast in Queensland, Australia, but takes regular trips west into the Outback, fossicking for gold or opal. These breaks in the beautiful and sometimes cruel red earth country provide her with an escape from the writing desk and a chance for her mind to roam free and supply the kernels of so many stories it's hard for her to stop writing!

New York Times bestselling author **Shirley Jump** didn't have the will-power to diet, nor the talent to master under-eye concealer, so she bowed out of a career in television and opted instead for a career where she could be paid to eat at her desk—writing… and she turned to the world of romance novels, where messes are (usually) cleaned up before The End.

The Forever Family

COLLECTION

July 2019

August 2019

September 2019

October 2019

A Forever Family: Falling For You

LIZ FIELDING

MEREDITH WEBBER

SHIRLEY JUMP

MIX
Paper from
responsible sources
FSC
FSC C007454

This book is produced from independently certified FSC™ paper
to ensure responsible forest management.

For more information visit: www.harpercollins.co.uk/green

Printed and bound in Spain by CPI, Barcelona.

MILLS & BOON

First Published in Great Britain 2019
By Mills & Boon, an imprint of HarperCollins *Publishers*
1 London Bridge Street, London, SE1 9GF

A FOREVER FAMILY: FALLING FOR YOU
© 2019 Harlequin Books S.A.

The Last Woman He'd Ever Date © Liz Fielding 2013
A Forever Family for the Army Doc © Meredith Webber 2017
One Day to Find a Husband © Shirley Kawa-Jump, LLC 2013

ISBN: 978-0-263-27681-7

THE LAST WOMAN
HE'D EVER DATE

LIZ FIELDING

With love
For my lovely daughter-in-law,
Veronique Allsopp-Hanskamp

CHAPTER ONE

Cranbrook Park for Sale?

THE future of the Cranbrook Park has been the subject of intense speculation this week after a move by HMRC to recover unpaid taxes sparked concern amongst the estate's creditors.

Cranbrook Park, the site of a 12th century Abbey, the ruins of which are still a feature of the estate, has been in continuous occupation by the same family since the 15th century. The original Tudor hall, built by Thomas Cranbrook, has been extended over the centuries and the Park, laid out in the late eighteenth century by Humphrey Repton, has long been at the heart of Maybridge society with both house and grounds generously loaned for charity events by the present baronet, Sir Robert Cranbrook.

The *Observer* contacted the estate office today for clarification of the situation, but no one was available for comment.
—*Maybridge Observer,* Thursday 21 April

Sir Robert Cranbrook glared across the table. Even from his wheelchair and ravaged by a stroke he was an impressive man, but his hand shook as he snatched the pen his lawyer offered and signed away centuries of power and privilege.

'Do you want a sample of my DNA, too, boy?' he demanded as he tossed the pen on the table. His speech was slurred but the arrogant disdain of five hundred years was in his eyes.

'Are you prepared to drag your mother's name through the courts in order to satisfy your pretensions? Because I will fight your right to inherit my title.'

Even now, when he'd lost everything, he still thought his name, the baronetcy that went with it, meant something.

Hal North's hand was rock steady as he picked up the pen and added his signature to the papers, immune to that insulting 'boy.'

Cranbrook Park meant nothing to him except as a means to an end. He was the one in control here, forcing his enemy to sit across the table and look him in the eye, to acknowledge the shift in power. That was satisfaction enough.

Nearly enough.

Cranbrook's pawn, Thackeray, hadn't lived to witness this moment, but his daughter was now his tenant. Evicting her would close the circle.

'You can't afford to fight me, Cranbrook,' he said, capping the pen and returning it to the lawyer. 'You owe your soul to the tax man and without me to bail you out you'd be a common bankrupt man living at the mercy of the state.'

'Mr North…'

'I have no interest in claiming you as my father. You refused to acknowledge me as your son when it would have meant something,' he continued, ignoring the protest from Cranbrook's solicitor, the shocked intake of breath from around the room. It was just the two of them confronting the past. No one else mattered. 'I will not acknowledge you now. I don't need your name and I don't want your title. Unlike you, I did not have to wait for my father to die before I took my place in the world, to be a man.'

He picked up the deeds to Cranbrook Park. Vellum, tied with red ribbon, bearing a King's seal. Now his property.

'I owe no man for my success. Everything I am, everything I own, Cranbrook, including the estate you have squandered, lost because you were too idle, too fond of easy living to hold it, I have earned through hard work, sweat—things you've always thought beneath you. Things that could have served you. Would have saved you from this if you were a better man.'

'You're a poacher, a common thief…'

'And now I'm dining with presidents and prime ministers, while you're waiting for God in a world reduced to a single room with a view of a flower-bed instead of the park created by Humphrey Repton for one of your more energetic ancestors.'

Hal turned to his lawyer, tossed him the centuries-old deeds as casually as he would toss a newspaper in a bin and stood up, wanting to be done with this. To breathe fresh air.

'Think about me sitting at your desk as I make that world my own, Cranbrook. Think about my mother sleeping in the Queen's bed, sitting at the table where your ancestors toadied to kings instead of serving at it.' He nodded to the witnesses. 'We're done here.'

'Done! We're far from done!' Sir Robert Cranbrook clutched at the table, hauled himself to his feet. 'Your mother was a cheating whore who took the money I gave her to flush you away and then used you as a threat to keep her useless drunk of a husband in a job,' he said, waving away the rush to support him.

Hal North had not become a multimillionaire by betraying his emotions and he kept his face expressionless, his hands relaxed, masking the feelings boiling inside him.

'You can't blackmail an innocent man, Cranbrook.'

'She didn't have to be pushed very hard to come back for more. Years and years more. She was mine, bought and paid for.'

'Hal…' The quiet warning came from his lawyer. 'Let's go.'

'Sleeping in a bed made for a queen won't change what she is and no amount of money will make you anything but trash.' Cranbrook raised a finger, no longer shaky, and pointed at him. 'Your hatred of me has driven you all these years, Henry North and now everything you ever dreamed of has finally fallen into your lap and you think you've won.'

Oh, yes…

'Enjoy your moment, because tomorrow you're going to be wondering what there's left to get out of bed for. Your wife left you. You have no children. We are the same you and I…'

'Never!'

'The same,' he repeated. 'You can't fight your genes.' His lips curled up in a parody of a smile. 'That's what I'll be thinking about when they're feeding me through a tube,' he said as he collapsed back into the chair, 'and I'll be the one who dies laughing.'

Claire Thackeray swung her bike off the road and onto the footpath that crossed Cranbrook Park estate.

The No Cycling sign had been knocked down by the quad bikers before Christmas and late for work, again, she didn't bother to dismount.

She wasn't a rule breaker by inclination but no one was taking their job for granted at the moment. Besides, hardly anyone used the path. The Hall was unoccupied but for a caretaker and any fisherman taking advantage of the hiatus in occupancy to tempt Sir Robert's trout from the Cran wouldn't give two hoots. Which left only Archie and he'd look the other way for a bribe.

As she approached a bend in the path, Archie, who objected to anyone travelling faster than walking pace past his meadow, charged the hedge. It was terrifying if you weren't expecting it—hence the avoidance by joggers—and pretty unnerving if you were. The trick was to have a treat ready and she reached in her basket for the apple she carried to keep him sweet.

Her hand met fresh air and as she looked down she had a mental image of the apple sitting on the kitchen table, before

Archie—not a donkey to be denied an anticipated treat—brayed his disapproval.

Her first mistake was not to stop and dismount the minute she realised she had no means of distracting him, but while his first charge had been a challenge, his second was the real deal. While she was still on the what, where, how, he leapt through one of the many gaps in the long-neglected hedge, easily clearing the sagging wire while she was too busy pumping the pedals in an attempt to outrun him to be thinking clearly.

Her second mistake was to glance back, see how far away he was and the next thing she knew she'd come to an abrupt and painful halt in a tangle of bike and limbs—not all of them her own—and was face down in a patch of bluebells growing beneath the hedge.

Archie stopped, snorted, then, job done, he turned around and trotted back to his hiding place to await his next victim. Unfortunately the man she'd crashed into, and who was now the bottom half of a bicycle sandwich, was going nowhere.

'What the hell do you think you're doing?' he demanded.

'Smelling the bluebells,' she muttered, keeping very still while she mentally checked out the 'ouch' messages filtering through to her brain.

There were quite a lot of them and it took her a while, but even so she would almost certainly have moved her hand, which appeared to be jammed in some part of the man's anatomy if it hadn't been trapped beneath the bike's handlebars. Presumably he was doing the same since he hadn't moved, either. 'Such a gorgeous scent, don't you think?' she prompted, torn between wishing him to the devil and hoping that he hadn't lost consciousness.

His response was vigorous enough to suggest that while he might have had a humour bypass—and honestly if you didn't laugh, well, with the sort of morning she'd had, you'd have to cry—he was in one piece.

Ignoring her attempt to make light of the situation he added, 'This is a footpath.'

'So it is,' she muttered, telling herself that he wouldn't have been making petty complaints about her disregard for the by-laws if he'd been seriously hurt. It wasn't a comfort. 'I'm so sorry I ran into you.' And she was. Really, really sorry.

Sorry that her broad beans had been attacked by a black-fly. Sorry that she'd forgotten Archie's apple. Sorry that Mr Grumpy had been standing in her way.

Until thirty seconds ago she had merely been late. Now she'd have to go home and clean up. Worse, she'd have to ring in and tell the news editor she'd had an accident which meant he'd send someone else to keep her appointment with the chairman of the Planning Committee.

He was going to be furious. She'd lived on Cranbrook Park all her life and she'd been assigned to cover the story.

'It's bad enough that you were using it as a race track—'

Oh, great. There you are lying in a ditch, entangled with a bent bicycle, with a strange man's hand on your backside—he'd better be trapped, too—and his first thought was to lecture her on road safety.

'—but you weren't even looking where you were going.'

She spat out what she hoped was a bit of twig. 'You may not have noticed but I was being chased by a donkey,' she said.

'Oh, I noticed.'

Not sympathy, but satisfaction.

'And what about you?' she demanded. Although her field of vision was small, she could see that he was wearing dark green coveralls. And she was pretty sure that she'd seen a pair of Wellington boots pass in front of her eyes in the split second before she'd crashed into the bank. 'I'd risk a bet you don't have a licence for fishing here.'

'And you'd win,' he admitted, without the slightest suggestion of remorse. 'Are you hurt?'

Finally...

'Only, until you move I can't get up,' he explained.

Oh, right. Not concern, just impatience. What a charmer.

'I'm so sorry,' she said, with just the slightest touch of sarcasm, 'but you shouldn't move after an accident.' She'd written up a first-aid course she'd attended for the women's page and was very clear on that point. 'In case of serious injury,' she added, to press home the point that he should be sympathetic. Concerned.

'Is that a fact? So what do you suggest? We just lie here until a paramedic happens to pass by?'

Now who was being sarcastic?

'I've got a phone in my bag,' she said. It was slung across her body and lying against her back out of reach. Probably a good thing or she'd have been tempted to hit him with it. What the heck did he think he was doing leaping out in front of her like that? 'If you can reach it, you could dial nine-nine-nine.'

'Are you hurt?' She detected the merest trace of concern so presumably the message was getting through his thick skull. 'I'm not about to call out the emergency services to deal with a bruised ego.'

No. Wrong again.

'I might have a concussion,' she pointed out. 'You might have concussion.' She could hope…

'If you do, you have no one but yourself to blame. The cycle helmet is supposed to be on your head, not in your basket.'

He was right, of course, but the chairman of the Planning Committee was old school. Any woman journalist who wanted a story had better be well-groomed and properly dressed in a skirt and high heels. Having gone to the effort of putting up her hair for the old misogynist, she wasn't about to ruin her hard work by crushing it with her cycle helmet.

She'd intended to catch the bus this morning. But if it weren't for the blackfly she could have caught the bus…

'How many fingers am I holding up?' Mr Grumpy asked.

'Oh…' She blinked as a muddy hand appeared in front of

her. The one that wasn't cradling her backside in a much too familiar manner. Not that she was about to draw attention to the fact that she'd noticed. Much wiser to ignore it and concentrate on the other hand which, beneath the mud, consisted of a broad palm, a well-shaped thumb, long fingers… 'Three?' she offered.

'Close enough.'

'I'm not sure that "close enough" is close enough,' she said, putting off the moment when she'd have to test the jangle of aches and move. 'Do you want to try that again?'

'Not unless you're telling me you can't count up to three.'

'Right now I'm not sure of my own name,' she lied.

'Does Claire Thackeray sound familiar?'

That was when she made the mistake of picking her face out of the bluebells and looking at him.

Forget concussion.

She was now in heart-attack territory. Dry mouth, loss of breath. Thud. Bang. Boom.

Mr Grumpy was not some irascible old bloke with a bee in his bonnet regarding the sanctity of footpaths—even if he was less than scrupulous about where he fished—and a legitimate grievance at the way she'd run him down.

He might be irritable, but he wasn't old. Far from it.

He was mature.

In the way that men who've passed the smooth-skinned prettiness of their twenties and fulfilled the potential of their genes are mature.

Not that Hal North had ever been pretty.

He'd been a raw-boned youth with a wild streak that had both attracted and frightened her. As a child she'd yearned to be noticed by him, but would have run a mile if he'd as much as glanced in her direction. As a young teen, she'd had fantasies about him that would have given her mother nightmares if she'd even suspected her precious girl of having such thoughts about the village bad boy.

Not that her mother had anything to worry about where Hal North was concerned.

She was too young for anything but the muddled fantasies in her head, much too young for Hal to notice her existence.

There had been plenty of girls of his own age, girls with curves, girls who were attracted to the aura of risk he generated, the edge of darkness that had made her shiver a little— shiver a lot—with feelings she didn't truly understand.

It had been like watching your favourite film star, or a rock god strutting his stuff on the television. You felt a kind of thrill, but you weren't sure what it meant, what you were supposed to do with it.

Or maybe that was just her.

She'd been a swot, not one of the 'cool' group in school who had giggled over things she didn't understand.

While they'd been practising being women, she'd been confined to experiencing it second-hand in the pages of nineteenth-century literature.

He'd bulked up since the day he'd been banished from the estate by Sir Robert Cranbrook after some particularly outrageous incident; what, she never discovered. Her mother had talked about it in hushed whispers to her father, but instantly switched to that bright, false change-the-subject smile if she came near enough to hear and she'd never had a secret-sharing relationship with any of the local girls.

Instead, she'd filled her diary with all kinds of fantasies about what might have happened, where he'd gone, about the day he'd return to find her all grown up—no longer the skinny ugly duckling but a fully fledged swan. Definitely fairy-tale material…

The years had passed, her diary had been abandoned in the face of increasing workloads from school and he'd been forgotten in the heat of a real-life romance.

Now confronted by him, as close as her girlish fantasy could ever have imagined, it came back in a rush and his power to attract, she discovered, had only grown over the years.

He was no longer a raw-boned skinny youth with shoulders he had yet to grow into, hands too big for his wrists. He still had hard cheekbones, though. A take-it-or-leave-it jaw, a nose that suggested he'd taken it once or twice himself. The only softness in his face, the sensuous curve of his lower lip.

It was his eyes, though, so dark in the shadow of overhanging trees, which overrode any shortfall in classic good looks. They had the kind of raw energy that made her blood tingle, her skin goose, had her fighting for breath in a way that had nothing to do with being winded by her fall.

She reminded herself that she was twenty-six. A responsible adult holding down a job, supporting her child. A grown woman who did not blush. At all.

'I'm surprised you recognised me,' she said, doing her best to sound calm, in control, despite the thudding heart, racing pulse, the mud smearing her cheek. The fact that her hand was jammed between his legs. Nowhere near in control enough to admit the intimacy of a name she had once whispered over and over in the dark of her room.

She snatched her hand away, keeping her 'ouch' to herself as she scraped her knuckles on the brake lever and told herself not to be so wet.

'You haven't changed much.' His tone suggested that it wasn't a subject for congratulation. 'Still prim, all buttoned-up. And still riding your bike along this footpath. I'll bet it was the only rule you ever broke.'

'There's nothing big about breaking rules,' she said, stung into attack by his casual dismissal of her best suit. The suggestion that she still looked the same now as when she'd worn a blazer and a panama hat over hair braided in a neat plait. 'Nothing big about hiding under the willows, tickling Sir Robert's trout, either. Not the only rule you ever broke,' she added.

'Sharper tongued, though.'

That stung, too. The incident might have been painful but come on... She'd been chased by a donkey and every other man she knew would be at the very least struggling to hide a grin right now. Most would be laughing out loud.

'As for the trout,' he added, 'Robert Cranbrook never did own them, only the right to stand on the bank with a rod and fly and attempt to catch them. He can't even claim that now.'

'Maybe not,' she said, doing her best to ignore the sensory deluge, 'but someone can.' And sounded just as prim and buttoned-up as she apparently looked. 'HMRC if the rumours about the state of Sir Robert's finances are to be believed and the Revenue certainly won't take kindly to you helping yourself.'

Buttoned-up and priggish.

'Don't worry,' she said, making a determined effort to lighten the mood, 'I'll look the other way, just this once, if you'll promise to ignore my misdemeanour.'

'Shall we get out of this ditch before you start plea bargaining?' he suggested.

Plea bargaining? She'd been joking, for heaven's sake! She wasn't that buttoned-up. She wasn't buttoned-up at all!

'You don't appear to have a concussion,' he continued, 'and unless you're telling me you can't feel your legs, or you've broken something, I'd rather leave the paramedics to cope with genuine emergencies.'

'Good call.' As an emergency it was genuine enough— although not in the medical sense—but if she was the subject of her own front-page story she'd never hear the last of it in the newsroom. 'Hold on,' she said, not that he appeared to need encouragement to do that. He hadn't changed that much. 'I'll check.'

She did a quick round up of her limbs, flexing her fingers and toes. Her shoulder had taken the brunt of the fall and she knew that she would be feeling it any moment now, but it was probably no more than a bruise. The peddle had spun as her foot had slipped, whacking her shin. She'd scraped her knuckles on the brake lever and her left foot appeared to be up to the ankle in the cold muddy water at the bottom of the ditch but everything appeared to be in reasonable working order.

'Well?' he demanded.

'Winded.' She wouldn't want him to think he was the cause of her breathing difficulties. 'And there will be bruises, but I have sufficient feeling below the waist to know where your hand is.'

He didn't seem to feel the need to apologise but then she had run into him at full tilt. She really didn't want to think about where he'd be black and blue. Or where her own hand had been.

'What about you?' she asked, somewhat belatedly.

'Can I feel my hand on your bum?'

The lines bracketing his mouth deepened a fraction and her heart rate which, after the initial shock of seeing him, had begun to settle back down, thudding along steadily with only an occasional rattle of the cymbals, took off on a dramatic drum roll.

CHAPTER TWO

'ARE you in one piece?' Claire asked, doing her best to ignore the timpani section having a field day and keep it serious.

If he could do that with an almost smile, she wasn't going to risk the full nine yards.

'I'll survive.'

She sketched what she hoped was a careless shrug. 'Close enough.'

And this time the smile, no more than a dare-you straightening of the lips, reached his eyes, setting her heart off on a flashy drum solo.

'Shall we risk it, then?' he prompted when she didn't move.

'Sorry.' She wasn't an impressionable teenager, she reminded herself. She was a grown woman, a mother... 'I'm still a bit dazed.' That, at least, was true. Although whether the fall had anything to do with it was a moot point. Forget laughing about this. Hal North was a lot safer when he was being a grouch.

'Okay,' he said. 'Let's try this. You roll to your right and I'll do my best to untangle us both.'

She gingerly eased herself onto her shoulder, then gave a little gasp at the unexpected intimacy of his cold fingers against the sensitive, nylon-clad flesh as he hooked his hand beneath her knee. It was a lifetime since she was that timid girl who'd watched him from a safe distance, nearly died when he'd looked at her, but he was still attracting and scaring her in equal quantities. Okay, maybe not quite equal…

'Does that hurt?' he asked.

'No!' She was too fierce, too adamant and his eyes narrowed. 'Your hand was cold,' she said lamely as he lifted her leg free of the frame.

'That's what happens when you tickle trout,' he said, confirming her impression that he'd just stepped up out of the stream when she ran into him. It would certainly explain why she hadn't seen him. And why he hadn't had time taking avoiding action.

'Are you still selling your catch to the landlord of The Feathers?' she asked, doing her best to control the conversation.

'Is he still in the market for poached game?' he asked, not denying that he'd once supplied him through the back door. 'He'd have to pay rather more for a freshly caught river trout these days.'

'That's inflation for you. I hope your rod is still in one piece.'

His eyebrow twitched, proving that he did, after all, possess a sense of humour. 'Couldn't you tell?'

'Your fishing rod…' Claire stopped, but it was too late to wish she'd ignored the innuendo.

'It's not mine,' he said, taking pity on her. 'I confiscated it from a lad fishing without a licence.'

'Confiscated it?'

As he sat up, she caught sight of the Cranbrook crest on the pocket of his coveralls. He was working on the estate? Poacher turned gamekeeper? Why did that feel so wrong? He would be a good choice if the liquidators wanted to protect what assets remained. He knew every inch of the estate, every trick in the book…

'Aren't they terribly expensive?' she asked. 'Fishing rods.'

'He'll get it back when he pays his fine.'

'A fine? That's a bit harsh,' she said, rather afraid she knew who might have been trying his luck. 'He's only doing what you did when you were his age.'

'The difference being that I was bright enough not to get caught.'

'I'm not sure that's something to be proud of.'

'It beats the hell out of the alternative.' She couldn't argue with that. 'I take it, from all this touching concern, that you know the boy?'

'I imagine it was Gary Harker. His mother works in the estate office. She's at her wit's end. He left school last year and hasn't had a sniff of a job. In the old days he'd have been taken on by the estate,' she prompted. 'Learned a skill.'

'Working for the gentry for a pittance.'

'Minimum wage these days. Not much, but a lot better than nothing. If the estate is hiring, maybe you could put a good word in for him?'

'You don't just want me to let him off, you want me to give him a job, too?' he asked.

'Maybe there's some government-sponsored apprentice-ship scheme?' she suggested. 'I could find out. Please, Hal, if I talk to him, will you give him a break?'

'If I talk to him, will you give me one?' he replied.

'I'll do better than that.' She beamed, aches and pains momentarily forgotten. 'I'll bake you a cake. Lemon drizzle? Ginger? Farmhouse?' she tempted and for a moment she seemed to hold his attention. For a moment she thought she had him.

'Don't bother,' he said, breaking eye contact, turning back to her bike. 'The front wheel's bent out of shape.'

She swallowed down her disappointment. 'Terrific. For want of an apple the bike was lost,' she said, as he propped it against a tree. 'Can it be straightened out?'

'Is it worth it?' he asked, reaching out a hand to help her up. 'It must be fifty years old.'

'Older,' she replied, clasping his hand. 'It belonged to Sir Robert's nanny.'

His palm was cold, or maybe it was her own that was hot. Whatever it was, something happened to her breathing as their thumbs locked around each other and Hal braced himself to pull her up onto the path. A catch, a quickening, as if his power was flooding into her, his eyes heating her from the inside out.

Just how reliable was the finger test as a diagnosis of concussion, anyway?

'I've got you,' he said, apparently feeling nothing but impatience, but as he pulled, something caught at the soft wool of her jacket, holding her fast.

'Wait!' She'd already wrecked her bike and she wasn't about to confound the situation by tearing lumps out of her one good suit. 'I'm caught on something.' She yelped as she reached back to free herself and her hand snagged on an old, dead bramble, thorns hard as nails. 'Could my day get any worse?' she asked, sucking at the line of tiny scarlet spots of blood oozing across the soft pad at the base of her thumb.

'That depends on whether your tetanus shots are up to date.'

Was that, finally, a note of genuine concern? Or was it merely the hope she would need a jab—something to put the cherry on top of her day—that she heard in his voice?

'That was a rhetorical question,' she replied, tired of being on the defensive, 'but thanks for your concern.' And he could take that any way he chose.

Right now she'd gladly suffer a jab that would offer a vaccination against dangerous men. The kind that stood in your way on footpaths, made you say blush-making things when you hadn't blushed in years. Made you feel thirteen again. Made you feel...

'Here. Use this,' he said as she searched her pockets for a tissue. He dropped a freshly ironed handkerchief into her lap then, as he stepped down into the ditch to unhook her from the thorns, he spoiled this unexpected gallantry by saying, 'You really should make an attempt to get up earlier.'

She turned to look at him. 'Excuse me?'

He was closer than she realised and his chin, rough with an overnight growth of beard, brushed against her cheek. It intensified the tingle, sent her temperature up a degree. Deadly dangerous. She should move.

Closer...

'It's gone nine,' he pointed out. 'I assumed you were late for work?'

His hair was dark and thick. He'd worn it longer as a youth, curling over his neck, falling sexily into his eyes. These days it was cut with precision. Even the tumble into the ditch had done no more than feather a cowlick across his forehead. And if possible, the effect was even more devastating.

'I am,' she admitted, 'but not because I overslept.'

His breath was warm against her temple and her skin seemed to tingle, as if drawn by his closeness.

She really should move. Put some distance between them.

She'd never been close enough to see the colour of his eyes before. They were very dark and she'd always imagined, in her head, they were the blue-grey of wet slate, but in this light they seemed to be green. Or was it simply the spring bright tunnel of leaves that lent them a greenish glow?

He raised an eyebrow as he opened a clasp knife. 'You had something more interesting to keep you in bed?'

'You could say that.' In her vegetable bed, anyway, but if he chose to think there was a man interested in undoing her buttons she could live with that. 'I'm more concerned about my ten o'clock appointment at the Town Hall with the chairman of the Planning Committee.'

He glanced at his watch. 'You're not going to make it.'

'No.' There were worst things than crashing into a ditch and losing her job was one of them. 'If you got a move on I could call him before I'm late and reschedule for later today.'

'Have a care, Miss Thackeray,' he warned, glancing up at her, 'or I'll leave you where you are.'

About to point out that all she had to do was undo her jacket and she could free herself, she thought better of it.

If Hal North was working for the estate he probably knew far more than the planning department about what was going on.

'I was going to talk to him about the Cranbrook Park estate,' she said, moving her hand away from her jacket button. 'There's a rumour going round that a property developer has bought it.'

The rumour of a sale was real enough. As for the rest, she was just fishing and most people couldn't wait to tell you that you were wrong, tell you what they knew.

'And why would that be of interest to you?'

Yes, well, Hal North hadn't been like most boys and it seemed he wasn't like most men, either.

'The estate is my landlord,' she said. 'I have a vested interest in what happens to it.'

'You have a lease.'

'Well, yes…' With barely three months left to run. 'But I've known Sir Robert since I was four years old. I can't expect a new owner to have the same concern for his tenants. He might not want to renew it and if he did, he'll certainly raise the rent.' Something else to worry about. It was vital she keep her job. 'And then there are the rumours about a light industrial estate at my end of the village.'

'Not in my backyard?' he mocked.

'Yours, too,' she replied, going for broke. 'I live in Primrose Cottage.'

'What about the jobs that light industry would bring to the area?' he replied, apparently unmoved by the threat to his childhood home. 'Don't you care about that angle? What about young Gary Harker?'

'I'm a journalist.' A rather grand title for someone working on the news desk of the local paper. 'I'm interested in all the angles. Protecting the countryside has its place, too.'

'For the privileged few.'

'The estate has always been a local amenity.'

'Not if you're a fisherman,' he reminded her. 'I assume, since you're covering local issues that you work for the local rag?'

'The *Observer*, yes,' she said, doing her best to ignore his sarcasm, keep a smile on her face. She wanted to know what he knew.

'All that expensive education and that's the best you could do?'

'That's an outrageous thing to say!'

Oops... There went her smile.

But it explained why, despite the fact that she'd been a skinny kid, totally beneath his notice, he had remembered her. Her pink and grey Dower House school uniform had stood out amongst the bright red Maybridge High sweatshirts like a lily on a dung heap. Or a sore thumb. Depending on your point of view.

The other children in the village had mocked her difference. She'd pretended not to care, but she'd envied them their sameness. Had wanted to be one of them, to belong to that close-knit group clustered around the bus stop every morning when she was driven past in the opposite direction.

'You were headed for Oxbridge according to your mother. Some high-flying media job.'

'Was I?' she asked, as if she didn't recall every moment of toe-curling embarrassment as her mother held forth in the village shop. She might have been oblivious, but Claire had known that they were both the object of derision. 'Obviously I wasn't as bright as she thought I was.'

'And the real reason?'

She should be flattered that he didn't believe her, but it only brought back the turmoil, the misery of a very bad time.

'It must have been having a baby that did it.' If he was back in the village he'd find out soon enough. 'Miss Snooty Smartyhat brought down to size by her hormones. It was a big story at the time.'

'I can imagine. Anyone I know? The father?' he added, as if she didn't know what he meant.

'There aren't many people left in the village who you'll remember,' she said, not wanting to go there. Even after all these years the crash of love's young dream as it hurtled to earth still hurt… 'As you pointed out, there aren't any jobs on the estate for our generation.' Few jobs for anyone. Sir Robert's fortunes had been teetering on the brink for years. Cheap imports had ruined his business and with his factories closed, the estate—a money sink—had lost the income which kept it going.

The Hall was in desperate need of repair. Some of the outbuildings were on the point of falling down and many of the hedges and fences were no longer stock proof.

Cue Archie.

'No one who'll remember me is what I think you mean,' he said.

'You're in luck, then.'

'You think I'd be unwelcome?'

He appeared amused at the idea and flustered, she said, 'No…I just meant…'

'I know what you meant,' he said, turning back to the delicate task of unpicking the threads of her suit from the thorns.

Ignoring the cold and damp that was seeping through her skirt, trying to forget just how much she disliked this part of her job, she tried again. This time, however, since he clearly wasn't going to be coaxed into indiscretion, she came right out and asked him.

'Can you tell me what's happening to the estate?' Maybe the subtle implication that he did not know himself would provoke an answer.

'There'll be an announcement about its future in the next day or two. I imagine your office will get a copy.'

'It has been sold!' That wasn't just news, it was a headline! Brownie points, job security… 'Who's the new owner?'

'Do you want a scoop for the *Observer,* Claire?' The corner of his mouth quirked up in what might have been a smile. Her stomach immediately followed suit. She might be older and wiser, but he'd always had a magnetic pull. 'Or merely gossip for the school gates?'

'I'm a full-time working single mother,' she said, doing her best to control the frantic jangle of hormones that hadn't been disturbed in years. 'I don't have time to gossip at the school gates.'

'Your baby's father didn't stick around, then?'

'Well spotted. Come on, Hal,' she pleaded. 'It's obvious that you know something.'

If he had been the chairman of the Planning Committee she'd have batted her eyelashes at him. As it was, she'd barely raised a flutter before she regretted it.

Hal North was not a man to flirt with unless you meant it.

Poised on the brink of adolescence, paralysed with shyness if he so much as glanced in her direction, she had not fully understood the danger a youth like Hal North represented.

As a woman, she didn't have that excuse.

'It'll be public knowledge soon enough,' she pressed, desperately hoping that he wouldn't have noticed.

'Then you won't have long to wait will you?'

'Okay, no name, but can you tell me what's going to happen to the house?' That's all she'd need to grab tomorrow's front page. 'Is it going to be a hotel and conference centre?'

'I thought you said it was going to be a building site. Or was it an industrial estate?'

'You know how it is…' She attempted a careless shrug, hiding her annoyance that he persisted in trading question for question. She was supposed to be the professional, but he was getting all the answers. 'In the absence of truth the vacuum will be filled with lies, rumour and drivel.'

'Is that right?' He straightened, put away his knife. 'Well, you'd know more about that than me.'

'Oh, please. I work for a local newspaper. We might publish rumour, and a fair amount of drivel, but we're too close to home to print lies.'

She made a move to get up, eager now to be on her way, but he forestalled her with a curt 'wait.'

Assuming that he could see another problem, she obeyed, only to have him put his hands around her waist.

She should have protested, would have protested if the connection between her brain and her mouth had been functioning. All that emerged as he picked her bodily out of the ditch was a huff of air, followed by a disgusting squelch as her foot came out of the mud, leaving her shoe behind. Then she found herself with her nose pressed against the dark green heavyweight cloth of his coveralls and promptly forgot all about the bluebells.

Hal North had a scent of his own. Mostly fresh air, the sweet green of crushed grass and new dandelion leaves, but something else was coming through that fresh laundry smell. The scent of a man who'd been working. Warm skin, clean sweat—unexpectedly arousing—prickling in her nose.

He was insolent, provoking and deeply, deeply disturbing but, even as the urgent 'no!' morphed into an eager 'yes...' she told herself to get a grip. He had been bad news as a youth and she'd seen, heard nothing to believe that had changed.

'If you'll excuse me,' she said, doing her best to avoid meeting those dangerous eyes as she clung to his shoulders, struggling for balance and to get her tongue and teeth to line up to form the words. 'I really have to be going.'

'Going? Haven't you forgotten something?'

'My shoe?' she suggested, hoping that he'd dig it out of the mud for her. He was, after all, dressed for the job. While the prospect of stepping back into it was not particularly appealing, she wasn't about to mess up the high heels she carried in the messenger bag slung across her back.

'I was referring to the fact that you cycled along a footpath, Claire. Breaking the by-laws without a second thought.'

'You're kidding.' She laughed but the arch law-breaker of her youth didn't join in. He was not kidding. He was... She didn't know what he was. She only knew that he was looking down at her with an intensity that was making her pulse race. 'No! No, you're right,' she said, quickly straightening her face. 'It was very wrong of me. I won't do it again.'

The hard cheekbones seemed somehow harder, the jaw even more take it or leave it, if that were possible.

'I don't believe you.'

'You don't?' she asked, oblivious to the demands of the front page as her upper lip burned in the heat of eyes that were not hard. Not hard at all. Her tongue flicked over it, in an unconscious attempt to cool it. 'What can I do to convince you?'

The words were out of Claire's mouth, the harm done, before she could call them back and one corner of his mouth lifted in a 'got you' smile.

There was no point in saying that she hadn't meant it the way it had sounded. He wouldn't believe that, either. She wasn't sure she believed it herself.

If it looked like an invitation, sounded like an invitation...

Her stomach clenched in a confused mix of fear and excitement as, for one heady, heart-stopping moment she thought he was going to take her up on it. Kiss her, sweep her up into his arms, fulfil every girlish dream she'd confided to her journal. Back in the days before she'd met Jared, when being swept into Hal's arms and kissed was the limit of her imagination.

No! What was she thinking!

In a move that took him by surprise, she threw up her arm, stepped smartly back, out of the circle of his hands, determined to put a safe distance between them before her wandering wits made a complete fool of her. But the day wasn't done with her.

The morning was warm and sunny but it had rained overnight and her foot, clad only in fine nylon—no doubt in shreds—didn't stop where she'd put it but kept sliding backwards on the wet path. Totally off balance, arms flailing, she would have fallen if he hadn't caught her round the waist in a grip that felt less like rescue than capture and her automatic thanks died in her throat.

'You've cycled along that path every day this week,' he said, in a tone that suggested he was right, 'and I don't think you're going to stop without good reason.'

'Archie is a great deterrent,' she managed.

'Not to those of us who know his weakness for apples. A weakness I've seen you take advantage of more than once this week. Being late appears to be something of a habit with you.'

He'd seen her? When? How long had he been back? More importantly why hadn't she heard about it when she called in at the village shop? There might be few people left who would remember bad, dangerous, exciting Hal North, but the arrival of a good-looking man in the neighbourhood was always news.

'Were you lying in wait for me today?'

'I have better things to do with my time, believe me. I'm afraid this morning you just ran out of luck.'

'And here was me thinking I'd run into you.' He moved his head in a gesture that suggested it amounted to the same thing. 'So? What are you going to do?' she demanded, in an attempt to keep the upper hand. 'Call the cops?'

'No,' he said. 'I'm going to issue an on-the-spot penalty fine.'

She laughed, assuming that he was joking. He didn't join in. Not joking…

'Can you do that?' she demanded and when he didn't answer the penny finally dropped. A fine… 'Oh, right. I get it.'

He hadn't changed. His shoulders might be broader, he might be even more dangerously attractive than the boy who'd left the village all those years ago, but inside, where it mattered, he was still the youth who'd poached the Park game, torn up the park on his motorcycle, sprayed graffiti on Sir Robert's factory walls. Allegedly. No one had ever caught him.

He was back now as gamekeeper, warden, whatever and he apparently considered this one of the perks of the job.

She shrugged carelessly in an attempt to hide her disappointment as she dug around in her bag, fished out her wallet.

'Ten pounds,' she said, flicking it open. 'It's all I have apart from small change. Take it or leave it.'

'I'll leave it.' Her relief came a fraction too soon. 'I'm looking for something a little more substantial by way of payment.' What! 'Something sufficiently memorable to ensure that the next time you're tempted to ride along this path, you'll think again.'

She opened her mouth to protest that parting with all the spare cash she had to see her through until the end of the month was memorable enough, thank you very much. All that emerged was another of those wordless huffs as he pulled her against him, expelling the air from her body as her hips collided with hard thighs.

For a moment she hung there, balanced on her toes.

For a moment he looked down at her.

'What would make you think again, Claire?'

Had she thought there was anything soft about those eyes? She was still wondering how she could have got that so wrong when his mouth came down on hers with an abrupt, inescapable insistence.

It was outrageous, shocking, disgraceful. And everything she had ever imagined it would be.

CHAPTER THREE

CLAIRE Thackeray abandoned her bike, her shoe and, as her hair descended untidily about her shoulders, a scatter of hair pins.

Hal knew that he would have to go after her, but it hadn't taken her stunned expression, or her stiff back as she limped comically away from him on one shoe to warn him that laughing would be a mistake.

It was as clear as day that nothing he did or said would be welcome right now, although whether her anger was directed at him or herself was probably as much a mystery to her as it was to him.

The only thing he knew with certainty was that she would never again ride her bike along this path. Never toss an apple—the toll Archie charged for letting her pass unmolested on her bike—over the hedge.

'Job done, then,' he muttered as, furious with himself, furious with her, he stepped down into the ditch to recover the shoe she'd left embedded in the mud. He tossed it into the basket on the front of her bike, grabbed the fishing rod he'd confiscated from Gary Harker and followed her.

It was the first time he'd lost control in years and he'd done it not just once, but twice. First when he'd kissed her, and then again as her unexpected meltdown had made him forget that his intention had been to punish her. Punish her for her insulting offer of a bribe. Her pitiful attempt at seducing what he knew out of him. Most of all, to punish her for being a Thackeray.

He'd forgotten everything in the softness of her lips unexpectedly yielding beneath his, the silk of her tongue, the heat ripping through him as she'd clung to him in a way that belied all that buttoned-up restraint.

Which of them came to their senses first he could not have said. He only knew that when he took a step back she was looking at him as if she'd run into a brick wall instead of a flesh-and-blood man.

Any other woman who'd kissed him like that would have been looking at him with soft, smoky eyes, her cheeks flushed, her mouth smiling with anticipation, but Claire Thackeray had the look of a rabbit caught in headlights and, beneath the smear of mud, her cheek had been shockingly white.

Her mouth was swollen but there was no smile and she hadn't said a word. Hadn't given him a chance to say... What?

I'm sorry?

To the daughter of Peter Thackeray? The girl who'd been too good to mix with the village kids. The woman who, even now, down on her luck and living in the worst house on the estate, was still playing the patronising lady bountiful, just as her mother had. Handing out charity jobs to the deserving poor. Sending the undeserving to the devil...

That wasn't how it was meant to be.

But she hadn't waited for an apology.

After that first stricken look, she'd turned around and walked away from him without a word, without a backward glance as if he was still the village trash her father—taking his cue from Sir Robert—had thought him. As if she was still the Cranbrook estate's little princess.

The battered wheel ground against the mudguard and stuck, refusing to move another inch. Cursing the wretched thing, he propped it up out of sight behind a tree, then grabbing her shoe he strode after her.

'Claire! Wait, damn it!'

Claire wanted to die.

No, that was ridiculous. She wasn't an idiot kid with a crush on the local bad boy. She was a responsible, sensible grown woman. Who wanted to die.

How dare he!

Easy... Hal North had always done just what he wanted, looked authority in the eye and dared anything, defying them to do their worst.

How could she?

How could she just stand there and let Hal North kiss her? Respond as if she'd been waiting half her life for him to do exactly that? Even now her senses were alight with the heat of it, the blood thundering around her body at the thrill of surrendering to it, letting go in a world-well-lost moment when nothing else mattered. Not her dignity, not her child...

It had been everything her youthful imagination had dreamt about and more. Exhilarating, a dream-come-true moment to rival anything in a fairy tale.

Appalling.

She clung desperately to that word, closing her eyes in a vain attempt to blot out the warm, animal scent of his skin, the feel of his shoulders, solid beneath her hands as she'd clutched at them for support. The taste of his hard mouth lighting her up as if she'd been plugged into the national grid; softening from punishing to seductively tender as her lips had surrendered without a struggle to the silk of his tongue.

'Didn't you hear me?'

Of course she'd heard him.

"Wait, damn it..."

He'd sounded angry.

Why would he be angry? He was the one who'd kissed her without so much as a by-your-leave...

'I brought your shoe,' he said.

She took it from him without slowing down, without looking at him. It was caked in wet sticky mud and she tossed it defiantly back into the ditch.

'That was stupid.'

'Was it?' Probably. Undoubtedly. She'd come back and find it later. 'What's your on-the-spot fine for littering?'

'Are you sure you want to know?'

She stubbed her toe on a root and he caught her arm as she stumbled.

'Get lost, Hal,' she said, attempting to shake him off. He refused to be shaken and she glared up at him. 'Are you escorting me off the premises?'

Bad choice of words, she thought as his mouth tightened.

'It's for your own safety.'

'Safety? Archie isn't going to bother me now I'm on foot, but who's going to keep me safe from you?' she demanded, clearly not done with 'stupid.'

'You've had a shock,' he replied, all calm reason, which just made her all the madder.

'Now you're concerned!'

Too right she'd had a shock. She'd had a shock right down to her knees but it had nothing to do with Archie and everything to do with crashing into Hal North. Everything to do with the fact that he'd kissed her. That she'd kissed him back as if she'd been waiting to do that all her life. Maybe she had...

How dare he be all calm reason when she was a basket case?

'It's a bit late to start playing knight errant don't you think?'

'You're mistaking me for someone else.'

'Not in a hundred years,' she muttered, catching her breath as she stepped on a sharp stone, gritting her teeth to hold back the expletive, refusing to let him see that she was in pain.

The last thing she needed was a smug I-told-you-so from Hal North.

It did have the useful side effect of preventing her from saying anything else she'd regret when Hal moved his hand from her arm and looped it firmly around her waist, taking her weight so that she had no choice but to lean into the solid warmth of his body, allow him to support her.

The alternative was fighting him which would only make things worse as she limped the rest of the way home, her head against his shoulder, her cheek against the hard cloth of his overalls. The temptation was to simply surrender to the comfort, just as she'd surrendered to his kiss and it took every crumb of concentration to mentally distance herself from the illusion of safety, of protection and pray that he'd put her erratic breathing down to 'shock.'

When they reached her gate, she allowed herself to relax and took the fishing rod when he handed it to her, assuming he meant her to give it back to Gary.

'Thank you…' The word ended in a little shriek as he bent and caught her behind the knees, scooping her up like some bride being carried over the threshold. Hampered by the rod, she could do nothing but fling an arm around his neck and hang on as he strode along the gravel path that led around the house to the back door.

'Key?' he prompted, as he deposited her with an equal lack of ceremony on the doorstep.

'I'm home. Job done,' she said, propping the rod by the door, waiting for him to leave. She was damned if she was going to say thank you again.

'Are you going to be difficult?' he asked.

'You bet.'

He shrugged, glanced around, spotted the brick where she hid her spare key. 'My mother used to keep it in the same place,' he said, apparently oblivious to her huff of annoyance as he retrieved it and opened the door. 'In fact, I'm pretty sure it's the same brick.'

'Go away,' she said, kicking off her remaining shoe in the scullery where the boots and coats were hung.

'Not before the statutory cup of hot, sweet tea,' he said, following her inside and easing off his own boots.

Her suit was damp and muddy, her foot was throbbing and her body, a jangle of sore, aching bits demanding her attention now that she'd come to a halt, responded with a tiny 'yes, please' whimper. She ignored it.

'I don't take sugar.'

'I do.'

Behind her, the phone began to ring. She ignored it for as long as she could, daring him to take another step then, with what she hoped was a careless shrug—one that her shoulder punished her for—she limped, stickily, into the kitchen and lifted the receiver from the cradle.

'Claire Thack…'

Hal pulled out a chair, tipped off the two sleeping cats and, taking her arm, eased her down into it before crossing to the kettle.

'Claire?'

'Oh, Brian…'

'Is there a problem?' Brian Gough, the news editor, sounded concerned rather than annoyed, but then she had always striven to be one hundred per cent reliable—hoarding those Brownie points that every working mother needed against the days when her daughter was sick and her needs had to come before everything, even the desperate necessity of making a career for herself. 'Only I've just had Charlie on the phone.'

Charlie… That would be Charlie Peascod, the Chief Planning Officer. Her important ten o'clock meeting. She caught sight of the clock and groaned.

Hal heard her and turned. 'Are you okay?' he asked, with what appeared to be genuine concern.

'No,' she hissed, swivelling round so that her back was to him in an effort to concentrate. 'I'm s-o s-sorry, Brian but I've had a bit of an accident.'

'An accident? What kind of accident? Are you all right?'

'Y-yes…' she said as, without warning, she began to shiver.

'You don't sound it.'

'I will be.' Behind her there was a world of comfort in the sound of the kettle being filled. The sound of the biscuit tin lid being opened. She refused to look… 'I was going to c-call you but…' But it had gone clean out of her head. Her important meeting, her job, pretty much everything. That's what a man like Hal North could do to you with nothing more than a kiss. 'I f-fell off my bike.'

'Have you been to the hospital?' he asked, seriously concerned now, which only added to her guilt.

'It's not that bad, truly.' And it wasn't. She just needed to get a grip, pull herself together. 'Just the odd bump and scrape, but there was rather a lot of mud,' she said, attempting to make light of it. 'Once I've had a quick shower I'll be out of here. With luck I'll catch the eleven o'clock bus.'

'No, no… These things can shake you up. We can manage without you.'

Her immediate reaction was to protest—that was so not something she wanted to hear—but for some reason she appeared to be shaking like a jelly. If she hadn't been sitting down, she would almost certainly have collapsed in heap.

'Take the rest of the week off, put your feet up. We'll see you on Monday.'

'If you insist,' she said, just to be sure that he was telling her, she wasn't begging. 'I'll call Mr Peascod now to apologise. Reschedule for Monday.'

'Oh, don't worry about Charlie. I'm taking him to lunch and, let's face it, he's much more likely to be indiscreet after a glass of wine.'

Of course he was. All boys together. On the golf course

or down the pub. No need for Brian Gough to make an effort with his hair, wear his best suit, flutter his eyelashes. He'd take Charlie to the King's Head and over a plate of their best roast beef—on expenses—he'd hear all about what was going on at Cranbrook Park. It was how it had always been done.

Forget the news desk. At this rate, she'd be writing up meetings of the Townswomen's Guild, reviewing the Christmas panto until she was drawing her pension. Thank goodness for the 'Greenfly and Dandelions' blog she wrote for the Armstrong Newspaper Group website. At least no one else on the staff could write that.

And that was the good news.

All that expensive education notwithstanding, it was as good as a single mother without a degree, a single mother who had to put her child first could hope for. Even then she was luckier than most women in her situation. Luckier than she deserved according to her mother.

The bad news was that the *Observer* was cutting back on staff and a single mother with childcare issues was going to be top of the chop list.

'All done?' Hal unhooked a couple of mugs from the dresser, keeping an eye on Claire while he filled a bowl with warm water. Despite her insistence that she was fine, she was deathly pale.

'All done,' she said.

'You don't have to call the Town Hall and make your apologies?'

'No need.' She looked at the phone she was still holding, then put it on the table. 'The news editor is handling it.'

'Right, well I'll clean up your foot.'

She frowned as he placed the bowl of water at her feet, then she rallied; he could practically hear her spine snapping straight. 'There's no need to make a fuss. I'll get in the shower as soon as you've gone.'

'It's cut,' he said. 'There's blood on the floor.'

'Is there?' She looked down and saw the trail of muddy, bloody footprints on her clean floor. 'Oh…' She bit back the word she'd undoubtedly have let drop if she'd been on her own. 'It must have been when I stepped on a stone.'

One sharp enough to cut her and yet she hadn't so much as whimpered. His fault. If he hadn't kissed her, if he'd just scraped the mud off her shoe, let her go…

'It might have been a piece of glass,' he said, not wanting to think about that kiss. About the button she'd been playing with or how she'd felt as she'd leaned against him as he'd helped her home. 'Or a ring pull from a can. I can't believe the litter down there.'

'A lot of it blows in from the towpath. It used to drive my dad wild.'

'It wasn't just me, then.' Before she could answer, he said, 'Stick your foot in this and soak off the dirt so that I can make sure there's nothing still in there.' She didn't bother to argue, just sucked in her breath as she lifted her foot into the water.

'Okay?'

She held her breath for a moment, then relaxed. 'Yes…'

He nodded and left her to soak while he made tea, adding a load of sugar to hers. Adding rather more than usual to his own.

He shouldn't have come to Cranbrook. He hadn't intended to come here. Not now. Not until it was all done. It had been his intention to keep his distance and leave it all to the consultants he'd engaged, but it was like a bad tooth you couldn't leave alone…

'Have you got any antiseptic?' he asked, setting the mug beside her.

'Under the sink, with the first-aid box.'

'Towel?'

'There's a clean one in the airing cupboard. It's in the bathroom at the top of the…'

'I know my way around.' He took a chocolate biscuit—it

had been a long time since breakfast—and handed another to her. 'Eat this.'

'I—'

'It's medicinal,' he said, cutting off her objection, opening the door to stairs that seemed narrower than he remembered. He glanced back. 'You might want to lose the tights while I'm fetching it.'

'Are you quite sure I can manage that all by myself?'

He paused, his foot on the bottom step, and looked back. 'You have a mouth that will get you into serious trouble one of these days, Claire Thackeray.'

'Too late,' she said. 'It already has.'

'It's not a one-time-only option,' he pointed out and as she blushed virgin pink, he very nearly stepped back down into the kitchen to offer her a demonstration.

Peeling down tights over long, shapely legs that he'd already enjoyed at his leisure as she'd lain sprawled on top of him with her skirt around her waist would have offered some compensation in a day that was not, so far, going to plan.

He'd arrived at sunrise and set out for a quiet drive around the estate, wanting to claim its acres for himself. To enjoy his triumph.

The rush of possessiveness, unreasoning anger, when he'd seen a lad fishing from what had once been his favourite spot had brought him up short. Or maybe it had been the fancy rod and antique reel wielded so inexpertly that had irritated him. The boy had sworn it had belonged to his granddad, but he was very much afraid that it had been stolen.

Not the most pleasant start to the day and, once the boy had gone, he'd stopped to look, remembering his own wild days.

That's when he'd noticed that the bank opposite had been seriously undermined by the torrential winter rain. He'd pulled on the overalls and boots that had been lying in the back of the Land Rover and crossed the stream to take a closer look at the damage and walked right into the Claire and Archie double-act.

And if it hadn't been part of his plans to come back to Cranbrook Park until he'd made it his own, that was doubly so with Primrose Cottage.

There had been no reason to come down a lane on the edge of the village, a lane that stopped at a cottage that was hidden unless you were looking for it. Forgotten by the estate.

Jack North had never been prepared to use good drinking and gambling money to decorate, repair a house he did not own and Robert Cranbrook would have seen it fall down before he'd have allowed his workmen to touch it.

He never could understand why his mother had stayed. Some twisted sense of loyalty? Or was it guilt?

In his head the cottage had remained the way it had looked on the day he'd fired up his motorbike and ridden away. But, like him, it had changed out of all recognition.

The small window panes broken in one of Jack's drunken rages and stuffed with cardboard to keep out the weather had all been replaced and polished to a shine. Windows and trim were now painted white and the dull, blistering green front door was a fresh primrose yellow to match the flowers that were blooming all along the verge in front of a white-painted picket fence.

There had always been primroses…

Weeds no longer grew through the gravel path that led around to the rear; the yard, once half an acre of rank weeds where he'd spent hours stripping down and rebuilding an old motorcycle, was now a garden.

Inside everything had changed, too. His mother had battled against all odds to keep the place spotless. Now the walls had been stripped of the old wallpaper and painted in pale colours, the treads of the stairs each carpeted with a neatly trimmed offcut.

He'd once known every creak, every dip to avoid when he

wanted to creep out at night and he still instinctively avoided them as he took the second flight to revisit his past.

Everything was changed up there, too.

Where he'd once stuck posters of motorcycles against the shabby attic walls, delicate little fairies now flitted across ivory wallpaper.

Did Claire Thackeray's little girl resemble her mother? All fair plaits and starched school uniform. Or did she betray her father?

He shook his head as if to clear the image. What Claire Thackeray had got up to and with whom, was none of his business.

None of this—the clean walls, stripped and polished floors, the pretty lace curtains—changed a thing. Taking it from her, doing to her what her father had done to him would be all the sweeter because the cottage was now something worth losing.

A towel…

The door to the front bedroom was shut and he didn't open it. Claire was disturbing enough without acquainting himself with the intimacy of her bedroom, but the back bedroom door stood wide open and he could see that it had been converted into an office.

An old wallpaper pasting table, painted dark green, served as a desk. On it there was an old laptop, a printer, a pile of books. Drawn to take a closer look, he found himself looking out of the window, down into the garden.

He'd hadn't been able to miss the fact that it was now a garden, rather than the neglected patch of earth he remembered, but from above he could see that it was a lot more.

Linked by winding paths, the ugly patch had been divided into a series of intimate spaces. Divided with trees and shrubs as herbaceous borders, there were places to sit, places to play and, at the rear, the kind of vegetable garden usually only seen on television programmes was tucked beneath the shelter of a bank on which spring bulbs were now dying back.

He looked down at the piles of books. He'd expected a thesaurus, a dictionary, whatever reference works journalists used. Instead, he found himself looking at a book on propagation. The other books were on greenhouse care, garden design.

Claire had done this?

Not without help. The house was decorated to a professional standard and the garden was immaculate.

He'd suggested that she was still all buttoned-up but her response to his kiss had blown that idea right out of the water. The woman Claire Thackeray had become would always have help.

He replaced the books, but as he turned away wanting to get out of this room, he was confronted by a cork board, thick with photographs of a little girl from babyhood to the most recent school photograph.

Her hair was jet black, and her golden skin was not the result of lying in the sun. Only her solemn grey eyes featured Claire and he could easily imagine the thrilling shock that must have run around the village when she'd wheeled her buggy into the village shop for the first time.

CHAPTER FOUR

'Did you have a good look round?' Claire asked, as he stepped down into the kitchen.

'I thought I'd better give you time to make yourself respectable,' he said, not bothering to deny it. 'It's all changed up there.'

It had changed everywhere.

Colour had begun to seep back into her cheeks and she raised a wry smile. 'Are you telling me that the young Hal North wasn't into "Forest Fairies"?'

'It wouldn't have mattered if I was,' he said. 'This house wasn't on the estate-maintenance rota and nothing would have persuaded Jack North to waste good drinking money on wallpaper.'

'I thought the cabbage roses in the front bedroom looked a bit pre-war,' she said. 'Not that I'm complaining. It was so old that it came off as easy as peeling a Christmas Satsuma.'

'You did it yourself?'

'That's what DIY stands for,' she said. 'I couldn't afford to pay someone to do it for me.'

'I didn't mean to sound patronising—'

She tutted. 'You missed. By a mile.'

'—but it's your landlord's job to keep the place in good repair.'

'Really? It didn't seem to work for your mother. In her shoes I'd have bought a few cans of paint and had a go myself.'

'She wouldn't…'

Hal's eyes were dark blue, she realised, with a fan of lines around them just waiting for him to smile. That bitten off "wouldn't," the snapping shut of his jaws, the hard line of his mouth, suggested that it wasn't going to happen if she gave way to her curiosity and asked him why a fit, handsome woman would choose to live like that.

'Sir Robert would only let me have the cottage on a repairing lease.'

'Cheapskate.'

'There was no money for renovations,' she said, leaping to his defence.

'So he got you to do it for him.'

'I had nowhere to live. He was doing me a favour.'

The cleaning, decorating, making a home for herself and Ally had kept her focussed, given her a purpose in those early months when her life had changed out of all recognition. No university, no job, no family. Just her and a new baby.

Cleaning, stripping, painting, making a home for them both had helped to keep the fear at bay.

'We both got a good deal, Hal. If the cottage had been fixed up, I couldn't have afforded the rent. He did get the materials for me at trade,' she said, 'and he replaced the broken glass and gutters himself.'

'Why am I not surprised?'

'I don't know,' she asked. 'Why aren't you?'

He shook his head. 'Are you ticklish?'

'What? No… What are you doing?' she demanded, confused by the sudden change in subject.

He didn't bother to answer but got down on one knee, soaped up his hands and picked up her foot.

She drew in a sharp breath as he smoothed his hand over her heel. 'Does that hurt?'

'It stings a bit.'

She lied.

With his fingers sliding over the arch of her foot, around her ankle, she was feeling no pain.

'Ally has started moaning about the wallpaper in her room,' she said, doing a swift subject change on her own account in a vain attempt to distract herself from the shimmer of pleasure rippling through her, an almost forgotten touch-me heaviness in her breasts, melting heat between her legs.

'Ally?'

'Alice Louise,' she said. 'After her grandmother.'

'Oh, right,' he said, and she knew he'd seen the photographs, put his own interpretation on her daughter's name.

'Apparently she's grown out of the fairy stage. It's hard to believe that she'll soon be eight.'

'Is eight too big for fairies?'

'Sadly.'

'So, what comes next?' She was mesmerised by the sight, the feel of his long fingers as they carefully teased the grit from between her toes. They were covered with small scars, the kind you got from knocks, scrapes, contact with hot metal. A mechanic's hands... 'Ballet?' he asked, looking up, catching her staring. 'Horses?'

'Not ballet,' she said quickly. 'She loves horses, but I can't afford to indulge her. To be honest, I don't care what she chooses, just as long as there is a stage between now and boys. They grow up so quickly these days.'

'They always did, Claire.'

'Did they? I must have missed that stage. Too much homework, I suppose.' And not enough freedom to hang around the village, giggling with the other girls, dressed to attract the boys. Not that they'd have welcomed her. The girls, anyway. She'd received sideways looks from the boys, but no one had been brave enough to make a move... 'The local girls my age seemed so much more grown up.' So much more knowing.

'You appear to have caught up.'

She shook her head. 'You never get that back.' She'd still

been hopelessly naïve at eighteen, believing sex and love were the same thing. Not wanting to think about that, she said, 'I'm taking Ally to the DIY store at the weekend to look around, see what catches her eye.'

'Shouldn't you wait and see what the new owner has in mind before you part with more hard cash on a house you don't own?'

'A few rolls of wallpaper won't break the bank.' And decorating would keep her mind off it. 'When he sees what a great tenant I am,' she added, 'he'll probably beg me to stay.'

He didn't comment, but instead turned another chair to face her, covered it with a towel and rested her dripping foot on it.

'Shouldn't you be at work?' she asked, as he tipped the dirty water down the sink and rinsed the bowl before refilling it with clean water to which he added antiseptic. Anything to stop thinking about the way his hands had felt on her foot, her ankle. How good it felt to be cared for.

The big hole that was missing not just from Ally's life, but her own.

'Not until I've dealt with this,' he said, washing her foot again, but this time when he lifted it up, he sat on the chair and set both towel and foot on his knee so that he could take a closer look at the damage.

It was one of those 'clean knicker' moments—except for clean knickers substitute nail polish.

'Never go out without painting your toenails in case you have an accident and some good-looking man decides to wash your foot…'

Who knew?

'No glass, it's just a nasty little cut,' he said, patting the heel dry before working the towel through her toes. She was really regretting the lack of nail polish… 'If you'll hand me a dressing?' he prompted.

She tore the cover off a big square dressing and handed it to him, shivering slightly as his fingers brushed against hers.

'You're cold. Drink your tea,' he said, as he placed the dressing over the cut, smoothed it into place and continued to hold her foot.

'It's too sweet,' she said, shuddering as she took a sip.

'Think of it as medicine,' he said as the phone in his pocket began to ring. He glanced at it. 'I have to go,' he said, without bothering to answer it, transferring her foot from his knee to the chair as he stood up. 'Keep an eye on that. Any redness, don't hang about, straight to the surgery for some antibiotics.'

'Yes, doc.'

He picked up the bowl, emptied it in the sink, dried his hands and was gone.

'Thank you, doc,' she said to herself, and the sound of his footsteps crunching on the gravel grew fainter and the silence returned.

She didn't move.

While she hadn't used her imagination in a long while, it was, apparently, still in full working order and if she kept still, concentrated very hard, she could still feel his hands on her foot, the sensual slide of his fingers between her toes.

Claire had just stepped out of the shower when a rap at the door sent her heart racing.

'Claire? It's Pen.'

Not Hal with her bike, her shoe, but a neighbour. She opened the window and called down, 'Hold on, Penny, I'll be right there.'

She threw on a sweatshirt, wincing as her shoulder reminded her that it, too, had been in the wars, and a pair of comfortable jeans.

'Are you all right?' Pen watched her limp across to the kettle and switch it on. 'I was in the village shop and Mrs Judd said she saw some man helping you home.'

Life in Cranbrook might have changed out of all recognition in the last decade but the impossibility of doing anything without everyone knowing in ten minutes flat remained a constant. Which meant that Hal North couldn't be living in the village. He wasn't a man you would miss when he pitched up in your neighbourhood and Penny, who was always urging her to get out and find someone, would have been full of it.

'Earth to Claire…'

'Sorry, Pen. I fell off my bike.'

'I wonder who he was?' Penny said, ten minutes later when, hands clutched tightly around a warm mug, she'd heard the severely edited highlights of her accident.

'You haven't taken on anyone new?' Claire asked. 'I hear the estate has been sold.'

'Who told you that?' she demanded. 'It's not being announced until Monday.'

'So who's bought the place? Don't worry, I won't say a word before it's official. I just want a chance to dig up some background details.'

Something to add a bit of sparkle to the two-page spread of the history of the house and the Cranbrook family that she'd been working on since it was evident that the estate would have to be sold. Without some background on the new owners, it was just that. History.

'Well…' Penny stretched the word like a piece of elastic as she helped herself to a chocolate-chip cookie and propped her elbows on the table. 'According to the solicitors' clerk it's been bought by a millionaire businessman.'

'Well, yes. Obviously.' Who else could afford it? 'He'll need millions if he's going to live there.' Spend millions to bring it up to modern specifications. That had to be good news for the local economy. 'What kind of business, do you know? Is he married? Does he have children?' They were the details that the *Observer* readers would want.

'Sorry, but I did have a call from a Ms Beatrice Webb this

morning, who wants to discuss my future with the estate on Monday.'

A woman? Well, why not…

'I should have asked for more information but to be honest I was too shocked to do anything other than say I'd be there.'

Claire curbed her impatience. 'That sounds hopeful.'

'Does it? With Steve on short time and Gary without a hope of a job, my few hours in the estate office and the money you give me for taking care of Ally after school is all that's keeping us afloat at the moment.'

'The estate will still need managing, Penny. The new owner, whoever he or she is, is going to need you.' She didn't mention her appeal to Hal on Gary's behalf. No point in raising false hopes.

Penny pulled a face. 'Ms Webb sounded capable of running the whole shebang with one hand tied behind her back.'

'She's probably got more than enough work to keep her busy in London.'

'London?'

'I imagine that's where the millions are made. A country estate is a plaything. A weekend retreat,' she added.

If Ms Webb planned to use it to hold shooting and fishing parties for business contacts she'd need someone who knew what he was doing to run the place. Take care of the game birds, the trout stocks.

Someone like Hal.

A tiny flutter of anticipation invaded her stomach and she grabbed a chocolate-chip cookie in an effort to smother it. The man was a menace and she had enough on her plate without getting involved.

Involved! That was a joke. Hal North was never going to be interested in a buttoned-up woman with a sharp tongue. The hot imprint of his lips on hers meant nothing.

'The rumour in the post office on Monday was that it's

going to be converted into a hotel and conference centre,' Penny said.

'There are all kinds of rumours flying around,' Claire said, 'but that wouldn't be such a bad thing and you have to admit that the Hall has got everything going for it. The location is stunning and there's probably room for a golf course on the other side of the Cran.'

'Really? How much room does a golf course take?'

She grinned. 'I've no idea, but look on the bright side. Whatever the future, a new owner means that there's going to be work for local builders, craftsmen, grounds men and that has to mean work for Steve.'

'Maybe Gary, too,' Penny said, cheered. 'There might even be more hours for me.'

'Absolutely.' Then, as casually as she could, she asked, 'Is Gary at home today?'

'According to him it's a study day although the only thing he's studying is how to cast a fly.'

Which answered that question. 'Well, if he could spare the time, I wonder if he'd pick up my bike for me. It's still on the footpath.'

'When he comes home to raid the fridge I'll ask him.'

The minute she'd shut the door on her Claire picked up the phone and dialled the number for the Hall.

'Cranbrook Hall.'

The unfamiliar voice was rich and plummy. 'Miss Webb?' On being assured that it was, she said, 'Welcome to Cranbrook Park. I'm Claire Thackeray—'

'Yes?'

No 'how can I help you?' No easy way in.

'—from the *Maybridge Observer*. I understand that Cranbrook Park has a new owner,' she said, pausing briefly. Nothing. 'As you can imagine, there are all kinds of rumours flying around at the moment and, inevitably, there are concerns about jobs.' The few that there were. 'The hope that if the Park is going to be developed commercially there will be work for local people,' she prompted.

Still no response.

'There has always been a very close relationship between the town and estate,' she continued, despite the lack of encouragement. 'Charity events, that sort of thing?' Good grief, this was like drawing blood from a very dry stone. 'I wondered if you could spare me half an hour to talk about the future of the estate? Maybe fill in some background detail for our readers?' she added hopefully.

'Don't you people talk to one another?' she replied, impatiently. 'Your editor called half an hour ago and I told him what I'll tell you. Mr North does not speak to the press.'

Ouch.

'I'm sorry, I haven't been in the office this morning and while the editor would be looking for facts, something to fill in the gaps in the announcement about the sale, I'm more interested in the human-interest angle. As I said the Park is a big part of the local community...'

And then the name sank in.

North.

No. She must have misheard. Or it was a coincidence. There was another North. It couldn't be...

'Did you say North?' she asked.

'Ask your editor, Miss Thackeray. He has all the details that are being released to the press.'

'Yes... Thank you,' she added belatedly as the dialling tone kicked in.

No...

No, no, no, no, no...

She repeated the word with every step as she ran upstairs to the office and turned on her cranky laptop. Kept saying it as it took an age to boot up. Even as she searched on the internet for Hal...no, Henry North.

It. Could. Not. Be. Him.

There was no shortage of hits—there were, apparently, a lot of Henry Norths in the world—and rather than plough through them, she switched to 'images' to see if she recognised any of them.

There were dozens of photographs, but one leapt out at her and it was the shock of seeing Hal face to face in the ditch all over again. That stop-the-world total loss of breath where the only thing moving was her mind, and that was spinning like a top. Seeing it in front of her she refused to believe it even when she clicked on the image to bring up the document it was attached to; a company report.

She knew it couldn't be true. But there he was. Hal North. In full colour.

The Hal North she'd knocked off his feet a couple of hours ago was, apparently, the Henry North who owned a freight company. Make that an international freight company.

The one with the sleek black-and-silver HALGO livery familiar to anyone who'd ever stood at a bus stop by a busy road watching the traffic thunder by.

Vans, trucks, eighteen-wheelers, not to mention air cargo and shipping.

Hal North, her Hal North, was the chairman of a household-name company with a turnover in billions.

'Hal! At last. Where on earth have you been?' Bea Webb rarely got agitated, but she was agitated now. 'I've organised the staff meetings for Monday, but I have to get back to London and so do you.'

'Sorry. I was looking around the Park and got sidetracked.'

'Collecting junk left by fly-tippers more like,' she said, as he lifted Claire's bike off the back of a Land Rover.

'I couldn't just leave it there,' he said. Easier than telling her what had really happened.

'Well, don't. The consultants have arranged for a contractor to come in and do a thorough clean-up of the estate, clear the outbuildings. Do you want me to organise someone to take a look through all this junk before they start?' she asked, with a dismissive wave in the direction of the ornate, eighteenth-century stable block. 'Just in case there's a priceless Chinese vase tucked away in a box of discarded china?'

'Don't bother,' he said. 'Cranbrook had experts go through it all with a fine-tooth comb in the hopes of finding buried treasure.' Anything to save him bankruptcy. Anything to save him from being forced by his creditors to sell to him.

It was knowing that Sir Robert Cranbrook wouldn't see a penny of his money that had made paying the price almost a pleasure. Once the tax man had taken his cut, the remainder would go to the estate's creditors; the small people Cranbrook had never given a damn about so long as he continued to live in luxury.

That and the fact that Robert Cranbrook knew that every moment of comfort left to him was being paid for by the son he'd never wanted. Whom he'd always refused to acknowledge. Knowing how much he'd hate that, but not having the moral fibre to tell him to go to hell, was the sweetest revenge.

'What I do need is a front loader. The public footpath running beside the stream has been seriously undermined and is in danger of collapse. We can use some of this stuff to make a temporary barrier. The last thing I need is for someone to get hurt.'

'Terrific,' she said. 'Tell me again why you bought this place?'

'The Cran is a great trout stream. I thought I'd take up fishing,' he said, removing Gary Harker's rod from the back of the Land Rover.

Her eyebrows suggested she was not convinced, but she confined herself to, 'Not today. You've got a board meeting at two-thirty and if we don't get moving you'll be late.'

'I gave Angus a call and asked him to stand in for me.' Her

eyebrows rose a notch. 'He can handle it and right now I'm needed here.'

'In other words you want to play with your expensive new toy.'

'Every man needs a hobby.'

'Renting a stretch of someone else's trout stream would have been a lot cheaper,' she pointed out. 'Besides, I thought you were going to leave all this to the experts. Keep a low profile.'

'This is the country. No chance of that.' Not when you'd just had a close encounter with the local press. 'Front loaders?' he prompted, picking up Claire's bike then, as Bea called up an app on her phone to search for a local hire company. 'Any messages?'

She shook her head, then looked up. 'Were you expecting a call?'

'No.' As far as Claire knew there was no one to take a complaint about uppity staff who took shocking advantage of maidens in distress. On the other hand... 'I thought you might have heard from the local paper.'

'No "might" about it. The editor rang, hoping for a quote to go with the announcement of the sale they're running in Monday's edition. Then there was some girl wanting "the personal angle" on the new owner of Cranbrook Park...' Her phone began to ring. 'Don't worry, Hal. I made it clear that you don't give interviews.'

Some girl.

No prizes for guessing who that was. Claire Thackeray hadn't been so shocked by her tumble, by her confrontation with him, that she'd neglected to follow up the news that the estate had been sold.

'Hold on, Katie...' She held the phone to her chest. 'Is there anything else, only I really do need to get home. There's an open evening at Katie's school this evening.'

'Don't worry. I've got it covered.' He picked up the bike.

'Tell Katie that she can come down for the half term if she likes. She'll enjoy the deer.

'You're staying down here?' she asked.

'For a week. Maybe two. The roof needs immediate attention. It's getting me out of the office,' he pointed out, when she would have protested. 'Something you're always encouraging.'

'Creating barriers for footpaths and dealing with a leaky roof wasn't quite what I had in mind. And thanks for the invitation but we're headed to Italy and guaranteed sunshine. Lying by the pool beats picking up rubbish hands down. There's plenty of space if you fancy a change of scene,' she said.

'I'll think about it,' he said, but they both knew he wouldn't. Travel was something he did because he had to, for business. Right now all he wanted to do was get on his Harley and ride around the estate the way he used to, although it wouldn't be as much fun without some furious gardener or gamekeeper chasing him on a quad bike.

Nothing was as much fun these days.

He blocked out Robert Cranbrook's mocking voice, and looked around. He had more than enough to get out of bed for. Everything was shabby, worn out. There were weeds growing out of what had once been perfectly raked gravel, and water stains on the walls where broken guttering hadn't been repaired.

When he was a kid this had been gleaming, cared for. A place where only the privileged few—and their staff—were allowed. Forbidden territory for the likes of him. Not that he'd taken any notice of that.

Ignoring the rules, going where he wasn't allowed, dodging the staff to explore the seemingly endless empty rooms had been a challenge.

He'd never taken anything, not even as much as a polished apple from a bowl; he'd simply wanted to tread the centuries-old floors, finger the linen-fold panels, look at the paintings, absorb the history that he'd been denied as he'd wandered through the empty, unused rooms.

There had been a moment of elation, triumph when he'd picked up the deeds and tossed them casually to his company lawyer that even Robert Cranbrook's outburst couldn't sour. But while he was now the proud owner of the Hall with its leaking roof and crumbling fences, ironically, the only place on the estate where the paintwork was glossy and well cared for was the house he'd once lived in.

And it was Claire Thackeray's unexpected response to his ill-advised kiss that was burning a hole in his brain; the memory of her slim foot, her ankle resting in his hands, playing havoc with his senses.

CHAPTER FIVE

CLAIRE stared at the screen.

Hal North had been turned off the estate by Sir Robert with nothing to his name but a motorbike and a bad attitude on his nineteenth birthday. Now he was back, the chairman of an international company. A millionaire. A millionaire she'd accused of fishing without a licence. A millionaire to whom she'd offered her last ten-pound note.

He must be laughing fit to bust.

Well, let him laugh, she thought, as she clicked furiously on the links, determined to find out all she could about where he'd been, what he'd been doing since he left. How he'd made his money.

She'd teach Hal North to make sarcastic comments about working for a local paper.

Human interest?

This was human interest in letters ten feet high. A story that she could write because she'd been there at the beginning. One that she knew hadn't been told because it would have been a sensation in Cranbrook. A sensation in Maybridge.

Headline material.

Prodigal returns, buys up the big house and has hot, sweaty sex with the girl he left behind…

Whoa, whoa!

She didn't write fantasy, she dealt in reality.

And she didn't write gossip. She had been told to stay at

home for the rest of the week and she'd use the time to get ahead on the G&D blog.

She was taking photographs of a particularly large slug—planning a piece on organic control—when her phone rang.

She took it out of her pocket, checked the caller. So much for putting her feet up...

'Hello, Brian,' she said.

'Claire... How are you feeling now?' he asked, all sympathy.

Having insisted that she was ready to come into work, she could hardly say she was hors d'combat. Not that he waited for an answer.

'Any chance you could do a bit of research on the new owner of Cranbrook Park? Nothing you'll have to leave the house for.'

Yes, well, she was the one who'd insisted that the Park was her territory.

'What do you want to know?'

'General background. Where he comes from, family, that sort of thing. I'll send you what we've got. Unless it's too much trouble?' he added, apparently picking up on her lack of enthusiasm.

'No, no, of course not. I was using the down time to catch up on my gardening blog, but it can wait.'

'Good girl.'

'Patronising oaf,' she muttered, but only when he'd hung up.

Back in her office, she checked her email and, just in case she was in any doubt, there was the press release, embargoed until Monday, telling the world that Henry North had bought Cranbrook Park.

The moment it emerged he was local—and there would be plenty of people who remembered him—it would become obvious to Brian that she would have known him. He'd want specifics, details.

She opened up a new document and began to makes notes. Everything she knew about Hal. His parents, school.

She fired off an email to the recently retired headmistress of the village school to get a quote, called Maybridge High and spoke to the school secretary who pointed her in the direction of teachers who would remember him. She left messages for them to call her back. That done, she hit the internet in order to find out what he'd been up to since he'd left Cranbrook. How he'd transformed himself from disaffected youth to millionaire. That was the big story.

She ran into a blank wall.

When Ms Webb said that Mr North did not speak to the press, she hadn't been kidding.

Hal wasn't one of those CEOs who courted publicity. He didn't date supermodels, big himself up on television talk shows, or appear in *Celebrity* magazine attending showbiz parties. Of course he didn't. If he'd done any of those things she would, undoubtedly, have seen him. And if he was happily married with a parcel of children he'd kept that to himself, as well.

The kiss that still burned on her lips suggested otherwise. Or, if he was married, the relationship was clearly more of a hobby than a full-time occupation.

No.

Despite the endless stream of girls who had made his life sweet when he was a youth living on the estate, she didn't see him as a man who'd play the field once he'd found his mate.

'Oh, get real,' she muttered.

She knew nothing about him. Only that he made the air sizzle. Made her pulse race, her heart pound. Which was as ridiculous now as it had been when she was a pre-pubescent fantasist who would have fainted if he'd as much as winked at her.

Okay. She had the boy, the youth and by the time she left to pick up Ally from school, she had school photographs, anecdotes from teachers and enough general background to email Brian and ask him if she could go to London on a quest to fill in the more recent past. The fact that he agreed so readily, suggested he had already drawn a blank himself.

She'd just opened the back door when she heard the crunch of gravel. Gary with her bike.

Not Gary.

Like iron filings, a gazillion cells turned in one direction as if someone had switched on an electro-magnet. That had to explain the sudden dizziness as Hal North rounded the corner of the cottage, stopped as he saw her.

'You're on your way out?' he asked.

'I was just going to pick up Ally from school,' she said, banging the door behind her and heading for the gate.

'How's your foot?' he asked, falling in beside her.

'What? Oh, good as new,' she said. Not. Her heel was throbbing and walking on the gravel was painful. 'What do you want, Hal?'

'To explain about your bike.' He looked at her foot, clearly not convinced. 'Can I give you a lift? We can talk on the way.'

There was an ancient estate Land Rover parked at the gate and he opened the door. It was high and as she put her weight on her foot to haul herself up, she gave a little gasp and he put his hands on her backside and gave her a boost up.

'Okay?'

Okay?

You went eight years without a man's hand on your backside and then it happened twice in as many days…

'Fine,' she snapped and reached to the seat belt, any excuse to look away.

He climbed in beside her, teased the cranky old machine into life, then turned it and headed into the village.

'So? What's the verdict on my bike?' she asked.

'It's a mess,' he said, above the noise of the engine. 'You're going to need a new wheel and front mudguard. I'm doing my best to locate one.'

'You could have phoned to tell me that.' Then, aware that she had sounded less than grateful, 'I meant you didn't have to come specially.'

'I was at this end of the estate.'

'Inspecting your domain?'

He glanced at her. 'Something like that,' he said.

Damn! There were a hundred questions she wanted to ask and she'd blown her chance with a snarky remark. But while it was easy enough to be focussed, professional when he was just a name, a face on her computer, up close and personal—with the imprint of his hand on her bottom still warm in the memory—it was difficult to be dispassionate. Professional. Cool.

'When were you going to tell me that you've bought Cranbrook Park?' she asked, doing her best to recover the situation.

'Would you have believed me if I'd told you this morning?'

'We'll never know,' she said, as he pulled up in front the school. Then, rolling her eyes she said, 'Probably not.'

'No.' Her honesty earned her one of those rare smiles. 'And I knew you'd read about it in the paper on Monday.'

A group of mothers turned as one to see who had arrived. Gossip city.

'I'd better go. I'm supposed to be supervising some workmen.'

'You're going to be a hands-on lord of the manor, then?' It had been a very long time since she'd given anyone anything to talk about so she might as well make the most of it.

'Just taking a few days out to play with my expensive new toy,' he said, with the merest edge of self-mockery in response to her sarcasm.

'Expensive, I have no doubt, but Cranbrook Park is not a toy.'

'No. Like all my investments, it will have to work for its keep.'

'How? What are you going to do with it?'

He leaned across her, threatening a sensory overload as his arm came within a whisker of her breast and she had a close-up of his cheekbone, a lungful of the scent of his skin, hair as he opened her door. 'I'll have someone bring your bike back when it's fixed.'

She slid down onto the pavement, turned to face him.

'Ask Gary,' she said. 'He might even be able to straighten out the wheel. He's like you, good with his hands.' And she blushed.

'Goodbye, Claire.'

'Goodbye, Hal. Thanks for the lift.'

She slammed the door shut and watched the old Land Rover move away through the village leaving her engulfed in the scent of hot metal and diesel.

Work for its keep...

Was that a warning that her days of paying a low rent in return for keeping the cottage in good repair were running out?

He'd warned her not to spend money on wallpaper...

All her hard work would mean nothing to him. Her cottage was pretty, her garden was a showpiece. It would fetch three times the rent she paid on the open market.

It wasn't just her job that was under threat, but she was being forced to seriously consider the possibility that she would lose her home.

'Mum!' Ally flung herself at her.

'Hi, angel. I'm home early so I thought I'd come and meet you. Do you want to ask Savannah if she'd like to come to tea?'

'Absolutely not. I am never talking to her again.'

Oh, terrific.

* * *

He could have phoned, should have phoned, Hal knew, but like coming back to Cranbrook Park, he was drawn to Claire Thackeray by something he couldn't explain.

Robert Cranbrook was right, he had obsessed about owning the Park, it had driven him and he'd commissioned plans for its future long before it had been on the market. He'd known it was only a matter of time.

It had all seemed so simple; what he'd do, how it would feel but then, this morning, he'd seen that boy—so like himself at that age. No respect. Full of what the world owed him. It had been like a kick in the gut.

And then he'd been run down by the Claire and Archie double act and the kick had been physical rather than meta-phorical.

Local Boy Saves Cranbrook Park

Solicitors acting for Sir Robert Cranbrook announced this morning that the Cranbrook Park estate has been sold to mil-lionaire businessman, Henry North.

For Mr North, founder and CEO of HALGO, the interna-tional freight company, this is a very special homecoming. Born in Maybridge, both his parents worked for Sir Robert Cranbrook and he went to both Cranbrook Primary and Maybridge High Schools before leaving the area to set up his own business.

Mrs Mary Bridges, retired Head Teacher of Cranbrook Primary School remembers Mr North well, describing him as 'full of life' and he's remembered at Maybridge High School as a promising student who, even as a youth, demonstrated a well-honed entrepreneurial spirit.

Former residents of the estate recall that he was a keen fish-erman and he will no doubt take full advantage of the excel-lent fishing in the famous trout stream for which the Park is named.

Henry North started his own motorcycle courier service upon leaving school and he swiftly fulfilled his early promise, rapidly expanding his business to compete with major freight companies at home and internationally. When his company was floated on the stock exchange three years ago, his personal fortune was estimated to be in nine figures.

Rumours have been flying around all week, suggesting that the estate will be transformed into a leisure facility but Mr North, 33, divorced, is keeping his plans for the estate under wraps for the moment. He did however confirm that it would, like all his investments, have to 'work for its keep,' which sounds promising for local jobs.

—*Maybridge Observer,* Monday April 24

'Excellent job, Claire.' Brian leaned back in his chair. 'Obviously we went to the internet, but it was pretty thin considering who he is and we missed the local connection. Of course you live on the estate. Did you know him?'

'He's a bit older than me,' she said.

'Of course. You must have been just a kid when he left. You did well to get hold of the school photographs so quickly.'

'Thanks.' She handed him her expense sheet for Friday. Her fare—cheap day return, receipts for copies of his birth, marriage and divorce certificates, as well her lunch in the café near his office.

She'd felt like a proper reporter as she'd struck up a conversation with the girl clearing the tables, pretending that she'd been offered a job with the company. As she'd hoped, most of his staff ate there at lunchtime and, no surprise, the women talked about their good-looking, eligible boss.

'I kept my expenses to the bare minimum,' she said, as his eyebrows rose at the amount. 'Worth it simply for the information that he's unattached, I'd say. How many copies is a front-page photograph of a good-looking, eligible millionaire in the neighbourhood going to be worth?'

'I don't know.'

'Women buy the local newspaper,' she pointed out.

'True, but how often can we use him on the front page? Until we know what his plans are he's not going to be head-line news.'

'You don't need headline news. I'll give you stories,' she promised. 'All you need on the front page is a photograph and a caption leading on to page two. It's how they use the royal family to sell papers.'

'Shame he doesn't have a title to go with all that money, but you can't have everything.' He grinned, signed the sheet and handed it back to her. 'With the way circulation is fall-ing, anything is worth a try, but no more trips to London.'

The phone rang once, twice, three times. He checked his watch. Ten on the dot.

He picked up the receiver, sat back in the leather chair worn smooth by generations of Cranbrook men. 'What do you want, Claire?'

'And good morning to you, Hal.'

'Is it good? I hadn't noticed.'

'Shame on you. I was earthing-up my potatoes as the sun rose with a robin for company.'

He was at his desk dealing with the reports and emails that, these days, seemed to multiply faster than he could deal with.

'I hope you weren't late for work again.'

'I was, but only because the bus was late. Any news on my bike?'

'I'll chase it up. If that's all?' he prompted, knowing full well it wasn't.

'How about an update on your plans for the future of Cranbrook Park?' she asked, in a clear, bright musical voice that was inextricably tied into a burning sense of injustice, of longing for something beyond his reach. Was Robert Cranbrook right? Was this the end rather than the beginning he'd envisaged? 'Just a little hint?' she prompted. 'Something I can use in tomorrow's paper?'

'It's none of your business?' he offered. That 'boy' in the *Observer*'s headline had been too reminiscent of Cranbrook's bile.

'No…I'm going to need more than that.'

Was she laughing?

'It's none of your business, Claire Thackeray?' he offered, restraining the urge to join her.

'Okay. We'll leave that for now but I was hoping you'd explain to our readers why you've blocked off the public footpath beside the Cran?'

'Do your readers care?' he asked. 'No one has complained.'

'Clearly you don't read our letters page.'

'I don't read the *Observer,*' he lied, 'but I have no doubt that "outraged of Maybridge" is an inside job.'

'How cynical you are. People do care.'

'No comment.'

'So that's a "no comment", a "no comment" and a "no comment," then. Okay,' she said—definitely laughing— 'That'll do nicely.'

'Claire… How's your foot?'

'I'm scarred for life. You'll be hearing from my lawyers any day now. How's your, um, rod?' she asked.

'I refer you to the answer I gave earlier.'

'It would make a great story. Millionaire Landowner Mown Down by Tenant. Archie has form, you know. He ran some quad bikers into the stream last year. I'll send you a link to the article.'

'You wouldn't rat on Archie,' he said, as an email popped into his inbox. 'How do you know my email address?'

'No comment and no comment. It's a good picture of him, don't you think?'

He clicked on the link, looked at the photograph of Archie, the picture of sweet innocence as he peered over the hedge.

'Believe nothing that you read and only half what you see,' he replied and thought he caught a sigh from the other end of the phone.

'Any progress with my bike?' she asked.

'Ask Gary. He's working on it.'

'I will and, Hal?'

'Yes?'

'Thanks for giving him a chance. The offer of a cake is still open. Any time.'

'Just stop ringing me and we'll be quits,' he said, hanging up before he relented.

The estimate for re-leading the roof dealt with the smile.

'Made the front page again, Claire?'

'Homing instinct,' she said, glancing at the pulls of the front page. The Maybridge Wish-List fairy might be draped over the masthead, but it was her story that was the lead. '"Closed for Fun…" It has a nice ring to it, don't you think?' she said, doing her best to sound enthusiastic.

'It was a slow news day.' Tim Mayhew, the sports editor, made a virtue of being a grouch.

'This is Maybridge, Tim. It's always a slow news day. The ambitious journalist has to get out there and create her head-lines.'

That would be the journalist who was desperate to hang on to her job. The journalist who wished she hadn't promised the news editor a constant feed of Hal North stories.

'There's nothing wrong with ambition,' Tim said, 'but you're going to have to come up with something better than local landowner closes footpath if you're going to repeat your local-boy-makes-good coup.'

She didn't need him to tell her that. Brian was already on her case.

'It's not the footpath that makes the story, Tim, it's the "new," "millionaire" and "landowner" that does the business.'

Along with the tall, dark. The classically handsome element was cancelled out by rich and available.

'People will soon get fed up of being fed a diet of Hal North stories.'

The sooner the better. She couldn't wait to get back to the WI meetings, meanwhile…

'I've just heard that he's cancelled the traditional Teddy Bears Picnic. Just who the heck does think he is?' she asked, trying to put some real feeling into it.

'Henry North? New millionaire landowner?' he said, quoting her own words back at her.

She stared at the front-page picture of the pile of scrap metal blocking the footpath across the Cranbrook estate.

The photographer had used a marker to write "Closed For Fun" on a piece of cardboard and propped it against a handy piece of junk. It made a great picture, she didn't deny it. And Brian had found a photograph of Hal at a white-tie dinner. The juxtaposition suggested arrogance, distance, a man who didn't care.

Tim grunted. 'Personally, I don't blame him for refusing to have dozens of kids running riot on his newly acquired country estate.'

'Next to you the Grinch is warm and cuddly.'

Hal wasn't like that.

She mentally rolled her eyes. She kept telling herself that 'Hal wasn't like that'; she hadn't a clue what he was like. All she had was this fantasy figure she'd created in her head—a cross between Prince Charming and the Beast. And if she'd cast herself in the role of Beauty, it was because she'd been a kid and didn't know any better.

What she did know was that it hadn't been 'Mr Henry North, millionaire businessman' who'd mocked her, reminded her that she had once had a goal in life. A place at a good university, every advantage, and she'd wasted it. And it sure as heck hadn't been 'Mr Henry North, millionaire businessman' who'd kissed her socks off. Well, her tights, anyway…

That had most definitely been Hal North, Cranbrook bad boy, doing what he did as naturally as breathing. She'd put his bad temper down to the fact that she'd run into him. That must have hurt. But having reinvented himself it must have come as quite a shock to discover that she was still on the estate and working for the local newspaper.

He'd got off lightly, she reminded herself.

She could have got a lot more quotes to liven up her original front page if she'd had a mind to, but she'd kept that to herself. She wasn't about to annoy the man who had it in his power to put up her rent.

'It's really tough on the charity that relies on the event,' she said. Concentrate on that. Not on Hal.

'It must have come as a real shock when Cranbrook Park was sold overnight to a man who doesn't buy into the whole noblesse-oblige thing.'

'It was quick, wasn't it?' Almost as if Hal had been watching, waiting…

'Once you're in hock to the tax man you're done for. They won't wait for the market to pick up. As long as they're covered they don't care how cheap they sell. And it would need to be cheap. The place is going to take a fortune to restore.'

'I suppose.'

'No doubt North will finance it with a high-end executive estate on that meadow running beside the May. It's a prime riverside location and out of sight of the Hall. Perfect.'

'What? But that's Archie's meadow!' she protested. He was right, though. It was perfect. Forget dancing on Sir Robert's grave. How much more satisfying would Hal find it to make Sir Robert watch as he trampolined a thousand years of Cranbrook family history into the dirt. 'He'd never get it through planning,' she objected.

'You think a man like North is going to let petty bureaucracy stand in his way? If the local planners prove obstinate, he'll put in a appeal to the Secretary of State on the grounds of the local need for jobs, houses.' He shrugged. 'They're probably mates. There's a story for you.'

'I can't print that!'

She wouldn't have to. All it would take was a photograph of them together and people would leap to their own conclusions. And there was nothing like a suggestion of dirty doings at the Town Hall to boost circulation.

She would be flavour of the month. And if it made her feel just a little bit soiled? The way she'd felt as she'd listened to gossip about him in the café near his office, well, it was her job. It paid the rent, kept Ally warm and fed.

'Besides, what will happen to poor old Archie?'

'Oh, please. If North has any sense that donkey was cats' meat within a week of him moving in. You should sue him for not keeping him under control,' he added. 'Or are you saving that for another headline?'

'Of course not. He's always been a lamb with me.' As long as she had an apple to buy him off. 'Archie,' she added, rubbing the back of her hand over her mouth. Hal North was something else...

'Kebabs, then. Millionaire Makes Mincemeat of Maybridge Mascot...'

'Shut up, Tim,' she muttered as Brian walked through the office.

'Children, children!' Jessica Dixon, the features editor raised her head from her PC. 'The only thing that should concern you on today's front page is who is going to be this year's Fairy Godmother. Or Godfather,' she added, looking at Tim over her spectacles. 'This is an equal-opportunity chance to volunteer.'

'Tim in a tutu and wings.' Cheered at the thought, Claire grinned. 'Now that I would pay good money to see.'

CHAPTER SIX

Maybridge wish week!

It's Maybridge Wish Week! Time for the *Maybridge Observer*'s Fairy Godmother to wave her magic wand and make some wishes come true for members of the community.

In the past few years, we've hunted down grant funding, drummed up support from local business and enlisted the help of a volunteer army from our community to refurbish the pensioners' day-care centre, built a modern, fully equipped sports pavilion on the old playing fields and turned a derelict cinema into an arts centre that is now a vibrant part of Maybridge life, as well as dozens of smaller projects to make life easier for groups and individuals.

So—what next?

We're asking you to tell us what project you'd like to see tackled this year...

—*Maybridge Observer,* April 27.

'Have you seen this?'

Hal glanced at the newspaper Bea Webb was holding up.

'The *Maybridge Observer* Fairy Godmother?' he asked blandly, ignoring the headline and concentrating instead on the cartoon fairy waving her wand and sprinkling gold sparkle over the newspaper masthead.

She looked exactly like Claire Thackeray.

'If only. According to this, Maybridge has become a "fun-free zone" since your arrival.'

He took the paper from her and dropped it in the bin, refusing to think about the way she called him every day at the same time to ask about his plans. To think about the fact that he was always at his desk, waiting for her call. Glancing at his watch if she was a little late.

That her voice, clear, confident, the product of all that expensive private education that had gone to waste in a moment of lust with a man who hadn't bothered to stick around and deal with his own mess, had taken up residence in his head.

'I need someone in the office full-time, Bea,' he said, firmly changing the subject. 'Will you ask Penny if she's prepared to do more hours?'

She shook her head. 'Why don't you stick to the plan and leave all this to the professionals, Hal?'

Good question.

Claire knew that Tim had just been winding her up, but she couldn't get Archie out of her head.

Okay, he was a bit—more than a bit—of a liability and while Sir Robert might have had a soft spot for the beast, Hal North had no reason to consider him anything but a pain in the fishing rod, but...

Just...but.

She looked up as Brian stopped by her desk. 'How far have you got with the Teddy Bears Picnic story, Claire?'

'I'm working on it,' she said. 'I thought I might run over and take some photographs of Cranbrook woods.'

'No need. I sent Marcus over there this morning. I want you to focus on the "all this and he won't share it for a day, not even for a good cause" angle.' Her heart was still sinking when he said, 'On the other hand, it wouldn't hurt to go and have a good look round. Take some pictures if you see any sign of surveying.'

'Have you heard something?' she asked.

'No. Charlie Peascod is being unusually close-mouthed. Why don't you pop along this evening and see what's going on? Take your little girl with you. You can always say you're on a nature walk or something.'

'I'm not taking Ally with me! Suppose we're thrown out for trespassing?'

'We couldn't get that lucky.' Maybe her expression betrayed just how far he'd stepped over the line because he said, 'It's nearly lunchtime. You might as well go now. But don't take all day about it.'

The minute Bea had left, Hal walked across the courtyard towards the garages.

Claire's bike was standing, upended, still minus a wheel, in one corner. It had been more than a week since her bike had been damaged, too long for her to be without any kind of transport. And when it was fixed she wouldn't have an excuse to ring him.

'Gary?'

There was a clank of metal, the familiar sound of a spanner hitting concrete, followed by a muttered oath.

He followed the sound to the workshop and the years rolled back as he saw the boy and an old motorcycle in pieces strewn all around him.

The minute Claire got home, she changed into jeans, boots and, with her camera tucked into her pocket, she walked down to the meadow.

It was a classic flower meadow. It hadn't been ploughed in centuries, just grazed by sheep, rabbits and Archie. Except that Archie wasn't there.

Forget looking for surveyors setting up levels, she had to talk to Hal, find out what on earth was going on.

* * *

'Okay, hand me the nut...'

'This one?'

Hal, lying on his side as he tackled an awkward connection, turned his head a little too quickly and nearly lost the assembly he was rebuilding.

Claire Thackeray, all legs in a pair of close-fitting jeans, was offering him a large wing nut.

'Don't be ridiculous,' he snapped. 'Anyone with half a brain cell can see that I need that one.'

'Pardon me.' She dropped the wing nut and bent to pick up the small nut he'd indicated, but instead of handing it to him, she closed her hand around it and straightened up. 'Where is Archie?' she asked.

Archie?

'The nut?' he prompted. It was taking a considerable amount of pressure to hold everything in place.

'He's not in his meadow.'

She was serious?

'I don't want another quad-bike incident.'

'I shouldn't have sent you that link,' she said, ignoring the irritable clicking of his fingers. 'What have you done with him, Hal?'

'Give me that nut and I'll tell you.' She offered it between finger and thumb. 'It may have escaped your notice,' he said, through gritted teeth, 'but I can't let go of this.'

She took a step closer, close enough for him to smell the crushed grass on her boots, see the way her jeans stretched across her hips, clung to a backside his hand remembered.

'Will you get down here?'

His voice felt as if it was wading through treacle.

She dropped to her knees and now he had the full impact of skin glowing from a brisk walk, wisps of cream-coloured hair escaping the clasp at her neck, huge grey eyes.

The wish-fairy come to life...

He closed his hand around the nut and discovered that her hand was shaking. Or was it his?

For a moment their gazes locked. It was his thumb, the one holding the spring assembly together, on the point of losing it, that reminded him what he was supposed to be doing. He took the nut, fastened it in place. 'Pass me a spanner.'

She glanced at the row of tools and, wonder of wonders, selected the right one.

'Now, hold this.'

'It's greasy,' she objected.

'Tough, it's you or Gary and I don't see Gary. What have you done with him?

'I made the magic sign of the teacup. I had to talk to you, Hal.'

'Nice try, Claire, but I don't...'

'No comment won't cut it. This isn't work.'

'It's not?' She really was worried about that stupid donkey? 'In that case we're both playing hooky. I'm recapturing my boyhood, what's your excuse?'

'The usual. Rumour, drivel...'

'Then it can wait until we've finished this.' And he kept her there for half an hour, handing him parts as he worked on the bike.

A smear of grease appeared on her cheek, on her shirt. She gritted her teeth as her hand slipped and she knocked a knuckle, but didn't complain. By the time they'd finished she was anticipating his next move and they were working smoothly as a team.

'Anyone would think you'd done this before,' he said, passing her a cloth to wipe her hands.

'I may have taken my lawnmower to bits once or twice.'

'You are full of surprises,' he said, standing up, offering his hand to help her to her feet. 'Shall we go and see if Gary managed to switch on the kettle?' He glanced back at her as they crossed the courtyard. 'I don't suppose you brought that cake you keep threatening me with? Or have you been too busy earthing up your potatoes?'

'Hal…'

'Archie's in the stables,' he said, taking pity on her. 'He's been confined to barracks until the hedging contractor has made the meadow escape-proof.'

'Oh.'

'Why? What did you think I'd done with him?'

'Nothing.' She said it too quickly. 'Just… One of my colleagues said something. Nothing.'

'Hardly nothing if it had you racing up here to check up on him.'

She pulled a face. 'Just a stupid throwaway remark.' He waited. 'It involved the phrase "cats' meat."'

He would have been affronted if she hadn't been so obviously embarrassed. If she hadn't been so desperately concerned.

'I suppose I should be grateful that you bothered to check rather just starting a hue and cry with a story about a missing donkey.'

'We're not so short of stories at the *Observer* that we're reduced to manufacturing them. I've been remarkably restrained.'

'Am I supposed to be grateful?'

'I haven't written a word about being attacked by livestock running wild on a public footpath, my trashed bicycle, the cuts and bruises I sustained without so much as a penny-piece in compensation from the landowner. On the contrary, it was the landowner who demanded—'

'Why not?' he asked, cutting short her list of complaints.

Claire looked at the cloth, rubbed at a stubborn grease spot, grateful for the interruption. If she reminded Hal about the on-the-spot fine he'd levied, he might also recall how enthusiastically she'd paid up.

'You know why not,' she said. 'He's had enough bad press.'

'That doesn't explain why you're going easy on me. Isn't it your public duty to warn your fellow citizens about my wicked past?'

He was closer. Too close...

'You haven't mentioned the poaching,' he pointed out. 'Or the graffiti on Cranbrook's factory walls, or the time I rode a motorcycle up the venerated steps of Cranbrook Hall and in through the front door. Why is that, Claire?'

'You were a kid. I'm more interested in what you're doing now.' Which was the truth. This was a different world, they were different people... 'Were you?' she asked. 'Wicked?'

His smile took her unawares and, as he caught her hand, the heat of it went straight to her knees, burning up her lips, firing the same melting ache between her thighs as his kiss...

'Do you want to come inside and repeat that question?' he offered.

'I'll take that as a yes,' she managed, her voice remarkably steady considering the fact that the rest of her appeared to be slowly melting.

'Good decision,' he said.

Was it? Right now melting was deeply appealing. The thought of being touched by those oil-stained hands, being kissed, being wicked...

'Did you really ride your motorbike through the front door of Cranbrook Hall?' she asked.

'You hadn't heard about that?' He seemed surprised.

'No one ever talked to me.' Oh, good grief, that sounded so pathetic. 'Was that why Sir Robert banned you from the estate?'

'It wasn't Sir Robert who did that, Claire, it was your father.' And his hand slid from hers, leaving her feeling oddly bereft.

'My dad?'

'Acting on Robert Cranbrook's instructions I have no doubt, but he enjoyed delivering the message.'

'I didn't know.' She swallowed. 'Not that it matters,' she added quickly. 'I'm far more interested in how you progressed from estate tearaway to millionaire businessman.'

'Are you?' His doubt suggested, worryingly, that he knew exactly the effect he had on her. 'Well, you're the journalist, if a somewhat ineffectual one judging by your performance so far. You won't get far in your chosen profession unless you toughen up, learn to be ruthless.'

'Is that how you succeeded?'

'There is no other way. The difference between us is that in your business it doesn't matter who you hurt so long as you sell newspapers.'

She opened her mouth to protest. Closed it. Took a breath. 'I told you, this has nothing to do with my job.'

'A real journalist is never off duty, Claire.'

'Then I guess I'm not a real journalist...'

There was moment of shocked silence as the reality of what she'd just said sank in.

'So, what? You're just playing at it?'

She shook her head, as if to deny it but her mouth was clamped tight and Hal felt a moment of pity for her. What the hell was she doing in a job she clearly wasn't cut out for?

'Would it reassure you if I told you that I was the one who used apples to train Archie to be my wing man?' he said.

He saw the ripple in her neck as she swallowed hard, taking a mental step back from what she'd just said.

'Wing man?'

'Once he got the hang of being bribed to be quiet, he kicked up a fuss whenever anyone came near.'

'Giving you time to disappear.' A smile broke through, lighting up her eyes. 'That would be the same apples,' she said. 'From the tree in my garden?'

'It would.'

She shook her head. 'Now I feel really stupid.'

'You look it. Here...' He took her chin in her hand, lifted

her face and taking the cloth she was holding, wiped at the smear of grease.

Her skin was warm against his fingers and her soft pink lips, parted as if to ask a question she'd thought better of, invited a kiss. Not the harsh, punishing kiss he'd inflicted on her that day on the path, that she'd subverted into something else, but the kind that could only ever have one conclusion.

'Has it gone?' she asked.

'No, I've just made it worse,' he said, dropping his hand, turning away.

Not in this lifetime.

'You'd better come inside and clean up. You don't want to be on the street looking like that.' Gary was in the kitchen, emptying the biscuit tin. 'Lunch break's over,' he said. The lad looked startled and Hal being aware that he'd been abrupt said, 'We'll finish your bike tomorrow.'

'Really? Gosh, thanks, Mr North... Hal. Actually...' He waited. 'Would you mind if I brought a mate with me to watch? We're hoping to start a scramble team and—'

'Yes, yes,' he said. 'Now get back to work.'

'That's kind of you,' she said, when Gary had gone.

'It's nothing. Pure self-indulgence.'

'Helping Gary isn't nothing. Recapturing your boyhood isn't nothing.'

'I don't have time for that.'

'No?' She gave a little sigh. 'Growing up isn't all it's cracked up to be, is it? I'd better go and wash my hands.'

'I'll be in the morning room.'

Claire used the staff cloakroom to clean up, splashing cold water onto her face and neck to cool herself down.

Standing out there in the courtyard she'd been sure that Hal was going to kiss her again and not to punish her this time, even if she deserved it.

For one reckless, forget-the-world moment, she'd wanted

him to. She scooped up more water, splashed herself again. Gathered the ends of her hair and re-fastened the clip. Tidying everything up. Restoring order out of the chaos of her thoughts, her life.

Blanking out that moment when he'd challenged her and the ground had seemed to open up in front of her. What on earth was she thinking?

Not a real journalist…

A glance in the mirror belied any hope of order.

She wasn't about to use anti-bacterial hand wash on her face and she'd been a bit too enthusiastic with the splashing. Her shirt was wet, almost transparent. She had to change, get back to work. Bad enough to be going back empty-handed, but late buses was an excuse that she could only take so far.

Hal wasn't in the kitchen and she pushed open the green baize door that divided upstairs from downstairs. She'd expected it to be stripped bare, but it was much as she remembered, family portraits and all.

'Having a good look round?'

'I'm just surprised it's all still here, but I don't suppose there's much of market for second-hand ancestors.'

'It depends whose ancestors they are,' he said.

She glanced at him.

'There's no one here important enough, distinguished enough to excite anyone who isn't a Cranbrook, and the previous owner's nursing-home room isn't big enough to accommodate them.'

'Poor man. It must be so difficult for him.'

'He made bad choices, Claire. He has to live with them.'

He sounded, looked so hard.

'Have you never made a bad choice?' she asked.

'I got married.' For a moment she thought he was going to say more, but he just looked at her. 'What about you?'

'I fell in love with the wrong man,' she said. 'I'm not sure that choice had much to do with it but I let down my family.'

'And Robert Cranbrook let down his.'

'I suppose.' She looked up at a portrait of Sir Robert's mother, holding her son. There was a faded border around it, where there had once hung a larger portrait of his father, replaced when it was damaged. 'So,' she said, turning away, looking around at the serried ranks of Cranbrooks rising up the stairs, 'the portraits were thrown in with the fixtures and fittings. Like unwanted carpets and curtains.'

'I can almost see the cogs turning in your brain. It's not a story, Claire.'

'Isn't it?' Something told her that it was, but she let it go. 'I told you, I'm off the clock.'

'So you did. Shall we take these into the morning room?'

He handed her a mug and led the way to a small, shabby but comfortable sitting room with French windows that stood open on to a sunken walled rose garden.

She carried her mug onto the terrace.

'It breaks my heart to see it in this state,' she said, sipping at her tea. 'It makes my fingers itch to get stuck in with the sécateurs.'

'You love gardening?'

'There's something about restoring order out of chaos that appeals to me,' she said. 'And then putting back just enough chaos to make it interesting.'

'You'll find all the chaos you need here. This has been neglected since Cranbrook's wife left him. Fortunately, it's not like the Hall, where every single item of architectural detail has to be approved before it can be replaced.'

'Replaced?' She looked up at him. 'Please tell me that you're not planning to grub it up? Plant tidy rows of bedding plants. All the same colour, the same height...'

'You said it. Order out of chaos.'

'I didn't mean… Some of these roses are really old, Hal. Heritage varieties.'

'Old, dying, heritage varieties.'

'It takes more than neglect to kill a rose. These just need some TLC. You should consult a specialist. You might be able to interest a grower in a restoration project.'

'And have sponsorship signs all over the place? I'll stick to the bedding plants, thanks.'

'All they'd want is a discrete little plaque somewhere, acknowledging their contribution. I've seen them in other great gardens.'

'So what do they get out of it?'

'In this case I imagine they'd love the chance to take cuttings, use modern methods to breed from your old varieties,' she offered. 'Their PR people would commission a book on the restoration project—you could sell it to your guests—and provide articles for gardening magazines, the Sunday supplements, lifestyle magazines. Everyone wins.' She put down the mug, aware that she was letting her passion run away with her tongue. 'I have to get back to work, Hal.'

'Next time bring cake.'

'Is that an open invitation? I do a great Victoria sandwich with homemade raspberry jam—'

'Goodbye, Claire.'

'I make the jam myself,' she said, her mouth running away with her, even while her head was saying, 'Go. Now.' 'With raspberries from my garden.'

'That would be perfect. And don't forget that you owe Archie two applies.'

'Two?' He'd remembered her desperate appeal as she was chased down the path? 'While I'd be the first to admit that Archie is a smart donkey, I doubt he keeps a tally,' she said. 'Besides, since he didn't deliver on the deal, I don't think he has a leg to stand on.'

'Then just come yourself. He gets lonely.'

'What about you, Hal? This is a big place to live in on your own.'

'Two apples, a Victoria sandwich,' he said, 'and you can send me the name of a rose specialist. Just in case I change my mind.'

CHAPTER SEVEN

HAL stood at the open French windows, listening to a blackbird sing, trying to blot out the image of Claire Thackeray.

Her concerns for an old donkey, a neglected garden, for Gary were beginning to eat away at his armour, undermine his determination to visit the sins of the father on her head.

Bea was right. He should have left this to the professionals.

Claire walked home, her head in a whirl, scarcely noticing where she put her feet. Talk about the good news and the bad news...

All she'd wanted to do was reassure herself that Archie was okay. Job done. But walking into the courtyard and seeing Hal on his back with a motorcycle in bits around him had been a heart-leap moment, a flashback to the boy in leathers astride his own bike. Today, though, she hadn't been an outsider. She'd been there, working alongside him and for a while had felt like a kid herself.

It couldn't last.

On some subconscious level, she'd always known that her father must have been involved in Hal's banishment. He'd been the estate manager, he ran Cranbrook Park. He engaged and dismissed staff, dealt with maintenance, arranged shoots and fishing parties.

Keeping order had been his responsibility.

She might be reduced to jelly-bones by Hal, but she could well understand why he'd been so peppery when they'd met. It hadn't just been the crash. She was a Thackeray and in his shoes she wouldn't have wanted to have anything to do with her, either.

She was amazed that he answered her phone calls. He could easily have left them to Penny, or let them go to voice mail. And he'd listened to her on the rose garden. That was good news. It would mean he was invested in Cranbrook Park, in the Hall.

As for that moment when he'd challenged her commitment to her job, being a journalist was what she did.

It put food on the table, kept Ally safe. It was what she'd always been going to do. She might not be working for the BBC, or be a high-flying correspondent for one of the broadsheets, but she was doing her best to fulfil the ambitions of her parents. Speaking of which—

She sat on a grassy bank, took out her phone and called Brian.

'Where on earth have you been?' he demanded.

'It's a big estate, Brian, but I haven't seen any sign of surveying so far.'

'Nothing?'

'Nothing.' Which was true. 'But I have heard a whisper that Mr North is thinking about restoring the rose garden.'

'And?'

'It's a famous garden. Bags of history.' She glanced at her watch. 'It'll be a waste of time coming back to the office. I'll do some research at home and maybe we can run something tomorrow?'

'We're running the Teddy Bear's Picnic story tomorrow.'

'I haven't finished it.'

'I have. Mr Mean Targets Teddies. The garden story can go in the home supplement on Saturday.'

She muttered an expletive she wouldn't have used at home and dialled again.

'North.'

'Hal…'

'Claire… Twice in one day.'

'Sorry, but I need to talk you out of cancelling the Teddy Bears Picnic.'

'Sorry.'

'Not a chance?'

'No.'

'That's a shame. The news editor's wife is the treasurer of the animal-rescue charity that benefits from the event.'

'Then I'll brace myself for tomorrow's edition.'

'Don't buy it unless you want to see a really sweet photograph of you, aged six, dressed as one of the three bears in a primary-school play on the front page,' she said,

'I take back everything I said. You are ruthless.'

'Absolutely,' she said, heart sinking.

'Why don't they hold it at Memorial Park?' he suggested.

'You're not getting it. We need woods. If you go down to the woods today…?' She sang a snatch of the song.

'You are not doing your case any favours.'

'You've got until the paper goes to press to reconsider.'

'Don't hold your breath.'

'No. Right. Breathing in and out.' She didn't want to hang up. 'I forgot to ask Gary when my bike will be ready.'

'Apparently they don't make wheels like that any more but he's doing his best to find a second-hand replacement. I'd buy you a new bike, but I'm sure you'd just tell the world I'm trying to buy your silence.'

'Not the world,' she assured him, saying goodbye to any chance of that. 'Just Maybridge.'

'Shame. I saw one on the Net that would have been perfect. Pink and white. Just like the one you had when you were a little girl.'

'I'm all grown up now, Hal.'

'Goodbye, Claire.'

Hal picked the newspaper out of the bin, looked again at the fairy lookalike. Claire's hair was still the colour of rich cream with a tendency to escape the tortoiseshell clip she used to hold it back and curl in soft tendrils around her face. It was the kind of clip that gave a man ideas. Which was, no doubt, its purpose.

Not that he needed any help.

At a distance, he could be rational about her. Remember that she was the daughter of his enemy.

Close up, with her scent—a combination of shampoo, soap, the memory of bluebells—blanking out the smell of motor oil, her eyes smiling even when her mouth was trying not to, her mouth smiling because she forgot to keep it in line, he'd wanted a re-run of a kiss that should never have happened. To feel her body soften in response to him the way it had that morning on the path.

Taking Claire Thackeray in a ditch... Against one of the estate's ancient oaks... In the Queen's bed...

All grown up and he knew that he'd dream about letting loose her lovely hair to fall over pale, naked shoulders.

Daydream when he should be concentrating on the ballroom ceiling.

Night dream about doing things with raspberry jam that would put it on the Women's Institute banned list but, more to the point, what was she going to do about him?

So far, she'd stuck strictly to the facts, although that first piece might have raised a wry smile amongst those who remembered him.

He'd anticipated some comeback to his crack about her not fulfilling her mother's inflated expectations. It had hurt her. It had been his intention to hurt her.

She had been the estate's little princess while he'd been the frog who was supposed to live under a stone.

So why hadn't she struck back hard? She knew that he'd been thrown off the estate and that was the story any real journalist would have told.

But then no real journalist would have warned him about what was going to be on tomorrow's front page.

He called up the *Observer*'s website and clicked on the link to the editorial staff. She was about halfway down the list, a cool blonde looking out at the world with a confident smile, very different from the mud-spattered creature, hair tumbled about her face that he'd picked out of the ditch. Full of sass and spirit one minute, flapping her eyelashes at him the next, when she thought he might be useful to her.

Still the estate princess despite her fall from grace. She might have been bright, but not bright enough to avoid the obvious trap.

Knowing her mother, he'd have thought an unwanted pregnancy would have involved a quick trip to the nearest clinic. But maybe it hadn't been an unwanted pregnancy. After all, she'd told him herself, she'd been in love.

Not wanting to think about it, he swept the paper up, but as he was about to drop it where it belonged, in the waste-basket, his attention was caught once again by the fairy perched on the masthead.

He was here to make her pay, but so far she'd been doing all the running. It was time to bite back.

'Okay, everyone. Can I have your attention for a moment?' Jessica Dixon, the assistant editor, stood in the centre of the large open-plan newsroom and looked around. 'As you all know we launched this year's "Make a Wish" campaign last week and we've had lots of interesting suggestions.' She glanced at the card she was holding. 'A facelift for the Guildhall—'

'That'll be the mayor trying to get it done on the cheap.'

'If it keeps the Council Tax down I'm all for that.'

'The Mums & Minis group are pushing for an undercover children's play area in Memorial Park and we've had several requests to restore the riverside gardens after last year's bad weather,' she continued determinedly, ignoring several more sarcastic remarks. 'There have also been a lot of great ideas to help individual people in need. It will be our Fairy Godmother's job to liaise with local youth groups and—' she looked around '—the really good news is that this year we have a sponsor for the Make a Wish scheme.'

'A sponsor? Does that mean our fairy will have to wear a company logo on her wings?' someone joked.

'No logo. Our sponsor isn't a company, but a private individual and we have Claire to thank for that.'

Claire, busy on a piece of village-school closures, looked up when she heard her name.

'What?' she asked. 'What have I done?'

'Quite a lot, apparently,' Tim said, with what could only be described as a snigger. 'It seems that your one-woman campaign to rouse the community spirit of a new arrival in the area has borne fruit.'

It took her a moment to filter through the background sound. The guildhall…sponsorship…her campaign…new arrival…

Hal?

'Are you saying that this year's Make a Wish is going to be sponsored by Henry North?'

'By George, I think she's got it!'

Hal was getting involved with the Make a Wish scheme? Why did that make her nervous?

'What exactly is he offering? His money, his time or his labour?' she asked, trying not to think about the powerful muscles beneath that green coverall, the soft cashmere. 'And, more to the point, what does he want in return?'

Jessica sketched the smallest of shrugs. 'All I know is that in return for supporting whatever major "Wish" we decide to undertake this year, Mr North has asked for just two things. One, that we help him with a Wish of his own—'

'A Wish? The man's a multimillionaire, what can we do for him?' someone asked.

'Give Claire the sack?' Tim suggested, dodging as she threw the latest edition of the paper at him. She missed him but clean-bowled his coffee cup, splattering him with cold dregs. A result.

Life was tough enough without him suggesting that she was surplus to requirements.

'And two,' Jessica continued, 'since he'll be working with her, he's asked to be allowed to choose this year's Fairy Godmother.'

'I bet it'll be some model he's dating...'

'Yes, please! That would guarantee us a mention in *Celebrity* magazine...'

'No!' Then as everyone turned to stare, Claire said, 'He doesn't do that kind of publicity.'

'Oh? And how would you know?'

'She's the local authority on Henry North,' Tim said again.

'Actually, it can't be an outsider,' she said quickly as she once again became the centre of attention. 'It has to be someone on the staff...'

Nooooooo... But even as the words left her lips she knew what was coming and instinctively slumped down in her chair, ducking behind her monitor.

'Quite right, Claire,' Jessica said, approvingly. 'This isn't a media circus, it's about community so if you could spare a moment? Mrs Armstrong would like a word.'

Tim, mopping up the sunrise splatter of cold coffee dregs from his shirt, paused long enough to shout an ironic, 'Goal!'

'Claire's been called out of the office,' she said, from behind her computer. If she was going to be the office joke, she was entitled to the laughs.

'Chasing down yet another investigative piece for the front page?'

Her trip to London on expenses had not gone unnoticed, or uncommented on.

'Only if she's investigating the dust under her desk.'

A ripple of laughter ran around the office and, straightening up, Claire held up a dust-coated finger. 'Actually, it's a vital and wide-ranging report on Health and Safety in the workplace.'

'Shouldn't that be "elf and safety"?'

'Who needs a duster when you've got a magic wand?'

'Everyone's a comedian,' she said, pushing her seat back and doing her best to put a brave face on things. 'If Mr North has seen the error of his ways and is prepared to salve his conscience by helping with a project that benefits the town, let's make it a good one. Something to make his eyes water.'

Toughen up, be ruthless...

Meanwhile, in return for sprinkling the fairy dust of publicity on local suppliers who supported the "Wish"—free promo in the paper in return for their generosity—and hours of extra unpaid work spent drumming up that support, chasing down grants, organising local youth groups, she was about to be working with Hal North. Given the choice, she wouldn't have done it dressed in a tutu and wings.

She paused just before she reached the door and, having pasted on a broad grin for her colleagues, she turned to face them and was confronted by the display of the week's front pages.

Mr Mean Targets Teddies leapt out at her.

Oh, well, brave face, Claire...

'Ladies, gentlemen...' She waved her ballpoint over them with a flourish before executing a low curtsey. 'I leave you to fight over the front page while I don my wings and fly away to part Mr Mean from his money.'

She'd anticipated an ironic cheer. At the very least a laugh. What she got was dead silence. She flicked a glance in Tim's direction. He was always good for a jeer, if nothing else. He'd paused in the act of mopping the coffee off his shirt but didn't respond with as much as a twitch of an eyebrow and with a sudden sick feeling in the pit of her stomach she turned around.

Behind her, Willow Armstrong, the CEO of the Melchester-based Armstrong Newspaper Group which owned not only the *Maybridge Observer,* the *County Chronicle* and dozens of other titles in the region, but the local commercial radio station, was standing in the corridor.

With her, Hal North, a head taller, was looking down his long, not-quite-straight nose; piercing her with eyes that were of a blue so intense, so dark that it sucked the breath right out of her body.

'Hal…' Willow Armstrong, ignoring the pregnant silence said, 'I believe you know Claire Thackeray?'

'We have met,' he said. His expression was grave, serious, but a gleam in the depths of those eyes suggested that he was enjoying the moment even if she was not.

No green coveralls today, not a trace of motor oil, but a lightweight grey tweed suit that was exactly right for the well-heeled gentleman about his business in a country town.

'Claire, Mr North has read about our "Make A Wish for Maybridge" programme and has generously offered to support us this year. Since you've shown such a passionate interest in Cranbrook Park,' she added smoothly, not suggesting by as much as a flicker of an eyelash that she'd seen that 'Mr Mean' headline, 'he has asked to work with you on the flagship project.'

This was her prompt to say something, but clearly not the word that had momentarily threatened to slip from her lips.

Fortunately, with his gaze holding her like a moth on a pin and the breathless silence of the editorial office behind her, words—as ridiculous as that seemed—had deserted her.

This was her big chance to get close to him, she told herself. Not in a ditch or over a motorcycle, but a chance to talk to him, find out where he'd been, what he'd been doing all these years.

Why he'd come back.

She could write an in-depth profile of a very successful, very private businessman. Something that mattered. Something bigger than the *Observer* could handle, but would make a colour spread in the *County Chronicle,* the group's glossy lifestyle magazine. Maybe even make a national newspaper. Something that would lift her career a notch or two.

She should be happy…

Jessica's surreptitious nudge in the back was sufficient to make her blink and the break in eye contact restored a little of her composure. She breathed in, placed her hand in his.

'Hal…' she said. 'How unexpected. You're always telling me that you never talk to the press.'

'Is that why you haven't called recently?'

'There seemed no point.'

'Never give up, Claire. Given sufficient incentive—' his hand closed around hers in what was less a conventional handshake, more a 'gotcha' moment as he held it a little too firmly for her to pull away without making it obvious '—I'm prepared to talk to anyone.'

'It was the Victoria sandwich that did it?'

'I expected you to bring it yourself.'

'I've been a bit busy.' She swallowed. 'What kind of support are you offering the Make a Wish project?' she asked, doing her best to ignore the continuing firm pressure of his cool fingers around her own.

Cold hand, warm heart?

Her own fluttered a little as she recalled the way her cold

lips had heated up as he'd kissed her, his long fingers encircling her ankle, sliding between her toes. That moment when he wiped the oil from her cheek.

Her knees buckled.

Her lips burned...

She rested her free hand on the door handle, told herself to get a grip. So, Brian had stuck a vile headline on a story with her name on it. It was Hal who'd told her that it didn't matter who you hurt as long as you sold newspapers.

'You're in the transport business, aren't you?' she managed, as if her file on him didn't contain the exact number of vehicles his company operated, the total tonnage of air cargo, shipping containers it had handled in the last tax year. When his transport company was floated on the stock exchange a couple of years back his business—if not his life—had become public property. 'We always need help moving the goods people donate.'

'I was thinking of something a little more hands on than that,' he replied.

There was the slightest tightening of his grip before he released her without warning, leaving her feeling weirdly off balance, as if she had been the one hanging on. Without his support the ground seemed to slip from beneath her feet and she found herself clinging to the door handle to stop herself slithering down it to the floor. Before she could take a step back, grab a breath, steady herself, his hand had shifted to her elbow. It should have helped.

No...

'Let's discuss it over a cup of coffee.'

'Coffee?' she repeated stupidly, her pulse quickening even as she clung to the door handle as if to a lifeline.

She was keen as mustard to discuss all and everything with him over coffee or any other beverage he had in mind—if he was going to make her pay for that headline, it was going to be a two-way street—but he was up to something. She needed to marshal her thoughts, marshal her knees, marshal everything before she could handle this.

Her boss, her editor were watching. It was vital to be professional.

Cool...

Who was she kidding? His hand was warming her skin through her sleeve, a flush of heat that was spreading up her arm, through her body, touching her with an intimacy that was disturbing, unnerving, arousing...

'Sadly, that won't be possible,' she said, hoping that she didn't sound as desperate as she felt. Breathe, breathe... 'Coffee will have to wait for another day,' she said, with every appearance of regret. 'I'm sure Willow has explained that Fairy Godmother duties are voluntary? My job has first priority and I'm interviewing a local woman who gave birth to triplets—' a story that had filled today's front page thank goodness '—in twenty minutes. It's one of those human-interest stories our readers love and, since I'll be walking to the maternity unit, I need to leave now,' she added.

After that, she was taking an early lunch so that she could take Ally home. It was half term this week and since Penny was now working five mornings a week for Hal, and Ally and Savannah had fallen out, childcare had become a lot more complicated.

Having demonstrated her independence, she managed a smile.

'Perhaps Ms Webb could give me a call and arrange a convenient time for a meeting?' she suggested. 'I'd be happy to come up to the Hall. I know how busy you must be. How's the motorcycle coming along?'

A small crease deepened at the side of his mouth, his eyes darkened imperceptibly, acknowledging the tiny prod about her bicycle, about not talking to the press, but it had been a mistake to mention the motorcycle.

'And the rose garden?'

Shut. Up.

'Why don't I give you a lift to the maternity unit and you can advise me on bedding plants over lunch?' he suggested. 'You do eat lunch?'

'Oh…' The sound escaped before she could stop it, betraying her annoyance that he refused to play by anyone's rules but his own.

She hated losing control. She'd done it once but had created order out of the chaos of her life, making a home, creating a garden, bringing up her little girl…

Belay that.

She'd lost control when she'd run into him on that footpath. Bad enough, but with nobody's job safe, having to rely on public transport to get anywhere and her childcare arrangements in ruins, she was juggling eels while running uphill.

'Don't worry about the triplets.' Willow stepped in before she could say something she regretted. 'I've been dying for an excuse to see them and I think I can still write a paragraph or two that won't shame the *Observer*.'

'Oh, but…'

'Jessica was telling me that you've got childcare issues?' Her smile was sympathetic. 'School holidays are a nightmare. Believe me, I know.'

Terrific! Thank you, Jessica.

'Actually, I've been talking to Brian,' she continued, 'and we're agreed that now the Make a Wish scheme has grown so large it needs someone whose sole responsibility is to coordinate it. Liaise with local companies, the voluntary and youth groups, keep an overview of progress, that sort of thing.'

'Yes?' *No!*

'He's offered to release you from his team for the next couple of months.'

Months!

'But…'

…I'm a journalist.

The words stuck in her throat as she realised exactly what Hal had done.

'You can handle the Wishes from home just as easily as the office, which will make life a little easier for you and,' she added, 'you will make a delightful Fairy Godmother.'

'Are you sure?' she said, making one last bid for her job. 'If it's authenticity you're after, maybe I could point you in the direction of Jessica?' If she was going down, she was going down fighting. 'She looks exactly like the grandmotherly FGM in Ally's book of fairy tales.'

Willow laughed, patted her arm as if she appreciated the joke, but then said, 'Hal has some really interesting ideas that you'll want to include in the voting list on Saturday, so I suggest you start there. Send me a weekly update and anything you need just ask.' She didn't wait for an answer but turned to Hal. 'I'll tell Mike that you're looking for local craftsmen, Hal. I'm sure he'll know someone who can help with your ceiling.'

'Thank you, Willow. I appreciate that.'

She glanced at her watch. 'The triplets!'

They both watched in silence as, having tossed her metaphorical hand grenade, she moved quickly to the front door to avoid the fallout.

'Impressive woman,' Hal said, finally.

'Yes. She is.' Her idol as it happened. They'd gone to the same school, although she'd been years later and Willow Armstrong had started as a journalist on their sister paper in Melchester, doing the 'human interest' stories, just like her. That was as far as the comparison went. Willow had been offered a job on a national newspaper but had turned it down, choosing instead to stay in Melchester and manage the Armstrong group. 'And a busy one,' she added. 'She's not just a figurehead, she really does run the whole show.'

'That would explain why you appeared to be so shocked that she would drop everything to meet me here this morning.'

'Not at all.' That wasn't what had shocked her and they both knew it. 'Let's face it, you're not some nobody to be fobbed off on a local reporter. You're…'

'Mr Mean?' he offered when she hesitated.

She'd hesitated because she'd been going to say 'the lord of the manor' but Sir Robert had always had time for her. Unlike Hal North, who had mocked her lack of ambition and then used his power to take her away from the news desk. Sideline her.

Taking her silence for agreement, he said, 'You're a local reporter, aren't you?'

'Not much of one according to you.'

'You've sharpened up your act since then.'

'I took your advice, Hal. Nothing personal.'

'I think Mr Mean is about as personal as it gets, Claire. The fact that you haven't been back to see Archie, asked Gary to deliver your cake, suggests you're aware of that.'

'I told you, I've been busy. There's so much to do in the garden at this time of year.'

'I know. The contractor is going to be clearing the rose garden next week.'

'Hal!'

He said nothing.

'Didn't you contact any of the rose specialists I sent you?'

'I've been busy. I have a company to run, as well as a house to restore.'

'And motorcycles to play with.'

'That, too.'

'I'll do it for you—'

'Not unless you can wave your magic wand. You're going to be far too busy granting other people's wishes to work on your own.'

Working with Hal North Rule Number One: Keep it businesslike.

'We'd better get on with it, then. I'll see if the conference room is free. How do you take your coffee?'

'Not from a machine,' he replied. The hand at her elbow tightened imperceptibly as he began to steer her firmly in the direction of the door.

The heat increased a degree, tingling dangerously.

Claire told herself that it was anger rather than attraction. The sizzle that seemed to fry the air whenever they were in the same room was real enough, but he wasn't interested in her. Nor, she suspected, was he interested in the Wish project.

Whatever fairy tale he'd told Willow Armstrong his return to Cranbrook Park was tied up with what Sir Robert had done to him. What her father had done to him.

He'd dealt with Sir Robert, but her father wasn't alive to answer for his actions. Apparently she was going to have to stand in for him.

Working with Hal North Rule Number Two: Keep it totally businesslike.

She pointedly removed her elbow from his hand. 'I'll call your office and arrange a formal meeting at the Hall.'

She didn't wait for his agreement but walked back to her desk and began tossing all her belongings into her bag.

'Well, well, well,' Tim said to nobody in particular, 'that was a turn up for the book. The ambitious Miss Thackeray reduced to a playing Tinkerbell.'

'Book? What book?' she asked, refusing to rise to the bait. 'I didn't realise you had ever read a book, at least not one without pictures.'

'Sweet. Does Henry North have any idea what he's getting himself in for? The man must be a glutton for punishment.'

'Have a care, Tim, or I'll wave my wand and turn you into a frog.' She turned to look at him, then put her hand to her mouth. 'Oh, noooo... Someone's already done that.'

She gave him a little wave, put her bag over her shoulder and went through to collect Alice who was safely tucked up in the library working on a project under the eye of one of the juniors who was on filing duty.

'Come on, sweetheart.' She'd held off Hal North for the moment, but he wouldn't stay held off for long.

CHAPTER EIGHT

'NOT rushing off on my account, I hope.'

'Oh, sugar!' The betraying words slipped out as Hal North straightened from the wall he'd been leaning against, out of sight until she was through the front door.

'That was heartfelt. Why do I get the feeling that if you'd realised I was waiting you'd have left by the rear entrance?'

'Why on earth would I sneak out the back way?' Claire demanded, all the more indignant because it was true.

'I don't know. The words "rabbit" and "headlights" came to mind when you saw me in your space for a change.'

'You're the one who avoids the press.'

'Oh, it was merely surprise? I thought perhaps you were worried that having poked your stick into my wasp's nest—'

'Don't worry, Hal, I get it,' she said. 'I've been stung.'

He hadn't complained about her, hadn't got her the sack. Instead, he'd got her taken off the news desk, placed at his beck and call for weeks on end and had himself officially transformed from Mr Mean into Mr Generous at a stroke.

There would be no more snarky headlines written by her, or anyone else.

A result in anyone's language.

'So, coffee,' she said briskly. 'Shall we try the café in the craft centre? It's Ally's favourite.'

'Ally?'

Ally, fed up with being taken to one boring place after another, having to be quiet and well-behaved instead of having fun like everyone else at half term, had been dragging her heels behind her, sliding down the wall with a sigh when she'd seen her mom stop to talk to someone. Not complaining, but thoroughly fed up.

Well, that was all about to change.

'Come and say hello to Mr North, sweetheart, he's going to buy you a milkshake.'

'A milkshake?' She scrambled to her feet, looked up at Hal. 'Seriously?'

'Seriously. You deserve one.' She picked up Hal's long, thoughtful look, smiled. 'I did give you every chance.'

'No. That would have meant you'd told me that you had your little girl with you,' he said in the same pleasant tone, his own smile pitch perfect. Then, before she could let him off the hook, tell him that she was going to drop her off at Penny's for the afternoon he turned to Ally and said, 'Tell me, Alice, is your heart set on a milkshake at the craft centre? Or could I possibly tempt you to lunch by the river?'

'Penny's making you lunch,' Claire said before she could answer. 'Spaghetti with meatballs. Your favourite,' she added, to soften the blow.

'But what about the milkshake?' she asked, with a confused little frown. Ally did a very good confused little frown.

'I'll make you one when I get home.'

'It's not the same,' she said. 'You can't make it so thick that you can hardly suck it through the straw.'

'Penny? Would that be Penny Harker?' Hal asked, rescuing her before she was promising double, triple scoops of strawberry ice cream in the shake. 'Gary's mother?'

'Yes. Of course you know her.'

'I know why she couldn't work this afternoon,' he said. 'Why she won't work full-time.'

'You asked her to work full-time?' Claire was shocked. 'I had no idea.'

'Well you do now so the least you can do is call and tell her you won't need her to babysit this afternoon. Make everyone's day.'

His day, Penny's day, Ally's day. She wasn't so sure about hers...

Leaving her to it, he turned to Ally and with the utmost seriousness said, 'Tell me, Alice, is the Birdcage still the best place in town for lunch?'

Ally's eyes widened. 'The Birdcage? Is that the place that looks like a birdcage? That has birds? In cages.'

'That sounds like the place.'

'I'm not sure I approve of birds in cages,' she said. 'Can they fly about? Not just hop around like Savannah's budgie?'

'Why don't you ask your mother? She used to go there all the time when she was your age.'

'I went there once!' Claire said, with a glare that warned him that making plans for her was one thing, making them with her daughter was quite another. 'And there is still a problem.'

'Why am I not surprised?' There was nothing in his voice, his manner to betray him and yet she sensed his impatience. He had a plan and she was messing with it. Tough. 'If you're worried about timekeeping I'll swear it was a working lunch.'

'What else would it be?' she snapped. Dammit, lunch with Hal should have been... Nothing. 'Unfortunately, and I'm really sorry about this—' it wouldn't hurt to apologise, no matter how insincerely '—but I imagine you were planning on going by car?'

'I wasn't going to walk,' he said, using the fob he was holding to unlock the doors of a glossy black Range Rover parked at the kerb.

'Well, that's it, you see. Ally doesn't have her booster seat with her and, as I'm sure you know, it's against the law for a child to travel in a car without one.' She waited for the count of three. 'I suppose, if your heart really is set on The Birdcage, we could catch the bus?'

'The bus?' Hal appeared to consider it. 'That's a possibility,' he said. 'Or Alice could use the booster seat that Bea had fitted for her little girl.'

He lifted an eyebrow, inviting her to counter his check.

Claire had none to offer. Her only thought was that the plum-voiced Ms Webb had a daughter who visited often enough for Hal to need a booster seat in his car.

No more than her journalistic antenna twitching. His relationships were news. There was no other reason for her to be interested. At all.

'Well…' she said. 'How great is that, Ally? I wasn't much older than you the one time I went to the Birdcage.' Emphasis on the 'one.'

'My mistake,' Hal said, as he lifted Ally up. She scrambled across onto the booster seat and quickly fastened her seat belt before any more objections were raised. 'Your mother talked about it so much that I assumed it must be a regular event. According to my mother,' he stressed, presumably to establish that he was not in the habit of gossiping with her mother. As if. 'Didn't you have a good time?'

She concentrated on checking Ally's seat belt then shut the door before turning to face Hal. 'Truthfully?'

'What else?' he asked.

'I hated every minute of it.'

'Really? Well, you weren't with me on that occasion,' he said as he opened the passenger door for her.

'My mother would never have invited you out to tea with a bunch of little girls.'

'With or without,' he agreed, with a wry smile. 'I was definitely not her type, a sentiment I returned with interest. But little girls would have been safe enough.'

'I don't doubt it. You had bigger fish to fry.'

She caught his eye and despite doing her best to be cool,

she discovered that what she wanted to do most of all was smile right back at him.

Despite the bad start, the prospect of lunch with Hal North at a pretty riverside restaurant had a ridiculously uplifting effect on her. Which was, well, ridiculous.

'Let's see,' she said, doing her best to keep her feet firmly planted on the ground. She had to remember that he hated her father, was messing with her career and she knew practically nothing about his life since he'd left Cranbrook Park. Who knew what ulterior motive was driving him? 'It was my eighth birthday so you must have been about fourteen or fifteen...' She pretended to think about it, but she could remember exactly what he'd been doing—or at least who he'd been doing it with—the year she was eight.

She'd seen him from the back of her mother's car that day. She'd been dressed up for her tea party in a pink frilly nightmare of a dress and as they'd driven through the village she'd seen him standing at the bus stop with his arm around a girl in a skirt so short that her legs had looked ten yards long.

Her mother had kept her eyes on the road, but there had been a distinct 'tut' as they'd passed.

She, on the other hand, had been green with envy, turning round in her seat to stare until her mother had spotted her in the mirror and told her to sit up straight before she creased her dress.

'That,' she said, 'if I'm not mistaken, was the year you were going out with the incredibly, um, precocious Lily Parker.'

'Was it?' His eyes creased into a smile that warned her she'd said too much, remembered too well, betrayed an interest she would have denied with her last breath. 'Possibly, although I can't imagine that even Lily, with her undoubtedly precocious assets, lasted an entire year.'

'So many girls, so little time,' she said, as he held the door and then as she hesitated at the high step up, placed his hand on her bottom and boosted her up into the front seat.

For a moment their eyes locked. It was like descending on a roller coaster. That sensation of falling, leaving your stomach behind...

Working with Hal North Rule Number Three: Don't make eye contact.

'I was desperately envious of her red-leather skirt,' she said, just so that he'd know that it was Lily she'd noticed, rather than him. 'I always swore I'd have one exactly like it when I was fourteen.'

'And did you?'

'Oh, please! Do you think my mother would have allowed me out of the house wearing something like that?'

'A clever girl like you would have found a way. Did you never climb out of your bedroom window?'

'Is that what Lily did?'

'That would be telling.'

In other words, yes, but by the time she was old enough there had been no one to be bad with. Make that no one she'd wanted to be bad with.

She shook her head. 'I had too much homework to spend my nights hanging around in Maybridge,' she said, turning away to pull down her seat belt. 'Okay, sweetheart?' she asked, twisting in her seat to smile at Ally as he shut the door and walked around to take the seat beside her.

Ally nodded but she was sitting very still, clearly anxious not to do anything to make this unexpected treat go away. She was really missing Savannah, but refused to talk about it.

'Okay?' he asked, when she'd called Penny.

'Fine.'

Not fine. He'd offered Penny a full-time job and she'd turned it down because she needed someone to look after Ally. She paid her, but not as much as Hal, who had apparently put all the estate staff on the same pay scale, and with the same benefits, as his HALGO staff. She couldn't match that kind of hourly rate.

'I'll talk to her about working full-time when I see her,' she said. 'So, what's wrong with your ceilings?'

'My ceilings?' He shrugged. 'A combination of old age,' he said, looking over his shoulder to check the traffic before pulling out, 'and a leaking roof.'

'Ouch. That sounds expensive.'

'It will be. You might be better occupied devoting your front page to the scourge of thieves who are stripping lead from the roofs of churches and listed buildings.'

'If you'd talked to me about it, I would have done.' She lifted her hand to her mouth. 'Oh, no. That's not possible. You don't talk to the press.'

'I'm talking to you.'

'Too late. I'm off the news desk.' She shrugged. 'Actually, with several million to spend on property I think I'd have chosen something rather less of a liability than Cranbrook Park.'

'Would you? And here was me thinking that you were in love with the place. All those Christmas parties in the great hall, picnics, gymkhanas courtesy of Sir Robert.'

'You can mock, but it's been the backdrop to my life since I was four years old,' she told him. 'It's a big part of local history and every stone is full of stories. That doesn't mean I'd want to be responsible for it. Or live in it.'

'I was born in Cranbrook,' he reminded her, 'which gives me a good few years on you, but you're in excellent company. My accountant would endorse the former sentiment and my PA would definitely agree with the latter.'

'Miss Webb doesn't enjoy country life? Or is that Mrs Webb?' she asked.

'Does it matter?'

'Not to me. Presumably it does to her.'

'She's Mrs Webb. Divorced but—'

'There's a lot of it about,' she said, not wanting to know about her 'buts.'

'Her problem isn't with country life, it's to do with country plumbing.'

'Wimp,' she murmured.

'I wouldn't let her catch you saying that,' he replied. There was nothing wrong with his hearing. Nothing wrong with any bit of him...

She was the problem. She had the wrong name.

She glanced back at Ally, but she was too busy looking out of the window to be interested in them.

'So?' She kept her voice light as she asked the big question. 'Why did you buy Cranbrook Park?'

They were paused at the traffic lights and he looked at her. 'Because I could?' he offered.

And then he smiled.

It was nothing spectacular as smiles went, no more than the tiniest contraction of lines fanning out from indigo eyes but the effect was like sticking wet fingers into a live socket and the fizz went all the way down to her toes.

'It's about power, then,' Claire said, doing her best to ignore the tingle. Was there anything more galling than getting that kind of a sexual buzz from a man you didn't want to fancy? That it would be crazy to fancy?

Working with Hal North Rule Number Four: Don't say anything that will make him smile.

'No, it's about a promise I made the day I left Cranbrook,' he replied. Clearly the memory was not a good one because he abruptly lost the smile and the tingle was reduced to something more like the aftermath of pins and needles.

It wasn't over, but you could breathe again.

'Really?' she said, working to keep it that way. 'Did you swear to return rich as Croesus and buy out the wicked baron?'

Bad mistake. As an anti-smile strategy it worked for him but she found her own imagination running wild with the mental picture of some over-the-top confrontation between Hal and Sir Robert as he parked his motorcycle on the marble floor of the entrance hall. The miscreant—in black leathers rather than armour—swearing a fierce oath to return and claim his rightful place. A modern version of the dispossessed knight.

No.

Really.

Why on earth would he do that? Besides, he'd already told her it wasn't that incident which had got him banned from the estate.

On the other hand he hadn't bothered to deny it. And why else would he ride in through the front door, if not to make some statement of intent.

'It's a bit of a cliché isn't it?' she suggested, pushing him to tell her what had really happened.

'Clichés are what happen in moments of high drama, Claire.'

True her own small drama had contained just about every cliché in the book, but it was his story she was interested in.

'What drama?' she asked. 'How high?'

More importantly, who had he made that promise to? His mother? Sir Robert? Or just himself? Who was still around who might know?

Her mother almost certainly, but they'd have to be on speaking terms before she could ask her.

His mother...

'How is your mother?' she asked.

He glanced at her, a slight frown buckling his forehead as, unsurprisingly he hadn't followed her thought processes. 'She's well enough. She's living in Spain.'

'Will we see her? What does she think of you buying the estate?'

'She doesn't know.'

'Oh.' Weirder and weirder... 'She was always very kind to me. I missed her when she left.' She looked at him, but his expression gave nothing away. 'After your father died.'

His mouth tightened. 'It was an accident waiting to happen. The towpath on a foggy night is no place for a drunk.'

'Hal…' she warned, with a touch to his arm, reminding him that they weren't alone. Curling her fingers back when he looked across at her. 'I'm sorry. I didn't know. About your dad.'

'Why would you? You were never around when he came home after closing time.'

'No.' Had he been a violent drunk, or a sullen one? She restrained a shiver. 'Even so it was a shocking thing.'

'Why don't you say what's really on your mind, Claire? Where was I when my mother needed me?'

'No… At least I assumed the ban was still in place,' she said. 'I begged my mother to speak to Sir Robert. It seemed so cruel.'

'Did you?' Was that a smile? Stupid question, her heart rate had gone through the roof… 'And did she?'

She shook her head. 'She said I didn't understand. That it wasn't that simple. That you'd never come back.'

'How wrong can you be?' He took the slip road off the ring road. 'Have you told her?'

'That you've bought Cranbrook Park? No.'

'Mothers. Always the last to know anything…' He shrugged. 'Well, when you do you can inform her that she was wrong on both accounts. It wasn't the ban that kept me away.'

He slowed for the roundabout, his hand brushing her leg as he changed down. She jumped as his touch shot through her like a charge of electricity but he didn't appear to notice.

'The boring truth is that I was in India on business when it happened and my mother made sure that I didn't hear about it until it was all over and done with. I had her out of here the minute I did.' He glanced at her. 'She wouldn't leave before. In case you were wondering.'

'Why would I wonder? I had no idea you were so successful. Or that she might be unhappy.' She swallowed. 'I'm sorry, Hal.'

'Don't be. At least not for me.' He picked up speed, reached for the stick shift to change up but before she could move her knees out of the danger zone, he said, 'Jack North wasn't my natural father.'

Claire, stunned, opened her mouth, but couldn't think of a thing to say and closed it again.

Hal, shockingly, laughed. 'Could that be you losing the power of speech?' he asked.

'No!'

Not his father?

Well, that made sense in a weird sort of way. They hadn't been a bit alike…

'Well, maybe. Just a bit,' she admitted, with a rueful smile.

So who was? Someone on the estate? Who did he look like? There was something flickering in the back of her mind. Something she'd heard, maybe, or seen…

'Was that your intention?' she asked, refusing to ask him outright. If she'd learned anything in her brief dealings with Hal North, it was that if he wanted her to know something he'd tell her. If he didn't, he'd change the subject.

Then, suspiciously, 'Was it even true?'

Working with Hal North Rule Number Five: Don't believe everything he says.

'If it was my intention, clearly I'm going to have to try harder,' he said, turning off the road and pulling into the riverside car park. 'But why would I lie?'

'To wind me up?'

'Why would I bother when you do such a great job all by yourself.'

Okaaay…

Working with Hal North Rule Number Six: Disregard Rule Number Five.

But why would he tell her something so personal? Did he

really believe that removing her from the news desk would totally silence her? Surely no man so careful of privacy would be that naive?

No way. He'd told her because it didn't matter. She'd mentioned the tragic accident in that first piece she'd written about him, but Jack North was a drunken labourer who'd fallen into the river and drowned one misty night. How much worse could it get?

No. He simply wanted to shock her. Send her off on some wild goose chase, no doubt. But while her curiosity was aroused she felt nothing but relief that she wouldn't have to write it.

Get this Wish thing over with and she'd happily report town-council meetings and agricultural shows until the cows came home.

He'd climbed out, opened Ally's door while she struggled to make sense of it. 'First one to the island gets an ice cream,' he said, as he lifted her down, then having wound her up, stood back to let her race away over the bridge.

'Oh, for goodness sake.' She scrambled down. 'Not before lunch!'

'And the milkshake you promised her?'

She glared at him. 'Don't go too close to the water, Ally!'

'Spoil sport.'

'Try responsible...' She sighed. 'Oh, never mind.'

He was right. She'd been happy enough to use a treat to wind up Hal and Ally was having a miserable half term. An ice cream would do no harm.

She walked on, Hal's hand still on her arm, holding her at his side as if fearing that she, too, might bolt, run on ahead.

'I'm sorry, Hal. It's half term. Jessie Michaels usually has her in the mornings. She and Savannah are best friends, were best friends. They've fallen out.'

'How are you managing?'

'Like every other woman in my situation. And every man.

With a combination of help from my friends, expensive child-care and, when all else fails, doing what I did today and taking her with me to the office.'

'Not ideal.'

'No. She's being good, but it's a bit like living with a volcano with the lid on. You know it's going to blow and that the longer it takes the worse it's going to be.' She sighed. 'At least now, thanks to you, I can work at home.'

'You don't sound particularly grateful.'

'Forgive me if I don't weep with gratitude, Hal, but I don't think you meant to be kind.'

They'd reached the far end of the bridge where Ally was waiting for them, jumping up and down with excitement.

'I won, I won…'

'You beat us,' Hal said, taking a handful of coins from his pocket. 'Okay, let me see… I think I'll have a ninety-nine…' He looked at her. 'Claire?'

She shook her head but said, 'The same. A small one.'

'Two ninety-nines and whatever you want for yourself,' he said, dropping the change into Ally's upturned hands.

'She'll buy something ghastly with a load of E numbers,' Claire protested.

'Fuelling the volcano,' he said, taking her arm and heading along the bank. 'We'll be looking at the ducklings, Alice,' he called back.

'This is ridiculous,' Claire said.

'The ice cream? Lunch? Or are you telling me that you don't want to be the Wish Fairy?'

Oh, fudge, here comes the smile again…

'I thought it was your aim in life to wave a wand over everyone and make their dreams come true.'

'If I wave it over the rose garden will you send away the contractor?'

'You can try.'

Alice caught up with them, walking carefully as she carried

a little cardboard tray supporting their ices. Hal took one and offered it to her. There was a momentary collision of fingers, fuelling the little personal volcano inside her. The ice should have melted on the spot.

He took one for himself, accepted his change, then, admiring the traffic-light coloured nightmare that would have her daughter spinning like a top, said, 'That looks interesting.'

Resisting the urge to snatch it out of Ally's hand, she bit off the top of the chocolate flake on her own ice. Seeing her spin and whoop, even if it was an additive-induced high, had to be better than the misery of the last week or two.

'Rose gardens, dog walkers, donkeys,' Hal said as he steered her along the bank in Ally's wake until they reached a bench.

'What are you talking about?'

'Magic-wand time. You appear to have a soft spot for dog walkers, donkeys, even teddy bears.'

'Especially teddy bears,' she said, sitting down on a bench strategically placed so that two weeping willows offered a theatrical view of the river. A stage set with brief walk-on parts by passing swans, oarsmen, a passenger boat on its way up-river to Melchester.

'Everyone, in fact, except me.'

CHAPTER NINE

HAL sat down next to her, stretching out in the sunshine, crossing his long legs at the ankles.

'You've got a wish in return for your sponsorship. Just say the word and I'll do my best to deliver.'

He turned his head, regarding her from beneath heavy lids. 'Anything?' he asked.

'Anything that's legal, honest and decent,' she replied to what was clearly a loaded question. 'Or have you already got what you wanted?' she asked. 'Me, sidelined.'

'You're not being sidelined, Claire,' he said, taking the chocolate flake out of his ice, using it to scoop out a dollop of ice cream, sucking it clean, then biting a chunk off the end. 'On the contrary. You are going to be centre stage, making Maybridge a better place to live. Isn't that what you wanted? What your teddy bears picnics and public footpaths are all about?'

She dragged her eyes away. 'All I want,' she said, 'is for you to accept the responsibility that goes with owning a great estate. And the Wish Fairy, as I'm sure you know, is a role for an intern.' Which was true. 'At least the dressing up bit. The features editor usually coordinates the whole thing and some pretty young thing fresh out of school and happy to make a fool of herself in return for getting her picture in the paper, dons the wings and sprinkles fairy dust.'

'You don't do fun?' he asked, watching Ally as, lolly in one hand, she gathered up sticks to drop in the river for a game of Poohsticks around the willow.

'No. Yes! What's that got to do with it? This is my career. I have to be taken seriously.'

'Do you? Always?' He propped an elbow on the back of the bench and turned to face her, his light eyes thoughtful.

'That was the plan, but once I'm in a tutu and wings with all my cellulite on show, there isn't a chance in hell of anyone treating me as anything but a joke.'

'Whatever happened to that little girl who yearned for a red-leather skirt, Claire?'

'The same thing that happened to the boy who rode up the steps of the Hall. She grew up and sadly, a knicker-skimming leather skirt isn't a great look once you've outgrown size zero.'

'You'd still look good in one.' He sucked, thoughtfully, on the ice. 'Perhaps not red.'

'It has to be red. That's the whole point of inappropriate clothing. It has to make the grown-ups tut.' The whole point of inappropriate behaviour, she thought, remembering the barely understood longing to be the girl at the bus stop with Hal North's arm around her.

This brand new desire to be anywhere with Hal North's arm around her. Here, now...

She didn't need her mother to warn her that he was just as dangerous now as he'd always been. More so. Back then she'd been too young, beneath his notice. Now...

From the first moment she'd set eyes on him there had been a frisson of awareness, a quickening that provoked this need to challenge him, make him look, make him see her. And he was here, she was here, sitting beside the river on a sunny day, eating ice cream.

'Growing up,' he said, 'how we all longed for it. The freedom to do what we wanted, be whoever we wanted. We had no idea how lucky we were, wasting precious time before life became all about responsibility with no time to kick back, goof off.'

'You don't become a millionaire by fooling around.' She never doubted that those threads of silver amongst the near-black hair had been hard-earned. She wasn't the only one who'd missed out on playtime. 'What would you do, Hal? If you could goof off for just one day.'

'You know. You were there, remember?'

'Taking a motorcycle to bits?'

'Putting it back together. Riding over the sandpits on the far side of the Cran.'

'Idiot.'

'I tickled a trout this morning. It's years since I've done that but I had it there between my hands, purring with pleasure before I let it go.'

'Really? Can you really do that?'

'Want me to teach you how?' he asked and her heart rate seemed to slow to match the way a smile moved across his face. The slow-motion deepening of the creases bracketing his mouth, straightening of his lips, lifting of hard cheekbones. The faintest contraction of lines fanning out from eyes that gleamed with a dangerous light. The kind of smile that could burn a woman who didn't have an asbestos guard around her heart. A warning that they were no longer talking about fish.

'I thought it was just a tall story, a fisherman's yarn,' she said.

'You have to know where the fish hide, stand perfectly still, be endlessly patient.'

And in her mind's eye she could see herself standing in the shallow water, Hal behind her, his arms around her as he guided her...

'You stroke them so gently that they don't know you're there. Mesmerise them with your touch, make them want more...'

'I hate fish,' she snapped, as her hormones jangled, uncomfortably, certain now that he wasn't talking about any old trout. 'Ally, be careful!' Hal caught her arm, keeping her at his side when she would have leapt up to pull her away from the bank. 'She'll fall in,' she protested.

'It's shallow and I'm watching her. She won't come to any harm.'

'She'll get wet.'

'It's warm. She'll soon dry off.'

'Are you suggesting that I'm an overprotective mother?' she said stiffly.

'Only because you are an overprotective mother,' he replied. 'It's understandable, but you need to fight it.'

'Why? What do you know about it?' she demanded, as she watched her daughter, ice lolly in one hand, Poohsticks in the other teetering on the edge as she leaned over to drop them in. 'I would never have been allowed...' She would never have been allowed to get that close to the water, to risk getting her feet wet, mud on her clothes when she'd been Ally's age. She caught herself. 'I'm responsible. She has no one else.'

'Relax,' Hal said softly and she felt the tension flow from her limbs.

She forced herself to take her eyes off Alice for the merest second.

'Don't do that! I'm not one of your blessed fish!'

'No.' What was that expression? Sympathy? She didn't need that. No... It was something else, something she couldn't quite put her finger on.

'It's hard to be everything. Everywhere. To keep her safe. I want so much for her...'

'Take care you don't turn into your mother, Claire.'

'What?' His words were like a slap, the shock of it taking the breath from her body, pushing her to her feet. 'Never!'

'I wonder if Alice ever longs for a red-leather skirt?' Hal sucked a smear of ice cream from his thumb with mesmerising slowness. She wanted to look away, couldn't... 'What does she dream about? Do you know? Have you ever asked her? Did your parents ever ask you?'

'Parents do what they think is best for their child,' she said, aware that she was on the defensive, that she knew too little about what her child was thinking. What was making her unhappy.

'Do they?'

'Mine did everything they could for me.'

'Lucky you.' He crunched up the remains of his ice. 'But even with the best of intentions they don't always get it right. How did they respond to Alice's arrival?'

Feeling rather stupidly way up on her high horse, she sank back onto the bench. 'My dad died a week before Ally was born.'

'Bad timing.'

She sighed. 'Is there a good time to die?'

'In bed at the end of a life well lived?'

'Yes, well, his was cut short by pancreatic cancer. Two years—' chemo, remission, more chemo '—it took two years. He kept working until weeks before the end,' she said. 'Refused to rest. He said he'd have all the time in the world for that.'

He didn't say he was sorry, but then her father had always been on his case. Had, it seems, been the one to deliver his banishment. What threat had he used to keep him away from his home? From his mother? It would have had to be something big.

His stepfather's job? The cottage had been tied to the job and while he might not have cared about the drunk everyone assumed was his father, Hal's mother would have suffered if he'd been sacked.

She was used to asking questions, it was her job, but she wasn't sure she wanted to know the answer to that one. She wanted, needed, to remember her dad as the one person in the world who'd understood her. Who'd loved her enough to stand by her when she'd most needed support.

'It must have been hard for you,' Hal said.

She tore her anxious gaze from Ally to glance at him. 'Harder on my dad. And my mother, too. I was able to escape, have fun, if only for a while.'

'With Ally's father?'

She swallowed hard. 'Yes.'

'Don't blame yourself for that.'

'Easier said than done.' It wasn't the fact that she was out having fun while they were suffering. It was the lifetime that came after. 'I have to live with them knowing that I'd lied about where I was, who I was meeting. Letting down parents who only wanted the best for you.'

'I never had that problem.' He finished his ice. 'The house went with the job, of course.'

'Yes…' She wanted to ask him about his childhood. How he'd suffered at the hands of a drunk who wasn't his father. Had he known? His expression suggested not and she said, 'Sir Robert offered my mother the chance to buy the house, my father was well insured, but she didn't want to stay.'

'While you, I imagine, wanted to be close to Ally's father.'

'It wasn't that.' She pulled a face. 'Jared was long gone, but I chose my baby over the future my mother had worked so hard to give me.' She watched Ally, hopping about, happy to be outside, playing. 'Morning sickness instead of a gap year with all those influential friends I'd made at Dower House. She couldn't forgive me for throwing all that away. Or for the fact that my dad had sided with me.'

'He was dying,' Hal said. 'That tends to focus the mind on what's important.'

'Yes.'

So few people had understood. Her mother, her teachers, her friends had all urged her to cut free, take her starred As and fly away from Cranbrook, out into the big wide world.

Her dad had been the only one who'd understood why she'd clung so desperately to a life she had made with love, with passion. A life she was responsible for. A life she had been given in return for the one she was about to lose.

Unexpectedly, Hal did, too.

Working with Hal North Rule Number Seven: Expect the unexpected.

'It couldn't have helped that Alice's father came from a different ethnic background,' he said.

'I met Jared at a party thrown by one of the girls at school. He was at university with her brother and quite the most beautiful man I'd ever seen. Golden, gentle.'

'And gone.'

'He really was desperately sorry when I told him that I was pregnant. And generous.'

'He supports Alice?'

'No…' She broke off, unable to say the words.

'He gave you money to make the problem go away?'

Something in his voice made her look up. 'He was going home to an arranged marriage. He thought I'd understood that our romance was no more than… Well, you get the picture.' She shrugged. 'I told him I understood, took the money he offered and he flew home assuming that I had used it for the purpose intended.'

'Is that what you used to improve the cottage?'

She shook her head. 'I put it into a fund for Ally. She'll need it when she's older.'

'Mothers…' He shook his head. 'Does she know? Who her father is?'

'Of course. I've kept photographs for her and we put together an impressive family tree when they did an ancestry project at school last term. Jared al Sayyid came from a rich and powerful Ras al Kawi family. Her great-great-great grandfather was a tribal leader who fought with Lawrence. I found loads of photographs on the Net…'

She stopped, frowned.

'What's the matter?'

'What? Oh, nothing. I was just wondering if that could have been the trigger for whatever happened at school.'

'The Arab connection?'

'No,' she said, shocked. 'It's just, well, Ally can be a bit of a drama queen and she did get rather carried away with the whole Arabian Nights thing. A bit princessy. It doesn't take much for the pack to turn on you...'

'It doesn't take much for it to blow over, either.'

'No. Just something to break the ice.' But what? The longer it went on the harder it became...

'Came?' Hal prompted, as if he'd said it more than once. She looked at him, confused. 'You said her father came from a powerful family. Past tense.'

'Oh, yes. Jared was killed in a car accident a year after she was born. I wouldn't have known, but it happened on the Melchester bypass. He was visiting the brother of my school friend... It was one of the first news items that crossed my desk when I started at the *Observer*.'

'You weren't tempted to contact his family?'

She shook his head. 'He didn't want that, Hal. I was something separate, never part of his real life. Just a few wild oats sown, rather carelessly, before he married the bride chosen for him by his family.' She looked across the grass at her long-limbed daughter. 'Keeping Ally was my decision. One that I never for a moment regretted.'

For some reason, that made him smile.

'So, your mother left Cranbrook and you moved into my mother's cottage. Extraordinary.'

'There was nothing extraordinary about it. It was empty, I needed somewhere to live.'

'No...' He shook his head. 'You don't see your mother?'

'Not much. She remarried quite soon after she moved and

she's busy with her new family.' She dug out a tissue, wiped her fingers. Glanced at her. 'Now you know all my secrets.'

'I doubt that.'

'More than most.' She looked across at him, still stretched out, totally relaxed while she was as taut as a bow spring. 'Now it's your turn to tell me one of yours.'

'Payback time?' he asked, unconcerned.

'Absolutely,' Claire said. 'I tell you mine, you tell me yours. It's only fair.'

'I think the word you're looking for is "show,"' he said. 'As in I show you mine... Or didn't you play that game?' Then, having extracted a blush from her, he said, 'I've already told you my biggest secret.'

She wasn't falling for that.

'That was no more than a distraction. Ancient history. What about now? I know you were married to Suzanne Parsons. Do you have any children?' She had been thinking particularly about Bea Webb's little girl, but afraid she had betrayed too much personal interest she quickly added, 'Where did you go when you left here? How did you turn a motorcycle courier service into an global business? What are you going to do with Cranbrook Park?'

Burying the big question in a heap of little ones. Except that none of them were little.

'Is that it?'

'No, but it will do to be going on with.'

'I don't doubt it. I'd be interested to find out how you found out about Suzanne. It hardly made a blip on the emotional radar.'

'Sorry, that's a professional secret.' She still felt uncomfortable about the way she'd drawn the information from staff who clearly adored him. 'How did you meet her?'

'She worked in the office. Ran the office for me when things started to take off. We were both working crazy hours and had no time for a social life. It just happened but all we had was work and sex. Mostly work. Looking back, I don't even know why we got married,' he said, taking her by surprise. She'd expected him to stonewall her, as he usually did, but maybe he took her demand for a secret seriously.

'It's what they call a starter marriage.'

He glanced at her. 'A what?'

'You know, like a starter home. Small, temporary, a practice run. Somewhere to find out what you really want,' she said.

'Right. Well, Suz has got that sorted. Good bloke who's never been on a motorbike, a couple of kids. Just as well we didn't make that mistake. You can't have starter children,' he said, standing up. 'Shall we walk off those ices?'

'Good plan. Ally!'

There was a smear of mud on one cheek, a dribble of something green on her cardigan and her foot was wet, a total mess. Her mother would be appalled.

'We're going for a walk. There are swings over there.'

'I'm a bit old for swings.' Then with a casual shrug, she said, 'although they're quite big.'

Claire couldn't stop herself from grinning as she walked nonchalantly over to the nearest one and began to gently sway backwards and forwards as if she was just sitting there.

'Will you need a push?' Hal asked.

Ally gave him a pitying look. 'I don't think so,' she said, before letting rip to show him that she was capable of swinging herself, thank you very much.

'You haven't been tempted to try again? Marriage?' she asked, anything to distract herself as Ally swung higher and higher. She would not call out, tell her to be careful…

'Marriage takes commitment, time, if you're going to do it properly,' he said. 'Sex is simpler. What about you?'

'Do I find sex simple?

He didn't answer and she turned to see what he was looking at.

Her.

He was looking at her and for a moment she was back on that roller coaster again, teetering on the edge under the intensity of a gaze that stirred the yearning empty ache low in her belly.

'Well? Do you?'

'Who has the time?' she said, abruptly, turning to look at the restaurant, anywhere but at him.

Built in the early years of the twentieth century as a summerhouse for boating parties from a grand estate on the far side of the river, it resembled an ornate, bamboo birdcage and was a popular spot on a sunny day, even mid-week.

Hal grabbed the chance to take a mental step back.

What the hell was he doing? His reaction to that headline had been to yank her out of the newsroom, turn her into that cartoon. Put her on display for once and see how she liked it.

Instead they were sharing confidences. And he was thinking the unthinkable about the last woman on earth he'd ever date.

'The terrace is beginning to fill up, I'd better grab a table,' he said, leaving her to gather up Ally. Give himself a moment to cool off, although short of a plunge in the river there wasn't much chance of that.

Hal handed each of them a menu when they joined him.

'Could I have a burger?' Ally asked him. 'One with cheese and all that other stuff?'

He looked at Claire.

'If that's what you want,' she said, avoiding his gaze.

'All that other stuff apart from the pickle.'

'Got it,' he said.

'And fries.'

'A burger with cheese and all that other stuff apart from the pickle and fries,' Claire said. 'Anything else?'

'Cola? I don't want a straw.'

'Make that two burgers,' she said, without even looking at

her menu. 'One with everything, one without the pickle, both with fries and a cola.'

'Can I go and look at the aviary?' Ally said, already fidgeting to be off.

'Stay where I can see you.'

'Righto!' She beamed a smile at him and then ran over to the aviary that was attached to the restaurant.

'Relaxed enough for you?' Claire asked.

He shook his head. 'I'm shocked. No attempt to steer Ally towards a healthier option? A jacket potato, water instead of cola? Whatever happened to responsible parenting?'

'She gets that twenty-four seven. Everyone needs a break.'

'Your mother would not approve.'

'I know,' she said, and without warning grinned, nearly blowing his socks off. 'I'm overwriting my memory's hard drive.'

'Was your birthday party that bad?'

'I was allowed to invite five carefully selected school friends. We all wore our best frocks and sat at a table with a white damask cloth and silver cutlery. Tea consisted of tiny cucumber-and-egg sandwiches, scones with clotted cream and pretty little cupcakes. We were allowed cordial, tea or milk to drink.'

'Sweet.'

She pulled a face.

'I was eight not six. I wanted a party at a burger bar. Fast food, fizzy drinks and giggling over absolutely nothing. And jeans. I wanted to wear blue jeans but my mother thought they were common.'

'No red-leather skirt, no blue jeans. Your life was blighted.'

'I was teased rotten about it for weeks afterwards. Little girls can be cruel.'

'Big girls can be cruel, too.'

That had been heartfelt and Claire, who'd been keeping an eye on Ally, gave Hal her full attention.

He'd brushed off his failed marriage, but clearly it hadn't been as simple as he'd made it sound. A man like Hal didn't commit without giving something of himself.

As if conscious of having revealed more than he intended, Hal pulled out the chair next to him.

'You'll be more comfortable if you sit here. You won't have to keep turning around to check on Ally.'

He was right, but sitting opposite him was bad enough. Looking at him was bad enough. Sitting close enough for their knees to touch, to smell his skin, was more than flesh could stand.

'No. It's fine,' she said. 'You're her new best friend. You watch her while I relax.'

'Three large burgers, hold the pickle on one, all with fries and colas,' he said to the waitress. 'We'll be over by the aviary.' Then when she'd gone he said, 'It's a shame you're not wearing jeans. We'll have to come again and do a thorough job.'

Working with Hal North Rule Number Eight: He can read your mind.

'Coming?' he asked, pushing back his chair. 'Just in case your little animal-rights warrior takes it into her head to set the birds free.'

'No danger. The aviary is glass fronted.'

Ally looked up as they joined her. 'What's that bird?'

'It's a lovebird,' Hal said.

'It looks lonely.'

'You're right. There should be a pair.'

'Like in the Ark... We've got two cats but they're both boys. Tom and Jerry. They're brothers so it would have been cruel to separate them. Do you have any pets, Mr North?'

'Why don't you call me Hal?' he suggested.

'Do you have any pets, Hal?'

'I've got a donkey. His name is Archie.'

'Oh, I know Archie. Mum takes him apples so that he doesn't chase her,' she said, dismissively. 'Have you got a dog?'

Hal, gallantly, responded to the cue. 'Do you like dogs?'

'I love them, but mummy is at work all day so we can't have one.'

'Well, that's a shame, but she's right, they're not like cats. Dogs need people.'

'Sometimes people need dogs. Seeing-eye dogs,' she said, 'hearing dogs, guard dogs. Just-for-company dogs.'

'Do you know, Alice, I was thinking only this morning, when I went for a walk, that I really needed a just-for-company dog. Would you help me to choose one?'

'A puppy?'

'I was thinking that I might go to the animal-rescue centre and see if there was a dog who didn't have a home. I'm sure that's what your mother would suggest.' He looked across Ally's head at her. 'Shall we go after lunch? See what they've got.'

Ally, unaware of the subtext, looked up. 'Can we, Mum? Pleeease.'

'I should be working.'

'Consider it a research trip,' he suggested. 'I'm sure the animal-rescue centre is in need of a wish.'

'What they need,' she said, 'is a wood. So that the teddies can have their picnic.'

'Sorry, I can't help you there. The tree surgeons will be surveying the woods next week, and then they'll be making if safe.' She stared at him. 'You wouldn't want a rotten branch falling on someone's precious Steiff, would you?'

CHAPTER TEN

'Hi, Claire, hi Ally. How are Tom and Jerry? I hope this visit doesn't mean—'

'No, they're fine, Jane. I've brought along my neighbour. He's just moved to the country and he's looking for a dog. Ally is going to help him choose.'

'Well, excellent.' Jane kinked a 'nice one' eyebrow in her direction and she shook her head quickly, smiling when Hal glanced round, clearly picking up the fact that signals were passing between them. 'What sort of dog did you have in mind, Mr—?' Jane said quickly.

'Just call me Hal,' he said.

'Hal.'

She smiled at him. Everyone smiled at him, Claire thought. The waitress at the Birdcage, women having lunch there, Willow and Ally. Especially Ally. Hell, she had smiled at him herself as he'd entertained them effortlessly over lunch. And not just smiled, she'd laughed and for the life of her couldn't have said why, or what they'd talked about. She'd just felt relaxed, happy, hadn't thought once about grilling him…

'Something man-size?' Jane guessed.

'It's not the size, it's the character,' he said. 'But it has to be well behaved. I don't have time to rehabilitate a neurotic dog.'

Jane looked doubtful. 'Dogs are full-time companions.

We're very careful where we re-home them,' she warned. 'You do have a garden? Good fences?'

'Hal has plenty of room,' Claire assured her. 'And there's always someone around.'

'Well, good,' she said, reassured. 'Why don't you give him the tour? I've got something special to show Ally.'

Ally hesitated, clearly torn.

'Don't worry, Alice, I won't choose anything until you've given your approval,' Hal said.

'You will regret that,' Claire said, as he stood back to allow her to lead the way.

'Probably, but you know what they say, a man with a couple of hundred acres, must be in want of a dog. Possibly two.' He put his hand on her shoulder and eased her through the door to the kennels. Left it there, a warm, unaccustomed weight that she wanted to lean into. 'Thanks for not ratting on me about the state of my fences.'

'Penny told me that you've got her husband laying hedges. You're obviously giving the estate a thorough overhaul. You could have told me about the woods.'

'You could have looked. A journalist would have checked her facts and seen for herself that it's in a shocking state.'

'My mistake. But I haven't got it wrong about the dog. I know you'll be a responsible owner.'

'Do you? How?'

'You had a dog when you were young. It stuck to you like glue and never put a paw out of place. A cross of some sort. A bit of lurcher, a bit of retriever?'

'The perfect poacher's dog.' He smiled at the memory. 'I haven't had one since Paddy died.'

They stopped at the first kennel. A rough-coated Jack Russell with a black patch over one eye looked up, sat up, grinned, his tongue hanging out.

'Cute,' Claire said, 'but they will dig holes. Murder on the garden.'

'Who'd notice a few more holes in mine except the rabbits?'

'That's just showing off,' she said, digging him in the ribs with her elbow.

He grinned. 'Maybe.'

'The rabbits would undoubtedly prefer if you gave him a miss.'

'Don't they dig up your garden? Eat your lettuce? Plunder your carrots?'

'You appear to be confusing me with Mr McGregor. Fortunately the cats keep Peter Rabbit and his cousins at bay.'

'They have to sing for their supper?'

'We all have to do that.' She hesitated. 'Does the rose garden come under the not-talking-to-the-press rule?'

'I don't think I'll be able to get away with that. Not if I do what you suggest.'

'No. But it would be the garden, the roses that people would be interested in.'

'On that understanding, I might be persuaded to let you cover the restoration in your Greenfly blog,' he said.

His hand on her shoulder had drawn her in and as she turned to look at him, she discovered that he was close enough for her to see the fine stubble on his chin, a small scar that ran across his cheekbone, the individual threads of silver running through his hair at the temples.

If she said 'it's a deal,' would he seal it with a kiss?

'It's a deal.'

'You're teasing me about the bedding plants,' she said quickly.

'Possibly,' he said, turning to the spaniel in the next kennel. His muzzle was turning grey and he rolled his eyes at them, sighed and didn't bother to get up.

A large cream Labrador ambled over to give them a friendly sniff, offer an ear to be scratched. A German Shepherd flung himself in desperation at the bars, a mongrel raised his eyes from a bone to growl a warning and something that looked as if it had had a brush with a French Bulldog rolled onto his back, inviting a tummy rub.

'Have you seen anything you like?' Jane asked, as they returned to the office having looked at a couple dozen dogs of all shapes and sizes.

'How can anyone choose? I feel a heel for not taking them all,' he told her.

'Everyone feels like that, but you mustn't feel guilty. You're doing a good thing just giving one of them a home.'

'Tell us about the Labrador,' Claire said. She'd seen the way he'd lingered, rubbed the dog's ears.

'Bernard. He's three years old, lovely temperament. Health certificate. His owners split up, moved from a house into flats.' She shook her head. 'We see it all the time.'

'You've got me,' Hal said, 'but I need Alice's approval.'

'Ally, you're wanted,' she called, pushing open a door to reveal her sitting on the floor with two tiny white puppies in her lap. Their mother, a West Highland terrier, was keeping an anxious eye on her.

'Look, Mum! Hal! Aren't they just too sweet!'

'The mother was found abandoned,' Jane explained. 'Only two of the puppies survived.' Then, catching sight of Claire's expression. 'Don't worry, they won't be going anywhere until they're weaned.'

'But they will stay together,' Ally insisted, anxiously.

There was an awkward moment of silence, then Hal said, 'Of course they will.' He turned to Jane. 'If I take the whole family, can they come home with me now?'

'You'll take all three? But I thought you wanted the retriever?'

'Him, too.'

'Really?' She was clearly torn between elation and concern. 'You do understand that even with Claire vouching for you we will have to come and check to make sure your home is suitable. Four dogs...'

'Of course.' He took out his wallet and handed her a card. 'How soon can you come?'

Jane looked at the card. Frowned. 'North? You're Henry North? Of Cranbrook Park?'

'Jane...' Claire began, but instead of telling this picnic-cancelling piece of work how he could get off thinking he could take her precious dogs, Jane was beaming up at him.

'Why on earth didn't you say who you were? How lovely to meet you in person. I can't tell you how grateful we are. So generous... And if there's anything we can ever do for you.'

'Actually,' he said, 'maybe there is. I'm looking for a companion for my donkey. What do you advise?'

'Well, now...'

'Four dogs and a one-eyed pony?' Claire shook her head. 'Are you quite mad?'

'Possibly. In fact this is where I'm going to have to play my personal Wish card.'

'Oh?'

'The terrier and her pups are going to need more time than I can give them until they're free-range, so I'm going to ask Alice to take care of them for me until they're weaned.'

'Ally?'

She looked across at Ally, who was talking to the puppies, already half in love with them. Half in love with this big man who had bought her ice cream and burgers and had made her day shine brighter with his attention, listening to her, encouraging her to chatter away.

Made her day shine brighter...

'No. Please don't do that, Hal, it'll break her heart when she has to give them up.'

He looked at her for a moment as if searching for something in her face, her expression, then, without turning away, said, 'Alice? Your mother is going to be working from home for the next few weeks so I'm leaving the terriers with you to take care of for a while. Can you handle that?'

'Oh, wow!' she said, completely losing her cool in her excitement.

'What on earth do you think you're doing?' she muttered.

'She'll enjoy looking after them.'

'Bastard!' she said under her breath.

'Obviously.'

No! Oh, God, bad word choice but he knew what she meant...

'What will you do with them, with Bernard, once you've made your plans, the Hall is a fancy hotel or conference centre—'

'Both.'

'—and you've gone back to your London penthouse?'

'For a clever woman, you can be remarkably stupid,' he said and there was a moment of utter stillness before he shrugged. 'Obviously Jane will find good homes for them when the time comes.'

Stupid. Got it in one. She'd allowed him to draw her in. Worse, draw in Ally, and this was the result. One nasty headline that she hadn't even written repaid in full.

'Well? Are you going to rush back and tell her not to let me have them?' he asked. 'After your glowing reference?'

'I ought to.' But then she would be the one who'd break Ally's heart. But she would, anyway...

'I thought not. Do you want to bring that box?' he prompted, before encouraging the Lab to jump up into the back of the Range Rover.

She picked up the box containing the leads and dog food he'd bought from Jane and put it beside Bernard, rubbing the Lab's silky ears to reassure him while Hal settled the basket of heartbreak beside Ally on the back seat.

'These dogs are going to need names,' Ally said.

'You're right. Why don't you make a list,' Hal suggested, 'and we'll choose tomorrow. I'll send a box for the pony, Jane,' he called, ignoring her, leaving her to climb aboard by herself and deciding to concentrate on Ally and the terriers when they got home.

'Hal…'

'We'll discuss the Wish-scheme tomorrow,' he said, finally deigning to notice her once the dogs were settled to Ally's exacting standards. 'Is nine o'clock too early for you?'

'I'm sure you'll knock loud enough to wake me if I oversleep,' she replied, matching the chill in his voice and lowering it ten degrees.

'Count on it.'

She heard him say goodbye to Ally, the sound of his footsteps rounding the cottage, the Range Rover turning in the lane and then the snuffling of the dogs.

'Ally, love, leave the puppies to rest now,' she said.

'Alice.'

'Sorry?'

Ally looked up from the basket. 'Hal calls me Alice.'

She'd noticed. 'But Ally is short for Alice Louise.'

'I know, but Alice is more grown up.'

Okaaay… 'Well, Alice Thackeray, it appears that the incredibly clever Hal North has driven away with the dog food, so we're going to have to walk to the village shop and fetch some.'

'Will they be all right on their own?'

'The mother has water—' she should be grateful that he'd remembered to bring in the dishes '—and the cats have had a look and decided the dogs are beneath them, so I think they'll be okay for half an hour. In fact they could probably do with a little peace and quiet after all the excitement.'

She certainly could.

No such luck. Jessie Michaels was at the post-office counter with Savannah. She had to find a way to talk to the woman, try and sort things out, but the village shop wasn't the place for it.

She handed Ally some dog food and headed for the counter, hoping to get away without the girls having to confront one another.

'What's this, Ally?' Mrs Chaudry, who'd known her all her life was looking at the can. 'Have you got a dog now?'

'Actually,' she said, in a clear, carrying voice, no doubt meant for Savannah's ears—so much for discretion, 'I've got three. A mummy dog and her two tiny, tiny puppies.' She cupped her hands to show how little they were. 'They're white and fluffy and totally gorgeous.'

Out of the corner of her eye, she saw Savannah turn and look, unable to resist the magic word—puppies.

'How lovely. What are they called?'

'They don't have names yet. I'm going to make a list when I get home and Hal and I are going to choose tomorrow. I'll get Mum to take a picture on her phone and we'll show you next time we come to the shop.'

'I can't wait.'

Claire, seeing Savannah edge a little closer, backed off and went to pick up a loaf she didn't need. As she turned, she caught Jessie Michaels watching the two girls standing side by side now, but ignoring one another, each waiting for the other to speak first.

Claire headed towards the freezer to give them space. Jessie, taking the hint, followed.

'How is she?' she asked anxiously.

'Alice? Fed up, bored, missing Savannah.'

'Girls… They get cliquey. Silly. Small things get blown up out of all proportion.'

'What was it, do you know?'

She shrugged awkwardly. 'Apparently Ally told everyone

that her father was a sheikh and that made her a princess or something…'

'Oh, good grief. It's my fault. I did go a bit over the top with the ancestry thing,' she admitted.

Attempting to make her father someone who mattered.

'I really wish they wouldn't do that family tree thing,' Jessie said. 'You start digging around in the past and all kinds of stuff comes up that you'd really rather not know about. How have you been coping during half term?'

'My boss has arranged for me to work at home for a few weeks.' Would she be missed from the news desk? Or once the Wish List thing was done and dusted would they realise that they'd managed perfectly well without her?

They both turned at the sound of a giggle from the counter. The two girls were head-to-head, instant friends again in the way that only children can be. Ally turned to look for her.

'Mum, can Sav come and see the puppies?'

'If her mother says it's all right.' Then she said, 'Maybe she'd like to stay to tea?'

Claire sat at her desk, phone in her hand.

Downstairs the dogs were asleep in their basket. On the floor above her, Alice and Savannah were choosing names for them. She couldn't put it off a moment longer…

She dialled the number of the estate office, the only number that was listed, and wasn't sure whether she was disappointed or relieved when, for once, it was picked up by an answering machine.

There was so much she could say, she thought, as she listened to Penny's voice inviting her to leave a message. So much she should say.

Clearly Hal hadn't forgotten to leave the dog food. He'd known that the puppies would be an irresistible draw to Ally's friends and that if she bought food in the village shop everyone would know about them by the next morning. She just got lucky that Savannah was there...

But she didn't have to say any of those things.

He knew what he'd done and although it had taken her a while to cotton on, so did she and when the beep sounded she kept it short.

Hal paused, looked up from his laptop as the answering machine picked up an incoming call.

'You are too clever by half, Hal North.' Miss Snooty Smartyhat. 'And you're right. I'm stupid. Thank you.'

'Too clever for my own good,' he muttered, reaching to delete the message and instead pressing Play Again.

Bernard lifted his head from his paws and looked at him, his eyebrows poetry in motion.

'What?'

He whined softly, sat up.

'You want me to call her back?' he asked, earning himself a woof of encouragement. The dog had been in the house for no more than three hours and already he thought he owned it. 'The trouble with you Labradors is that you are just so easy,' he said, forcing himself to hit Delete; it wasn't something he wanted Penny to hear when she arrived in the morning. 'You're anyone's for the rub of an ear.'

As for him, easy wasn't the word.

Another thirty seconds and he'd have been hitting Call Back, just to make sure that the puppies had settled, that Alice was coping, to hear her say thank you again in that sweet, musical voice that seemed to whisper over his skin.

His intention had been to give her a hard time, use her newspaper to show her two could play dirty, knowing how much she'd hate dressing up as a fairy, being cut off from the news desk.

Instead, he'd taken her to lunch, lumbered himself with a

menagerie and, in the process, had completely forgotten who she was, why he wanted to hurt her, until she'd turned on him.

He had been so sure she'd instantly pick up on what he was trying to do, but he'd seriously underestimated the defence mechanism of the mother defending her young from the possibility of pain.

Stupid. He was the one who was stupid.

How often had his mother stepped between him and Jack North, taken the blows until he'd been big enough to strike back. But then it was Jack his mother had rushed to comfort, bathing his lip, crooning to him.

Bernard pushed impatiently at his hand.

'Behave, or I'll trade you in for that Jack Russell,' he warned, even as his hand rested on Bernard's broad head. 'We both know that if I suggested a good long walk right now you'd forget about Claire Thackeray in a heartbeat.'

Bernard was on his feet and at the door a second after the word 'walk' had left his lips and abandoning his laptop he headed for the mudroom and picked up a lead before following him out into the soft evening. With luck, a walk would have a similarly amnesia-inducing effect on him.

Claire worked late, dealing with comments on her "Greenfly and Dandelion" blog, answering queries.

She had no formal training, did not pretend to be an expert, but her mother had studied garden design at the same college as her father had studied estate management and, between them, she'd absorbed a lot of practical knowledge.

In the period between Ally's birth and the time she started at pre-school, she'd had a lot of time to fill, but no money and she'd put all her efforts into making her home, creating her garden.

Blog done, she sent Brian an update on the teddy bears picnic story—turning Hal North from villain to something more like a hero.

Just because she was off the news desk didn't mean she couldn't contribute. Besides, he was right. She should have looked for a reason.

Cranfield Wood had been hit hard during the storm, but she remembered her dad complaining that there had been no money to restore it. The truth was that it had been neglected for years and it was all about Health and Safety these days.

Was that the problem with the footpath, too?

She would look, she promised herself, turning to the box of her father's things that she'd brought down from the loft. It contained his journals, the photographs he'd taken of the estate and with luck there would be photographs of the damage caused by the big storm back in the nineteen-eighties that she could scan and attach to her piece.

That done, she went on looking, searching for one face. Not Hal, he'd never been in those group shots of beaters, estate workers, but someone else might be there. And she turned the pages long into the night, searching for a resemblance, a clue...

CHAPTER ELEVEN

DESPITE her late night Claire was up at sunrise planting out the summer bedding she'd been hardening off.

There was nothing like back-breaking work to take your mind off the parts that were stirring, demanding some attention.

Fat chance.

Hal had expected her to know what he was thinking and she'd blown it. Well, she'd finally caught on, thanked him and she half expected him to call back and tease her on her slowness. Hoped…

'You're early,' she said, glancing at the clock as, having rapped on the open door, Hal walked in without waiting for an invitation. She'd heard him coming—the gravel made a good burglar alarm—had time to still her beating heart. 'It's only eight-thirty. What's up? No one to keep you in bed?' she asked.

'Sadly, no. Not that it would have mattered one way or the other. The contractors arrived at seven to start emergency work on the roof. If it didn't sound paranoid, I'd swear that Cranbrook sold the lead himself when he knew he'd lose the house.'

'You're right,' she said. 'That does sound paranoid.'

'You didn't see him the day he signed the contract.'

'He was there?' she asked, surprised, a little shocked. 'I heard he'd had a stroke. How was he?'

'In surprisingly good voice,' he said, turning away, looking out of the window. 'The reason I came to knock you up early is because I have another meeting at ten.'

'Sorry, you're hours too late to have that pleasure. Have you had breakfast?' she asked.

'Yes, thanks, but I wouldn't say no to a cup of coffee if there's one going. Is Alice around?'

'Working on a school project. Half-term homework. Just to keep us parents up to scratch.' She switched on the kettle, turned to face him. 'Hal…'

'I got your message,' he said, before she could say any more.

'I'm sorry I was so slow on the uptake,' she said, turning to lean back against the counter, refusing to let him brush the subject aside. 'The puppy wheeze worked a treat but it still doesn't solve the problem of what you'll do with all this livestock when you go back to London.'

'Who said I was going back to London?' he said. And looked as shocked as she felt; almost as if his mouth had bypassed his brain and spoken from some deeper instinctive place.

"The heart has its reasons which reason knows nothing of…"

For some reason the quotation had been running through her head.

'Hello, Hal!'

He turned, almost with relief she thought, as Alice bounced into the room clutching the list she'd been working on.

'Hello, Alice.'

'Excuse me, young lady,' she said, trying very hard not to resent the fact that her daughter had got a much warmer greeting from Hal than she had. That Ally—Alice—had interrupted a moment when he might have said anything. 'You are supposed to be working.'

'I have been working. I've been working for hours,' she

said. 'It has to be break time. There are rules about that sort
of thing, you know. A children's charter. Human rights, loads
of stuff...' She put the sheet of paper on the table, and poured
herself a mug of milk, raided the biscuit tin. 'Besides, Hal and
I need to settle on some names. We can't go on calling the
dogs Mummy Dog, Baby Dog One and Baby Dog Two forever, can we?

'Certainly not. Show me what you've got,' Hal said, pulling out a chair and sitting down.

'Well, I thought we could call the mummy dog Dandelion,
because she's all white fluff.'

'I like it.'

She gave him a big smile. 'You could call her Dandy for
short.'

'I really like it.'

'And then Savannah and I drew up a list of names for the
puppies. I was thinking maybe Thistle for Baby Dog One.'

'Thistle?'

'I was thinking Purple and Prickly,' Claire said, helping
him out, 'but apparently we're doing seed heads.'

'So that would be Thistle, short for Thistledown? It works
for me,' Hal said.

Well, great...

'Now,' Alice said, 'the next one is a bit tricky. I like
Parsley...'

'Parsley?'

'That's cow parsley, of course, not the green stuff that Mum
grows in the herb garden, but Sav wanted Bramble.'

'Savannah is Alice's best friend,' Claire explained. 'She
came to tea yesterday. To see the puppies.'

'Bramble flowers are white but there's no fluff,' Alice said.
'Just blackberries.'

'I see your problem.'

'They're doing a wild-flower project this term,' she said,
refusing to be ignored. 'Endangered habitats. There are bee or-

chids, cowslips, fritillary in the long meadow, did you know? We'd have lost them without the rabbits to graze it.'

'It's a good job we didn't go for the Jack Russell, then,' he said, finally raising his head to look at her. There was a moment of connection over a good memory, shared, before he turned back to Alice. 'I really like Parsley, but if it would make Sav happy maybe we should go with her choice.'

'Dandelion, Thistledown and Bramble,' Alice said, ticking their choices. 'Okay. They'll need name tags for their collars. Will you organise that?'

'I'll get it done straight away. Great job, both of you.'

Alice beamed. Then, looking around, said, 'Did you bring Bernard to visit them?'

'No. He's been out for a long walk this morning and decided he'd rather take a nap under Penny's desk.' Seeing her disappointment, he said, 'The pony's arriving after lunch if you want to come up and say hello. You can say hello to Bernard then. Bring Sav, too, if you like.'

'Great. Mum, can I use your computer? I want to look up West Highland terriers, just to make sure I'm doing all the right things.'

'Help yourself.' She poured out a couple of mugs of coffee, sat down. She wanted to thank him again, but it was probably better to stick to business. 'The Wish scheme. Willow said you had some ideas?' she prompted, head down, pen at the ready.

He didn't respond and she looked up.

'I'm really sorry about calling you a bastard.'

'Are you?'

'What will it take to convince you?' she asked and remembered, too late, another moment when she'd said that. Another moment, right here in this kitchen, when he'd told her that her mouth would get her into trouble.

Hal's face was giving her no clues as to what was going

through his mind, but if she had to gamble, she'd have said that he was thinking much the same thing.

He held her gaze for a moment that seemed to stretch like an elastic band, with the same breath-holding uncertainty about when it would snap.

'I'll let you know,' he said, finally, looking away. 'In the meantime, tell me what you think about a cycle path across the estate. From the village right into the town.'

'A cycle path?' Gratefully seizing the reprieve, she said, 'Where did you have in mind?'

He took a map of the estate from his pocket and unfolded it on the table. 'Here, on the far side of the Cran,' he said and she leaned forward so that she could follow the route he traced with his finger.

'Across here?' she asked.

He looked up, catching the note of confusion in her voice.

'Yes. Do you have a problem with it?'

His eyes were particularly blue this morning, his hair had grown out of the perfect trim and he was beginning to look less like a man who'd strayed from his city office into the country, more like a man who was at home there.

'Claire?'

The lines of his face had relaxed into a smile, his mouth into the sensuous curve of a man whose thoughts had nothing to do with cycle paths.

He lifted his hand to her cheek, slid his fingers through hair escaping untidily from the band she used to keep it out of her face while she was in the garden, cradled her head. The noises of the countryside drifted in through the open doorway.

A chainsaw whining as it cut through a branch somewhere, a thrush declaring territorial rights, a tractor...

She heard none of them as his lips touched hers. All her senses were concentrated on Hal. On the touch of his fingers, entangled in her hair, on the taste of toothpaste, fresh and sharp against her mouth, the scent of his skin… He'd come to her fresh from the shower after his early walk.

Her lips parted of their own volition, her tongue teased gently inside his lip and there was nothing in the world but the two of them as he kissed her, sweetly, thoroughly, with total conviction until a thud from the room above brought them crashing back to their senses.

'Okay,' he said casually, 'we'll call that a down payment. Now, you will please concentrate on the cycle path.'

He had to be kidding…

'What, exactly, is your problem with the route?'

She blinked, swallowed. Concentrate? He expected her to concentrate when he was still looking at her as if…

'A down payment!'

'I'm almost convinced,' he said, 'but your apology still needs a little work. Now the cycle path?' he prompted, as if what had happened was the most ordinary thing in the world. Maybe, almost certainly, for him it was…

Focus, Claire!

'I don't have a problem with it,' she said, doing her best to be as blasé as Hal. 'It's perfect except…'

What?

There had been something and she dragged her gaze from his, looked at the map. The route. Oh, yes…

'What about your golf course?' she asked.

'What golf course?'

'Isn't there going to be a golf course for your hotel and conference guests?'

'I hope not. I've earmarked the sandpits area as a scramble course where local lads can let off steam on their motorbikes in safety. Learn maintenance. There's a keeper's hut up there that would make a good clubhouse. It's on my list of ideas for the town to vote on.'

'And if they don't like it?'

'I'll do it anyway.' He waited. 'And the cycle path?'

'Is a brilliant idea. The kids could ride in safety to the high school instead of catching the bus. I could ride safely to work. If I was going to work.' She paused. 'If I had a bike.'

'Well, um, great. So, which one is going to be your personal "Wish"?'

'Neither. I want the town to approve of the scramble club, and the cycle path is a public amenity. If they want, they should put in a bit of effort. My personal "Wish" is for help to restore the temple beside the lake.'

'Oh.'

'I'm getting that look,' he said. 'The one that says I can afford to pay someone to do it.'

'Well, you can. At least I'm hoping you can, because that's going to be peanuts compared to the cost of repairs and renovations to the Hall with every move monitored by English Heritage. You won't be able to get away with that PVC guttering you've put up at the back of the house.'

'It's temporary. The replacements will have to be specially cast.'

'Good grief. How much will that cost?'

'Not peanuts,' he assured her. 'But it's not about the money. You keep telling me that Cranbrook Park should be available for the community. I think the community should prove that they care about it enough to put something back, don't you?'

'Is Cranbrook Park going to be available for the community?' she asked.

'You're just going to have to trust me on that, Claire,' he said, getting up.

'Like the wood and the puppies and no doubt some perfectly good reason for closing the footpath?'

'Here's my list of project ideas,' he said, placing an envelope on the table. 'Take a look, let me know what you think when you bring the girls up to the Hall this afternoon to meet the pony.'

'I'm included in the invitation?'

'Only if you bring another cake. Gary ate most of the last one.'

She laughed. 'I knew that would get you in the end.'

'You don't know a thing, Claire Thackeray,' he said, 'or you'd be a lot more worried.' He paused in the doorway. 'There is one more thing.'

She rose slowly to her feet. 'Yes?'

'I have to go to a charity dinner on Saturday night and I need a partner.'

'Dinner...' Was he asking her on a date?

'It's in London,' he warned. 'A black-tie event. Is that a problem?' he asked. Almost as if he immediately regretted mentioning it. Wanted her to turn him down.

She ought to turn him down.

'I may not have fulfilled my potential, Hal, but I do possess a long frock. I bought it cheap in a sale for the *Observer* Christmas party,' she added. 'It's dark blue and everyone wants black.'

'I don't care if you bought it in a charity shop,' he replied. 'I just need someone to fill an empty seat.'

'And having wondered who you knew who wouldn't have a date for Saturday night, you thought of me.'

Sweet.

'Have you?' he asked.

'Got a date? Hold on, I'll check,' turning to unhook the calendar from the kitchen wall,

She knew she should tell him that she was busy. No woman should be free on a Saturday night, it said so in all the dating manuals, but he wouldn't be fooled. She was never going to have a date any night of the week.

The big question was why didn't he have one?

Who cared? When would she ever have another chance to place a tick in her fantasy-date box?

'Well?' he asked impatiently.

'I do have bingo in the church hall pencilled in for Saturday,' she said, 'but you're in luck.'

'You'd give up bingo for me?'

'No, but the village hall had a plumbing disaster last week and it's been cancelled.'

'Can you get a babysitter?'

The single parents' get-out-of-jail-free card. No babysitter, no date...

'I'll let you know.'

'This is my mobile number,' he said, writing it on the back of the envelope. 'Call me.'

She waited for the sound of his feet on gravel, but it didn't come and when she glanced out of the window, she saw him walking through her garden. He stopped in the play area and she half hoped to catch him doing hopscotch. Maybe it was a girl thing...

He took his time, doing a little looking of his own, before he climbed over the fence and walked up the hill towards the Hall.

Claire filled a bucket with hot, soapy water and sat on the doorstep washing her plant trays. Not until they were spotless and drying in the sun did she get out her phone and call Penny to ask her if she was up for a Saturday night babysitting job.

'You've got a date?' she asked, delighted.

'Oh, no...' She'd been left in no doubt on that score. This wasn't 'convincing' Hal part two—at least not in that way. Her punishment was an evening at a dull dinner that he wasn't going to inflict on any woman he cared about. But one man's punishment was another woman's...research opportunity. 'It's work,' she said.

'Why don't I have a job like that?'

'The thing is, it's going to be a late one. Is that going to be a problem?' Now she was the one sounding as if she was hoping for a reprieve.

'Of course not. Ally can stay over with us. I've got a ton of baking to do for the school Spring Fayre and she can help me.'

'She'll love that except…'

'Yes?'

'She's taking her responsibility for the puppies very seriously. I think she'll insist on them coming, too.'

'No problem. I might even be tempted to have one of the puppies if Ally will let them be separated.'

'You are a star.'

Hal's phone bleeped, warning him of the arrival of a text.

Sitter sorted. Time?

Uncharacteristically economical with words for Claire Thackeray and interesting that she had texted rather than called him. Could it be that she was still so mad that she couldn't trust herself to speak to him?

Or had she picked up on his own uncertainty and didn't want to risk saying something that would give him an excuse to change his mind?

He still didn't know why he'd asked her instead of one of half a dozen women whom he could have called, who would have been happy to fill the seat beside him even at such short notice. And his bed, when the dinner was over, if it was on offer. Infinitely simpler.

Or maybe he did.

He'd told Claire that sex was simpler than getting involved in an emotional relationship, but it was soulless, too. Little more than going through the motions while his exchanges with Claire raised his pulse, left him wanting more.

Her tongue was sharp but her eyes were soft and her anger was the kind that only needed a touch to explode into rip-your-clothes-off desire. Then there was the added edge in knowing that she wanted something from him. His story. His life. The suspense in wondering how far she'd go to get it.

Would she flutter her eyelashes at him again?

Flirt?

Risk another meltdown kiss?

The thought of her touching close in the dark rear of the car, touching close as they sat shoulder to shoulder over dinner, thigh-to-shoulder close as they danced, had him achingly hard. That he was sure she felt the same way lent Saturday night a dangerous, touchpaper volatility that made him feel like the kid that had, once upon a time, run wild in Cranbrook Park.

She might be the last woman on earth he'd ever date, but he hit Reply, thumbed in—6:45 I won't wait.

CHAPTER TWELVE

At exactly fifteen minutes to seven on Saturday evening there was a long ring on the doorbell.

Claire took a last glance in the hall mirror, checked her hair, pulled on an artfully arranged tendril, putting off the moment for as long as she dared. Then she took a deep breath and opened the door.

The breath wasn't enough. What she needed was a quick blast of oxygen as she got the full effect of Hal North in a dinner jacket. It should be a criminal offence for any man to look that good.

'Ready?' he asked impatiently. Clearly he wasn't reduced to similar gibbering incoherence by the efforts she'd made with her hair, her make-up, her bargain-basement dress. 'No last instructions to the babysitter?'

Dating Hal North Rule Number One: This is not a date.

'Alice and the dogs are having a sleepover with Penny.' She handed him the heavy naval officer's dress cloak that had belonged to her great-grandfather. 'Didn't she tell you?'

'Penny? We don't gossip over the ledgers.'

'Neither do we,' she said, turning so that he put it over her shoulders. 'I would never ask her anything about Cranbrook Park. Or you.'

'Discretion. How rare these days.' His fingers momentarily brushed her naked shoulders as he settled the cloak into place, then, as she turned to face him, he looked her up and down, raised an eyebrow. 'Shouldn't you have a sword to go with that?'

'Yes, but it tends to cause havoc when I'm dancing.'

'Then I'm glad you decided to go unarmed.' He stepped out onto the path, waited while she picked up a small clutch purse, made sure the door was shut, then, with his hand to her back, followed her down the path to the waiting car. 'Who does she think you're with? Penny.'

'I told her it was work.' She smiled at the driver who was holding the door and stepped inside, gathering the cloak around her as she sat down. 'Which of course, it is.'

'If that's a warning that I'm going to be talking to the press all evening,' he said, sitting beside her, 'this could be a very quiet journey.'

'That would be a pity. Just think of me as your fairy godmother. Which means, unfortunately, that this car will turn into a pumpkin at twelve.'

'That should prove interesting if we're on the motorway at the time.'

'Hopefully it will concentrate your mind,' she said. 'I promised my daughter I wouldn't stay out after midnight.'

'And she believed you?'

'Of course. I'm her mother. So, tell me about this dinner we're going to.'

'It's a charity event. There's going to be an auction to raise funds for the homeless.'

'You should have told me. I didn't bring my chequebook. Just a little emergency money tucked into my underwear.'

'Don't worry,' he replied. 'I'll look away while you retrieve it. If anything catches your eyes.'

'My emergencies don't come that expensive,' she said.

'Well, if anything catches your eye just say and I'll bid for you. You can always settle up later.'

'Thanks. I'll remember that.'

Settle up? There was something about the way he said that…

Dating Hal North Rule Number Two: Sit on your hands.

'And I asked you because I don't go to clubs or parties or any of the places where you meet up with unattached women.' He looked across at her. 'Pretty much like you, I imagine.'

'Oh, I'm not into women.' She raised her hand in a dismissive little gesture. 'Not in that way.'

'I got that impression,' he said. 'Is there a man in your life?'

Weird question. Did he think she would have kissed him like that if she'd had anyone even remotely attached to her? Obviously he did. Which meant that she shouldn't take his kiss too seriously.

'It's Saturday night and I'm out with you filling an empty chair,' she said with what she hoped came across as careless indifference. 'What do you think?'

'I thought we'd already established that for you this is work,' he said. 'As it is for me. You're right, Bea does usually fill in on these occasions but she's started leaving details of dating websites on my desk, so I'm taking the hint that she has better things to do on a Saturday night. Have you ever tried that?'

'Online dating?' She shook her head. 'A colleague persuaded me to go speed dating with her once, but Alice had an earache so I had to miss it.' She sighed. 'I was devastated.' Then, when he didn't respond, she said, 'That was your cue to laugh, Hal.'

'Was it? I appear to be sadly out of practice with this.'

She doubted that. Just as she doubted the fact that his assistant acted as his walker on these occasions. No man as good-looking as Hal North, as rich as Hal North, would ever have to go hunting for a date.

'Your assistant doesn't have to be entertained?' she asked.

'We usually talk about work.'

'No wonder she bailed out,' she said, firmly suppressing

a tiny 'hooray.' 'That would be the plummy Ms Webb?' she enquired. He probably had more than one assistant.

'Plummy?'

'Plummy. "Don't you people ever speak to one another?"' she quoted in a particularly rich level of plum. '"I've already told your editor that Mr North does not speak to the press…"'

Her performance earned her an appreciative chuckle.

'That's better.'

'I'm a fast learner.'

'She didn't tell you that I'd called, did she?'

'Maybe she didn't think you were important enough.'

'That was the impression I got.' It was warm in the car and she unhooked the cloak, pushed it back off her shoulders. 'Tell me, Hal, how did you make the leap from a youth with a bad attitude to multimillionaire?'

'You don't subscribe to the subtle school of interview technique do you, Claire? I thought the idea was to put people at their ease, draw them out gradually until they were answering your questions without noticing.'

'Oh, please. That would be a complete waste of time. You're on your guard, waiting for the questions, so I thought I might as well get them out of the way and then we can relax and enjoy ourselves.'

'Good plan. You can tick that one off. How's your foot?' he asked.

'Fully healed, thanks. You give great first aid.'

'No excuse not to dance, then.'

'Dance?'

'I assumed, since you left your sword at home, that it was your intention to tango.'

'I was making conversation,' she squeaked as, for a moment, her carefully worked out plan of attack deserted her and all she could think of was Hal holding her, her hand in his, his hand at her waist, sliding lower as he pulled her close against his hips…

Dating Hal North Rule Number Three: Carry a fan at all times.

'You do dance?' he persisted.

'I may need reminding... How's the pony settling in?' He hadn't been there when she'd taken Alice and Savannah to see him after school. He'd been called away to London according to Penny. Urgent business. How long would he stay?

'Archie is teaching him the ropes. What happened to the cake I was promised?'

'The guys working on the roof had a tea break. Who gave you your start?' she asked.

'My start?'

'In business. There must have been someone. You can't make the kind of leap you've done without a hand up.'

'I don't recall any hand being involved. Only a metaphorical boot in the backside from your father.' He thought about it. 'Forget the metaphorical.'

She'd hoped that by disarming him with her candour, maybe making him laugh a little, Hal would relent and tell her his story. It wasn't going to happen and bearing in mind that all those girls who'd giggled at the bus stop, who'd called her names, would die to be where she was now, in a limousine, going to a black-tie dinner in London with Hal North, she gave it up.

Instead of worrying about her story she should just seize the moment, enjoy it. And with that decided, she half turned and propped her elbow against the back seat so that she was facing him.

'Okay, here's a novel idea, Hal,' she said. 'Let's call a truce for tonight, forget about the past, the future and simply enjoy ourselves.'

'You're suggesting that we should go for fun?'

If she'd wanted to surprise him, then she'd apparently scored a bullseye.

'Isn't that the idea? Eat a little, dance a little, spend loads of your money on a good cause.'

He shifted in his seat so that he was facing her. 'I notice you didn't say "our" money.'

'We both know that I don't have any, but I'll be cheering you all the way.'

'No past, no future, just the present?'

'Until the clock strikes twelve,' she said, offering her hand to seal the bargain.

'Until midnight, Cinderella,' he said, taking it. 'And this time, let's try to get you home with both shoes.

Claire was wearing her hair pinned up, but not in that frightful schoolmarm way she'd had it when she ridden into him on her bicycle.

It was a tumble of curls from which tendrils escaped to coil softly against her cheek. Her only jewellery was a pair of long dark blue enamelled and silver earrings which drew attention to a neck that begged to be stroked and her dress might have been a bargain but it had the kind of elegant simplicity that emphasized her slender figure, her height. Better still, there were no buttons, just tiny straps which had a tendency to slip off her shoulders when she shrugged in a way that gave a man all kinds of inappropriate ideas.

One slipped now as she laughed at something her neighbour said to her and she left it dangling, more interested in conversation than clothes. She had been a hit with these people. She talked to the women about the things that interested them, laughed in all the right places. Charmed the men without alienating their wives.

Why was he surprised?

She might not have gone to university but she was well educated, had a job requiring empathy, as well as intelligence.

He would do well to remember the intelligence.

No doubt she was simply biding her time, hoping that he

would crumble and reveal some dark secret, but having made her deal, she had thrown herself into the evening with enthusiasm. And just as he had when they'd had lunch together, he'd forgotten who she was.

She turned, caught him looking at her. 'What? Have I got spinach between my teeth?'

'Was there spinach? I didn't notice.' He hadn't been noticing much of anything. All he could think about was holding her as they danced. No... 'Elizabeth was admiring your earrings,' he said. He really mustn't think about holding her. His hand at her back, his body betraying what she did to him. Elizabeth, thankfully, turned at the sound of her name. 'I was telling Claire that you were asking about her earrings.' She'd assumed that he'd bought them for her. And put the idea in his mind of dressing her naked body in jewels... Possessing her.

'Aren't they gorgeous?' Claire said enthusiastically, not girly or coy. 'I wrote a piece about a local jewellery designer for the women's page of my newspaper and I couldn't resist treating myself. Every piece is different,' she said, taking a pen out of her purse to write something on the menu. 'That's her website,' she said, putting her hand on his arm as she leaned across to hand it to the woman.

The move exposed the delicious curve of neck and shoulder and all he could think about was touching his lips to the point where they met, about tasting her skin, sinking his teeth into the smooth flesh and sucking it into his mouth.

Only the sharp rap of a gavel from the television personality conducting the auction saved him from making a complete ass of himself.

'Okay, everyone. We've softened you up with good food and good wine and before we let you loose on the dance floor we're going to part you from your money for a great cause.'

Claire straightened. 'Uh-oh. That's the cue for me to sit on my hands.'

He caught one before she could carry out her threat, wrapping his fingers around it. 'Don't do that. I want you to bid for me.'

'Really?' She sounded wary, but her eyes were sparkling with excitement. 'Suppose I get carried away?'

'That's the whole idea. It's for charity.'

'Okaaay…' She used her free hand to pick up the list of lots to be auctioned. 'What takes your fancy? A sporting trophy for your office wall? A cricket bat signed by the Ashes-winning team?' She looked up and he shook his head. 'Not interested? Maybe something from the world of transport. A spoiler from an F1 car? An early Rolls Royce mascot? Or are you interested in a different kind of trophy?' She grinned. 'How about a bra which was worn by—'

'I don't think it would fit me,' he said.

'It's not to wear, it's to drool over.'

'If I'm going to drool over a bra, Claire, I want the owner to be inside it.'

'Bad luck. I'm not…'

'I know,' he said. And, never taking his eyes from hers, he hooked a finger beneath the strap that had slipped from her shoulder and lifted it back into place.

He had barely touched her and yet every nerve ending was alight with anticipation. How long had it been since he'd felt that way?

Was it the uncertainty? He had done a little research of his own and knew a lot more about Claire Thackeray than she knew about him.

Penny had been a mine of information. Not gossip, but responding to carefully phrased questions she had let slip far more than she knew. An admiring comment about Claire's garden had, for instance, had her waxing lyrical about how she'd transformed the rank half acre of weeds that had been Jack North's legacy into a garden entirely on her own.

And her response to the, 'She must have had help with

the heavy work. A boyfriend?' had been a firm negative. Apparently there had been no one. Which made the way she responded to his kisses rare. Real...

Claire shivered.

Hal had barely touched her and yet, as his fingertip brushed the shoulder, her skin had goosed and just the thought of dancing with him had her simmering. Scarcely any wonder that she'd blurted that out about her lack of a bra...

She took a sip of water. Held the glass to her cheek.

Until then she'd been doing so well. Being a good dinner guest, talking to the women, drawing them out—well, it was her job—laughing at the men's jokes when all she'd wanted to do was look at Hal. Lay her fingers on the smooth dark cloth of his jacket sleeve as she leaned a little closer as if to catch what he was saying. To breath in the faint citrus scent of his aftershave.

Dating Hal North Rule Number Four: Do not mention underwear.

Dating Hal North Rule Number Five: Do not mention the fact that you're not wearing a bra...

'When I say I'm not...' she said.

'Lot number one is an England rugby shirt worn by Johnny Wilkinson. Who'll start me off at—'

'Put your hand up, Claire.'

'What?'

'Put it up now.'

'—a thousand pounds. And we have a great starting bid from the lovely lady sitting just below me.'

'No...' She realised that everyone was looking at her. 'Did he say a thousand pounds?' she asked, snatching her hand down. 'It's not even clean!'

'Don't be shy, gorgeous.' The comedian leaned on the podium. 'Stand up and let everyone see what a generous woman looks like.'

She swallowed, glanced at Hal.

'Do as the man says. Gorgeous.'

'Bastard,' she mouthed as she forced herself up on rubber legs, but this time he smiled.

'What's your name, darling?'

'Claire…' She cleared her throat. 'Claire Thackeray.'

'Well, there you have it. The gorgeous Claire Thackeray has set the benchmark for tonight's auction with an opening bid of a thousand pounds. But you're not going to let her get away with this shirt, this muddy, sweaty shirt straight from the back of one of England's finest for a mere thousand pounds are you ladies?' He put his hand to his ear. 'Are you ladies?'

'Did you enjoy that?' Hal asked, as the bidding raced away and the auction took off.

'Are you kidding?' she demanded. 'Playing patsy to an auctioneer is not my idea of a good time.'

'Someone has to break the ice and we were both in need of a distraction. It was that or a jug of cold water in my lap.'

So it wasn't just her…

'If that's your problem, Hal,' she said, 'buckle up for an expensive night, because I'm going to have to keep on bidding.'

'I've got a better idea.' He seized her wrist and stood up, attracting the attention of the auctioneer. 'Ten thousand pounds,' he said, heading for the door before the gavel came down.

'Sold to the man exiting left in a hurry with the lovely Claire Thackeray. We'll catch up with you later, Hal!'

'What did you just bid for?' Claire gasped as the lift doors closed on them.

'Who cares?' he said, bracketing her with his arms on the mirrored wall of the lift, his body pinning her against it.

She thought he was going to kiss her, but he didn't. He just held there, her breasts crushed against his chest, his thighs containing her, the tumescent evidence of his need rigid against her abdomen. He held her with his body, with his eyes and the hot, sweet ache of desire surged through her veins, liquefied between her legs…

'But your guests…' she gasped, in a last-ditch attempt at sanity.

'Will have to provide their own distractions. I have to get you home by midnight…'

'We're never going to make it.'

'My home.'

The lift came to a halt, the doors opened, someone cleared their throat and he must of thought of something very painful to have regained such swift control before he stepped back and, nodding to the couple waiting for the lift, walked her into the foyer where her cloak was produced while she was still fumbling in her purse for the ticket.

He didn't touch her in the taxi that the doorman had waiting, didn't even hold her hand. He didn't touch her in the small lift that whisked them to the top of his riverside apartment block. He didn't have to.

Everything that was between them had been acknowledged, accepted as they'd ridden the lift down from the banqueting suite and now the air was vibrating with something primal, ancient; she was shaking with the need to feel the roughness of his skin against hers, the velvet, the silk, the steel…

Knowing him was her destiny. Here, now was the moment and when they touched there would be no stopping, no going back.

By the time they'd reached the top floor and the door of the apartment had been kicked shut, every nerve ending was tingling. Her breasts were hard peaks that not even the bra built into her dress could disguise. They demanded to be touched, kissed, pinched. Her body was a melting inferno and she took no more than three paces into the apartment before she turned and let the heavy cloak fall at her feet.

Hal discarded his jacket, took a step towards her, let his hands rest momentarily on her shoulders, his thumbs stroking her neck as his eyes ate her up. She anticipated a fierce hunger, wanted it, was practically screaming for it, but his kiss was the antithesis of that moment on the footpath when his mouth had first punished her, then aroused her, then stolen her wits.

His mouth descended with tormenting slowness as if he wanted to savour every moment, his lips barely brushing hers, here, there, parting softly in an erotic tango that became darker and deeper as he pulled at her lower lip. He slid his tongue along it, sucked it into his mouth setting up a chain reaction of responses that left her weak, trembling with longing.

Eyes closed, she found his tie, pulled it loose with shaking hands, blindly unfastening studs, scattering them in her desperation to touch his skin, feeling its warmth beneath her hands, against her own.

'Look at me, Claire...'

She opened her eyes and he let his hands slide slowly over her shoulders, brushing aside the straps.

'Look at me...'

His breath was soft against her cheek, his mouth trailed moist kisses down her throat, in the hollow of her shoulder as he slowly lowered the zip.

'Say my name...'

As her dress slithered over her body, pooled around her ankles, Claire let her head fall back in invitation, wanting his mouth on her breasts, wanting it everywhere...

'Dance with me, Hal North,' she murmured, putting her arms around his neck. 'Dance with me.'

CHAPTER THIRTEEN

HAL opened his eyes to the familiar panorama of the Thames, pink in the predawn glow. There were still lights twinkling along the water's edge but scarcely any movement on the river itself.

Beside him, Claire was sleeping, his arm holding her against his chest, his hand cradling a breast. Utterly vulnerable. Completely his. Soon, very soon, she would wake and the perfect moment would be broken in her panic to get home, to be there for Alice, but for now he could watch her sleeping.

'Don't move,' he said as she stirred.

'I don't want to.'

Her body was responding to his own. All he had to do was move his thumb, tease a nipple that was hardening beneath his palm and she'd forget everything, be totally his for another half an hour maybe.

He resisted the temptation, kissed her shoulder. 'I'll make some coffee while you take a shower.'

He rolled away quickly, while he had the strength to let her go, unhooked a gown from behind a door and turned to toss it to her. She had clutched the sheet to her breast, already slipping away from him.

He put the kettle on, bread in the toaster, went to find her something to wear.

'Shirt, sweater, jeans, socks and a new pair of boxers,' he

called, dropping them on the bed. 'They'll be a bit on the big side, but they're clean. Shame we didn't bid on that bra…'

His mouth dried as she walked back into the bedroom, bringing with her the scented steam of the shower.

'No problem. It would have been too big for me, anyway.'

'I'm afraid these will be, too, but you'll need them on the bike.'

'Bike?' she said, picking up the pack containing a pair of soft jersey shorts.

'Relax, I don't expect you to cycle home, but by the time a car gets here we can be halfway home.'

'You've got a motorbike?' she asked, a little breathlessly. He hadn't lost her quite yet…

'I'm the local bad boy, remember? Of course I've got a bike.'

She looked up at him. 'You're not bad, Hal…'

'No?'

Her skin was damp, her hair dripping. She smelled of his body wash, his shampoo, she was his and taking a hank of hair, wrapping it round his hand he back her against the wall and proceeded to demonstrate just how bad he could be…

She didn't object as he leaned into her, kissed her, pulled loose the belt of the robe she tied around her so carefully.

Didn't object as he stroked his hand over the length of her body from her neck to the warm, melting apex of her thighs. Holding her with nothing more than his gaze, he stroked her to a juddering climax then wiped his hand across his chest, anointing himself with her essence.

'Not bad…' She had that soft, dreamy smile of a woman completely satisfied. 'Very, very good…'

'Coffee, toast in the kitchen,' he said abruptly before he forgot himself completely. She did that to him. Made him forget who he was, who she was…

Claire roused herself, pulled on the clothes he'd brought her. The too big boxers, a soft woollen shirt that came down practically to her knees. She rolled up the legs of his jeans, cinched in the belt to hold everything together.

There had been a moment, in the middle of the night, when they'd raided the fridge for smoked salmon, champagne, but it took a moment to find the way. Or maybe she wanted the excuse to wander through Hal's lovely apartment, feel the fine Persian rugs beneath her bare feet, touch his things.

A Knole sofa. A Sheraton sofa table with a wonderful bronze of a horse. A Hockney on the wall.

'Had a good look round?' he asked as he handed her a big breakfast cup filled with richly scented coffee.

'You have a beautiful home, Hal. You've come a long way from Primrose Cottage.' Then, when he didn't answer, she said, 'I've never been on the back of a bike.'

'You've never sneaked back into the house at dawn, either. Shame about the leather skirt.'

'You can't have everything.'

'No. There are always sacrifices.' He patted a stool. 'Hop up.' He took the socks she'd been carrying.

'My sandals won't go over them,' she said. 'I thought I might put them over my sandals.'

'No need. I've got an old pair of boots you can have.'

She looked at the pair of biker's boots on the floor beside the central island. 'Those? They're going to be a mile too big.'

'I've stuffed some spare socks in the toes.' He took the socks she was carrying and slipped them on over her feet. Buckled the boots in place. Helped her into a thick, padded jacket, fastening the zip up to the neck.

'I feel like the Michelin man,' she said.

'Do you?' He leaned forward and kissed her. 'Make that a Michelin woman. Come on, it's time to go.'

The drive back to Maybridge was fast, thrilling and Claire clung to Hal like a teenager, her arms wrapped tightly around his middle, leaning into the curves, practically screaming with excitement.

It was madness. She was a mother. She was supposed to be responsible; not flying home at dawn, ripping up the quiet of the village, tearing across the estate, scattering deer, rabbits before Hal finally brought the bike to a swinging, giddy halt by her fence.

He pulled off his helmet.

'Don't move,' he said as she attempted to dismount. For a moment they looked at one another, both remembering when he'd said that before. How his hand had been gently curled around her breast, what she'd wanted…

He slid from the bike, unfastened her helmet, then removed it. Her hair was crushed to her scalp and she pulled off an oversized gauntlet, tried to lift her hand to loosen it. Her arm was stiff, her legs were stiff, too and he lifted her clear of the bike and deposited on the far side of the fence.

'Okay?' he asked, holding her for a moment, then, when he was sure she could support herself, he used one hand to casually vault it, found the spare key, opened the door. And suddenly she didn't know what to say.

'It's a good thing I didn't have to shin up the drainpipe and climb in through the window wearing all this stuff,' she said.

'Easy. You strip off and I take the evidence away with me.' He grinned. 'Want to try it?'

And be caught wearing his underwear by her daughter galloping home at the crack of dawn? 'I'm good, thanks.'

'Sensible answer.'

Yes, well, that was her. Good old sensible Claire.

Except for last night when she'd lost her mind, lost her reason, lost herself.

'Here you go, Cinders,' he said, taking a bag from inside his jacket. Her clothes, her handbag, her shoes.

'Hal…'

He waited.

'See you tomorrow?'

'Tomorrow?'

Today, now, anytime...

'It's the Wish List photo-shoot,' she said. 'Me in the tutu with my magic wand...' She broke off, feeling stupid. 'I thought you might enjoy your big moment.'

'I've had my big moment, Claire,' he said, touching her cheek, briefly. 'Right now I have to get back to London.'

'Oh, but...'

'I've been neglecting things.'

'Of course,' she said. 'Take care.'

She watched him walk away, vault over the fence, fire up the bike, her invitation to stay, have breakfast, left unspoken.

It was just as well. It wouldn't do for her daughter, her neighbour to come walking in on them sharing breakfast.

Sensible Claire would never let that happen.

She swallowed, turned away. Whatever happened now, she would never be the same. Never be that carefully focussed woman who had always only ever had one goal in life.

To pass her exams and be the daughter her mother wanted her to be. To protect her child and be the mother she had always wanted to be. To be good at her job, make a name for herself...

It was like shattering glass.

She'd put herself back together the first time it had broken. When she'd abandoned the strict rules laid down by her mother and her world had fallen apart. Her father had died, her mother had abandoned her.

She'd carefully sealed up the cracks. Learned to focus again. On her baby, her home, her career. Starting at the bottom.

This time was different.

The glass had not just broken, it had fragmented, been blown to the four corners of the wind and in a sudden panic she opened her evening bag, dug out her phone.

There were no missed calls, no messages.

No. She had done the unthinkable and hadn't been struck down by lightning. Yet.

It would be a while before Penny brought Alice home, she could take a nap, catch up on her sleep, but if she went to bed she would think about Hal, dream about Hal.

Instead she changed into jeans that fit, a T-shirt, a pair of Wellington boots, pulled on Hal's woollen shirt over them, rolling up the sleeves. She'd wash it in the morning, but for now she wanted to keep him close.

Look...

Taking her camera, she went for a walk, crossing a footbridge over the Cran, walking along the far bank until she saw exactly why Hal had closed the footpath.

She took photographs using her phone, attached a text to Hal— I looked.

A sort of apology for doubting him.

She told Alice about her evening—some of it—making her laugh about her bidding for a rugby shirt. She gave her the chocolates—hers and Hal's—that she'd saved for her. Then, since there was no response from Hal, she decided to write up a piece for Monday's newspaper about the footpath being undermined by the winter rains.

She thought better of it. She wasn't on the news desk and Hal was right. Nobody actually cared.

'Who are these people?' Alice asked, rooting around in her father's box, picking out one of the photographs.

She glanced at it. 'Some of the men who used to work on the estate when your granddad was alive.'

'And this?'

She glanced at it. It was a picture of a small boy on a pony with a man holding the leading reins. She couldn't think why it was in the box. It was too old to be one of her father's pictures.

'I think the boy is Sir Robert,' she said. 'Doesn't he look sweet?'

'And who is the man?'

His clothes were that of a country gentleman rather than a groom and the posture had a careless arrogance.

'His father, I should think. Sir Harry Cranbrook.'

'Are you sure?' Alice examined it closely. 'He looks an awful lot like Hal.'

Hal?

'It's an old picture, Alice,' she said. 'It can't be Hal.'

'But he has the same hair!'

'Lot's of people have dark hair,' she said, taking it for a closer look. Lots of people had dark hair, but not dark hair that grew in just that way, that slid over the forehead just so. Or a mouth that lifted at the corner...

'And he's the same shape,' Alice insisted.

What?

'Can I keep it?' she asked.

'No.' She took the photograph from her. 'It belongs in granddad's archives.' With his journals. She'd started reading them, but they had just contained weather reports, details of maintenance, hiring and firing of staff, shoot records...

Look...

The phone rang and she snatched it up. Not Hal but Jessie Michaels asking if Alice could go with them to the safari park.

It was all the distraction Alice needed, and forgetting all about the photograph, she rushed off to get changed. She took another look at the photograph.

The same shape?

The same wide shoulders. That way of holding his head. Sir Robert did that, too, but he hadn't had the striking colouring, the strength of features. He'd clearly favoured his mother, although she'd never seen a picture of Sir Harry before.

She'd once asked Sir Robert if there was one but he'd said it had fallen, been damaged beyond repair.

Looking at this photograph, an entirely different explanation leapt to mind. That the genes had skipped a generation. That the likeness had been too obvious to ignore and he'd removed it.

Was that why Lady Cranbrook had left him? Because he'd had an affair with his cook? She'd always thought of Hal's mother as old, but heading downhill towards thirty herself she had a different view of age.

Looking back it was obvious that she'd been something of a head-turner with her dark, Gypsy looks. Far too much woman for a man like Jack North to handle...

She finally found the entry she was looking for written not in the daily log, but in the back of her father's journal for the year Hal had been banished from the estate.

I did a despicable thing today. I told young Hal North that if he didn't leave the estate Sir Robert would demolish his mother's house. Leave both her and Jack North without a job.

Clearly something had to be done after he rode his bike into the house, parked it in front of the portrait of the man who is, undeniably, his grandfather.

I never liked the boy, he's arrogant, full of himself and helps himself to my game at will, no matter what traps the gamekeepers set, but this was a dreadful thing to do to him. If I had somewhere else to go, I'd leave tomorrow, but the house goes with the job and Sir Robert pays Claire's school fees. Laura would never forgive me for giving all that up on a matter of principle.

One thing I didn't do—destroy Sir Harry's portrait. I've hidden it in the rafters of the hayloft. It's not much, but I've told his mother where it is and, maybe, one day young North will have justice and I will be able to rest easy.

She closed the book, held it close, remembering horrible days when her father hadn't talked to anyone. When her mother had been more demanding. It had passed, but her father had never been quite the same again. She'd always assumed that it was the beginning of the cancer that eventually killed him. But there were other things that ate you up from the inside…

'Mum, where's my…' Alice erupted into the room then came to an abrupt halt. 'Why are you crying?'

She shook her head. 'No reason. I was just remembering your granddad, Alice. I wish you'd known him. He'd have loved you so much.'

'Sav's got six grandparents,' she said. 'One set got a divorce and married again. She's got loads of aunts and uncles.' She flopped down on a chair. 'Why don't we have any family?'

'Your grandparents were both only children. And grandma… She thought I let her down.' But family was important and they had so little of it. A few distant cousins. Maybe it was time to build bridges… 'I'll call her later.'

But first she had to call Hal. She wanted him to see this. There were no excuses, but she wanted him to know that her father had loathed himself for what he'd done. That the picture was still there, somewhere.

There was no reply from the house and she hung up when the answering machine cut in; this wasn't something for anyone else to hear.

His mobile phone went straight to voicemail and she left a message asking him to call her back.

Hair done, nails done, make-up done…

Being a fairy wasn't all downside, Claire decided. And, in deference to her advanced age, she'd been allowed to choose a ballerina-length dress. Lots of tulle in the skirt and a soft gold bodice with minimal flesh on display. Very family friendly…

Brian was skimming through the photographs on his computer. 'That one, I think.'

'I can live with that.'

He nodded. 'Good, good… We'll need you in full fig at

the Mayoral parlour tomorrow morning. His worship wants to gather a little of the glory for himself.'

'Will expenses run to a taxi? I don't fancy travelling on the bus.'

'I'll pick you up if you like.'

'Thanks...' He seemed oddly distracted, seemed unable to look her in the eye. 'Brian, is there something you're not telling me? I do still have a job?'

'What? Oh, yes... You're our star investigative reporter,' he said, attempting a laugh. It wasn't convincing.

'But...' she persisted.

'I shouldn't tell you...'

'What?'

'You'd better see this,' he said, handing her a large envelope. Her heart was beating a little too fast as she put her thumb to the flap, but he stopped her. 'Don't open it here.' Which didn't do her heart rate any favours.

'Actually, I have to get home. I've exchanged babysitting Alice for babysitting puppies.' And this time she was the one attempting the unconvincing laugh.

'Off you go, then. But you didn't get that from me, okay?'

What on earth... She sat on the bench at the bus stop and opened the envelope, peered inside, afraid that it would be covered with red TOP SECRET stickers.

Nothing that exciting.

It was a photocopy of a planning application made by Mr Henry North to demolish the dwelling known as Primrose Cottage, Cranbrook Lane, Cranbrook.

Her house...

The home that she'd made for herself and for Alice.

Hal was going to knock it down. Drive a bulldozer through the rooms that she'd decorated, where she'd hung the curtains she'd made from remnants. The rooms for which she'd bought furniture from junk shops and car boot sales.

He was going to rip up the floors that she'd sanded, smash

the basins whose taps no longer dripped only because she'd taught herself how to change washers, tear out the pipes she'd crawled in the loft, braving spiders to insulate against the cold. Send bulldozers through the garden she had created...

She'd known, when Sir Robert was forced to sell the estate, that her future was uncertain, that her rent would undoubtedly go up. Unlike Sir Robert, Hal was a hard-headed businessman and he was determined that the estate support itself.

She understood that.

But to discover that all the while he was making friends with Alice, making love to her he'd known about this... And not just known about it. This didn't have anything to do with the redevelopment of Cranbrook Park as a hotel and leisure facility. This wasn't the work of some anonymous consultant.

Hal North had planned this. Planned to hurt her as her father had hurt him. Take his pain out on her hide.

I've had my big moment, Claire...

Oh, yes...

It had been a big moment for her, too. She'd thought, hoped that it was more than a one off, but she'd left a voicemail yesterday morning and he hadn't called back.

There had been no texts, no messages.

She'd always known, deep down, that there was something going on, something dark driving him, but she'd forgotten all her misgivings as he'd teased her, romanced her, taken her.

No. Not taken. His ultimate revenge was that she had given herself, heart, body and soul, freely, joyfully.

And now he was gone. Back to London. Back to his real life.

CHAPTER FOURTEEN

CLAIRE'S experience of lagging pipes in the loft stood her in good stead as she searched through the rafters of the elegant eighteenth-century stables—the horses had been housed far more grandly than the humans who did the manual work—for the painting her father had hidden.

Cobwebs, spiders, she brushed them aside without a thought.

It never occurred to Gary to query what she was doing there and when she finally found the crate, nibbled at the corners, covered in dust, cobwebs and mouse droppings, he helped her down with it. Went and found a screwdriver for her so that she could open it.

Being a seventeen-year-old boy, he wasn't interested in a boring old painting of some boring old bloke and went back to the old motorbike he was stripping down.

He looked so young, but Hal was only a few months older when he'd been turned out to fend for himself.

She turned away. She couldn't afford to think like that, think of him. Only what he was doing to her and Alice, but as she lifted the painting out, peeled back the wrappings, she felt her heart squeeze tight in her chest. Trailed her fingers briefly along the familiar features, the hard cheekbones, that firm jaw…

When had Hal seen it? Discovered the truth? Had his mother told him, or had he found out by chance and ridden into the house, parked his bike beneath it on his eighteenth birthday, an adult staking a claim to his inheritance. Refusing to be ignored...

Scarcely any wonder that Sir Robert had wanted him, this portrait, out of sight.

She stood it up on a bench, took photographs, then carried it inside and left it on Hal's desk.

That done, she went home and, about to become homeless, fired up her computer and had her own 'big moment.'

Henry North Revealed As Son Of Bankrupt Baronet

It was today revealed that media shy, multimillionaire, Henry North, founder of international freight company, HALGO, whose background has always been something of a mystery, is the love child of Sir Robert Cranbrook.

As a boy he lived in a humble estate cottage with his mother, Sarah—Sir Robert's cook—and his stepfather, Jack North.

Sir Robert Cranbrook, who refused to acknowledge his son, had him turned off the estate after an infamous incident in which he rode his motorcycle up the steps of the Park and into the front hall on his eighteenth birthday and parking it beneath a portrait of Sir Harry Cranbrook, his grandfather. The portrait, pictured here, and which Sir Robert ordered destroyed, has now been rediscovered hidden in a stable and leaves no doubt of the connection.

In a remarkable turn of fortune, Henry North recently purchased Cranbrook Park—occupied by the Cranbrook family for nearly five hundred years—for an undisclosed sum when creditors forced the sale. Sir Robert, divorced, with no legitimate heir, is now living in a nursing home.

Mr North could not be contacted today for a comment on his plans for Cranbrook Park but he is quoted as saying that, like all his investments, '...it will have to work for its keep...'

Local sources suggest that he will use the property as a hotel and conference facility.

This will be just one more step in the history of a property that was granted to Sir Thomas Cranbrook on the dissolution of the monasteries by King Henry XIII for services to the Crown...

It was all there. The potted history of Cranbrook Park, the motorcycle incident, photographs she'd found in her father's box of Hal's mother, his stepfather, Sir Robert.

There was the portrait of Sir Harry Cranbrook, beside the head shot of Hal at his desk. There were photographs of Hal at school. A photograph of Primrose Cottage that she'd taken when she first moved in.

All she had to do was call the *Herald*, tell them what she had and she would be paid handsomely for this prime piece of gossip about a man who had, until then, appeared gossip proof.

A fat cheque that she'd need when she was forced to move, a byline in a national newspaper, a chance to move on, be the journalist her mother always wanted her to be.

And if it hurt Hal, well he'd told her himself, it didn't matter who you hurt as long as you sold newspapers.

She had the phone in her hand. All she had to do was make the call. It was what a real journalist would do.

'Claire? Are you okay? The mayor is waiting for you.'

'I'll be right with you.'

Just press the button. Say the words. What was her problem?

She'd wanted to write his story...

A story about a boy who had made good despite his bad start. A story to inspire. To be proud of.

This was just sleazy gossip. It wasn't the kind of journalist she wanted to be. Looking at this, she realised that right now she would rather be turning her compost heap...

'Look,' he'd told her. Don't just accept what's on the surface. Maybe she'd got it wrong… And if she hadn't she would fight it.

She tossed her phone into her bag and followed the secretary who'd come to hunt her down in the loo.

There was a small group of people in the Mayor's Parlour. Willow Armstrong, who smiled a welcome. The Mayor. The *Observer*'s editor. And Hal North.

'There are you, Claire,' he said. 'We thought you'd got lost.'

Her mouth moved, but her tongue appeared to be stuck to the roof of her mouth. What on earth was Hal doing here? He was gone, job done…

'Come and stand here. By me.'

On the surface he sounded all charm, his mouth was smiling, but there was no warmth in his eyes and as he rested his hand on her shoulder he leaned close.

'Where were you, Tinkerbell? Counting your pieces of silver?'

'What?'

'Look this way, everyone. Claire, lose the bag, darling and let's see your wand.'

Hal took the bag she was holding and she raised her wand, gave it a little wave.

'It doesn't work,' he said. 'I didn't disappear in a puff of smoke.'

'Okay, big smile… And again… Hold it for one more…'

Hal moved first, his hand around her wrist before she could move. 'If you'll excuse me, Mr Mayor, I need to have a word with Claire about the project list.'

'Actually, Mr North, I was hoping we might…'

'Call my office,' he said, heading for the door. 'Penny will arrange a time for you to come up to the Hall. Lunch?'

'Oh, yes… Thank you.'

'Hal…'

'Not one word,' he said. 'Not one more word.'

He opened the door of the Range Rover, tossed her bag onto the floor and waited while she climbed aboard, blocking any chance of escape.

He had her wrong. She didn't want to escape. She wanted answers.

If he'd told her he was planning on bulldozing her home into the ground, she wouldn't have fallen in love with him.

How could any woman get it so wrong twice in one lifetime?

When they arrived at the cottage she didn't go around to the back. In the country, the back door was for friends and she stopped at the front, took out her key, as pointed a message as any how angry she was with him. With herself.

Inside, she went straight into the living room—no more kitchen comfort for him, no more cake—and turned to face him.

'Why?' she demanded. 'Why are you doing this?'

'Me?' Apparently she'd taken him by surprise. She was the one who was supposed to be on the defensive. 'You're the one who plastered my name, my family, across the tabloids.'

'Excuse me?'

He tossed a copy of the *Herald* on the table, open at a headline almost identical to the one on her computer.

'I didn't write that!'

'You climbed up into the stable loft and found the picture they've used. Gary helped you. He told me.'

'Hal, I admit that I wrote a story, had it lined up to send, but it's still in my draft folder. You can see for yourself.' She didn't wait, but turned and ran up the stairs, determined to show him. And then, when she saw the folder was empty, went cold. 'It's gone.' She turned to him. 'I didn't, I swear. I came so close, but I couldn't do it. I told you I wasn't a real journalist...'

She checked the time it had been sent.

'Alice… She was using the computer to surf stuff for home-work. She probably sent an email to Savannah while she was up here…'

'What's this?' Hal said, picking up the planning document.

She glanced at it. 'You should know. It's your application to raze my home to the ground.' She looked up at him. 'What are you going to do, Hal? Sow the ground with salt? Do you really hate my family, me, that much?'

He took the paper, looked at it, and then muttered some-thing scatological.

'Pretty much my first reaction,' she said.

'Where did you get this?'

'Privileged information.'

'Your friend the Chief Planning Officer, I suppose.'

She didn't say a word.

'And the portrait? Where is that?'

'On your desk. Haven't you been home? To the Hall, I mean.'

'I went to straight to the Town Hall. I've been working all weekend with the consultants, making changes to the plans. I wanted to get everything right before I talked to you.'

'Changes?'

'There was your cycle path. The scramble track. If I can get it through planning.' He looked at the document he was holding. 'Actually, considering this indiscretion I might be able to twist Charlie Peascod's arm.'

'No need. Buy him lunch. He's anybody's for the Red Lion's roast beef.'

'I think that's probably slander.'

'Undoubtedly,' she said. 'Roast beef and a good claret. Are you going to tell on me?'

'I ought to,' he said. He was looking at her, but it was im-possible to know what he was thinking. What he would do. 'How did you find out? That Robert Cranbrook was my fa-ther.'

'It was Alice who spotted the likeness. I was trying to find something, anything, in my father's journal about you, about what happened, and she picked out an old photograph of Sir Harry. She thought it was you.'

'Did you find anything? In your father's journals?'

'Yes. Dad wrote something the day he made you leave. He was supposed to destroy the portrait but he hid it. He was so ashamed of what he'd done. He told your mother what he'd done. Where it was.'

'She never told me.'

'You'd made your own way. And he didn't deserve a son like you,' she said. 'And now I'm standing in my father's shoes, but shame doesn't undo anything.'

'No...' He took a step towards her.

'I tried to call you, Hal. I wanted to show you, wanted to tell you.'

'I lost my phone on Saturday night. Apparently I dropped it in the hotel. Leaving in a hurry...' He dragged his hand over his face. 'This morning is not going the way I planned.'

'No. Me, either. I didn't expect to see you. I thought you'd just been stringing us all along. That Saturday night was part of it...'

'I can see why you might think that. A few weeks ago you might have been right.' He drew in a slow breath. 'You would have been right. I was going to evict you, smash this place down, clean the earth...'

'It was that bad?'

'Yes, Claire, it was that bad. Jack North knew he was a cuckold and he made my mother pay every day he lived. Drank every penny she earned. All she kept from him was the money Cranbrook gave her to get rid of me.'

'But she didn't. And she saved the money for when you needed it.' She reached out a hand to him. 'That's what you meant, isn't it? When you said it was extraordinary?'

He took her hand, drew her close so that they were leaning against one another, supporting each other.

'Why did she stay, Hal?'

'Passion?' he suggested. 'I used to roam the house as a boy and I saw them once...' He drew in a long, shuddering breath. 'He said that she was a whore. When he signed the contract on this place. Called me trash—'

'No, no!'

'I could have forced the paternity issue at any time, but I never wanted that man as my father. I just wanted him to look at me, see me, to know in his heart—always assuming he had one—that he'd made a mistake...'

'What changed, Hal?'

'I told myself that I wouldn't have to look you in the eyes when I evicted you. You didn't matter enough for that.' He eased back so that he was looking straight at her. 'But then Archie got into the act and I was looking into your beautiful grey eyes and I was so angry with you, because you did matter.'

'Did I?'

'Then you took out a ten-pound note to bribe me and that was fine, because I could be angry with you all over again.'

'It was all I had to last me until the end of the week, but it wasn't that. I was so disappointed in you. I was so sure that you were bigger than that...'

'And then I saw what you'd done here and hell, I was still angry because I needed to destroy this place.'

'And now?' she asked. 'Do you still feel that way?'

He lifted his hand to her cheek, laid her head against his chest. 'It's not the house, Claire. It's not Cranbrook Park. He said it would destroy me, said that my anger would eat me up, leave me hollow... Maybe it would have, but for you.'

'And now everyone knows and it's all my fault...'

'Who cares? Tomorrow some footballer will cheat on his

wife and all this will be nothing more than something to wrap the potato peelings.'

She looked up. 'It's going to be "no comment," then?'

'Always. But there is one thing,' he said, wrapping both his arms around her, holding her close.

'Oh?'

'I'm afraid you're going to have to sacrifice some of your garden.'

Her garden. She was going to be staying...

'Actually, I'm doing you a favour,' he assured her.

'Oh. How, exactly?'

'You're going to be busy organising the restoration of the Rose Garden at Cranbrook Park to be double digging your vegetable plot.'

She would? 'I will?'

'Double digging is so last century,' she said. 'What plans do you have for my garden?'

'I'm going to extend Primrose Cottage.'

'Extend it?'

'Think about it, Claire. Four dogs, two adults, a little girl who's growing every day. Then there's your office, my office. It's just not going to be big enough.'

Four dogs, two adults...

'The Hall isn't big enough for you?'

'I'm not going to live in a hotel.'

'So you've decided you'll move in with me?'

'It's a start. Of course it will be very tight until the extension is finished. People will talk...'

'The sofa is a pull-out...'

'I want a home, a family, Claire. I've found what I've been looking for and it's you.' His blue eyes burned with a fire that heated her to her toes, stole her breath, made her feel as if her wings were real... 'The deal is marriage. Not a practise run until something better comes along, not a tryout, but the real till-death-us-do-part deal. That's the one wish that only you can grant.'

'I'm a novice fairy, Hal. I haven't been issued with my fairy dust...'

'Forget fairy dust, a kiss will work all the magic we need,' he said. And he waited.

She lifted her arms and wrapped them around his neck.

'Marriage, forever...'

'Marriage, forever...'

And he was right. They had no need of fairy dust, because as her lips touched his, and her dream came true, the world turned gold.

They were married in the ruins of the ancient abbey in Cranbrook Park on the last weekend in August.

Alice and Savannah were bridesmaids, Penny was matron of honour. The bride's mother and the groom's mother outdid one another in the hat department.

There was no pink.

According to the reporter from the *Observer,* the only member of the press invited to the wedding—well, apart from the entire staff—the bride was wearing a dress of silver grey lace with a sash of a blue that exactly matched the groom's eyes.

The bridesmaids were wearing dresses in the same material as the sash. The dogs, a donkey and a pony had bows, ditto.

The groom must have been wearing something but the only thing anyone noticed was his smile.

* * * * *

A FOREVER FAMILY
FOR THE ARMY DOC

MEREDITH WEBBER

When my sister and brother-in-law discovered they were unable to have children, they began adopting babies and fostering older children, eventually adopting all six of them. The family they blended together became very special, not only to each other but to our wider family, and brought fun and joy and laughter to all our lives. This particular sister has been my greatest support as a writer, and the first reader of all my books, so to Jenny, and all her family, this book and those that follow it, are for you.

CHAPTER ONE

IZZY PACED HERSELF on the run along the coastal path, which, right now, bordered a small sheltered beach. Ahead, the path rose high over headland cliffs, and further on it wound through coastal scrub. A truly beautiful part of the world—the place she loved, the place she belonged.

She'd been working nights, so this early-morning run was in the nature of a reward. A little treat before returning to her real world—making sure Nikki was ready for the start of the new term, catching up with her parents to get the latest family news, walking the dogs across the lush paddocks around the house—relaxing!

Nikki!

Her daughter would be thirteen next month—thirteen going on thirty—sensible, loving, doing well at school. So why was there always a little knot of worry tucked beneath Izzy's sternum where Nikki was concerned?

Izzy stopped—well, jogged on the spot—peering down onto the beach where an unidentifiable lump of something lay just beyond the lapping water.

Too big to be a body, she told the lurch in her stomach, but best she check.

Scrambling down over lumpy rocks from the path to the sandy beach, she caught a glimpse of movement up ahead.

Someone else heading towards the unknown object?

Or someone leaving the—

No! It was definitely too big for a body; besides, the movement had now resolved into a person, tall, dark-haired—lots of dark hair—definitely heading for the lump.

Izzy was the first to reach what was now apparent as a beached mammal, and knelt beside it, speaking quietly, touching it gently—a baby whale? Surely it must be because dolphins were a different shape, sleeker, their faces pointed, beaked…

Although the sun was not yet high in the sky, the animal's skin was hot. Izzy ripped off her T-shirt, dunked it in the waves and spread it over the animal's back.

'Good idea,' a deep voice said. 'I've a towel in my pack, I'll get that.'

He'd turned and was gone before Izzy could get a good look at him, nothing but an impression of a very unkempt man with a lot of facial hair and plenty more in a tangled mess all over his head.

'Bring something like a bottle or a cup if you've got one, and clean water, too.'

She yelled the order after him then returned to studying the animal, trying to remember things she'd learned when she and Nikki had visited Sea World some years ago.

Sea mammals usually stranded themselves on their side.

Tick!

This one certainly had.

The stranger returned.

'Porpoise,' he said in an authoritative voice.

'You think? I thought maybe baby whale.'

A shout of laughter made her look up, and up, to the tousled-haired man standing above her.

'Whale calves are three times the size of this fellow and weigh a ton or more.'

'Know-it-all,' Izzy muttered to herself, but as the man had dunked his towel in the water and was efficiently covering the animal she could hardly keep arguing with him.

And why *was* she arguing?

Did it matter?

'I think the first thing is to get it onto its belly.'

Bit late now to tell him she'd already thought of that.

'But the fresh water?'

Ha, something she knew that he didn't!

Deep inside she wondered at the petty thoughts flashing through her head but hopefully he wouldn't have noticed the momentary pause before she answered.

'Just pour a little over each eye, like where he'd have an eyebrow, so it will run down. I seem to remember you need to keep the eyes moist but—'

'The salt gets encrusted on them if you use sea water,' he finished for her, smiling, so white teeth flashed in the mess of dark hair.

And something gave a tiny tug in the pit of Izzy's stomach...

No! Not that! No way!

Carefully he poured water to a point above first one eye, then the other, allowing the water to run down over both eyes.

'I'm Mac,' he said, screwing the lid back on the bottle to preserve the rest of the water.

'Izzy,' Izzy replied, lifting her hand towards his so they shook above the body of what was apparently a porpoise. 'We'll have to roll him this way, towards the sea, to get him on his belly and I think if we dig a hole along this side, he might turn easily.'

'You've done this before?' Mac asked, joining Izzy on the seaward side of the animal, and digging into the sand.

'Nope, but I once went to a lecture about beached mammals. Big ones you shouldn't roll because you can break their ribs, and, oh, you should keep the tail and flippers and this fin on the back wet because they cool themselves through these thinner bits of their body.'

Mac, who'd brought a billycan as well as the bottle of water, began filling it and tipping it carefully onto the fins and tail while Izzy kept digging, focused on what she was doing so the tremor of—what? Awareness?—that tickled through her body when Mac settled beside her again, scraping sand away, almost passed unnoticed.

Almost!

What malign fate had brought him to this precise spot at this exact moment in time? Mac wondered as he knelt far too close to the half-naked woman and pulled sand away from the stranded animal.

A three-week trek down the coast path had been an opportunity to clear his head and prepare himself for the new job that lay ahead—literally ahead, for this particular section of the coastal path ended at Wetherby, not far from Wetherby District Hospital, currently awaiting its new director.

'Director' was a glorified title when the hospital, from what he'd learned, only boasted two doctors, with a private practice of four GPs in support—

'I think he's tilting this way.'

He glanced towards the speaker, who was completely oblivious to the effect she was having on his libido. She was kind of golden—like he imagined a sprite might be. She had golden skin, reddish-gold hair pulled ruthlessly back into a knot at the back of her head, but already escaping its confinement with damp little corkscrew curls flopping around her face. And golden eyes—well, probably brown, but with golden glints in them…

Better to think of the whole of her than individual bits, like the soft breasts, encased in a barely-there bikini top that brushed his arm as they dug—

He stood up, too aggravated by his wayward thoughts—not to mention the apparent return of his libido—to remain beside her.

'I'll lift the towel and shirt off it so we can replace them when it rolls,' he said, and congratulated himself on sounding practical and efficient.

'Good idea,' the sprite said, stopping her digging and scraping for a moment to smile up at him.

Oh, for Pete's sake, she had a dimple…

Fortunately for his sanity, the porpoise rolled into the hole they'd dug and now lay, snug on its belly, the rising tide sending wavelets splashing onto it.

The sprite had leapt away just in time, but she'd caught the full brunt of the splash, so water and sand were now splattered across her skin as she danced up and down in delight, clapping her hands and telling the uncaring animal how clever he was.

'Why do you assume it's a male?' Mac demanded, his reaction to the sight of her capering happiness making the words come out grouchier than he'd intended.

Golden eyes lifted to his.

'Honestly,' she said, a smile barely hidden on her lips, 'do you think a girl porpoise would be stupid enough to get into a fix like this?'

'Hmmph!'

He couldn't recall ever making a 'hmmph' noise before but that was definitely how it came out, but it was time to be practical, not argue over male versus female in the stupidity stakes. He'd certainly been the stupid one in his marriage, assuming it had meant things like love and fidelity on both sides...

Annoyed by the thought, he concentrated on the porpoise.

'What do we do next?'

Izzy studied the still stranded animal. At least it was right way up now, but was she keeping her eyes on it, so she didn't have to look at the man—Mac?

She'd been so delighted when their plan had worked, she'd looked up at him to share the success—straight into the bluest eyes she had ever seen. Right there, deep in the tangled mess of dark hair, was a pair of truly breathtaking blue eyes. She was pretty sure her heart *hadn't* stood still, even for an instant, but it sure had seemed like it...

Think about the porpoise!

'Maybe if we dig a trench, kind of extending our hole towards the sea, he might be able to slide forward as the tide rises.'

'Or perhaps we should get help,' the man with the

blue eyes said, giving the impression he was done with the animal rescue business.

Or maybe he was just being practical.

'We're three kilometres from town and I don't have a phone—do you?'

He looked put out as he shook his head, as if admitting he didn't have a phone was some kind of weakness, but who in their right mind would want to carry a phone on a wilderness walk? There were small fishing and holiday villages along the route and anyone walking it was obliged to report each day's destination so a search could be mounted if the walker didn't turn up. And at this time of the year there'd be other people on the path—

She looked up towards it—hopefully…

No people right now.

'So, it's up to us,' she said, hoping he'd stay so there'd be an 'us'. 'I don't suppose you're carrying a sleeping bag?'

'A sleeping bag?'

He seemed confused so she added quickly, 'Thing you sleep in—the nights have been cool, I thought you might—'

'I *do* know what a sleeping bag is,' he growled, 'I just can't see why you're asking.'

Grouchy, huh?

'For a sling,' she explained, although the bemusement on his face suggested he still wasn't with her. 'Can you get it?' she asked, very politely, and smiling as she spoke because she needed this man's help and didn't want to upset him any more than she already had.

'We'll try to slip it under him,' she explained. 'We

probably should have done it before he rolled but it's too late now, so we'll just have to build a little pool for him. I don't think we could lift him with the sleeping bag, but once the water rises and takes some of the weight, we'll be able to guide him into deeper water.'

'You want me to put my sleeping bag into the water for this animal?'

The disbelief in his voice stopped all thoughts of politeness.

'Oh, stop complaining and go get it. This part of the track ends at Wetherby. I'll buy you a new sleeping bag there.'

He didn't move for a moment, simply looking at her and shaking his head, as if she, not the stranded porpoise, was the problem.

Muttering something under his breath—something that could have been about bossy women—he turned and strode away, long, strong legs eating up the distance back to the track.

Izzy realised she was staring after him, shook *her* head in turn, and returned to digging with renewed determination.

Better by far than thinking of the blue eyes or strong legs or the fact that the rest of him, now his T-shirt was wet and clung to a very well-developed chest, wasn't too bad either.

Aware that he was behaving like a loutish imbecile, Mac returned to his already diminished pack and pulled out his sleeping bag, unrolling and unzipping it so it was ready when he reached the water.

Her idea was a good one—he should have thought of it himself.

Was he annoyed because he hadn't?

Or because of his inexplicable awareness of the woman who *had*?

Wasn't he done with that kind of attraction?

Not with women in general—he had several good women friends, some of whom, from time to time, he had taken to bed.

Until that had become awkward—more than physical attraction creeping in—though not on his side.

And the one thing he'd learned from his marriage was that physical attraction was dangerous. It messed with a man's head, leading him to make rash decisions.

And wasn't his head holding enough mess already? The Iraq posting, then finding out about his wife and *her* physical attractions...

Ex-wife!

He shook his head to free it of the past and studied the animal as he approached, determined to take control of this situation.

Wasn't that what ED specialists did?

'I'm deepening the hole—not easy because the sand just washes back in with the next wave but I think if we persist we can do it,' the woman, Izzy, said. 'Do you mind wetting his eyes again?'

So much for taking charge!

But as the tide rose and the water in their porpoise paddling pool grew deeper, he forgot about messy heads and wars and women, determined now to get this creature back into the deeper water where it belonged. He dug until his arms ached, pushing the sleeping bag beneath the heavy body, reaching for Izzy's fingers, grasping towards his from the other side.

By the time the water in the hole was knee deep they had their sleeping bag sling in place, each holding one side, lifting as the waves came in and easing the docile creature inch by inch into deeper water.

'Look, he's floating now,' Izzy said, and Mac was surprised to realise the weight had gone from their sling.

'You're right,' he said, feeling a surge of relief for the animal. 'But just keep the bag underneath him. We need to roll him back and forth so he gets the feel of his body moving in the water. Well, I think that's the idea. I just know when you catch, tag, and release a big fish, you have to ease it back and forth in the water until it swims away.'

He pushed at the huge body and Izzy pushed back, the pair of them moving into deeper and deeper water until, with a splash of his tail, the rescued animal took off, diving beneath the surface and appearing, after an anxious few minutes, further out to sea.

'He's gone! We did it—we did it!' Izzy yelled, leaping towards Mac and hugging him so the sloppy, wet sleeping bag she was still holding wrapped around him like a straitjacket and he sank beneath the waves.

But once untangled and in shallower water, he returned the hug, the success of their endeavour breaking the reserve of strangers.

He was beginning to enjoy the armful of woman and wet sleeping bag when Izzy eased away, hauling the sleeping bag out of the water and attempting to fold it.

'I don't usually hug str—' she began, then frowned as if something far more important had entered her head.

'Oh, I do hope he doesn't come back,' she said anxiously. 'I hope the rest of the pod are somewhere out there looking for him and he can find them. Do you know that when a whole pod is beached, and rescued, they try to let them all go at once so they can look after each other?'

Well, that got us over the awkwardness of the 'stranger hug'.

He'd have liked to reply, *Not our problem*, but now she'd mentioned it, he did feel a little anxious that the porpoise—*their* porpoise—would be all right.

Nonsense—he wasn't even certain porpoises swam in pods, and probably neither was she. The job was done and he needed to resume his walk—without his sleeping bag and without drinking water.

Alone?

'I don't suppose you'd like to walk with me as far as Wetherby, or as far along the track as you're going?'

She looked up at him and he noticed surprise in the gold-flecked eyes.

Noticed it because he'd felt it himself, even as he'd asked the question. Wasn't he off women?

Taking a sabbatical from all the emotional demands of a male-female relationship?

Not that it mattered because she was already dismissing the idea.

'Oh, no,' she was saying—far too quickly, really. 'I have to run. I'm just off nights and I've got to check my daughter's ready for school on Monday and my sister's up from Sydney for the weekend, and I think my brother might be in town—'

'Okay, okay!' he said, holding up his hands in surrender, then he smiled at the embarrassment in her face, and added, 'Although in future you might like to remember something my mother once told me.

Never give more than one excuse. More than one and it sounds as if you're making them up on the spot.'

'I *was* not! It's all true.'

Indignation coloured her cheeks and she turned to go, before swinging back to face him.

'There's a fresh water tap just a few hundred metres along the track; you can refill your bottle there.'

After which she really did go, practically sprinting away from him along the track—

For about twenty paces.

'Oh, the sleeping bag,' she said, pointing to the wet, red lump on the beach. 'You can't carry it wet, so hang it on a tree. I'll be back this way in a day or two and collect it so it's not littering the track, and if you tell me where you'll be staying I'll get you a new one.'

Izzy was only too aware that most of her parting conversation with the stranger had been a blather of words that barely made sense, but she *did* need to get back, or at least away from this stranger so she could sort out just what it was about him that disturbed her.

Had to be more than blue eyes and a hunky body— *had* to be!

'I won't be needing the sleeping bag.'

The shouted words were cool, uninterested, so she muttered a heartfelt, 'Good,' and turned away again, breaking stride only to yell belated thanks over her shoulder. Duty done, she took off again at a fast jog, hoping she looked efficient and professional, instead of desperate to get away.

By the time she slowed to cool down before reaching the car park, she'd decided that the silly connection she'd felt towards the man had been nothing more than the combined effects of night duty and gratitude that there had been someone to help her with the porpoise.

Which, hopefully, would not re-beach himself the moment they were out of sight!

Mac resumed his walk with a lighter pack.

But vague dissatisfaction disturbed the pleasure he'd been experiencing for the past three weeks. Maybe because his solitude had been broken by his interaction with the woman, and it had been the solitude he'd prized most. It was something that had been hard to come by in the army, even when his regiment had returned from overseas missions and he'd been working in the barracks.

Strange that it had been the togetherness of army life, the company of other wives and somewhat forced camaraderie, that had appealed to Lauren—right up to his first posting overseas.

'But you're a doctor, not a soldier,' she'd protested, although she'd seen other medical friends sent abroad. 'What will happen to me if you die?'

He could probably have handled it better than promising not to die, which he didn't on his first mission. But by the second time he was posted to Afghanistan she'd stopped believing—stopped believing in him, and in their marriage—stopped believing in love, she told him later, while explaining that the excitement of an affair gave her a far bigger thrill than marriage could ever provide.

On top of the disaster that had been his second deployment, this news had simply numbed him, somehow removing personal emotion from his life. He knew this didn't show, and he had continued to be a competent—probably more than competent—caring doctor, a cheerful companion in the officers' mess and a dutiful son to both his parents and whichever spouses they happened to have in their lives at the time.

He'd always been reasonably sure that his parents' divorce, when he was seven, hadn't particularly affected him. He'd seen both regularly, lived with both at various times, got on well with his half-siblings, and had even helped them, at different times, when their particular set of parents had divorced. Walking the coastal path, he'd had time to reflect and had realised that perhaps it had been back then that he'd learned to shut his emotions away—tuck them into something like a memory box and get on with his life.

Had this shut him away, prevented him from seeing and understanding what had probably been Lauren's very real fear that first time he'd been sent abroad?

She'd contacted him, Lauren, when she'd heard he was back this time—an email to which he hadn't replied.

He'd wondered if the thrills she'd spoken of had palled, but found he didn't want to know—definitely didn't want to find out. In fact, their brief courtship and three-year marriage seemed more like some fiction he'd read long ago than actual reality.

A dream—or maybe a nightmare...

Not wanting his thoughts to slide back into the past where there were memories far worse than that particular nightmare, he shut the lid on his memory box and turned his thoughts to what lay ahead.

Inevitably, to the golden girl—woman—who'd popped into his life like a genie from a bottle, then jogged right back out again.

She must live in Wetherby, he realised, but the seaside town and surrounding area had a population of close to ten thousand, probably double that in holiday time.

It was hardly likely they'd run into each other...

And he'd be far too busy getting used to his new position, getting to know his colleagues and learning his way around the hospital and town to be dallying with some golden sprite.

Besides which, she had a child to get ready for school so was probably married, although he *had* checked and she didn't wear a ring.

Not that people did these days, not all the time, and there were plenty of couples who never married, and women, and men, too, he supposed, who had a child but weren't necessarily in a relationship.

But she *had* a child, and even if she wasn't partnered, he was reasonably certain that women with children would—and should—be looking for commitment, for security, in a relationship.

Not that he did relationships.

He was more into dallying, and since he'd been a single man again, the only dalliances he'd had were with women who felt as he did, women who were happy with a mutually enjoyable affair without any expectation of commitment on either side.

The path had wound its way to the top of a small rise and he halted, more to stop his rambling, idiotic thoughts than to look at the view.

But the view was worth looking at, the restless ocean stretching out to the horizon, blue and green in places, fringed with white where the surf curled before rolling up the beach.

Off the next headland he could see surfers sitting on their boards, waiting for the next good wave, and beyond that what must be the outskirts of the town.

Wetherby!

CHAPTER TWO

THE KITCHEN TABLE at the Halliday house could have seated twenty people quite comfortably, but Izzy and her sister Lila were under orders to set it for eight.

'I thought it was just us—how did we get to eight?' Izzy asked, as she obediently laid placemats while Lila added cutlery.

'Uncle Marty's coming and he'll probably have a new girlfriend,' Nikki, who was arranging a bowl of flowers for the centre of the table, volunteered.

'But that's you and me, two, and Lila, Hallie and Pop, five, then Marty and presumably his latest flirt, that's seven.'

'Plus the new doctor from the hospital. As chairman of the hospital board it seemed only right I get to know him,' the woman her foster children all called Hallie explained.

'She's matchmaking again,' Lila whispered to Izzy.

'Hopefully for you, not me,' Izzy retorted.

'But Lila doesn't live here,' Nikki pointed out. 'And, anyway, Mum, he might be The One.'

Izzy groaned. Thirteen-year-olds—*nearly* thirteen-year-olds—shouldn't be acting as marriage managers for their mothers!

'Now, don't start that again. I am perfectly happy
with my single state, besides which he's the new doc
and I'll be working with him, and while some people
seem to manage to combine their work and social lives,
it's always been a disaster for me.'

'It was only a disaster once,' Hallie reminded her,
'and that was probably my fault. He seemed like such
a nice man when the board interviewed him. How was
I to know he had two ex-wives he didn't happen to
mention?'

'Two ex-wives and a jealous lover who damned near
shot our Izzy.'

They all turned towards the back door and chorused Marty's name as he spoke. Nikki was first into
his arms for a hug.

But Izzy hung back, shuddering at the memory of
that ill-fated relationship, only looking up when Marty
added, 'Okay, I'm home and it's great to see you all
but just stand back, girls, because I found this bloke
out in the garden, looking a little lost, and apparently
he's come for dinner. Hallie's latest stray, I'd say, the
new doc in town. Says his name's Mac.'

Izzy could feel her face heating while her body
went stiff with shock. A long drawn out *no-o-o-o* was
screaming somewhere inside her, while her hitherto reliable heart was beating out a little tattoo that had more
to do with how the stranger looked than who he was.

Clean-shaven, with his long shaggy hair trimmed
and slicked neatly back, his blue eyes framed by dark
arched brows, he was possibly the most attractive man
she'd ever seen.

Any woman's body would react to him, she told herself, glancing at Lila to see if she was similarly struck.

But, no, her beautiful, dark-haired, doe-eyed sister was shaking hands with the man called Mac and asking where he'd come from, where he'd trained, doctor-to-doctor questions.

Not that Mac had time to answer them, for Hallie had taken charge and was introducing him to the family.

'Marty you've met—he doesn't live here, just arrives from time to time, though usually not alone…'

Hallie frowned and looked around as if realising for the first time that Marty hadn't brought a woman.

'I took Cindy straight upstairs,' he explained. 'She wanted a shower before dinner, then I went out to see Pop in the shed and met Mac on the way back.'

'Ah,' Hallie said, nodding as if the world was now back in its rightful place. 'So, Mac—you do like to be called Mac, don't you? Isn't that what you said at the interview?'

The poor bewildered man nodded, and before Hallie could go off on another tangent—something they were all only too used to—Marty stepped in.

'Mac, the smallest of the women in the room is Nikki, and the redhead cowering in the corner is her mother, Izzy. It's not your fault that the last hospital director had a mad ex-lover who tried to shoot Izzy.'

Marty waved his arm.

'Come on over, Iz, and say hello to your new boss.'

'We've already met,' Izzy said bluntly, her anger at Marty for singling her out overcoming all her weird reactions to Mac.

'And I'm Lila.'

Bless her! She'd read the tension in the room, had

probably felt it emanating in waves from Izzy, and had stepped in to defuse things.

Now she was doing doctor talk again with the newcomer, smoothing over the earlier awkwardness and giving Izzy time to recover.

Mac tried to make sense of the place and people around him. He'd been directed to walk up the hill from the hospital and the only place on the hill was a big, old, stone-built building that looked as if it could house the hospital as well as all the staff.

He'd walked around it, wondering if the chairman of the hospital board might have a real house hidden somewhere behind it, and had ended up in a huge vegetable garden.

The man called Marty had rescued him, leading him into the old building through a cave-like back entrance and directly into a kitchen where, amidst what seemed like a dozen chattering women, stood his sprite. She had clothes on now, stretch jeans that hugged her legs and lower body and a diminutive top that showed a flash of golden skin at her waist when she moved.

Mrs Halliday he recognised, and the young girl with long golden-brown hair—okay, that was the daughter—while the real beauty of the room, the exotic dark-haired, black-eyed Lila, was finding it hard to hold his attention so his replies to her questions were vague and disjointed.

The sprite rescued him.

'This is the man I was telling you about,' she said to the room at large. 'The man who helped me with the porpoise.'

After which she finally turned her attention to him.

'Sorry about the chaos here tonight, Mac, but with—'

'With your sister up from Sydney, and your brother might be home…yes, I know,' he teased.

He saw the colour rise in her cheeks, but the flash of fire in her eyes suggested anger rather than embarrassment.

Bloody man! Izzy muttered inwardly. Now the whole family was looking at her.

Waiting for her famous temper to flare up?

No way! She would *not* react to this man's teasing. Bad enough her body was reacting to his presence, sending messages along her nerves and excitement through her blood. If this kept up she'd have to leave— town, that is—given that a distracted nurse was no help to anyone.

But Nikki—school…

Pop saved her from total, and quite ridiculous, panic by appearing through the kitchen door with a long, and remarkably dangerous-looking spear in his hand.

It stopped both the conversation and the sizzle in her blood.

'This's the best I can do, Nik,' he said, passing the lethal weapon to Izzy's daughter. 'I don't know if the aboriginals in this area made ceremonial markings on their spears but old Dan at the caravan park will know. You can ask him, and he'll show you what it needs.'

'Put that away right now!' Izzy ordered as Nikki began to caper around the room, flourishing the spear dangerously close to several humans.

Nikki disappeared, Hallie introduced Mac to Pop, she and Lila finished setting the table, and peace reigned, if only momentarily, in the Halliday kitchen.

Pop was explaining to Mac the project Nikki would be doing when school resumed, and why she needed a spear.

'I've made so much stuff for so many kids over the years,' he added. 'Izzy, was it you who was the robot? That was probably my most ingenious design, although I did go through a lot of aluminium foil.'

Any minute now he was going to dig out the old photos and she'd be squirming with embarrassment all night!

'Okay, dinner is ready.'

Hallie saved the day this time. She set the roasted leg of lamb on the table and handed Pop the carving knife and fork, Lila brought over dishes filled with crisply roasted potatoes and sticky baked pumpkin, while Izzy did her bit, taking the jugs of gravy from the warming drawer in the big oven and setting them on the table.

'Right!' Hallie said. 'Guest of honour—that's you, Mac—at the head of the table. Izzy, you'll be working with him so you might as well get to know a bit about him. You sit on one side and Lila on the other, and no descriptions of operations of any sort, please, Lila. Pop, you sit next to Lila, and then Nikki, and on the other side Marty and Cindy, and I'll sit at the end because—'

'Because you have to get up and down to get things,' the family chorused, and Izzy began to relax.

This was home, this was family, this was where she was safe, so who cared if her body found Mac who-ever he was—did he *have* a last name?—attractive? Of course she'd felt attraction before—although not for quite a while, now she thought about it.

'Are you going to sit?'

Heat crept up her neck and with her hair piled haphazardly on top of her head, the wretched man would see it! How was she to know he'd hold her chair for her?

She thumped down in the seat, too quickly for him to guide it into place, pulled it in herself and turned to offer a brusque thank you. She met the blue of his eyes and felt herself drowning.

This wasn't attraction, this was madness.

'So, why Wetherby?'

Lila saved her again, asking the question that had been in Izzy's mind, only hers had been phrased more as 'Why the hell Wetherby?'.

Now he was smiling at Lila—well, what man didn't smile at Lila?—and the kind of dark voice she remembered from the beach was explaining in short, fairly innocuous sound bites: army doctor, Middle East on and off over the last few years—

'—so when I decided to get out of the service I looked for somewhere green, and close to the surf, yet small enough to be peaceful.'

'Well, it's certainly that—I'm guessing a month here and you'll be bored to tears,' Cindy told him.

'Hey, Cindy, this is my home!' Marty protested.

'And this is only the second time you've been here, Cindy, and then only for a night,' Nikki pointed out.

'Are all small-town people as defensive as Wetherbyans?' Mac murmured to Izzy, who felt the heat of his body radiating towards her and the breath of his words brush against her skin so all she could do was look blankly at him.

'Of course,' Lila said briskly, and although she'd once again saved the day, she was also studying Izzy closely. Probably trying to work out what was happening.

As if I know, Izzy thought desperately, passing the potatoes to their guest, while Lila piled slices of meat from the platter Pop had filled onto Mac's plate.

Mac took the offerings of vegetables as they arrived and passed them on, poured gravy on his meat, and when his hostess picked up her knife and fork, he began to eat.

He tried to make sense of this family—anything to forget the woman by his side and the effect she was having on him. But how big, blond, blue-eyed Marty could be related to the beautiful Lila, let alone the petite redhead by his side, was beyond him.

'We're foster kids.'

He wasn't sure whether he was more surprised by Izzy speaking to him or the fact that she'd read his thoughts.

'*All* of you?'

'Oh, yes, and there's heaps more of us. It was a nunnery, you see, and Pop bought it for a song when he and Hallie married, and they intended filling it with their own kids, but that didn't happen so they went out and found the strays that careless parents leave behind, or kids whose parents died, in Lila's case. And they gave us all unquestioning love, and stability, and the confidence to be anything we wanted to be. But more than that, they gave us the security of a home, a family.'

'It's true,' Lila said, nodding from his other side.

'And it's been the best thing that happened in all of our lives,' Marty put in, although Hallie was telling them to hush, it was nothing anyone else wouldn't have done.

But for some reason Mac's thoughts had stopped earlier in the conversation so although he'd heard the rest, and been impressed, the question that came out was, 'A nunnery?'

How could these beautiful women be living in a nunnery? Except it wasn't a nunnery, of course it wasn't, it was just that his brain wasn't working too well. There was nothing immodest about the sprite's clothing, but from where he was sitting he could see the tops of the soft roundness of her breasts, and blood that should have been feeding his brain was elsewhere.

'It was cheap,' the man they all called Pop offered. 'And not that hard to knock two or three of the little cells together into decent-sized bedrooms.'

'You're a carpenter? Builder?'

Pop smiled and shook his head.

'Truckie—mainly long haul. I've taught all the kids to drive trucks.'

'I'm learning now,' Nikki announced, adding, rather to Mac's relief, 'Though only in the paddocks behind the house at the moment.'

The talk turned to the animals kept in the paddocks—did Mac ride? That was Nikki. Hallie mentioned the vegetable garden—'Feel free to help yourself to any vegetable...we always have far too many!'— and with the simple, delicious meal, and the general chat, Mac found himself relaxing in the midst of this strange family.

'You've family yourself, Mac?' Pop asked.

'Parents, of course,' he said. 'Though I don't see much of them. The army, you know—you never know from one day to the next where you'll be.'

He didn't add that their regular divorces and remarriages had dulled any filial emotion he'd ever felt for them.

'Married?'

This time the question came from the beautiful Lila and he didn't miss the wink she sent to Izzy.

Best to get that sorted once and for all, and quickly.

'Was once,' he replied, forcing himself to speak normally, although what felt like a very unsubtle third degree had his temper rising.

'And once was more than enough,' he added, to underline the point.

He glanced at Izzy, who was blushing furiously, and realised the questions weren't so much for him but to tease her.

Marty put a stop to it.

'Enough!' he said, directing the word at Lila. 'Pop asked a normal, everyday question, but all you're doing, Lila, is teasing Izzy.'

He turned to Mac.

'Izzy had an unfortunate experience with a doctor we had here a few years ago and it's become a bit of a family joke.'

The shrill tone of a mobile phone broke up the conversation, and it was Marty who pulled one from his pocket, glancing at it and moving away.

'Work. I'll probably have to go,' he explained as he moved into a small room off the kitchen.

'Marty's a pilot on the rescue helicopter,' Lila explained, as the whole family turned anxious eyes towards the small room.

He returned briskly, grabbing a jacket from the back of his chair.

'Got to go! Cindy, you coming or staying? If you're coming there's no time to get your stuff.'

Cindy, too, pushed back her chair.

'Coming,' she said.

The pair had barely left the room when another mobile sounded, and, having been free of its tyranny for three weeks, it took Mac a moment to realise it was his.

He glanced at the message on the screen before he, too, stood up.

'Looks like I'm starting work early. I'm sorry, Mrs Halliday. The meal, what I managed to eat of it, was wonderful.'

'Wait, I'll come with you,' the sprite announced.

'I know the way.'

He didn't really snap, it just came out a bit sharp, images of the tops of her soft breasts still lingering in his head.

'Sure, but you only arrived in town this morning so I doubt you know your way around the hospital. Hallie might have given you the basic tour, but if it's an emergency—and it will be if Marty's flying someone in— then you need the best help you can get, and that's me.'

She paused, then added with a teasing smile, 'So, lucky you!'

She couldn't possibly have known what he was thinking—not possibly, but it was obvious she intended coming with him as she rushed around the table kissing Hallie, Pop, Nikki and Lila, before linking her arm through his and practically dragging him out the door.

Escaping?

It certainly seemed that way as she led him headlong down the hill to the small hospital.

'But aren't you just off night duty?'

Good, he'd not only remembered something she'd said this morning, but had also managed a question, so his brain must be back in gear.

'Yes, but in case you didn't notice there was a certain amount of conspiracy stuff going on around that table tonight.'

'Conspiracy?'

He didn't want to admit he'd been more than slightly distracted by his neighbour at the table.

'Never mind,' Izzy said. 'Silly family stuff! I was just glad to get away.'

She moved a little further from him now she had him out of the house.

Sitting next to him, conscious of every movement of his body, had been torture, especially since she'd noticed the silky hairs on his forearms.

Dark, silky hairs...

Mesmerising dark silky hairs...

She shook her head, glad of the darkness so he didn't see her shaking loose her thoughts.

They were going to work and this was actually a good opportunity to see if she could detach herself from the idiotic attraction and concentrate solely on whatever they had to get done.

Never in her twenty-six years with the Hallidays had she been diverted from the sheer gluttonous enjoyment of one of Hallie's roast dinners, yet there she'd been, her fork toying with a piece of pumpkin as she'd wondered if his arms would feel as silky as they looked.

'But you *have* just come off night duty?' Mac asked, successfully getting her mind off silky hairs—though only just...

'Yes, but I've had a good sleep today. It's why I jog.

The steady pace seems to get rid of any leftover work tension and I can sleep like a baby.'

'Some babies don't sleep all that well,' Mac muttered.

What babies did he know?

Not that it mattered…

'We can go in this way,' she told him, leading him to the kitchen door at the rear of the building. 'We've only eleven patients at the moment with another seven in the nursing home at the back, so there'll be two registered nurses and two aides on duty in the main hospital, with another RN on call. Actually, there should be one of the local GPs on call, but there's a wedding…'

She led him down a short corridor, waving to a woman sitting at a curved desk in a room to the left.

'That's Abby,' she told him. 'Abby, Mac, Mac, Abby.'

'Good thing you had your phone on,' Abby told him. 'I wouldn't have known where to find you otherwise. I know you haven't officially started work but there's been an RTA on the highway, helicopter will bring in one patient for stabilisation and onward transport, and there are two ambulances also on the way.'

A patient requiring stabilisation was a tough introduction, but Mac was intrigued.

'And how do you get this information? Know to be prepared?'

He'd asked the question into the air between her and Abby, so Izzy answered him.

'First on scene is almost always police. They radio for ambulance support, a paramedic with the ambulance team assesses the injured and organises everything until the patients are safely removed.'

'He can order a helicopter?' Mac asked.

'Providing one can land,' Izzy responded. 'And Marty can land just about anywhere. Roads are great if they're flat and straight, but around here it's been dairy country since for ever, and there are fields close to the roads even in the hills.'

Izzy was leading him towards the large room that was their 'emergency department', as she explained. The room had a desk, curtains that could be drawn to allow privacy for patients and on the far side, three small rooms.

'The first one is the resus room,' Izzy told him. 'Next to it is a quiet room for mental health patients who sometimes find other people disconcerting, then a kind of all-purpose room, used for everything from resus to upset kids, to talking quietly to relatives when necessary.'

Mac heard a hitch in her voice and knew that talking to relatives—usually with grim news—wasn't one of her favourite things. In a small town, a death would probably be someone she knew...

He wanted to touch her shoulder, say he was sorry, but why?

An excuse to touch her?

To feel that golden skin?

Fortunately, while totally irrational and unmedical thoughts flashed through his mind he heard the *whup, whup, whup* of the helicopter.

Not a big army helicopter carrying injured troops— a smaller chopper, light, one patient. He was fine, but as sweat broke out on his forehead he wondered why he hadn't considered rescue helicopters when he'd chosen Wetherby.

Because he'd thought it was too small?

Or because he'd doubted the noise of the little dragonfly helicopters he'd encounter in civilian life would affect him?

'You okay?'

He shook his head, then realised she'd probably take it as a negative reply, so he said, 'Of course,' far too loudly and followed her out the door, presumably to meet their patient.

The rotors were still moving when a crewman ducked out to open the door wider so they could access the stretcher. Marty appeared from the front cabin to help and Mac was left to follow behind as his patient was rushed with admirable efficiency into the hospital.

Following behind, in the lights that surrounded the landing circle, he could see the patient was in a neck brace and secured onto a long spine board, with padded red supports preventing any head movement. One arm was in a temporary splint, and a tourniquet controlled blood loss from a messy wound on his left leg.

Mac's mind was on procedure, automatically listing what had to be done before the patient was transferred on to a major trauma centre.

'No obvious skull fracture,' the paramedic reported, 'but the GCS was three.'

So, some brain damage! A subdural haematoma with blood collecting inside the skull and causing pressure on the brain?

A CT scan would assess head injury, but would moving him for the scan cause more complications?

This was a patient with spine and head secured and moving on to a major hospital.

Leave the CT scan to them!

Intubation?

Definitely!

A young woman, presumably the paramedic, was using a manual resuscitator to help his breathing.

'The paramedic is intubation trained,' Izzy explained, somehow picking up on his thoughts once again, 'and I know the literature is divided about whether or not to intubate at the scene, but if we're doing the main stabilisation here, the paramedics tend not to intubate as that way they get the patients to us faster.'

Mac nodded. The patient's worst enemy, with severe trauma, was time. The sooner he or she had specialised help, the better the outcome.

So, intubation first, Izzy already checking for any obstruction in the mouth, before passing Mac what he needed for rapid sequence intubation. While he checked the tube was in place, she attached it to the ventilator.

The medical personnel from the helicopter were assisting, one taking blood for testing, the other setting up for an ECG.

'We coordinate our rosters,' Izzy explained as she set up the portable X-ray machine. 'Ambulance, helicopter and hospital, so we always have emergency-trained personnel to assist in a crisis. These two both work at Braxton Hospital when they're not rostered on ambulance or helicopter duty. The helicopter is based at Braxton, an hour and a half away, but the patient was brought here for stabilisation because we're closer.'

Mac wanted to ask why the helicopter pilot was in Wetherby if he was on call, but the screen was in place, the picture showing a shadow that suggested a subdural haematoma and, anyway, he had other things to worry about.

Do a CT scan to be sure?

It meant moving the patient to the radiography room, maybe doing further damage to his spine—

No time!

Mac had already decided he'd have to drill a small hole into the patient's skull and insert a catheter to drain off some blood to relieve the pressure before he could be sent on.

Apparently Izzy had also read the situation correctly and had already shaved and prepped the area of scalp the shadow indicated.

The two paramedics—Mac had decided that's what they must be—had been making notes of all the findings, although all the information would also go directly into the computer. Mac knew the notes would travel with the patient in case of computer glitches.

'Are you okay in helicopters? Did Hallie ask you that?' The gold-flecked eyes were fixed on his face as Izzy asked the questions.

'Practically never out of one,' he told her as he carefully drilled through the patient's skull. 'Why?'

He sounded confident but Izzy was sure he'd gone pale and sweaty when the helicopter had come in.

'Well,' she said, 'another statistic shows better outcomes for serious trauma patients if a physician travels with them. I can stay here and Roger—have you even met our other resident doctor, Roger Grey?—he'll come if I need him. Would you be okay with going along?'

She paused, watching for any hint of a reaction, but Mac's attention was on the delicate job of inserting a catheter into the wound he'd created.

That done, he looked up at her, his eyes fixed on a point somewhere above her head so she couldn't read any reaction in them.

'Of course,' he said, but so shortly, so abruptly she guessed he'd rather poke a needle in his eye. 'We'll start a drip, and make sure there's saline, swabs and dressings available on the chopper. I'll look at his leg on the way.'

She went off to check, returning in time for Mac to give the order to return the patient to the chopper. However, a grim set to the new doctor's face made her wonder just what horrors he had seen in the helicopters that were used to ferry casualties in war zones.

A wailing ambulance siren recalled her to the other casualties coming in. Megan, the most experienced of the two paramedics, had given up her place in the helicopter for Mac and stayed at the hospital to help with the incoming patients.

There were three, none too serious, but two needing limbs set and the other slightly concussed. Izzy and Megan began the initial assessment, GCS and ECG, palpated skulls for signs of injury, set up drips with analgesia. One by one they were wheeled through to the radiography room for X-rays, and for the concussion patient a CT scan, Izzy blessing the radiography course she'd completed.

It was painstaking work, but needed to be completed swiftly in case some major problem showed up, so time passed without them realising that dawn was breaking outside the hospital, the sun rising majestically out of the ocean.

They were studying the films of the second of the

limb injuries, a compound fracture of the ankle, when they heard the helicopter returning.

'That's your lift home,' Izzy told Megan. 'And I think you should take Mr Anderson back to Braxton with you. That ankle will need pins and plating, and you've got an orthopod on tap up there.'

'Good idea. Of course we'll take him. I'll get Marty and Pete in to give a hand loading him.'

Izzy started on the paperwork for admitting the other two patients, one for observation, the other to have further X-rays then a temporary cast fitted on his leg, which would keep the bone stable until the swelling went down and a firmer cast could be used.

'And now we're all done, here comes the cavalry.' Megan nodded to the door where Roger Grey had appeared, accompanied by two of the day-shift nurses.

'Big night, do you need a hug?' Roger said, heading for Izzy with every intention of providing one.

She ducked away. Not that there was anything remotely sexual or untoward in Roger's hugs—he was just a touchy-feely kind of man, and there were often times when a member of the staff appreciated a quick hug.

But ducking away had her backing into someone else—someone who'd come in through the patient entrance, someone with a rock-solid body who steadied her with his hands, holding her in such a way she could see those dark silky hairs...

Moving hurriedly—escaping, really—she made the introductions, gave Roger a brief précis of what they'd already done for the two new patients, explained the third would go to Braxton, then, as exhaustion suddenly struck her, she turned towards the cloakroom.

There'd be a bikini, shirt, shoes and socks in her locker. She would run off the tension of the night, then swim, before heading home to sleep.

She peeled off the scrubs she'd been wearing since the ambulances had come in and threw them into the bin by the door—the opening door.

Mac's head poked around it.

'Sorry,' he said, though in bra and pants she was quite respectable. 'I wondered if you were going for a run. It's definitely what I need and we'd look silly running separately along the path.'

She'd have liked to say she was taking the path south but that would sound petty; besides, she wanted to collect the sleeping bag.

So she nodded, in spite of knowing that she was making a rash decision.

'I imagine you'll have to go home and change. I'll wait by your gate.'

CHAPTER THREE

I'LL WAIT BY your gate!

How stupid could she be?

This man, Mac, was causing her enough problems without her agreeing to go jogging with him—actually making arrangements to be *with* him instead of as far away from him as possible, which would have been the really sensible decision.

Although they'd be colleagues so she couldn't escape him forever.

She began some routine stretching so she wouldn't have to think about him—well, not as much...

He emerged in shorts and a faded T-shirt, his hair loose and tangled again, hanging just long enough to hide his ears.

Her body reacted with the little flutters and zings, but she was getting used to them now.

Nearly!

'Sorry to keep you waiting, and sorry to barge in on your run as well, but there were things I wanted to know.'

He brushed against her as he shut the gate, and, yes, the hairs were just as silky as they looked, and, no, she was *not* going to touch them...

'Such as?' she said instead.

'If your brother was on duty last night, shouldn't he have been in Braxton where the helicopter is based?'

They were walking briskly through the town and fortunately it was too early for many of the locals to be around.

'He has his own—his own helicopter, I mean. He can be back in Braxton as quickly as if he'd driven from his house there to the hospital. The paramedics load any extras he might need while his crewmate checks the machine. All he really does is get in and fly the thing, although he was a trained paramedic as well as the pilot.'

She paused, wanting to ask her own question about helicopters, but realised it was probably far too personal.

So she stuck with Marty.

'Even when he was young he had a passion for them. Pop made him a little model one that had some string around the rotor stem and you wound it up then pulled and the helicopter took off. But most of the time he just ran around with it in the air, making helicopter noises, diving, and rising, and chasing the rest of us.'

They'd reached the track and set out in a slow jog.

'You were a happy family, then?' he asked, turning to look at her as he asked the question, his eyes studying her face.

Looking for a lie?

'Very,' she said firmly. 'Oh, we had our fights like any family and there were always kids who found it hard to fit in.'

She faltered, paused, looked out to sea before adding, 'Some of them had been so traumatised, so badly abused, they hated being happy, I guess.'

Mac nodded. You couldn't get through training as a doctor without seeing the horrific things people could do to one another—could do to children. At least, that was what he'd thought until he'd gone to war.

'Hallie and Pop must be remarkable people,' he said, forcing his mind back to the present as they resumed their jog, speeding up slightly.

'They are,' Izzy agreed, and the simple confirmation, the love in her voice, told him far more than the words.

They jogged in silence, and he breathed in the sea air and marvelled at the might of the waves crashing against the cliffs, the beauty in the scraggly, wind-twisted trees along the path, the little cove…their porpoise cove?

'The helicopter bothered you last night?'

He'd been so lost in his contemplation of the scene—concentrating on the details of the beauty around him to avoid his reactions to the woman beside him—that the question startled him.

He didn't have to answer it, he decided, but within a minute realised his companion—colleague, as he should be thinking of her—wasn't so easily silenced.

'Just the sound of it coming in made you go pale, yet you agreed to accompany the patient to the city.'

She was stating a fact, not asking a question, so now he didn't have to…

Except…

Except he wanted to!

For some reason, in this beautiful place, with this

woman he barely knew by his side, he *did* want to talk about it.

'It wasn't fear so much as memory,' he said, stopping to look out to sea while he found the words.

Not the words for the unimaginable horror—no words could cover that—but enough words to explain, to her and to himself.

'On my last tour one crashed—not a medical evac chopper but a big Chinook, carrying troops. One guy died and the others were badly injured. Getting them out of there was surreal, like living a nightmare. We weren't in much danger, weren't under direct attack, but putting men who'd been through what they'd been through into another bird, well, some of them just couldn't handle it.'

A hand slid into his and small fingers squeezed his.

'Were you able to sedate them?'

He nodded, then admitted, 'Only some.'

She removed her hand, stepped away to look more closely at him, folded her arms—to stop her hand straying again?—and shook her head.

'Well, I think given that experience, plus all the other things you've seen, you were remarkably brave going off last night.'

He had to smile at her fierce defence of him, a man she barely knew, but smiling at her brought a smile to her face, too, and the dimple peeped from her cheek.

And there was no way he couldn't touch it—just reach out and brush his forefinger against it.

She lifted *her* hand. To smack his away? But, no, all she did was brush her fingers across his forearm, then she beckoned with her head so once again they began to jog.

But the touches, unexpected yet somehow intimate, had changed something between them. It was acknowledgement certainly, but was it also acceptance of the attraction that had inexplicably sprung up between them, right back when they'd first met?

Or was he being fanciful?

Did she feel it or was her touch nothing more than a casual gesture?

Did it matter when he'd decided he didn't do attraction any more?

And he certainly didn't dally with colleagues...

He shook his head—he didn't do fanciful thinking either. Somewhere along the coast path to Wetherby he'd lost his common sense.

But glancing towards her, her strides lengthening now, the golden limbs moving with such grace, he felt a tightening in his gut, *and* in his groin if he was honest—

Tricky when they worked together.

Especially tricky when he knew the danger of physical attraction...

He lengthened his own stride, catching up and keeping pace with her, but they were beyond casual conversation now; it was a sprint, an unspoken challenge, and when she muttered, 'To the she-oak,' in laboured tones, he understood the challenge.

They sprinted, and male pride made sure he won, although she wasn't far behind, collapsing against the rough bark of the tree, fighting for her breath, while he was bent, hands on knees, dragging air into his depleted lungs.

'Well, if that doesn't help us sleep, nothing will,' Izzy finally had breath enough to say.

Mac, still bent, turned his head towards her.

'That was torture. I'm a walker, not a runner.'

But he was smiling as he spoke, and Izzy knew for certain she was lost. It had been bad enough when he'd touched her cheek and she'd reacted by feeling those silky hairs, but bent over, smiling up at her—a teasing smile—she understood that whatever it was she was feeling it was mutual.

And dangerous!

Especially now, when getting involved with a man was the last thing she needed—well, wanted…

And as for attraction, that was just a fleeting thing, and too easily confused with love, and love would be downright impossible just now.

Ignoring it seemed the best option, so she stood up straight, pulled off her shirt, kicked off her runners, and headed for the beach.

'It's a safe swimming spot if you don't go out too far, where there could be rips and undertows.'

Mac had straightened up and now he looked around.

'Isn't this our beach?'

Dear heaven, surely they weren't going to have an 'our' beach! Not yet, not already—this was moving far too fast and she wasn't even sure what 'this' was…

Although she knew for sure she didn't want it.

'No,' she said firmly. 'The porpoise cove—' no *our beach* from her! '—was the last one we passed, and someone had already removed your sleeping bag.'

But he'd stripped the T-shirt off his chest, and the sight of his upper body, a six-pack, no less, left her too breathless to say more.

She raced down the beach and dived beneath the

first wave, the cold water providing a cooling balm to her overheated body.

Not that he was going to let it go, she realised as he, too, dived in and emerged beside her.

'A cold swim is as good as a cold shower, I guess,' he said, smiling down at her, and while she was deciding that the man was just a flirt who went for any woman within reach and she should steer very clear of him, he tucked a strand of hair back behind her ears, then licked his fingers.

'Mmm...salty,' he murmured, before diving beneath the water again.

Well, that was weird, but didn't it prove that he was *definitely* a flirt who went for any woman within reach, and she *definitely* should steer clear of him?

More chilled by her thoughts than the water, she headed for the beach, crossed the rocks that guarded it, then pulled on her shirt. She'd carry her runners back to the fresh-water tap and clean her feet of sand before putting them on.

Mac was still in the water, swimming strongly back and forth across the little cove, but heeding her warning not to go too far out.

Realising he couldn't stay there for ever, Mac reluctantly left the water, walked up the beach, and along the path to join Izzy at the tap. That touch on her errant curl had been a mistake, and given that he *was* attracted to the woman, such touches were to be avoided in the future.

They barely knew each other, and he really should be putting all his efforts into getting this, his first civilian job, sorted. He'd managed the emergency situation the previous evening satisfactorily—even managed the helicopter flight—but responding to an emergency was automatic. It was the rest of the job he had to get on top of, things like who did what, and when, and where.

There'd be rosters and staff duty statements and daily, weekly and monthly targets—all the bumf so beloved of bureaucrats everywhere, not only those in the army.

He eyed the woman standing waiting for him. It was a wonder she hadn't jogged away, but as she hadn't…

Keep your distance? suggested his sensible self. But surely the thought in his head would count as sensible!

'I don't officially start work until tomorrow, but you obviously know your way around the hospital, so I wondered if, after we've both had a sleep, you'd mind showing me around and telling me how things work and who's who, and how the GPs fit in and—'

'Who's good and who isn't, who's lazy and who's great?'

'No, no, I'm sure they're all great but it's more about—I don't know. I've an appointment with the hospital manager tomorrow morning but I have a feeling that will be all facts and figures and paperwork, not patients and staff and—'

He halted suddenly, mainly because those brown-gold eyes were fixed on his face.

Studying him or drinking in every silly word he was muttering?

'More to get a feel for the place,' she offered politely, and he laughed, not so much at the mock politeness but that she'd picked up on what he'd been trying to ask.

Not that she'd said yes…

'Four o'clock?' she suggested, and he felt a surge of pleasure—well, he was pretty sure it was just pleasure.

'Great! Maybe we could even have dinner afterwards—you can show me the best places to eat in town.'

Had he gone too far? She hesitated.

She had a daughter.

A partner as well?

'Okay,' she said, 'but I can't be late home. Nikki goes back to school tomorrow and she can twist Hallie and Pop around her little finger and they'll let her stay up as late as she likes.'

She paused then added, with a smile, 'They never let *us* stay up late before a school day!'

And in spite of the complaint, Mac read the love for the people who'd brought her up in her voice and saw it shining in her eyes.

Was she out of her mind?

Her body was already attracted to this man, so what would happen if she got to know him better?

Did he read her hesitation in her agreement that he asked, 'What's the problem?'

'Well, at the risk of sounding embarrassingly ridiculous, I'd like you to understand it's just dinner, not a date.'

His eyes twinkled—and her stomach churned.

'I don't date, you see,' she added, hoping to stop the churning with practicality. 'Well, not at the moment.'

'So dinner, not a date, that's okay.' A smile playing around the words only added to the stomach churning!

'Although at the risk of *my* sounding ridiculous,

why don't you date? Not that I expected it to be. A date, you know—'

Of course he wouldn't—a guy who looked like him could have any woman he wanted, so why waste time with a scrawny redhead, especially one encumbered with a daughter?

So she'd made a complete fool of herself even mentioning dates.

And had a question to answer!

She looked at him and sighed.

'Long story but I'll definitely take you over the hospital this afternoon.'

'And tell me the long story over dinner!' he said firmly. 'Stories are good over dinner, and it's *just* dinner!'

She sighed again, shrugged, and finally said, 'We'll see, but I still can't be late home.'

And if he thought she hadn't noticed the satisfied expression on his face as she finally agreed, he'd be wrong.

Used to getting his own way, was he?

A sure sign this was a man to be wary of.

The hospital tour turned out to be fun. Mac insisted on meeting all the patients, and had sat and talked to the men and women in the nursing-home section. It didn't take long for one of the men to winkle out the information that Dr Macpherson—'Please call me Mac'—was an ex-military man and as two of the residents had seen service in Vietnam, topics of conversation weren't hard to find.

The women were equally impressed by the fact that Mac's grandmother had belonged to the Country

Women's Association, and the conversation shifted to scones.

'Izzy here makes beautiful lemonade scones,' someone said, and Mac's eyebrows rose.

'Really? Well, those I'll have to try,' he said. 'But right now I've persuaded her to have dinner with me so she can tell me all about Wetherby, and the hospital, and probably you lot!'

One of the men chuckled.

'Is a good gossip all you want?' one of the men teased, and the rest laughed, although as she and Mac departed, her cheeks pink with embarrassment, another of the residents called out, 'Now you take care of her, mind. She's a special girl, our Izzy.'

Izzy expected Mac to laugh it off, but instead he walked slowly away, turning his head from time to time, as if to study her.

Searching for her specialness?

As if!

Interesting, Mac decided.

Were all the patients as protective of this one nurse as the nursing-home residents obviously were?

And what had someone said at that chaotic introduction to the Halliday family?

Something about someone trying to shoot her?

'As you left me to choose where to go for dinner, I decided the Surf Club. They have the best dining room in town as far as position goes, right by the beach, looking out over the ocean.'

Practical—she was practical, he decided, half listening while still following his train of thought.

'It only does basic stuff, like steak and fish and usually a roast, but it's quality food and well cooked.'

She didn't turn towards him as she spoke and he sensed she was still a bit put out about the man's remark.

He walked beside her, through quiet streets towards the beach, avoiding the centre of town, such as it was.

'Are there many restaurants in town?'

Her pace slowed and now she turned to look at him.

'You've really been thrust in at the deep end,' she said. 'You've barely had time to settle into the house, let alone see the town.'

'My own fault,' he told her, hoping his voice was steadier than he was feeling, because a ray of light from the streetlamp was lighting up the side of her face, and the curls he now realised would always escape her attempts to tame them, glowed red-gold against the paler gold skin of her cheeks.

Or was it the line of her profile that had started attraction stirring again? A clean line, smooth forehead, straight nose and soft pink lips above a chin that, while not too obvious, suggested determination.

What would it take to break her determination not to date?

He swung back towards the sea.

What on earth was he thinking?

His head was still a mess, and anger over Lauren's behaviour still simmered somewhere deep inside.

He knew the anger was more to do with humiliation than infidelity, an army base being such a hotbed of gossip, but that didn't make it easier.

And marriage definitely wasn't on the cards—not again. But dating—provided they both knew that was all it was—was different. Dating, and a dalliance, on a short-term basis, could be fun.

Except he didn't dally with colleagues.

Or with women who had children...

Izzy was talking about the town—had been for some minutes, he suspected—while his mind bounced between the present and the past.

'So recently we've had all kinds of new places spring up—offering Paleo and vegan food, as well as more exotic fare from the Middle East and North Africa. It's a result of people making what they call a "hill change" and coming to live in the country outside the town, growing weird and wonderful new fruit and vegetables, and refugees from other countries settling here.'

Fortunately, they'd reached the beach and there, on the right, was the Surf Club. But out in front was the ocean, and above it a nearly full moon, marking a path of silver out to the horizon.

'Magical, isn't it?' Izzy breathed, stopping to admire the view.

'Magical indeed,' Mac agreed, but he was including the moonlit woman beside him in his reply.

Maybe he was bewitched!

Didn't witches have red hair?

Or maybe black—

'Come on, we can see it from the restaurant,' the witch was saying, and he turned and followed her, dragging his thoughts from the mystical to the practical.

All the business of his discharge from the army, getting a job, the three-week walk—it had been a while since he'd been with a woman, that's all it was...

She should have chosen the Moroccan restaurant in the back street of the town, Izzy decided as the young waiter showed them to a table on the front veranda. The view out over the ocean, the white curl of the waves crawling up the curving beach, the surf crashing on the rocky headlands made it far too romantic a backdrop for what was 'just dinner'.

Studying the menu, deciding what to eat, these were helpful, practical things to get romance out of her head.

She didn't date!

Not at the moment anyway...

Not until...

Fortunately Mac seemed similarly intent on the offerings and choices so conversation was avoided until the waiter departed, leaving them a bottle of iced water and taking their orders with him.

'So,' Mac said, as the waiter disappeared, 'why don't you date?'

She frowned at him.

'Is that really any of your business?'

'Nope!' A cheeky smile accompanied the word and undid the little scrap of common sense she'd managed to regain with the decisions about eating.

'But you did say you'd tell me over dinner,' he reminded her.

She wasn't sure she *had* said any such thing, but she'd already realised this was a very persistent man, so she might as well get it over with.

'Nikki isn't mine,' she began, then realised that hadn't come out the way she'd meant it to. 'Well, she is but she wasn't.'

This was getting worse and heat was rising in her traitorous cheeks.

'I mean, I'm not her birth mother. Her birth mother was one of our sisters. She came to live with us when she was seven and not even the love Hallie and Pop gave so freely could make up for the horrific abuse she'd suffered as a young child. It was as if there was something broken inside her, too broken to ever be fixed...'

She'd been playing with her fork as she spoke but now glanced up at Mac, worried she'd begun this story in the wrong place and was boring him.

But his expression held interest, and also understanding, so, encouraged by a slight nod of his head, she ploughed on.

'Nikki was drug addicted when she was born. Her mother died soon after, asking me to care for her baby. As if she needed to ask—the baby was family. But drug-addicted babies are sick and fractious and Nikki demanded so much attention that any relationship was out of the question. In fact, I gave up my pre-med course and spent two years just looking after Nikki. Hallie and Pop were wonderful, of course, but she needed...'

The words dried up, and a lump the size of Ayers Rock had formed in her throat as she remembered that time.

'A mother,' Mac said quietly. 'I can understand that.'

Izzy nodded.

'Anyway, she got better, and life settled down. I decided I'd do nursing—I had credits from the pre-med course—and Hallie and Pop were happy to babysit.'

'So then you were too busy studying to date?'

Izzy returned the smile that accompanied his words,

although exchanging smiles was dangerous when even
a smile could knot her stomach.

'Go on,' he encouraged, and she shrugged.

'There's not much more to it,' she said.

'Nikki's nearly thirteen years old,' he pointed out.

This time it was a sigh, not a shrug—a huge sigh!

'You know, I'd never thought about it before I had
Nikki, but it's darned hard for a single mother to have
normal relationships. Not only because you have to
cancel if the child throws a fever, or starts coughing,
or falls over and needs stitches, but because you start
to worry about introducing strange men into her life.'

'*Strange* men?'

Another smile and this time a tweak along Izzy's
nerves!

'I mean different men—not family. And what happens if she gets to know and like one of them, then the
relationship falls apart and he's gone? There was no
way I was going to bring a string of men into Nikki's
life—not that I've ever had a string of men—but somehow it seemed easier not to bother.'

'So you never dated?'

Blue eyes dared her not to answer.

'Are you always this persistent?' she demanded,
'But if you must know, yes, I did—well, occasionally. Then—'

'Then? And, yes, I am always this persistent.'

Izzy had to smile, although memories of her last di-
sastrous almost-relationship made her shiver.

'Someone with a gun?'

She looked up into the blue eyes.

'How did you—? Oh, dinner last night—bloody
Marty opening his big mouth. Yes, another doctor,

a couple of years ago—since him we've had agency doctors. Nikki was ten, and somehow I had decided I needed a man in my life—well, in both our lives. She'd been asking questions about her father but I had no answers, then I began to worry what might happen if she *did* have a father.'

She put down the fork, straightened it carefully, fiddled with the knife, then continued, 'Well, of course she'd have a father, everyone does, but what if he suddenly appeared from nowhere? What if he took her?'

Mac heard what sounded very like panic in her voice and reached out to cover her restless fingers with his hand.

'I thought if she already had a father—a stepfather, but someone she might come to consider a father—then—'

'She'd be safer?'

Mac was rewarded with a blinding smile, although he suspected the shine in her eyes was from unshed tears.

'Exactly,' she said, her voice stronger now. 'I mean, Nikki's always had male role models in her life with Pop and all the brothers, but I kept thinking maybe if we were a family—a mother, father and daughter— she'd be safer.'

Mac could see a kind of weird logic in this, but he was caught up in the story and wanted to know more.

'So?' he prompted.

The gold-brown eyes met his, clear now but dubious, then she shrugged and continued.

'The man—the new doctor—came. Hallie matchmaking, I suspect. Anyway, he asked me out, and we… we got on well. We'd dated exactly four times when his ex-girlfriend turned up. She threatened Nikki as well as me.'

Now her eyes held memories of the horror and he tightened his hold on her hand, while anger at a man he'd never met gripped his gut.

'So, the man you went out with thinking it might end up being a good thing for Nikki ended up putting you both in danger?'

Her eyes widened with surprise and a small smile replaced the tension around her lips.

'That's exactly how I felt! Talk about an idiot! Anyway, it put me off all thoughts of relationships, at least until she's away at university or travelling overseas.'

Their meals arrived, barramundi for him and lamb cutlets for Izzy, and tackling the tantalising offerings brought the conversation to a halt.

But Mac couldn't help considering the things he'd just learned as he ate his fish—delicious fish. Izzy was busy cutting the meat from her cutlets so he could watch her as he ate.

Not obtrusively, but glances, checking out that she was as attractive as he'd first thought, but also wondering what else was going on inside her head, because she certainly hadn't told him *all* the not-dating story.

Not that he was interested in dating either—well, not a colleague anyway. Far too incestuous somehow! Small hospital, small town—very like an army base— far too easy for stories to spread.

And the attraction thing bothered him. He knew he was attracted to her, and suspected it was mutual, but he knew only too well how attraction could blind a man to other facets of the 'attractee's' personality. Hadn't he and Lauren met and married within eight weeks?

And wasn't he determined not to make the same mistake again—the getting-married mistake? Attraction was fine. Short, mutually enjoyable affairs could be fun, although he doubted that would be possible in a town this size.

'The problem was...'

He was so lost in his own thoughts it took a moment to realise Izzy was speaking to him.

Well, who else could she be speaking to?

He lifted his head, raising his eyebrows.

'The problem was?' he repeated.

She sighed, looked out to the ocean for inspiration, before eventually meeting his eyes.

'Losing Nikki!'

He could hear the tears clogging her voice and reached out to touch her lightly on the arm.

Maybe not a good idea as she flinched and drew her arm away, swallowed hard and finally looked at him again.

'She's not legally mine, you see, so for the last few years—since then—I've been trying to adopt her, which isn't easy when I'm not a blood relative, I'm single, no one knows who or where her father is, and the law says both parents have to agree. I don't even have a formal agreement from her mother—all I have is a note on a piece of grubby paper, asking me to look after her.'

Mac felt his gut tighten in empathy for this woman's fears for the child she so obviously loved.

'I'd been vaguely looking into adoption when the other doctor came along and I knew if I was married it would be easier.'

She frowned, but possibly more at her thoughts than at him.

'I thought if it worked—with the doctor—we'd be a family. Not like our big family, though that's essential to both of us, but a kind of regular family...'

'Mother, father, children kind of family?' Mac asked, wanting to tease with the words but sensing she was very serious about this.

'Exactly!' she said, her smile lighting up her face, obviously delighted he'd somehow understood.

Not that he had!

Although he was reasonably sure it was all to do with Nikki and her safety.

Protection in case some drop-kick birth father turned up and wanted to take her away?

'So I went out with him, the other doctor, had those four dates and we got on okay, but then the gun thing happened and—'

He waited, sure there was more.

And there was...

'The woman threatened Nikki as well—the both of us, in the flat—and the thought I might have lost her, well, I went back to pushing the adoption idea. To adopting her as a single parent.'

'But surely in this day and age, adoption isn't all that hard, even for single women.'

Bewitching golden eyes met his.

'Don't kid yourself! Quite apart from the fact that Nikki's father appears to be untraceable, and she has never formally been handed over to the state for adoption, there are formidable background checks on all adoptive parents, on their homes, their friends, their social life.'

'Ah,' Mac said, as the penny dropped. 'So a string of lovers in your life could rule you out?'

'Even one could, because that would show there could be a string in the future and would that be in the child's best interests? Not to mention the invasion of privacy that the one lover might suffer.'

She sighed, then added, 'So...'

'It's easier not to bother,' Mac finished for her.

He considered this for a moment.

'But isn't that hard on you?'

His answer was a brilliant smile.

'Not really,' she said, shaking her head. 'You get out of the way of it, dating I mean, and I have heaps of men in my life with my brothers and their friends and friends at the hospital, so there's always someone who'll take me along to anything that needs a partner. In fact, I'm very happy with my life.'

Hmm, Mac thought, but he didn't say it, although Izzy's story had affected him deeply.

But not deeply enough to stop the attraction?

As if that mattered. If she did get involved with a man, he'd need to be committed both to her and to a future with her—to marriage—and apart from the fact that the helicopter ride had proven to him he wasn't over the effects of PTSD, he'd decided that he was probably genetically unsuited to marriage, given his parents' and his own failures.

And why was he considering marriage at all? It was a first date—well, not even a date...

CHAPTER FOUR

IZZY STARED OUT at the limitless ocean, wondering why on earth she'd told this man—this virtual stranger—things she'd never voiced to anyone, not even Lila.

The family knew she'd talked about a formal adoption, but although they may have guessed, she'd never voiced her fear of losing Nikki.

'Does this happen with all the women you take out to dinner?' she asked, turning back to her companion. 'Do they all pour out their deepest, darkest secrets to you?'

She hoped the words came out lighter than they felt inside her head, because inside her head was a mess, what with having to resist the attraction and then the unguarded conversation, and the totally unnecessary moon over the ocean.

'Not usually on the first d—dinner,' he said, a smile in the words, eyes twinkling, although he was serious when he added, 'but I do understand how you must feel. I've seen drug-addicted babies before so those first years must have been hell, and having fought for her to stay alive, to be well at the end of the withdrawal time, it would make her extra-special to you.'

'I had good teachers in Hallie and Pop. Most of the

kids they took in had problems, some of them horrendous ones, yet they showered us all with love.'

'And you, did you have problems?'

The question was so unexpected, she answered automatically.

'Not really. My mum dumped me on Gran when I was about three—we never quite figured out when—then Gran died when I was six, and after a while in temporary foster homes I was lucky enough to be given to Hallie and Pop.'

'You make is sound like an ideal childhood, which it can't possibly have been.'

He was frowning, but Izzy couldn't help smiling at his words.

'Compared to some it was, and the love we all got from Hallie and Pop made us a happy family and our world a very happy place.'

She checked the moon again—still there—*and* the ocean, silvered in its light, and sighed.

'We should probably go.'

Not that she wanted to, but the scene must have bewitched her and she'd already told Mac far too much about herself. Stay here and who knew what else might come out?

'I suppose we should. Will I see you at the hospital tomorrow?'

Izzy repeated the words in her head. Did he sound as if he wanted to?

Not that it mattered, of course! No dating!

'Not tomorrow. I'm still on days off, and with Nikki back at school it's a chance to do a big spring clean.'

'You do know it's autumn?' he teased, smiling at her again.

One smile, that's all it took to put her heart back into fibrillation! She had to get over this. Every fibre of her being was yelling at her to keep right away from him. He was a dangerous distraction and the less she saw of him the better.

Work would be okay—well, kind of okay—and unavoidable—but she could handle things at work.

'Autumn clean would sound stupid, but spring clean—well, people know what you mean.'

It was such an inane remark she wasn't surprised he raised his eyebrows at her.

But that was better than him smiling.

And he'd pushed back his chair so they were leaving.

Which meant she could get out of there without making an even bigger fool of herself.

She caught up with him at the bar and reminded him it was just dinner and they should go Dutch, but the beautiful surfie chick behind the bar had already taken his credit card and given him a dazzling smile.

He returned the smile with a pretty good one of his own, and Izzy walked away, reminding herself it didn't matter who Mac smiled at, they were colleagues, nothing more.

But that made walking along the esplanade towards the hospital, and Mac's house beside it, very uncomfortable, because the presence of moonlight and rolling surf and the old lighthouse on the hill was a scene for romance, and the presence of Mac's body, so close to hers, was an agonising distraction.

'I was looking at pictures of the old hospital when you were showing me around,' he said. 'I hadn't realised that the nuns had once run the place.'

Well, that tells me there will be no further personal

conversation, Izzy realised, *which isn't fair because he now knows far more than I'm comfortable with about me and I know zilch about him.*

'Yes,' she said, playing the game. 'The church used to be the other side of the hospital so the three—church, hospital and doctor's house where you live—formed a curve of the old brick and stone buildings. The church burned down and there was damage to the rear of the hospital so it was all rebuilt, keeping the old façade. Your house was saved, and although it's been renovated from time to time, it's pretty much as it was when it was built.'

'It's certainly a lovely old building,' Mac confirmed. 'I'm lucky to be able to live in it.'

Tension tightened Izzy's body. This matter-of-fact, almost tourist talk felt wrong after all they'd shared.

Well, after all she'd shared...

Somehow during their dinner—during most of the time they'd spent together—Mac had shown he was a kind and caring man, not a robot mouthing platitudes about old buildings.

It's just attraction, Mac reminded himself, when his determined discussion of the old hospital buildings had failed to distract him from thoughts of the woman by his side.

And she's a colleague...

And she doesn't date, let alone dally—

The stupid thoughts were brought to an abrupt halt as the blare of a horn split the night air, and a roaring sound filled his ears.

Some sixth sense made him grab Izzy and together they rolled back onto the road, while a massive semi-trailer ploughed straight past where they'd been standing and crashed into the massive fig tree that was a feature of the hospital's grounds.

'Are you all right?' he asked, as he helped Izzy to her feet, steadying her for a moment as tremors of fear, or perhaps relief, ran through them both.

'Fine!' she said, 'But whoever was behind the wheel of that rig isn't.'

But Mac was already on his way, running towards the crushed cab, as staff came hurrying from the hospital.

The driver's-side door was jammed, but he could see the driver slumped sideways in the seat, his hand still on the steering wheel, on the horn that had warned them of danger.

Then Izzy was there, climbing into the cab from the passenger side, gesturing him to join her.

Not altogether easy, as the tree prevented him from going around the front of the vehicle, and getting around the back would take too long.

He went over the top, using broken branches of the tree to steady himself, sliding off the bonnet and into the cab.

'Faint pulse at first, but I lost it. His feet are trapped,' Izzy said, as she pumped the man's chest, counting her compressions.

'I'm too big to get down there, but I'll do the CPR if you can edge your way in and maybe release them.'

He watched her squirm her way down into the compressed foot space.

'It's no good.'

Her voice was muffled by the sound of the engine. Engine!

'Can you reach up and turn off the engine?'

The silence was almost more deafening than the noise had been.

'Now, tell me exactly what's holding his feet in place.'

A nurse Mac hadn't met had arrived from the hospital with a resus bag, and a siren told Mac that help was on the way—hopefully a fire truck with cutting equipment.

'It's the engine block, I'd say—come back with the impact. I can see his feet, just can't budge them.'

Mac's mind flashed through dozens of road accidents he'd seen, some caused by carelessness, others by the dreaded IEDs.

'Try taking off his shoes,' he suggested, as he slipped a mask over the man's nose and mouth while the nurse attached the tube to the small oxygen tank in the bag.

You try taking off his shoes! Izzy wanted to retort, but she could see it was a good idea—just not easy to do. She wriggled and squirmed, finally getting one shoe off the size-twelve foot, and, like magic, the foot was free.

The other was harder, but by now she could hear voices outside the cabin, and knew more help was at hand. Metal shrieked as some kind of tool was used in an attempt to pry the driver's door open, and although the door remained shut there must have been some movement, because now she could reach the other shoe—well, steel-capped boot, in fact—and pulling a boot off was far harder than removing a shoe, something she must remember to tell Mac.

'Who's in there?' she heard someone ask.

'Driver and a nurse,' Mac replied. 'Driver's feet are trapped.'

'Get her out. We have to start cutting and although we've got foam to cover the cab, if there's spilt fuel, the welding torch could still spark a fire.'

'You hear that, Izzy? Out now!'

It was an order, but—

'One minute. Give me one minute,' she said, as fear for the trapped driver gripped her. She grabbed the boot with both hands and gave an almighty tug, crashing backwards into Mac as the boot came off.

Her held her for a moment, then lifted her bodily out of the cab, passing her to a fireman as if she was a weightless bundle of skin and bones. The fireman set her on her feet, grinning as he recognised her.

'Seen you looking better, Iz!' he teased, passing her over to Roger, who was on call for the night.

'You okay?' he asked, and she nodded, easing away from his side so the comforting arm he'd put around her shoulders fell away. Roger's hugs were fine, but if she'd wanted a hug right now it wasn't from him.

Dangerous thoughts!

She walked back towards the crash site, keeping out of the way of the ambos now lifting the driver onto a trolley. Mac was there beside it, keeping the resuscitator tube free from kinks, checking oxygen flow and the rise and fall of the patient's chest.

'Have you brought some kind of curse down on us?' Roger was asking Mac. 'Two nights here and two accidents! We can go months without an emergency!'

Mac shrugged, passed the tube and oxygen bottle to Roger, then stepped back, looking around, his gaze coming to rest on Izzy.

Remembering the ambo's comments, she realised she should have gone straight home once the cavalry had arrived. Now Mac was going to see her in whatever state she must be in.

And just *why* was that bothering her?

She wasn't interested in Mac.

Attracted to him, yes, but interested?

Definitely not!

'I'll walk you home,' the person in whom she was *not* interested was saying, and although she'd have liked to refuse, her legs were suddenly shaky and the hand that took her firmly by the elbow was comforting.

'Had he had a heart attack, do you think?' she asked, to distract herself from comforting.

'I'd say so.'

'He must have known something was wrong,' Izzy suggested. 'Big rigs don't usually come through town but he was headed for the hospital and he was giving everyone warning that he was on the way. His hand was definitely on the horn.'

She hesitated, then added, 'It could have been Pop! We all keep telling him it's time to retire and he's not driving as much these days, but when you see something like that...'

Mac heard the tremor in her voice and shifted his hand from her elbow to put his arm around her shoulders—comforting her, nothing more.

Although when the fireman had mentioned fire, he'd felt his lungs seize up.

'Thanks,' she said to him when they'd climbed the path behind the hospital and reached the nunnery. 'And thanks for dinner. I'm sorry I talked so much. You know my entire life story and I know nothing more about you.'

It was too dark in the shadow of the building to see the flush of embarrassment he was sure was colouring her cheeks, and he knew, for certain, that he should let things go right there.

So what prompted him to speak again?

To say, 'Well, we could fix that. You could show me one of the other restaurants tomorrow night—and I'd let you pay half to prove it's not a date. I have meetings at the hospital in the morning but if I know anything at all about hospital meetings, mine will probably go on all day and I'll have no time to shop. So, shall we say six o'clock? Helping out a new colleague, nothing more. Please?'

He heard her sigh and held his breath. Though every functioning cell in his brain was telling him he needed to see less of her, not more, he wanted her to come, wanted to get to know more about the woman to whom he was so inexplicably—and inconveniently?—attracted.

'Okay,' she finally agreed, 'six o'clock.'

And with that, she vanished.

Well, she probably hadn't vanished, there was obviously a door somewhere along the wall that he hadn't noticed and certainly couldn't make out in the darkness.

Izzy escaped into the building, heading quietly up to the small suite of rooms that Pop had turned into a flat for her and Nikki. She looked in on her daughter, thankfully sound asleep, then headed for the bathroom, turning on the light and seeing her dirt-streaked face and scratches here and there where she'd obviously rubbed against something.

At least the path home, mostly in the shadow of the nunnery, had been dark so Mac might not have noticed.

Mac might not have noticed?

The question shrieked in her head. She wasn't interested in Mac. It was attraction, nothing more, and right now, with the adoption process under way, the last thing she needed was a man making things difficult.

She stripped off her clothes, showered, and went to bed. In five hours she'd have to be up, getting Nikki organised and off to school.

Life would return to normal, whatever normal was.

Mac woke bathed in sweat and shivering uncontrollably. The nightmares he thought he'd left behind somewhere on the coastal track had returned, possibly because of the near miss he and Izzy had suffered when the big rig had crashed.

He closed his eyes and breathed deeply, murmuring the words he'd adopted as a mantra—'truthfulness, compassion, forbearance.'

He'd first heard them used at a meditation session his psychologist had suggested he attend, and for some reason they had made sense to him. Now they helped to clear his mind and calm his body so meditation could be followed by dream-free sleep.

Sometimes!

Tonight his mantra didn't work.

Concern over a new job?

He didn't think so.

Regret over the mess his marriage had been because

surely Lauren wouldn't have gone looking for excitement if their marriage had been better?

No, he'd been down that track so many times he'd accepted it was just one of those things.

Which left Izzy.

Hearing her story—he'd seen drug-addicted babies and knew just how much they suffered and how big a task it must have been for her to take on—had added admiration for the person she was to the attraction that had sprung between them in the beginning.

But he also understood just how important her daughter was to her, and he had to be careful not to cross any lines that might put Nikki's adoption into danger.

And apart from that, the nightmare had been a reminder that he hadn't fully recovered—another reason not to get involved with an attractive redhead!

Who definitely didn't want a man in her life!

Just now, or any time?

'Get over it, Mac, get back to truthfulness, compassion and forbearance, breathe in, breathe out, breathe...'

Izzy was slipping a casserole into the oven when Nikki returned from school.

'Yum,' her daughter said, sniffing the air in their small flat. 'Chicken Marsala. Pity I'm going out. Sorry, Mum, I forgot to tell you. Shan and I need to work on our new media assignment so I'm sleeping over at her place.'

'The new media assignment you were going to do in the holidays?'

Nikki laughed.

'We *did* make a start—we decided on a topic. Has the rise in the ocean temperature contributed to the increasing number of great white sharks off east coast beaches?'

'That's media, not biology?'

'Oh, Mum, of course it is. What makes the biggest headlines in a newspaper these days? Four people injured in a traffic accident or a surfer bitten by a shark?'

'Shows how much I know,' Izzy said. 'Well, the casserole will do for our dinner tomorrow night, because I'm showing Mac around town tonight and thought we might end up at the new Moroccan place.'

'Mac? Two nights running? You're dating! And another doctor! Oh, Mum!'

Izzy knew she should have kept quiet, but when did she not react to Nikki's teases?

'I am *not* dating the man,' she said firmly, although the disbelief in her daughter's blue eyes suggested it hadn't been firmly enough. 'If and when I decide to go on a date with a man, I will let you know.'

'Well, if and when you do decide, I hope you know not to go too far on a second date—that's coming on too strong, Mum.'

'Coming on too strong?' Izzy growled. 'It is *not* a date and, anyway, who made you an expert?'

'It's in all the magazines, Mum, and people talk about it in online chat rooms—the ones you let me join.'

Izzy smiled. This was an easier conversation—her daughter's grievance that she had limited online options was a common argument. And one in which she'd held the line—so far!

But tonight Nikki wasn't going to air it, flitting

away with, 'I've got to change and pack a few things,' and popping her head back into the combined kitchen and living room to say, 'Just check there's no mad ex-lover in his life.'

Cheeky brat! Izzy thought, but she was still smiling, pleased that she could have these conversations with her daughter—pleased Nikki could have them with her.

She knocked on the bathroom door, and opened it a crack.

'Do you want me to run you down to Shan's?' she asked.

'No, Hallie and Pop are going to the restaurant for dinner, so they'll drive me, but thanks.'

Izzy was closing the door when Nikki spoke again.

'Do *they* know about your non-date?'

'Well, no, but that's only because I haven't seen them today. There's no reason not to tell them.'

'Good,' Nikki called after her, 'because everyone in town will know, probably before you get to his house.'

Brat indeed, but she was right.

Izzy sighed. How on earth had she got herself into this situation? *Why* on earth had she said yes? He was a grown man, ex-army, he could find his way around a small town!

So this would be the last time they had a—what? A rendezvous?

And to ensure he couldn't use the 'no time to shop' excuse again, she'd take the car, and they could do his shopping either before or after dinner.

Which was possibly one of the stupidest ideas she'd ever had, she realised later as she pushed the trolley around the supermarket while he threw in things he wanted.

Too domestic by far!

Too intimate somehow, especially as she kept running into people she knew and having to introduce Mac.

Which was when she realised that shopping together—although they weren't *really* shopping together—made them look like a couple. She couldn't keep adding 'I'm just pushing the trolley' to the end of every introduction, now, could she?

'What kitchen paper do you use?'

She was so lost in her 'couple' conundrum it took a moment to realise he was talking to her.

'Whatever's on special usually, although I do like it to be three-ply.'

'Kitchen paper comes in different plies?'

'Of course—the more plies, the thicker it is.'

'Well, what do you know?'

Mac was shaking his head, but now searching each pack for the little sign that gave the ply.

And Izzy, looking into the trolley for the first time and seeing the random selection of goods, forgot her worries over how shopping with him would look to the town and began to sort the contents.

'You've not shopped much?'

'Hardly ever,' he admitted. 'Maybe for coffee, or some biscuits for my quarters, but the army does meals rather well.'

'So you can't cook either?' Izzy demanded, and saw the hesitation on his face.

'Maybe just a little—bacon-and-egg sandwich and that kind of thing,' he said. 'But I've bought some books and one of my stepsisters said that if you can read you can cook, because cookbooks have very clear instructions.'

Izzy shook her head.

'So did you read the book before you came shopping? Write down a list of what you might need in order to cook something you'd read in your book?'

Mac grinned at her.

'Books—I bought two, and, yes, I read one of them on the walk and it all seemed easy enough, but I didn't know until you arrived that we were going to shop.'

'Heaven save me from a helpless male,' Izzy muttered. 'Is there any food at all in your house?'

Mac nodded.

'I've got bread, butter, honey, tea bags and coffee, biscuits, and some milk—most of it left over from the walk, although the milk's fresh.'

'Great start! But to even get the basics, we need time and a list, so what say we abandon this trolley and get some dinner? We can make a list of basics while we're eating and come back later.'

CHAPTER FIVE

SOUNDED GOOD TO MAC. Wandering around the supermarket with Izzy had been a weird experience, but one he'd found himself enjoying more and more. It felt comfortable—right, somehow—and it was impossible to drop things into the trolley without the occasional brush of skin on skin, which added sizzle to the exercise.

Not that he should be thinking of sizzle—not with Izzy. She was definitely off limits!

'So, where shall we eat?'

'Do you like Moroccan food?'

They were walking out of the store, and she'd turned to look at him.

'Love it,' he said, glad for it to be true. 'In fact, one of the cookbooks I bought was a Moroccan one because we had a cook at one time whose family was Moroccan and it was some of the best food I ever tasted in the army.'

She smiled and shook her head.

'Most men would have stuck to steak and sausages—barbeque stuff—but, no, you go for something that a lot of women wouldn't try! At least that will make writing the list easier.'

She was still smiling, and there was something about a smiling sprite that did weird things to his intestines, but he manned up.

'It will?'

'It will,' she confirmed, leading him to the right, along what was obviously the main street in town. 'We'll know what spices to get, and things like dates, and dried apricots, and couscous, and rose water—'

'Rose water? You've got to be kidding!'

This time she laughed, and that felt good—good that he could make her laugh.

But it was treading on very dangerous ground, this being pleased about something so trivial.

Not that making someone laugh was trivial, but it all felt too...

Domestic?

'It's here—not very imaginatively named but great food.'

Izzy pushed through a curtain of glass beads then held them for him to enter the Marrakesh.

He eased past her, careful not to touch—well, not too much—and breathed in the odours of spice and sauces.

'Wonderful!' he said, as Izzy greeted a man who was obviously the owner, dressed in a smart suit with a dazzlingly white shirt.

'This is Hamid,' she said to Mac, and introduced the two of them. 'Hamid's son, Ahmed, is going to be Australia's next great surfing champion. He's still only young, but beating professionals quite regularly in local competitions.'

Hamid waved away the compliment with eloquent hands but his chest had puffed out and Mac knew he was secretly delighted. Once settled at the table, menus in hand, he realised the scope of Moroccan food.

'I might need guidance,' he said.

Izzy glanced up and smiled.

'No menus in the army?'

'Certainly not this size!'

So she explained the different dishes, asked if he wanted something before the main meal.

'Hamid's mezze plate is wonderful, although it's not specifically Moroccan, more a general Arabic dish, with dips and lovely breads, olives and other bits and pieces.'

'Sounds good, and after that I'll have the chicken with prunes and apricots. Apricots seem to grow wild in Afghanistan and there's nothing as wonderful as a fresh one plucked from a tree. We even had them growing in our compound in Iraq.'

Izzy shook her head.

'We see war as such a terrible thing, and I know it is, but the pictures in the media here show things being blown up, or ruined vehicles or buildings, not a soldier reaching up to pluck an apricot from a tree and biting into it. That's so normal!'

Mac grinned at her, something she wished he wouldn't do as grins seemed to make people complicit—as if they shared a secret.

'Actually,' he admitted, 'there's more time than you'd believe for things like apricots. "Hurry up and wait" is an old army saying. Yes, things are unbelievably hectic at times but in between...'

He shrugged, drawing far too much attention to broad shoulders in a blue shirt that stretched across a well-muscled chest.

She closed her eyes momentarily, mainly to banish an image of the chest beneath the shirt. Was there a god or goddess way back in ancient history or maybe a wise woman spirit guide on a tropical island she could call on to banish attraction? Or maybe a spell—some potion she could take...

She couldn't think of any kind of help so opened her eyes to find Hamid had arrived to take their orders.

That part was easy, but sharing a mezze plate meant inevitable touches of fingers. Izzy could feel tension spiralling along her nerves, tightening every sinew.

This had to stop!

She would help him shop, then cut all ties outside work hours. Even at work she could probably avoid him, and surely she was professional enough to handle things when she couldn't.

She was sufficiently distracted that she didn't see Hamid remove the much-depleted mezze plate, but when he returned with the chicken for Mac and a couscous and baked vegetable dish for her, she knew she'd have to pull herself together and make polite conversation.

Or perhaps a list!

A list would be much easier.

She dug a pen from her handbag, pinched a paper serviette from the table next to them and folded it into note-size.

'So,' she said, brightly, 'exactly what do you have in the way of supplies already?'

His eyes narrowed slightly as if maybe he'd guessed she needed a distraction.

'You can eat your dinner first,' he said, spooning

food into his mouth. A pause while he chewed and swallowed, then, 'Mine's delicious.'

Izzy obediently ate a few mouthfuls.

'There,' she said, 'now we can both eat and talk. Basics are bread, butter, milk, tea and coffee, which you seem to have covered.'

'The bread's going a bit green.'

'Okay, so bread…'

She wrote it down.

'Now, breakfast—what do you eat for breakfast?'

Mac held up a hand, obviously giving his full attention to his food.

'It's wonderful,' he eventually said. 'Maybe I can persuade Hamid to give me some small containers of this dish and I could have it for breakfast, lunch and dinner.'

'You'd grow to hate it,' Izzy suggested, and he smiled.

Smiles affected her, but it was, she decided, better than the grin.

'Probably,' he admitted. 'What do you have for breakfast?'

'Totally boring,' Izzy told him. 'Cereal, yoghurt, fruit.'

Another smile.

'That would do me. Write it down.'

Izzy sighed.

'You can't possibly be this hopeless,' she grumbled. 'You must know there are choices. There must be hundreds of types of cereals alone, not to mention plain and flavoured yoghurts—'

'And all kinds of fruit,' he finished for her, shaking his head and laughing. 'Don't look so serious. I can make those choices in the shop. I'll just grab something that looks good and if I don't like it, I'll get something different next time.'

She didn't want to smile at him but a laughing Mac was hard to resist. The problem was that smiling at him arrested the laughter and something passed between them—nothing more than a quick clash of gazes—but it worried Izzy more than all the other sensations that being with Mac caused.

'Lunch?'

She spoke firmly, wanting to bring things back to normal between them. 'A sandwich? Cheese, ham, tomato, lettuce?'

And suddenly he was as decisive as she was.

'Ham and cheese—they'll last longer.'

Mac wasn't sure what had just happened, but something had—something that had been more than attraction—something dangerous, although not darkly so…

He scooped more of his meal onto his spoon and ate in silence, only half listening as Izzy added practical things—dishcloths, soap, washing powder—to his list.

Mac used her concentration on the list to study the woman across the table from him, a little frown drawing her eyebrows together. She wasn't a classic beauty, or even stunningly attractive, yet his body responded to every move she made, and every word she spoke. It was as if they were attached to each other with invisible wires—which was such a ridiculous fantasy he couldn't believe he'd thought it.

He had to get his head straight.

He had to keep things light between them. He knew her well enough by now to know she wasn't a dallying kind of woman, even without the vulnerability of her position in regard to Nikki's adoption.

And there were still too many dark places in his psyche to think beyond dalliance with any woman.

They finished their meals—and apparently the list—he wiping his plate clean with some thick, fresh-baked bread, though Izzy seemed too distracted to have eaten all of hers.

But she pushed her plate away and said, 'Come on, let's go. You paid last night so it's my turn.'

He protested that she was doing him a favour but she ignored him, handing her credit card to Hamid to stop any further argument.

But back in the supermarket—shopping with her—it seemed dangerous again.

She had to get out of here, Izzy decided. Finish this as quickly as possible and get out—get home. For some obscure reason an ordinary wander around a super-market was beginning to feel like a date—more like a date than dinner had.

She knew it wasn't, of course, but—

'That should keep you going,' she finally declared, heading resolutely towards the checkouts.

'That's if I can pay for it and don't end up in debt-ors' prison.'

'What, this little lot?' she teased, waving her hand at the almost full trolley. 'Back when we were young, we'd have Hallie pushing the lead trolley with three or four of us trailing along behind, each with a trolley.'

'The mind boggles,' Mac said, easing Izzy away from the handle and taking over the pushing, his body still close and warm.

'Oh, I need some toothpaste!' She dashed away,

grabbing two tubes, although she knew there was plenty at home.

Anything to get away from that warmth—that closeness—that somehow, even when he hadn't been near her, she'd been feeling.

'Throw them in with mine as thanks for all the help, not to mention the lift you're going to give me,' Mac suggested, and rather than argue—and get close again—she threw them in.

Once back at his house, she helped him unload the bags.

'I'll leave you to unpack so you know where you've put everything,' she said, backing towards the door as escape finally beckoned.

'None of this will go off if left for a few minutes, so I'll walk you home.'

'I've got a car,' Izzy reminded him. 'But thanks for the offer.'

'Then I'll walk you to your car,' he said, and did just that, opening the driver's door for her so their heads were close. She met his eyes and knew something was passing between them…like the promise of a kiss that couldn't be…

CHAPTER SIX

IZZY WAS STILL MUTTERING, 'Promise of a kiss, indeed...' to herself when she reported to work the next morning. The walk down from home had been pleasant, dawn breaking, the first rays of the sun peeking from below the horizon.

She loved the town when it was like this, barely awake, and the early shift, beginning at six, was her favourite.

Abby, still on nights, was waiting for her in the ED.

'Ambulance on its way in—four-year-old with febrile convulsions. Little Rhia Watson—Sally and Ben's daughter. I've written down all the handover stuff—it's on the desk—and the other night nurse will do a proper handover to Chloe, who's on with you today—I think an agency nurse is coming for the swing shift.'

The conversation ended as the ambulance pulled up outside, and both women hurried out to meet it.

'She woke up crying in the night,' Sally explained as Ben carried his daughter into the room. 'Her temperature was up so I gave her some children's paracetamol and sponged her down, but nothing seemed to help. We stayed with her, trying to keep her cool, and she drifted off to sleep then about half an hour ago she cried out and when we went in she was all stiff and shaking.'

'I called the ambulance,' Ben added, as he carefully laid his listless daughter on the examination table. 'She'd stopped shaking by the time they got there.'

The ambo was handing over his report to Abby, and although Izzy knew it would have all the details of Rhia's temperature, pulse, and oxygen saturation she knew she'd have to do it all again.

After she'd examined the little girl.

She took Rhia's hand. 'I'm Izzy and I'm a nurse and I'm going to look after you. Mum and Dad are still here. Now, can you tell me if you're hurting anywhere?'

'My head hurts…and my neck.'

'Get a doctor in here,' Izzy said quietly to Abby. She didn't want to alarm Rhia's parents but with neck pain or stiffness in a child this age there was always the possibility of meningococcal.

'Now, I'm just going to look at your tummy, is that okay?'

Dark brown eyes dulled by pain or fatigue looked blankly at her as Izzy checked the little girl's skin for any sign of a rash.

None, but that didn't mean anything at this stage.

'I'd like to give her an antibiotic injection just to be sure,' she said to the parents, who nodded, willing to go along with anything to make their little girl better.

'You're thinking meningococcal?' Mac asked quietly.

He had appeared from nowhere, but had obviously heard her.

'Or not,' Izzy said, 'but we usually start with an antibiotic just in case, then do the tests.'

He nodded, and she went off to get the penicillin while Mac introduced himself to the family and began his examination of their patient.

'Has she been vaccinated against meningococcal?' he asked, and Sally held out her hands in a helpless gesture.

'I think she had a needle for that when she was one but I'd have to check.' Fear brought a quaver to the words. 'Do you think that's what it is?'

Mac reached out and touched Sally's shoulder.

'We don't know but the fever means an infection and starting antibiotics straight away will help no matter what it turns out to be.'

He nodded to Izzy, who told Rhia about the needle, and waited until Ben had lifted his daughter into his arms before swabbing the skin, using deadening lotion, then slowly administering the antibiotic.

Rhia cried, but it was a half-hearted effort, and her listlessness made Izzy fear the worst.

Mac was explaining that he would need to take blood and some cerebrospinal fluid for testing, and Izzy suggested they move to the small room that was sometimes used as a second resus room.

Mac nodded, then smiled down at Rhia.

'Do you mind if *I* carry you instead of Daddy?'

There was no objection so he lifted her and carried her gently into the more private space. Izzy asked Ben to wait and with his help she filled in the admission form before leading him to join the others.

Mac had settled Rhia on a high table and with Izzy's help secured an IV port in their patient's little hand. He handed Izzy a vial of blood to be sent off for testing, then explained to Rhia that he needed her to lie on her side so he could put another needle in her back.

'I'm sorry sweetheart,' he said, smiling at the little girl, 'but we need to find out what's making you sick. I'll do my best not to hurt you.'

But Rhia was beyond caring, she simply stared at Mac with those big blank eyes, while Sally cried quietly on her husband's shoulder.

So Izzy held their patient curled on her side on the table while Mac numbed the site with local anaesthetic, then inserted the needle to test CSF pressure before withdrawing a sample. Izzy cleaned and covered the site with a dressing before gently rolling Rhia onto her back.

Mac was putting details on the chart, so Izzy labelled and packed the fluid container, added the blood sample to the package and passed it to the courier she had phoned earlier.

'Now we wait,' Mac said quietly, as Rhia's parents moved closer to their daughter, one on either side, holding her hands and talking quietly.

Mac followed Izzy out of the room.

'If it's confirmed as meningococcal we'll have to find out who's been in contact with her for the last week and give them all a dose of clearance antibiotics—starting with her parents. And if it *is* meningococcal there'll be a run on the vaccine. Is it subsidised by the government or will people have to pay for it?'

'If she had the vaccine, and she probably did, it would have been Type C. Since that's been on the free list the most common strain in Australia is B and although there's now a vaccine for it, you have to buy it.'

Mac nodded.

'We'll have to admit her, if only for observation—at least until the test results come back.'

'She could go into the family room, and that way her parents could stay with her. She's an only child and Sally's a stay-at-home mum so she could be here all the time and Ben go to work from here.'

Mac grinned at her.

'Family room, huh? I did wonder why one of the rooms had a double bed.'

Was it the grin or the mention of a double bed that raised Izzy's heart rate?

'It's a very useful room to have,' she said reprovingly. 'Apart from making it easier for hospitalised children to have their parents with them, it's been great for elderly people especially. Imagine being married for sixty years and suddenly your spouse is hospitalised twenty miles away. It's too much to expect them to visit for an hour or two each day.'

Mac's smile was back and with it Izzy's heightened pulse.

'I'm still back at the imagining being married sixty years part—I didn't make it to three.'

'Didn't work out?'

She remembered him saying he'd been married—back at that embarrassing dinner. And something else—that he wouldn't marry again?

His marriage must have been bad.

And the wretch was still smiling.

'I think you'll find in your statistics that something like forty percent of marriages fail.'

'You're wrong, it's one in three marriages fail so that's thirty-three percent,' Izzy muttered, disturbed by the conversation, although she couldn't work out why.

Mac's life, former, present, or future, had nothing to do with her.

Mac watched her walk along the passage that gave entry to the rooms that made up the ward. He liked the design of the hospital, with an enclosed courtyard garden on the other side of the passage. And along the outside of the patient rooms was a long veranda so those well enough could sit outside, enjoying the sunshine and the view over the town to the ocean.

Halfway down was the nurses' station, well set up with computers, monitors and light boxes. Someone had taken the trouble to make the new hospital, in the damaged part of the old building, into a relaxed and pleasant place for patients, and a great working environment for the staff.

'You're Mac, I believe,' a voice said from behind him, and he turned to greet a young Asian woman, the crisp white coat and the stethoscope slung around her neck a dead giveaway that she was a doctor.

'I'm Aisha Narapathan,' she introduced herself, holding out a slim hand for him to shake. 'I've a patient in Room Fourteen, and I pop in to see her most mornings.'

Mac introduced himself, and smiled.

'You're from the local GP group?'

Aisha nodded.

'We act as on-call doctors when you and Roger are off duty and although our patients are happy with the treatment they get in hospital, I like to check up on them myself. At times when there's been only one doctor employed at the hospital, and we've been rostered on for morning rounds. It might seem a clunky system at first but it works.'

She smiled again, and added, 'Most of the time. You've had a busy weekend, I hear. Normally one of us would have been on call—we cover weekends as well—but Saturday night was our receptionist's wedding and, it being a country town, we were all invited.'

'We managed,' Mac assured her.

'I'm sure you did,' Aisha said. 'With Izzy around, even the most helpless of the contract doctors we've had at the hospital can manage.'

She moved on but not before Mac caught the flash of a bright diamond on the ring finger of her left hand.

Was she the doctor engaged to Roger Grey?

His thought was confirmed when he saw her as she was leaving.

'You must come to dinner one day. Roger and I would love to have you. I'll tell him to arrange it with you.'

An aide arrived with a message. There was a phone call for him in his office.

He headed in that direction, pausing only to say goodbye to Aisha.

Was this job going to turn into a deskbound one? Surely not—and not if the weekend was anything to go on.

But interaction with people—with patients and their relatives—was the part of medicine he enjoyed the most.

The voice on the phone introduced himself as the pathologist at Braxton Hospital.

'I've emailed the results to you but thought it would be good if we spoke.'

He introduced himself, asked the usual questions

about where Mac had trained, seeking acquaintances in common, then explained.

'It's meningitis meningococcal for sure. The bacteria are present in the spinal fluid but none in the blood.'

'Thanks, mate,' Mac said. 'I owe you one for getting it done so quickly.'

But as soon as he'd hung up he wondered if the hospital would have ceftriaxone on hand, or whether he should have ordered some for Braxton.

There were optional drugs, but lately it had been the one of choice for meningococcal attacks on the brain.

He looked up from doodling the name on his desk pad to see Izzy flash past the door.

'Izzy!'

She turned, stopping in the doorway. For the first time he realised just how horrible the dark blue uniform tunic looked on a redhead, although he still felt his groin tighten just looking at her.

'Ceftriaxone?' he asked.

'So it *is* meningitis,' she said, her voice flat with the anxiety she felt for the child. 'We've some in stock. I'll set up a drip.'

'I'll do it,' he said, 'but come with me while I tell Rhia's parents. They'll feel better with someone they know in the room.'

Will they? Izzy wondered, but she accompanied Mac back to the family room, where Mac explained the result.

He did it well, she realised, listening to his explanation of what was happening inside their daughter's body, then moved swiftly on to treatment.

'We've got it early,' he told them. 'You were right to get help immediately she had the seizure. There are good drugs to treat it and we'll start a drip straight away so the antibiotic is going directly into her bloodstream. I'll also give the pair of you antibiotics and later the vaccine.'

He turned his attention to the small patient in the big single bed in the family room.

'I know you're feeling bad right now,' he said, stroking strands of pale brown hair off her face, 'but we're going to get you better.

'She'll be here for a few days, probably longer,' he said quietly to Ben on his way out the door. 'You might want to get some toys she's familiar with and her own pyjamas and a few clothes for her and the pair of you.'

'And books. I'll get books—she loves us reading to her.'

Hmm…Izzy thought to herself when she heard Ben's voice strengthen at the thought of having something to do to help. She knew already that Mac was a good doctor, he'd shown that in the emergencies over the weekend, but he was also a good psychologist.

Or perhaps just a caring man, sensitive to how Ben must have been feeling?

Whatever! She didn't need to be seeing these compassionate sides of him, they would add depth to the silly attraction she was already feeling.

But right now at least she could get away from him—she had a job to do in the pharmacy.

Except he caught up with her on the way and it was hardly a pharmacy, just a room where drugs were kept.

A very small room!

She paused outside the door.

She didn't *have* to go in!

Of course she did, she knew where it was kept.

He'd stopped beside her and she was so conscious of him her skin itched.

This was crazy—there was no other word for it. She'd been attracted to The Rat, as her family now called the last man in her life, but not like this—not as if the attraction was a tangible thing, not only causing responses inside her body but in her skin as well.

'What's the protocol?' she asked, forcing her mind to matters medical, fumbling with her keys to find the right one as if that, and not her disinclination to be in a very small room with him, was the hold-up.

'Seven days' IV for Rhia, in saline, not Ringer's, because it doesn't mix well with anything that has calcium in it. Then we'll have to give antibiotics to any people who've been in close contact with her in the last week, and check all of their statuses as far as vaccination goes. We'll get a list of friends and relations from her parents. Was she at childcare of any kind that you know of?'

Whatever was affecting her couldn't be affecting him that he was being so practical.

She could do practical!

'She's four. She'd be at the local pre-school probably three days a week. I'll get our secretary to phone the director and get a list.'

'Of teachers, too,' Mac reminded her as she finally got the key to fit into the keyhole and unlocked the door of the pharmacy.

They stepped inside together—close—and without turning to face her Mac said, 'I understand your reluctance to be going out with men because of the adoption business, and I know it's bizarre, but I've never felt an attraction like the one I feel for you. I thought maybe if we gave in to it, say for a week or two, it might go away. That's if you feel it, too, of course...'

His voice was only slightly strangled, but Izzy knew any words she said would come out far worse—if at all.

He'd touched her lightly and somehow they turned to face each other, not touching, not close enough to cause a scandal should anyone walk past, but Izzy could feel the shape of him in her skin, catch the warmth of his breath on her lips.

'You *must* feel it,' he said. 'Something this strong can't be one-sided.

She almost nodded—no way could she deny it. But caution, memory of the last disaster—and somewhere in her head and heart concern for Nikki—held her back.

'The ceftriaxone should be in here,' she said, moving towards a cupboard where she knew the powder was kept. It would be dissolved in the saline solution and dripped slowly into Rhia.

Then Mac was right behind her, peering into the cupboard, examining its contents, taking his cue from her—now totally professional.

'I have had a look inside these cupboards and the refrigerators but, as yet, couldn't put my hand on anything.'

'Which is why you have staff,' Izzy told him, so rattled by his presence she was shaking.

'Staff I can put my hand on?' he teased, touching her lightly on the shoulder. Not *quite* professional!

Was he another Rat or just another touchy person like Roger?

Izzy doubted it—this was something they both felt.

'We can't talk here,' she said desperately, a vial of the yellowish powder in her hand.

'Then later?' he asked, his breath now warming her neck.

'Sometime!' she said, almost shouting, desperate to get out of the room, away from Mac, if only so her body could settle down and her brain regain some thinking power.

He moved away, finding a bag of saline for all he'd said he didn't know his way around.

Izzy glanced at her watch—it had been less than five minutes since they'd left the corridor, yet it had seemed like a lifetime.

But was he right? Could a short—short what? Affair? Liaison?—kill the attraction?

She had no idea but as it was impossible to think while he was in such close proximity, she chose escape.

'I'll leave you to mix it if that's okay? I've other patients I need to check. They'll be thinking no one cares about them.'

And she fled, although her excuse hadn't been entirely true. Patients in a small hospital knew the staff could become caught up in emergencies and they bore it well, knowing it could be them or one of their loved ones who needed urgent attention next time.

And Mac was probably intuitive enough, from what she'd seen of him, to know it, too.

Was he avoiding her as assiduously as she was avoiding him? Izzy wondered later, when she was sitting in the secretary's room, working out how she could juggle the rosters for the week.

They would need more nursing staff on duty to handle vaccinations and antibiotics for adults and children who'd been in contact with Rhia, and the budget didn't have much wriggle room.

'Here's the list from Sally and Ben. They've included phone numbers where they knew them.'

She looked up to see Mac hovering over her desk, a piece of paper in his hand.

'One of the aides could have delivered that,' she said, disconcerted to have him back in her space when she'd thought she'd escaped.

She'd been looking up at him so saw from a half-smile that he was about to say something silly, then he glanced towards Belle at the desk at the back of the room and must have thought better of it.

Instead he tilted his head to see what she'd been doing. 'Have we enough staff to help out with the vaccinations when people hear about it and start coming in?'

Izzy pointed at the sheet.

'It's a juggling act, but staffing at small hospitals always is so, yes, we'll manage.'

A soft chime told them they had a patient in the ED and the enrolled nurse on duty there needed help.

'I'll go,' Mac said. 'You keep juggling, and maybe Belle can start on the phone calls.' He took his list from Izzy and passed it over to Belle, talking to her in a quiet voice, suggesting what she might say, emphasising it was a precautionary move but it was better to be safe than sorry.

As he whisked out of the room, Izzy let out the breath she'd been holding. What *was* it about this man that had her so uptight? So dithered and confused?

Another soft chime and she knew she was needed.

The rosters would have to wait, and as for unanswerable questions—well, those she had to put right out of her mind.

What was quite a large room for a country ED was filling up rapidly—filling up with worried-looking mothers or fathers, each clutching a small child by the hand.

'Dr Mac told me to phone the pre-school earlier,' the enrolled nurse on duty told her, 'and they must have started contacting parents straight away.'

Izzy could see Mac in a curtained alcove already, speaking to an anxious father. He saw Izzy, excused himself, and came across to her.

'We'll do antibiotic jabs today and ask parents to check their child's immunisation schedule and come back if they need the vaccine.'

'Sounds good,' Izzy said. 'I'll rustle up a few more nurses or aides to organise this scrum.'

As the day wore on, the trickle of people who'd been in contact with Rhia became a flood. Mac had contacted Braxton for more antibiotic and warned they could also be needing vaccine.

He was, Izzy realised when they had a break in customers late afternoon, the most organised doctor she'd ever worked with, and his efficiency seemed to make the whole process move more smoothly.

Swing shift nurses and aides had come in, taking over from anyone who had to go off duty on time to collect children or meet appointments, but the flood was once again a trickle and all but Izzy had returned to normal duties.

Mac was sitting behind the reception desk, eating a sandwich that had grown stale enough to have the edges of the bread curling up in a most unappetising manner.

'Want some?' he said.

'Eugh! No way! I did grab something earlier but I'm going to make a cuppa while the place is quiet. Do you want one?'

He shook his head, lifting a can of soda that was sitting on the desk.

But the image of him, sandwich in one hand, soda in the other, stayed with Izzy as she hurried to the tea room.

He was just a man, an ordinary man—good doctor, though—but still just a man!

So why was he affecting her the way he was?

Why so instantly?

Why him when other men roused no emotion whatsoever?

It must be, she finally decided, just one of life's mysteries to which there was no answer—no logical explanation.

CHAPTER SEVEN

MAC WATCHED HER disappear out the door and wondered about attraction. Why one woman and not another?

He looked at the curling edge of the sandwich and decided she'd been right—it wasn't worth eating. Dumping it and the empty can in the bin, he picked up the ED admissions book, looking back through the pages, seeing more than one night a week when they had no patients at all.

Had he brought the rush of emergencies to this small town?

That was nearly as ridiculous a thought as the attraction one he'd had earlier!

But forcing himself to focus—so as not to think about the other matter—he could see that this time of the day was always quiet. Patients, it seemed, came into the ED late afternoon, three to five, then the numbers dropped off until six-thirty when another trickle might arrive.

With the news about Rhia spreading, tonight's trickle would more likely be a flood.

'Will we have extra staff on this evening in case the people Belle phoned start coming in?' he asked Izzy, who was coming through the door with her cup of tea.

'Yes, we will,' a voice that wasn't Izzy's answered, and he realised Roger was right behind her. 'But I mean "we", not "you". Time the pair of you were off. The hospital can't afford overtime, you know.' He smiled, then added, 'Well, not the amount of overtime you've racked up over the weekend. Izzy doesn't count as she wasn't even on duty so how could she possibly claim overtime?'

As a nurse Mac had met, but whose name he couldn't remember, had followed Roger into the room, it was hard to argue.

'I'm happy to leave you to it,' Mac said, then turned to Izzy. 'And as I've just thrown my lunch into the bin and I know you haven't eaten, how about we duck into town for an early dinner at that Thai restaurant you mentioned? I've a few things to go over with Roger, so you'd have time to slip home and change.'

He hesitated, then added, 'Nikki might like to come, too—save you having to feed her.'

Was it nothing more than a friendly gesture, or was it a test? Izzy wondered. She'd told him she hadn't dated because she didn't want men coming in and out of Nikki's life, so asking Nikki made it just a casual dinner.

Didn't it?

And asking in front of other staff, that was casual, too—or had he done *that* to make it hard for her to refuse?

'Go and change, the man said.' Roger's voice broke into her muddled thoughts. 'No one in their right mind wants to be seen eating in town with someone in that appalling uniform.'

'It's practical and not that appalling!' She automatically defended the uniform Hallie had chosen, although Izzy had never yet met anyone it suited.

'Just go!' Roger ordered, and she went.

Befuddled, that was what she was.

And tired now the let-down after a busy day was seeping into her body.

Better tiredness than the things she felt when she was with Mac.

So why was she going to dinner with him?

Again!

With him and Nikki—that sounded better, and felt better, too, the tiredness leaving her as she wondered whether the two would get on well.

'Fab!' was Nikki's reaction. 'Shan and I can get on with the project.'

'After you've eaten,' Izzy told her firmly. 'Mac was good enough to ask us both so you'll sit and eat with us. It's an early dinner so if you like Shan could come back here with us and stay over if you've work you'd like to do.'

Nikki surprised her with a warm hug.

'You're the greatest, Mum!'

And Izzy's heartbeats went erratic again, although a very different kind of erratic from the way it reacted to Mac.

Enough! Shower and change, go downtown and eat with the man, then home to bed.

Inviting Nikki to dinner was nothing more than kindness.

As for the attraction—well, that was nothing but chemistry, a reaction.

Like a nuclear explosion?

Ridiculous, but that was how it felt—sudden and totally inexplicable, but so powerful...

She *really* shouldn't be seeing him again tonight!

She left the shower and dressed quickly, pulling on a long shift that swirled about her ankles.

Hair!

Always a problem, but tonight there was no time to fight it so she rammed combs into each side to hold the rebellious curls back off her face. If she hadn't spent so long in the shower, pondering imponderables, she could have put it up, but it was too late for regrets.

She grabbed a shawl to put around her shoulders in case the night turned cool, and walked into the living room, calling to her daughter.

Rather to her surprise, Nikki's clothes were, for her, remarkably conservative—jeans and a blue and white striped top.

'What, no holes or rips in your gear?' Izzy teased, and Nikki laughed.

'I didn't want to embarrass your doctor friend on our first family date.'

'He is not my friend and it's not a date,' Izzy retorted, then plunged into further trouble. 'Well, he is a friend the way colleagues become friends but it definitely isn't a date.'

They were walking down the path to the doctor's house by now, so Izzy couldn't see Nikki's face when her daughter asked, 'Why not a date, Mum? Is it because of me?'

Izzy sighed.

'Not really, although probably, early on, yes, I worried you might get to like a man I was seeing then he'd disappear, then later I worried—'

'About me being affected by you having someone else? Shared love? Possible abuse?'

'You're too smart for your own good,' Izzy said, putting her arm around Nikki's shoulders and giving her a hug.

'Not really,' Nikki told her. 'You can't help hearing and reading about all that kind of thing, but it's time you had someone special in your life, Mum. I'm old enough and we're close enough for me to tell you if I thought anyone was creepy. I mean, I know Roger's always giving me a pat but he's not creepy, not like that cleaner you had at the hospital a few years back. He was an old man—'

'At least forty,' Izzy put in.

'Old!' Nikki reiterated. 'He used to give Shan and me lollies and then we'd run away.'

Sheesh! Izzy knew exactly who Nikki meant but this was the first she'd heard of the lollies. The man hadn't been there long, mainly because other staff members were uneasy about him, but if she hadn't known *that* about her daughter what else might she not know?

'Mum, we're here, and there's Mac waiting at his gate and I know you're thinking bad mother thoughts but, really, we were fine and if we'd told you, you'd have put a stop to it and we liked the lollies.'

'You okay?' Mac asked, touching Izzy lightly on the shoulder.

Fortunately she was so numbed by what Nikki had just told her that the electricity that flashed through her body was only a half-charge, although her knees felt wobbly and she was pleased when he hooked his arm through hers, his other arm through Nikki's, and led them down towards the town.

'Not often I get to take *two* beautiful women out to dinner,' Mac said.

Then he laughed when Nikki retorted with, 'Flatterer!'

She then asked him about the meningococcal, having heard about it at school.

'I've had the vaccine—actually, I've had every vaccine ever developed, thanks to an over-anxious mother.'

She was teasing Izzy, Mac knew, but there was a gentleness in it that suggested a maturity beyond her age.

Growing up in a house with grandparents, as Hallie and Pop surely were?

Not that he had time to ponder the question, for she was speaking again.

'Sorry, miles away, what did you ask?' he said.

'Do you know anything about global warming?'

'Nikki!' Izzy protested, 'Let's just have a nice peaceful dinner without any debates on the problems of the world.'

'It's for my project, and he's a doctor—he'd know a lot of science.'

Time to intervene, Mac decided, though he'd far rather just keep walking, feeling the warmth of Izzy by his side, imagining how things could be—might be?

Probably wouldn't be...

'But not how to cure global warming, Nikki,' Mac told her. 'It's something that's going to take a lot of research and there still won't be a vaccine for it, but what, apart from sharks and global warming, do you do at school? You're in high school, right?'

Nikki listed off her subjects, gave character sketches—not always good but none too bad—of her teachers, and by that time they'd reached the restaurant and he had to relinquish his hold on Izzy.

Which was just as well, because seeing her in the bright advertising lights outside, his body tightened, his lungs seized, and he rather thought he might be shaking.

This was ridiculous!

Or was it, when she looked so ravishing? Red hair pushed back so it was a mass of rioting curls behind her head. A long dress with swirling patterns of what looked like autumn leaves, skimming across her lithe figure, emphasising pert breasts, a slim waist and hips that were designed to be held, in order to draw her closer.

'Are we going in, or are you going to stand there all night, staring at Mum?'

Had he been staring?

Surely not—he wasn't some schoolboy seeing his first woman.

Besides, the last thing she wanted in her life right now was a man...

He shuffled the pair of them in front of him into the restaurant, although it was an effort not to feel the silky material of that miraculous dress.

Miraculous dress?

He was losing it!

Or maybe he'd spent so many years seeing women in camouflage or uniform or khaki fatigues that the dress had affected him.

The dress or the woman inside it?

Nikki was introducing him to Shan's mother, who ran the front of house at the restaurant. She led them to a table in a quiet alcove, leaving them with menus and a bottle of cold water.

'You've had too big a day,' Izzy said to him. 'You look punch-drunk!'

'You've had a bigger day and you look magnificent!'

'She does, doesn't she?' Nikki said, adding, with the candour of youth, 'That's Mum's favourite dress.'

Izzy blushed and shook her head, then filled her water glass and drank deeply, thankful she didn't have a coughing fit or embarrass herself in some other way, given that her daughter had already mortified her.

Mac's head was bent over the menu, Nikki's close to his as she pointed out the best dishes, and seeing the pair of them Izzy felt a pang of conscience.

Maybe she should have done something about finding a father for Nikki earlier. Back when she was little—starting at pre-school where other kids had fathers—she'd sometimes asked about hers, but as none of them had a clue who'd fathered her sister's baby, Izzy could only tell the truth, that not even her sister had known.

At four, Nikki had accepted it, but Izzy knew that any day now Nikki would begin to wonder about a mother who hadn't known who her baby's father was. She knew her mother had been sick and died, but not about the drugs—something else that would have to be a conversation soon.

Izzy sighed, and Mac turned towards her.

'You don't have a favourite? It's too hard to choose?'

He smiled and her toes curled obligingly and she was glad they were sitting, with her feet tucked safely under the table, so no one could see *that* reaction. Perhaps in future she should wear shoes, not sandals, when out with Mac.

Although there was no real reason why she should be out with Mac again, and plenty of reasons why she shouldn't.

'I'm having the chicken pad Thai and coconut prawns,' Nikki announced, and, too bamboozled by her emotions, Izzy took the easy way out.

'I'll have the same,' she said, then caught Nikki's questioning look.

'You're going to eat noodles in front of Mac? And in your favourite dress?' her daughter said, in a voice that couldn't have been more incredulous. 'You know what a mess you always get into with noodles.'

'Not always,' Izzy said weakly, but with Mac now looking at her she wasn't about to back out.

She got into a mess with the noodles. For reasons beyond her comprehension, where other people could manipulate their spoons and forks to get them neatly into their mouths, the best she could manage was to get one end in and slurp the rest, leaving the juice all down her chin.

Or the whole lot fell out of the spoon as she lifted it towards her chin and she splattered herself, the table-cloth and anyone within arm's length of the disaster.

Nikki refrained from saying 'I told you so', and Mac was super-helpful with extra napkins, but if she'd thought her daughter's mention of her favourite dress was mortifying, this was fifty times worse and probably had a special name but she didn't know it.

The meal was delicious, and Shan's mother insisted it was on the house, but as they left Izzy realised that suggesting Shan return with them to stay the night hadn't been such a good idea. The pair went on ahead, way ahead, and the chatter and laughter drifting back grew fainter and fainter.

'Are they making sure we're left on our own for the walk home?' Mac asked.

'I'm afraid so,' Izzy answered gloomily. 'It seems Nikki's decided I need a man in my life and as long as you don't have a demented ex-lover then you'll do!'

'I'm flattered. And, no, no demented ex-lover.'

Their stroll had slowed so much they were dawdling and as they reached the deep shadows of the old fig tree he paused, touching her lightly on the shoulder to turn her towards him.

'And what about you?' he asked quietly. 'Would I do for you?'

It was too dark to see any reaction on her face but he watched her shake her head.

'It's all too hard just now,' she murmured. 'And you really don't want this either, for all the attraction there is between us.'

'So you do feel it?'

His voice was rough with some emotion he didn't understand, but the kiss he dropped on her lips was nothing more than a breath of air—the brush of a butterfly's wing.

Yet he felt the tremor that ran through her body, felt it in her shoulder where his hand still rested lightly.

He wanted her in a way he'd never felt before, yet knew it couldn't be. She wouldn't—couldn't—take the risk of losing her child, although how realistic that risk was he wasn't sure.

Neither was she a woman he could dally with—she was too fine, too caring, too loving and the way he was, his head still in a mess, nightmares roaring through his sleep—he'd end up hurting her.

Yet he couldn't let her go—couldn't ease her away when she leant into him—couldn't *not* kiss her when she raised her face to his, her lips an unseen invitation in the gloom beneath the tree.

Long and deep, this kiss! He probed her lips, tasted them with his tongue, felt her mouth open to the unspoken invitation and was lost. His arms wrapped around her, clamping her body to his, and his heart beat with a frenzied tattoo against his ribs.

She breathed his name, her fingers on his face now, moving across his cheeks, his temple, learning him through touch while he learnt the secrets of her mouth, the taste of her, her soft shape against his hardness.

It knew no bounds, this kiss, until the need to breathe, to replenish empty lungs with air, forced their heads apart. Knees weak, he stepped back to rest against the massive trunk of the tree, Izzy moving with him, still in his arms.

And with her hands now framing his face, which he knew would be nothing more than a faint oval in the darkness, she whispered, 'Do you really think a short affair would cure this? Do you think it would ever be enough?'

He drew her close again, his lips moving against her hair, kissing as he answered.

'I have no idea,' he said, because honesty was suddenly important. 'I'd be willing to find out, but you're the one with most at stake, my lovely one, so it's up to you.'

He felt her slump, as if her bones had melted, felt her head shake against his chest.

'I don't know!'

The plaintive response cut into him, as painful as a knife wound.

'Then let's just wait until you do,' he told her, straightening up from the tree, steadying her with his hands, brushing his fingers over her hair, then his thumb across her lips.

'We'll wait,' he repeated, then took her hand and led her out of the darkness, seeing the redness of her well-kissed lips, the glow of colour in her cheeks, and the doubt that shadowed the happiness in her eyes.

Back on the footpath, hands unlatched, they walked briskly up past the hospital and onto the path to the old nunnery.

'I'm sorry to be such a wuss about this,' she muttered as they reached the place where she'd disappeared before. 'But I really don't know where I stand and whether the adoption could be threatened and—well, I don't know anything at all right now—my brain's stopped working.'

'It's been a long day,' Mac told her, although what he really wanted to do was kiss away the hopelessness he knew she was feeling.

'Too long,' she agreed, then straightened up and actually smiled at him.

'Thank heavens I invited Shan back for the night. It means the two of them will be shut away in Nikki's room and I can sneak in without a post mortem of the evening and an inquisition on why it took us so long to get home.'

He smiled and touched her dimple.

'Good luck with that,' he said, and watched as she

did the disappearing thing again, although this time he did see the door through which she vanished.

Izzy made her way slowly up to the flat. She knew her hair would be a mess but hoped, in case she did run into Nikki or Shan, she didn't look as well kissed as she felt.

It had been a mistake, kissing Mac, but that oh-so-light touch of his lips on hers had weakened her to such an extent she could do no more than slump against him, and lift her lips...

For more?

Of course for more!

The man was right, this attraction—or chemical re-action—that had sizzled between them from that first meeting on the beach was too strong to be ignored.

Yet ignore it she should.

Unless he was right, and having a quick affair might let it fizzle out...

How quick was a quick affair?

Nikki probably knew more about relationships than she did—from second-hand experience admittedly.

Not that she could discuss this with Nikki...

Or anyone really...

Although—

She ran her mind quickly over the much-loved people she considered sisters and brothers. Lila had absolutely no experience with men, determined to find out who she was before she became someone else as part of a pair. Marty was an expert on affairs and would undoubtedly say, *Go for it, Iz!* because that was how he lived his life.

Stephen, now...

Sir Stephen they'd always called him when they

wanted to tease, because of all of them he had family that actually wanted him—two families, in fact—wealthy ones at that—two sets of grandparents fighting for the right to bring him up, in and out of courts, while Steve fitted himself awkwardly into Hallie and Pop's chaotic family.

She had no idea about Steve's love life. Nikki's mother had always been the one closest to Stephen, living with him in Sydney off and on, infuriating him with her behaviour, her addictions, her irresponsibility. Yet he'd always taken her in whenever she'd needed a bed, helped her when she'd needed help.

Perhaps that's why he'd been so good to her, Izzy, when she'd struggled with Nikki as a baby. And remembering that, she knew he'd say don't jeopardise the adoption!

She sighed. Fat lot of help her family were!

She showered, ran a comb through her hair, and climbed into bed, exhausted by the day and the emotions but unable to sleep because the kiss played over and over in her head, remembered ripples and tremors of desire tormenting her body.

CHAPTER EIGHT

Mac felt at a loss, arriving at the hospital the next morning to find it an Izzy-free zone. A quick check of the rosters showed she wouldn't be on until two, which was, he decided, probably a good idea.

But a recent idea?

He checked again and, yes, there'd been a shuffle in the rosters.

Was she avoiding him?

Had she spent the night reminding herself of all the reasons why getting involved with him could harm her adoption plans?

His night had been tortured not by nightmares but by thoughts of a single kiss, and by images of where that kiss might lead in the future.

Not that he had reason to be optimistic. He was well aware just how important Nikki was to her, and understood her reluctance to jeopardise the adoption process.

But even if they had to wait—surely what was just paperwork couldn't take too long...

'Are you with us or off with the fairies?'

He looked up from his desk where he'd been staring blankly at Izzy's name on the roster, and assured Abby he was all present and correct.

'Very army,' she said. 'Anyway, there are people stacking up in the ED for antibiotic shots and although Aisha—a local GP, have you met her?—is helping out, it's getting hectic.'

'Yes, I've met Aisha and, yes, I'll come,' he said, pushing himself up from the chair, pushing away memories of a splinter of time beneath the huge old tree, and turning his mind to what lay ahead.

At least he'd checked on Rhia and the Watsons when he'd first arrived, pleased to see the little girl was no worse.

Somehow he and Aisha got through the flood of panicky residents, many of whom, he guessed, hadn't had any contact with the Watsons, and by the time they stopped for a late lunch things had settled down. But Izzy's arrival coincided with the local ambulance, bringing in a ten-year-old boy who'd fallen in the school playground, suspected broken arm.

Izzy heard the ambulance approaching as she walked down to work. No flashing lights and sirens but she knew its noise as well as that of her own car.

Would Mac be in the ED, alerted ahead of the new arrival?

She'd woken in a stupid panic, unsure how to face a man with whom she'd shared such a fiery kiss the night before, and, given how the rosters had been disrupted the previous day, it had been easy to switch her shift time.

But she had to face him sometime—face him in daylight or the bright lights of the hospital—and put the kiss behind her. Behind them both.

The ambulance attendant was bringing a small boy through the doors, a white-faced, frightened small boy clutching at his right arm, which was stabilised in a sling.

Izzy went to him immediately, all thoughts of kisses gone from her head.

'And what have you done to yourself, Kurt Robson?' she teased, kneeling beside him and putting her arm around his shoulder.

'Fell over, that's all, but it hurts.'

'Of course it does.'

She looked up at the ambo.

'Have his parents been contacted?'

'His mum's on the way.'

'That's great, isn't it, Kurt?'

Kurt's face suggested it might not be that great.

'Mum might be angry,' he muttered. 'When I hurt my foot she was. She said I was playing too roughly, but this time, truly, I just fell over.'

'That's okay, we'll sort things out with Mum.'

'We gave him seven mils of paracetamol for the pain but that's all he's had,' the ambo said, handing the paperwork over to Izzy and heading for the door, and probably a late lunch.

Kurt's mother and Mac arrived at the same time, one through the front ED entrance, the other from the hospital.

'He had a fall,' Izzy told Mac, trying desperately to remind her body that this was work and she could handle colleague-to-colleague stuff for all that her blood was singing through her veins at the mere sight of him.

Who knew what a casual touch might do?

Turn her brain to mush, that's what, she realised when he brushed against her as he, too, knelt to talk to the boy.

Okay—enough's enough!

She breathed deeply and moved away to greet Mrs Robson, then Mac was by her side, speaking quietly to her.

'It should just be a simple X-ray; we do that here, don't we?'

Izzy nodded, the deep breath not quite stabilising her yet.

'I can actually do a bit more than that. With my pre-med degree I added a thirteen-week radiography course—before Nikki. We don't have an MRI machine but we can most other radiography.'

'Wonder Woman!' Mac teased softly, undoing the small amount of good that deep breathing had effected.

'Not really,' Izzy responded, letting a little of the irritation she was feeling because of him seep into her voice. 'You're probably just as capable of most radiography stuff as I am. Every doctor can do a simple X-ray.'

He grinned at her but she refused to be charmed.

Colleagues, they were colleagues! She'd work out the rest later.

Much later…

But thoughts of charm and singing blood disappeared when Izzy shoved the X-ray film into the light box. The same picture would be on the screen at the ED's front desk and she knew Mac was looking at it there.

'Mac!'

He came immediately and she wondered if he'd seen what she'd seen and realised it wasn't something to discuss in front of the Robsons.

'What are you seeing?' he asked, and she pointed to the fine line that showed a break in the humerus.

'That's the obvious one, but look at the elbow joint—isn't it slightly distorted?'

Mac ran his finger over the picture then turned his attention to the shoulder joint.

'That seems loose as well. Has the boy had other fractures, do you know?'

'None that have been reported here, but he said Mum got angry when he hurt his foot.'

'Okay, let's get him back in here and look at the foot,' Mac said, leaving with a touch on her shoulder that was so light she might have imagined it.

She heard him talking to Mrs Robson and Kurt, explaining they wanted to do some more checking.

'Is there anyone in your family that's had broken bones before?' he was asking Mrs Robson.

'Well, most kids do, don't they?' she said. 'I know I had a broken leg when I was younger.'

'And you went mad at me when I hurt my foot!' Kurt put in, and his mother laughed.

'Mothers worry,' she said, patting down his unruly brown hair.

Mac lifted Kurt onto the X-ray table while Izzy focused the camera over the foot he'd hurt earlier. Mac escorted Mrs Robson from the room while Izzy checked she'd get what she wanted.

'Hold still again,' she said, slipping into the side room and pressing the button to activate the camera.

She took different angle shots, propping the little foot with foam pads, and when she was satisfied she returned him to his mother, who by this time was getting anxious, although someone had given her a cup of tea and plate of biscuits.

This time they studied the shots on the computer in the radiography office, enlarging details so they could easily see the two metatarsals that had thickened areas where breaks had healed.

'Brittle bones?' Izzy asked. 'I've heard of it but wasn't sure it existed as a condition.'

'OI,' Mac replied. 'Osteogenesis imperfecta—there are eight levels of it, with the first four being the most common. OI One is the best to have, and probably what young Kurt has, and often people can go through all their lives without knowing they have it.'

'Genetic?' Izzy asked, so absorbed in learning something new that the fact that she was shoulder to shoulder with Mac wasn't bothering her at all.

'Usually, but not always. The problem is, we could set his arm but with OI I'm not sure that it shouldn't be pinned. I think someone said the other day that there's an orthopaedic specialist in Braxton.'

'Paul Kent,' Izzy told him. 'Very good. Should we get the ambulance back to take them?'

Mac had straightened and now turned towards her, a slight smile greeting her question.

'I think that's best, don't you? Although it leaves Mrs Robson stuck there without a vehicle.'

Colleagues, Izzy reminded herself, ignoring the effect of that slightest of smiles.

'If Paul decides to operate, Mrs Robson will want to stay anyway, and her husband has a ute so he can take over anything they need when he finishes work.'

Mac nodded and left the room, leaving Izzy to turn off machines and tidy up.

He was on the phone to the specialist when she returned to the ED and the ambulance was pulling in.

'Can I phone someone to pick up your car?' she asked Mrs Robson, who shook her head.

'I've called my sister—she only lives down the road, she'll walk up and get it. She has the extra set of keys to it and the house so she can pack things for me and Kurt—better than my husband would.'

She smiled and Izzy realised that however Mac had explained the situation it had left the woman at ease, not anxious and distracted as many mothers would be.

'Osteogenesis imperfecta—I like learning new things,' she said to Mac as the ambulance departed. 'I know we covered something about brittle bones in the course I did but I'm sure I didn't hear that name.'

'It's not that common,' Mac told her, 'but learning new things—well, that happens all the time.'

She knew he was teasing—suggesting—but also knew she had to ignore it. That kiss last night—and where it might lead—was something she had to think seriously about.

'Then I'd better go and learn new things about what's been happening at the hospital all day. I haven't even signed on for my shift, let alone had any kind of handover.'

'Of course,' he said, and something in his voice told her he understood she was backing off, trying to ignore what had happened between them.

Mac headed for his office, only too aware that there was paperwork multiplying on his desk, pleased to have a really boring distraction.

Seeing Izzy—a far from boring distraction—had reminded him that a relationship with a colleague was not a good idea. In fact, it was a dreadful idea! Especially when he was new to the job of being a civilian doctor, and really needed to concentrate on doing that job well.

Belle came in with a message for him. Paul Kent had received the X-rays and would phone him after he'd seen Kurt.

He thought of Izzy repeating the diagnosis, her face alight with learning something new, and his gut knotted.

The thought of *not* having a relationship with that particular colleague was far too depressing to even contemplate. Somehow they had to make this work—not only the being colleagues part of it but the hesitation they both felt about involvement.

Very reasonable hesitation!

'Are you sighing over the paperwork?' Belle asked, bringing in a sheaf of more bumf. 'One thing I can tell you, if you don't get onto it, it just multiplies. Worse than rabbits, paperwork.'

He laughed but knew what she said was true, so he set aside all thoughts of the redhead beetling around somewhere in the building and concentrated on sorting the urgent from the non-urgent, the notices of new procedural policy from the important things that needed a response.

Izzy started her catching up with a visit to Rhia. As Mac had said, she was holding her own, although she was still pale and from the chart slightly feverish. Ben was in the room with her.

'I've sent Sally home to get some sleep.'

He twisted his hands together as he spoke then looked up at Izzy.

'She *will* get better, won't she?' he asked, and the desperation in his voice touched Izzy's heart.

'We'll do everything we can to make sure she does,' she promised. 'She's getting the best of care, the drugs we're giving her will be fighting the infection, and...'

She hesitated, mainly because she hated making promises she couldn't keep.

'They usually win,' she finished, hoping he had missed the pause. 'It just takes time,' she told him, 'so you and Sally have to look after yourselves because even after she's out of here, she could need a long convalescence.'

'We'll make sure we're there for her,' Ben promised. Then his head lifted again and his dark eyes met Izzy's. 'I know all parents think their kids are special, but she's especially precious to us. Sally had a couple of miscarriages before Rhia and hasn't been able to get pregnant since. We've thought about IVF because we'd love another child, but we'd have to go to the city, and it's so expensive.'

'It's becoming more affordable, so who knows,' Izzy told him, not mentioning that her brother Steve was already talking about setting up a private IVF clinic right here in Wetherby.

She smiled as she thought about his grandiose plan of building a relaxing seaside resort where couples could stay while they underwent fertility treatment or IVF programmes. He believed that the failures in IVF conception were often brought on by stress and his clinic resort could alleviate a lot of that.

So Steve was in her mind when she ran into Mac in the tea room.

'Shouldn't you be at home, cooking up a Moroccan delicacy? Your shift's long finished.'

'Paperwork,' he said succinctly, turning from the urn where he was making a coffee to offer to make one for her.

'No, tea for me at this time of the evening,' she said. 'I don't need any stimulants to keep me from sleep tonight.'

He found a teabag and made her a tea, raising a milk bottle in silent query.

She shook her head and he passed her the rather battered mug.

Inevitably their fingers touched, and he raised his eyebrows as he asked, 'Something keep you from sleep last night? Stimulation?'

Izzy gave a huff of laughter.

'Not that so much as where it could lead,' she told him as one of the enrolled nurses came looking for Izzy.

'It's Mrs Warren in bed nine,' she said. 'Says she's feeling right poorly, whatever that might mean.'

'I'll see to her,' Izzy said quietly, setting her tea down on the table and leaving the room. Mrs Warren should really be in a hospice, but the nearest one was in Braxton and she didn't want to leave her friends and family.

She *was* poorly, her skin sagging around her bones, her old eyes clouded with pain and confusion. Three months earlier she'd been an extremely fit and spritely ninety-three-year-old living by herself, capable of managing her house and garden, getting a little help with shopping and occasional visits from a social worker.

An accident in the bathroom, a fall that had left her

with a broken hip, bruised ribs and a bang on the head
had changed all that. Lying in bed, she was a prime
victim for pneumonia, and although she seemed to have
fought that off, she was still far from well, her organs
slowly closing down.

Izzy slipped into the chair beside her and took her
hand, talking quietly to her.

'I see someone's brought you flowers from your
garden,' she said, nodding towards the big bunch of
colour on a shelf on the wall.

'Jimmy,' Mrs Warren whispered. 'He's a good lad.
He comes every day and often brings a mate so we can
have a laugh, but I don't want to laugh any more, Izzy.
I've had enough.'

'I know, love,' Izzy soothed. 'I know.'

Mrs Warren's health directory had been explicit that
she didn't want measures taken to keep her alive, but
her heart refused to give in, still beating strongly in
the old woman's skeletal body.

Izzy sat with her until she drifted off to sleep, then
she checked the other patients under her care. With everything quiet she returned to Mrs Warren, sitting with
her through the night until, at four, her heart finally
gave in, and the old woman passed away.

Technically, one of the GPs was on call for the night
shift, but why wake him just to certify death when
Mac would be here at six? Possibly earlier, knowing
Mac. Declaring Mrs Warren dead could wait, as could
breaking the news to her family.

Izzy had wanted to call them earlier, but Mrs Warren had insisted she didn't want wailing relatives sitting around her bed.

'I'm happy to go,' she'd told Izzy, 'so there's no reason for tears.'

She was phoning Mrs Warren's eldest daughter when Mac arrived.

'What are you doing here?' he demanded. 'Have you done a double shift?'

Izzy held up a hand to silence him as someone answered the phone and she began her explanation.

Mac shook his head and left the nurses' station, but when he returned it wasn't to chide her. Instead, he touched her lightly on the arm.

'You sat with her all night?'

Izzy nodded.

'She didn't want the family, just someone to be there.'

'You should have had the coffee,' Mac said, but the glint in his eyes and the smile tugging at his lips told her he approved.

Probably would have done the same, Izzy realised, and the warmth his light touch had generated blossomed into appreciation.

He was a good man.

It was a refrain that stayed with her as her feet pounded on the coastal path. She'd had to run to clear her head and have any hope of sleep but the 'good man' thought stuck and she knew it tipped the scales in his favour in the matter of any relationship between them.

Mac got on with his working day with a certain sense of relief. Relief because he'd see much less of Izzy while she was on the swing shift from two till ten, but qualifying the relief was a touch of let-down.

Damn it all, he *liked* seeing her at work! Enjoyed a

glimpse of her red curls as she flashed past a door, enjoyed the feel of her by his side as they studied notes or discussed a patient.

The worst of it was he'd see even less of her out of working hours. It was unlikely she'd want to try his Moroccan tagine at ten-thirty at night.

He fought an urge to check the nursing rosters again—he'd checked twice already today and she was definitely on the swing shift. And today he wouldn't see her come on duty. He had a district hospital meeting—some kind of meet and greet the new guy, he guessed—at Braxton Hospital at two this afternoon.

Belle had booked him into a motel in Braxton for the night as apparently there was always an informal dinner held after these meetings.

The paperwork following Mrs Warren's death diverted him for a few minutes and a visit to the nursing home took up a little more time, but the day still loomed as a very long one without Izzy.

Until a very attractive blonde bounced into his office.

'I'm Frances, I'm your physiotherapist—well, not yours particularly but the hospital one. I do two days a week in Wetherby, one here at the hospital and tomorrow in a private practice. I'm based in Braxton, so some of the patients here I've already seen at the hospital there.'

'Like the young man whose ankle was pinned and plated in Braxton last weekend? I heard he was coming back to us today.'

'And you've got another man from the same accident—simple tib and fib break who'll be seeing me here as an outpatient.'

Mac nodded. He'd discharged the patient with the simple break after fitting a full cast and had talked to him about needing physio once the cast came off, but apparently Frances would have exercises he could do now.

He walked with her as she visited the occupied rooms, introducing the Watsons and little Rhia, pleased that Frances spoke mostly to Rhia, telling her she'd be back to give her some toys that would help her stay strong in hospital.

'You probably haven't explored the physio cupboard,' Frances said as they left the room.

'I've seen a room that looked to be full of toys, and I did wonder just how many children might ever be here at any one time to warrant so many.'

Leaving Frances to go about her work, Mac returned to his office, aware of how much he didn't know about the hospital he was supposedly running. What other visiting therapists might they have? How did he contact one if he needed someone for a specific patient? An OT for a stroke patient, for instance?

All the information he needed would be here in his office somewhere, but he'd avoided being in it, doing only the absolutely necessary paperwork—and then only when bullied into it by Belle.

True, there had been emergencies to be dealt with in his first few days, and Rhia's diagnosis had led to a flood of outpatients, but now things had quietened down, it was time to learn his job—his real job—especially as the other district doctors would expect him to know *something* at this afternoon's meeting.

'Let's start at the beginning,' he said to Belle when he'd summoned her to his office. 'Tell me everything I need to know about how the place runs. I know who's in charge of Housekeeping, and I have met the cooks, but apart from Frances what other visiting professionals do we have? Where do I find their information?'

He smiled at her.

'I fear I've been leaving everything to you.'

'Not your fault,' Belle assured him. 'You've hardly had a moment to breathe since you arrived.'

But she ran him through the normal weekly and monthly routines, through the visiting professionals, and volunteers who worked mainly in the nursing home, playing board games and doing craft projects with the residents.

'It's all in there somewhere,' she said, waving her hand at the filing cabinets banked against one wall, 'but generally you only need to ask me and I'll either find it for you or find out what you want to know.'

'In fact, you really run the place,' Mac said, smiling at her. 'I had a sergeant like that in the army.'

They talked a little longer, Mac realising just how much was involved in running even a small hospital.

Frances appeared at the door, greeted Belle like an old friend, then handed Mac a knobby ball.

'Stress ball,' she said. 'You just squeeze it in your hand—one hand at a time—you'll be surprised how much it will relieve that tension in your neck and shoulders.'

What tension in my neck and shoulders? Mac wanted to ask, but with Belle there…

And Frances was right, although how she'd noticed it he didn't know.

'Thanks,' he said, taking the ball and squeezing it in his right hand then throwing it across the table to

Belle, wanting to make light of it—to not have people thinking he couldn't cope.

'Want a go?' he said, but Belle only tossed it back.

'I've got one of my own,' she said, 'only mine's hot pink. Frances keeps an eye on all of us.'

Enough of an eye to see tension in his neck?

Tension that was part of his PTSD, or new tension caused by his attraction to a certain redhead?

He wondered if the visiting professionals included a psychologist...

Mac kept squeezing, one hand and then the other, while Belle and Frances were now discussing a barn dance to be held that weekend at a property out of town.

'It's to raise money for the animal shelter,' Frances explained. 'Do come, I'll email you the directions. They have a kind of auction and you can bid on the different animals and if you win the bid your money goes towards its keep for the year.'

He agreed it sounded fun and was about to ask if he could take Izzy along when he realised that being linked with him was probably the last thing she wanted.

Or needed...

'It's very casual,' Frances was explaining, while he squeezed hard on his stress ball.

Because he was thinking of Izzy?

'It really *is* in a barn out on the animal refuge,' Belle added.

'As long as I don't have to wear a hat with corks dangling off it,' Mac told them, and the laughter broke up the meeting.

So, off to Braxton! *And it will probably do you good not to see Izzy for a whole day,* he thought. *That* situation was getting way out of control...

CHAPTER NINE

'WHY ARE YOU doing the swing shift?' Nikki demanded the next morning while Izzy was packing her lunch for school. 'You never do it because it's a quiet one, and working at the weekend means you won't be able to take me to the barn dance.'

'Hallie and Pop will take you,' Izzy said firmly, not answering the real question because she didn't want to admit she'd changed shifts to avoid Mac.

'There's no need because I'm going with Shan and her older brothers and sister,' Nikki informed her, but Izzy barely listened, her mind back to trying to work out why one kiss had affected her so badly.

Badly enough to change shifts in an effort to avoid the man causing her mind and body so much trouble!

Not that she could avoid him for ever. But she'd hoped the break would give her time to work out what was happening—to rationalise the feelings in her body and remind herself that her first priority was getting through the three- to six-month process of officially adopting her daughter.

Not that it was working—the shift change. She missed seeing Nikki after school, although now she had mornings to catch up with her and hear the latest school news, and she could make sure Nikki was taking a nutritious lunch, but Mac's absence from her life wasn't helping her sort out her thoughts or her feelings.

Even thinking about the kiss sent tremors down her spine, and she couldn't think about the situation without thinking about the kiss so, in truth, she was in a muddle.

A muddle made worse when she saw him as she came on duty that afternoon!

'You avoiding me?' he asked, just enough edge in his voice to tell her it wasn't really a joke.

'Trying to,' Izzy answered honestly, if weakly, as her brain lit up like a fireworks display and her body was rattled by more reactions than it could handle.

'Working, is it?' he asked, so genially she wanted to hit him. How could he be so composed?

Because he was a man?

Because he was used to kissing women he barely knew?

'How was the meeting?' Izzy managed to ask, determined to get her mind focused on work. She'd leave her body till later and run it to exhaustion...

'Very educational.'

Izzy raised her eyebrows, sure he was being facetious.

'No, I mean it,' he assured her, with a smile she really, really didn't need. 'I had no idea of the complexities of coordinating health services in regional areas. Whoever set this all up was a genius. The army couldn't have done it better.'

'High praise indeed,' Izzy said drily.

'No, I mean it. The way they manage to coordinate the staffing of the emergency services, like the ambulance and helicopter, with staffing at the hospitals so there's always a paramedic available to go out to accidents—that alone must take endless fiddling and adjustments.'

'It's a lot of paperwork,' Izzy agreed, and won another unnecessary smile.

'Which most doctors and, I imagine, nurses hate. Yet it all gets done.'

'Because the office staff know the system and have their own procedures in place,' Izzy told him. 'It took quite a while, but at the moment it's working. Most of the time!'

'I'm still mightily impressed,' Mac said.

'Good, but I've got to get to work. Rhia's drip will need changing and apparently the chap who had his ankle fixed in Braxton is complaining about cramps.'

She turned away but not quickly enough to miss Mac's last words, quietly spoken but sneaking into her ears and, damn it, into her heart.

'I've missed you, Izzy!'

The shift was quiet, a few visitors to the ED that Izzy could handle on her own—a footballer with a strained wrist, X-rayed to make sure it wasn't broken, and just before she went off duty, an older man with chest pain but no history of heart problems or angina.

Roger was on call, but by the time he arrived Izzy had ascertained that the ECG was normal, blood pressure and oxygen sat both good, but a blood test showed high troponin levels.

'That's ringing a bell for me,' Roger said. 'We'll admit him anyway and do half-hourly obs but I'll check back through his file.'

Izzy started the process of admitting the man, chatting to him in between the questions she needed to ask.

Yes, he'd been before, feeling the same way, and had stayed three days while the doctors did tests. He'd been to a cardiologist in Braxton who had done more tests, but found nothing.

'And how are you feeling now?' Izzy asked, as a wardsman arrived to move the patient to a hospital bed.

'The pain's gone but I just don't feel well,' the man explained. 'Just not right.'

Scary, was Izzy's first thought. With no symptoms to treat apart from giving him the blood thinners, there was little they could do but wait and see.

Roger returned as she was accompanying the trolley to a patient room.

'I've found the records of past blood tests. Turns out his blood tests always show a higher level of troponin than is normal. He's had every test under the sun, but the cardiologist found nothing.'

'But we keep him here?'

'My word we do,' Roger said. 'And keep him hooked up to the monitors so we can see if there's the slightest change in his status. High troponin levels could be an indicator of an imminent heart attack, but there've been no studies done on abnormally high levels in an otherwise well person.'

Izzy settled the man into what they considered their 'cardiac ward', a room with monitors already set up so it was only a matter of attaching the leads to their new patient's legs, chest and arms, slipping a blood oxygen monitor onto one finger, and watching information come up on the monitor screen.

'You should be gone,' the night shift nurse told her.

'I've called in an extra nurse so we can keep an eye on him, and Roger's staying awhile, just to be sure.'

Izzy glanced at her watch and realised it was after eleven. Tiredness swamped her suddenly. Adrenalin seeping out, she knew that, but it wasn't helping her put one foot in front of the other as she collected a jacket and headed out the back door for the short walk home.

'Izzy!'

She muffled the shriek that the soft murmur of his voice had caused and turned to see Mac standing in the light shed from the hospital's kitchen window.

'I thought I'd walk you home.'

The moment the words were out of his mouth Mac knew it was probably the lamest thing he'd ever said, but he'd been lurking around the back of the hospital for over an hour, wondering if this constituted stalking, feeling incredibly stupid but needing to see the woman who had him tied in knots.

'May I walk you home?'

She was standing on the path, apparently bemused by his sudden appearance, but then she smiled and he forgot his doubts about stalking, and all but forgot his name.

'That would be nice,' she said, 'although it's quite stupid for you to be doing this. You've got an early shift tomorrow and I imagine the district meeting went on to a dinner and a few drinks last night and you didn't get to bed till all hours.'

But she hadn't said no, so he took her arm and drew her close, felt her warmth, while the effect her body had on his sent blood racing under his skin.

They reached the shadows of the old nunnery and stopped of one accord, turning to each other as if there was nothing else to do, kissing gently at first, touches of lips on lips, remembering, revelling in their own restraint.

But restraint couldn't hold back the attraction, and the kiss deepened, until Mac heard a low groan from Izzy and she pressed closer, slid her arms around his back, pulling him into her, or her into him, the kiss saying things for which there were no words.

'I want you, Iz,' he murmured when they paused for breath. 'My body aches for you, and I'm sure you feel the same. I know you've got real reservations—that you could be risking the adoption—but surely we could work that out if something happened.'

She stopped his words with kisses, but he pulled away again, smitten by a wild idea.

'We could even get married if things were dicey,' he said, 'and you'd have that family you thought you might get with that other doctor. Mother, father, daughter—a family.'

Izzy sighed but this time didn't kiss him, leaning her head against his chest instead.

'You don't want to get married,' she reminded him.

'Only because the Macphersons, or my branch of them, seem to be genetically challenged when it comes to marriage. My parents have both had plenty of practice at it—the getting married part—but don't seem able to make it stick, and I was obviously a hopeless husband, but if it made things right for you and Nikki we could do it. It wouldn't have to last for ever.'

'Go home,' Izzy told him, stepping backwards so she couldn't touch him again—kiss him again—weaken...

She didn't add that they were just the words every

woman wanted to hear—the 'wouldn't have to last for ever' ones.

As if!

She opened the door and slipped inside, without another word to the man she'd been kissing. No way could she tell him that beyond her dream for Nikki had always been another, buried deep because for so long it had seemed impossible—a dream of love and happiness and a marriage that *would* last for ever...

Aware he'd said something wrong, Mac took himself home. Unfortunately, his disappointment at the abrupt end to the kisses wasn't enough to cool his blood or release him from the tension the kisses had caused.

Izzy's body seemed to have imprinted itself on his, so he could feel her pressed against his chest, a ghost lover...

Perhaps the nightmare was inevitable, the roar of planes, the thud of bombs landing, the explosive roar of the devastation that followed.

And he'd mentioned *marriage*?

Expected some woman to put up with the movies that mangled his head at midnight?

His shrink had suggested a relationship might help, hence the dallying, which did seem to stop them.

But would it work for ever?

Could he take the chance?

And why was he even considering it, given how hurriedly Izzy had shied away from the suggestion?

Unable to sleep, he found solace in a book, an easy-to-read mystery he'd found in the house's book-shelves when he'd moved in, so when sleep did come, his thoughts were turning over clues, seeking an answer to the mystery, not thinking of the past, or of a red-headed woman with skin like silk and kisses like magic.

No sign of Mac when Izzy went to work the next afternoon, but it was Saturday, he was off duty although probably on call.

She hoped she didn't need him!

She went about her work, calmly and efficiently, spending some time with Rhia while her parents went out for a walk. The little girl had recovered so quickly Izzy was surprised Mac hadn't discharged her so she could spend the weekend at home, but maybe he feared a relapse.

The young man with the pins and plates in his ankle was complaining about pain, but after checking he'd had pain relief only an hour earlier, she decided it was probably boredom and found one of the 'toys' in the physio cupboard that would test his skill—tipping a board to get little balls to run into holes.

It was totally frustrating and she'd only ever seen one patient do it successfully, but she knew that because it *looked* easy most patients, young men in particular, refused to be beaten by it, so it would occupy him for a few hours.

And help him forget his pain...

She caught up with paperwork, told Shan and Nikki they both looked fabulous when they popped in to show off their barn dance outfits—battered jeans, hardly unusual these days, and checked shirts, while the tattered straw hats over cute pigtails completed the look.

'Behave yourself,' she said as Nikki kissed her

goodbye, not really worried that her daughter would get up to mischief. All that lay ahead!

But as she handed over to the night shift and prepared to leave work, she was looking forward to getting home and a good night's sleep—undisturbed by memories of kisses from a—

Non-for-ever-and-ever man?

Was that what she could call him?

Definitely a non-marrying type.

He'd spelt that out.

So walking out the back door and hearing the whispered 'Izzy' sent her blood pressure soaring.

'What *are* you doing here?' she demanded. 'You're supposed to be at the dance. They're taking bets at the nursing home on you and Frances getting together.'

'They're what?'

Mac sounded so horrified, Izzy had to laugh.

'They're easily bored,' she said. 'But you should be at the dance. It's expected of the local doctor.'

'I went but you weren't there.'

The words tingled down Izzy's spine.

You can't let him affect you, she told herself, but her body was beyond listening, especially to anything that might be common sense.

'I did leave some money with Belle to buy an animal. I rather fancied the three-legged goat.'

'That's Arthur,' Izzy responded, hoping some normal chit-chat might settle her nerves. 'I kept him a couple of years ago.'

'Lucky Arthur,' Mac murmured, and Izzy knew no amount of chit-chat would work. Her shoulder was already leaning towards his and when he took her hand, her fingers gripped his, joining, intertwining—to-gether...

They walked up the hill, their immediate future as inevitable as it was unspoken. He'd seen her family at the dance, would know—because Nikki was a loud-mouth—that the flat would be empty, and suddenly she didn't want to fight this any more. She wanted him in a way she'd never felt before—never even imagined she *could* want someone.

And at this moment for ever was a foreign land, it was the now, and what lay ahead, the now she wanted—needed.

'It's this way,' she said, her voice shaking as, fingers still linked, she led him through the door...

And into her bedroom...

The hospital grounds were well lit so some light came through the windows, enough for Izzy to see Mac's face as he sought her lips.

She raised her hands and ran them through his hair, holding his head to hers—wanting, needing the kiss to last.

His hands explored her body, her back, her breasts, passing softly over her as if to imprint her on his mem-ory. But as the kiss deepened, the touches, hers and his, became more urgent, more demanding, her fin-gers tugging at his shirt so she could feel his skin, his easing open the buttons on her uniform to hold one breast in his palm.

A brush of thumb across the nipple and she could feel it peak, moaned softly, then slid her hand between them to find his hardness.

Restraint fled, and hands tore at clothes until they stood naked, close, not touching anywhere but with their lips. Kissing, breathing heavily, his hand between her legs now, hers holding his length in her hand.

'Bed?'

One whispered word, yet she knew he was asking, not suggesting—asking her if it was really what she wanted.

It was to be her decision!

'Bed!' she confirmed, and they fell together, finding each other's bodies close, touching, kissing, prolonging the anticipation, increasing the level of desire to near explosion point.

Mac held her close, felt the moisture in the softness between her legs, heard the gasp of breath, the whisper of need—and knew this wasn't dalliance, though dalliances in the past had left him prepared.

A brief pause, long enough to ensure safe sex but also to wonder why it *wasn't* dalliance, why it felt different. But the moment passed, Izzy's body arching up to his, her pleas for more, for proper contact, inflaming his desire.

Too quickly over, lying together, panting slightly, drained but content to simply lie, touching, breathing.

No words, but stirrings, too soon surely, but slowly now, with teasing fingers and gentle touches, they drew more pleasure from each other, until Izzy's cry of release was echoed by his own groan of enjoyment, a confirmation of some kind, but of what, he didn't know.

Relaxed together, their talk was general—lovers' talk, of pleasure given and received, widening to talk of their lives, so different, hers made great by the love of strangers, his not really settled until he'd found a home in the army.

How had Wetherby come up?

Later he would ask himself that question a hundred times, but it had, and they talked of the town, the locals, the incomers seeking respite from city life, the refugees rebuilding lives shattered by oppression and war.

So for her to ask, 'How did you come to choose the town?' was almost inevitable, and for him to answer—no problem at all.

She was lying on her side, pressed against his chest, held in the half-circle of his arm, her golden skin asking for the occasional kiss, a light brush of fingers—eyelids, nose, ears.

'Long ago, so far back it seems like another life,' he told her as he touched, 'I'd just finished my degree, felt freed at last from books and studies and responsibilities. I had leave before I went back to the army, and, like a couple of million other young Aussies do every year, I went to Bali. Have you been?'

He felt her head shake a no against his chest.

'I've heard it's beautiful.'

'It is, a kind of magical place where the real world no longer exists—it's all about the now, and fun, and laughter—beautiful beaches, great surf, nightclubs, and dancing, and gentle people smiling at your antics. It was so relaxing, as I said, another world, with everyone living for not even the day but for the moment.'

Izzy had snuggled closer, and even when he continued, 'I met a girl,' she seemed unbothered.

In fact, she laughed and teased, 'Of course.'

'We spent our time together—two short weeks, two Aussies having fun—until we walked into the hotel one day and one of the receptionists called out to me. "You're Nicholas Macpherson?" she said, and when I agreed she told me that my father had been hospitalised with a major heart attack and the family wanted me back home.'

He was remembering that time—that moment—so didn't realise Izzy had pulled away, until in the dim light he saw she was sitting on the bed.

'*What* did you say your name was?' she demanded.

Mac stared at her, puzzled by the abrupt change in the mood and by something in her voice.

Should he make light of it?

'Hey, you know me. I'm Mac—we've just made love. Twice.'

'I meant your other name, your whole name?'

This wasn't light—not at all.

Mac sat up, reaching out for her, wanting to hold her, to see her face, but she scrambled off the bed.

'Izzy, what's up?' he asked, totally bamboozled.

'Just tell me your name, your whole name!'

He heard an edge of hysteria in the words, and responded to it.

'Nicholas Edward Macpherson.'

If he'd thought this might calm her down he was totally wrong. Instead, she scrambled around the room, picking up items of clothing and pulling them on, whispering, 'I've got to go, I've got to go. I've got to get out of here, I've got to think.'

He stood up, found his own shorts and pulled them on, then walked tentatively towards her, touching her shoulder to calm her down.

'Iz,' he said gently, 'you live here. It's your place, not mine. But let me help you, tell me what the problem is. Surely there's nothing we can't talk about.'

She turned away from him, shoulders slumped,

pressed her head against the window pane and whispered, 'Just go, please, just go!'

He went, although he worried about leaving her alone.

Should he call someone?

Hallie?

And tell her he'd just made passionate love to her daughter but now she seemed to have cracked?

Hardly.

And if there was one word that described Izzy it was sensible. She wouldn't do anything silly.

Would she?

He walked down to his house, poured a whisky, and sat down with it to think.

But where to start?

It was his name that had upset her, but she'd always known his name.

The Macpherson part anyway.

He went back over the conversation and, yes, it was definitely his name that had upset her, but why...

No amount of thinking answered that one so he sent a text, saying he was there for her and please to contact him, any time, because he really needed to know she was okay.

No point in telling her he loved her, although somewhere along the way, maybe halfway through the whisky, it had occurred to him that that was what he felt for her.

Love!

Could it really be?

It felt like love...

A whole new kind of love...

CHAPTER TEN

NIKKI MAC... NIKKI MAC... The words pounded in Izzy's head as she ran the coast path.

Stupid really when only yesterday—*was* it yesterday?—the refrain had been, 'He's a good man...'

But maybe she was wrong, maybe she should have asked him when he was in Bali, although the sums all added up in her head. She knew his age, and could work back to when he'd got his degree and, anyway, she knew she wasn't wrong.

Nikki Mac. Her sister had texted almost daily about the glory of this Nikki Mac—and of the holiday romance that had no future, although why, she'd never said. She'd been well when she'd gone, had been through a detox programme in Sydney, then given herself the holiday as a reward.

And she'd come back clean, they'd known that, and had stayed clean for months, or so they'd thought because she'd returned straight to Sydney, at first staying with Stephen, then finding a flat and working for a web designer, her dream job.

Until the sleaze bag, as Stephen called her on-again off-again boyfriend, had come back into the picture, tempting their fragile sister with promises of fame—singing in a night club where drugs were plentiful…

Izzy sighed, remembering the lost soul they'd all loved so much. As well as drugs, there'd been a brush with anorexia, and episodes of cutting, so no one had been surprised that Liane, their lovely Liane, hadn't realised she was pregnant.

And hooked again on drugs!

Hallie had flown to Sydney, Stephen had tried to step in, and everyone had forgotten Nikki Mac until the baby came, and with her a grubby piece of paper on which she'd asked Izzy to look after her baby, Nikki.

Izzy's even stride faltered and she brushed tears from her eyes.

Now she knew, it was so obvious—Nikki's blue eyes, the same dark, clear blue…

She shook away the useless thoughts and ran on. She had to think, to work out what to do.

Did she tell?

She *had* to tell?

But who first?

Nikki?

Izzy's usual easy stride faltered again.

What if Nikki chose her father…?

What if Mac *wanted* her?

Mac didn't *do* for ever…

What if Mac *didn't* want her?

Wouldn't that be worse for Nikki?

Worse than not knowing?

Squelching down the howl of agony the thought of losing Nikki caused, Izzy pounded on.

She wouldn't think about it now!

She'd think about it tomorrow…

And having decided that, she turned and headed back towards town, forcing herself to blank out the turmoil in her head, looking at the ocean, drinking in the beauty of her surroundings, smelling the salt in the air, the faint scent of eucalyptus from the scrub, thinking nothing, nothing, nothing...

She heard the ambulance before she saw it, and as she came over the last headland, realised it was heading down to the beach.

A crowd of surfers, boards slung across the sand in a far too haphazard way—Nikki and Shan's project—sharks!

Her feet flew towards the now stationary ambulance, although she knew they'd do everything she'd be able to. She pushed through the gathering crowd, saw the anonymous figure in a full black wetsuit, one leg showing torn, lacerated fabric, skin, blood—

'It's Ahmed,' someone told her. 'Luckily the jet ski had been taking surfers out to the big point break and the rider saw it happen and headed straight over, frightening off the shark and bringing Ahmed in to the beach.'

As she left the beach, Izzy took out her phone to call his family, then saw Hamid heading down from the esplanade—someone else had already called.

So she went to the hospital instead, showered and pulled on some scrubs, coming out of the staffroom as Mac was asking the ambos to take the trolley through to the resus room.

'Shark bite,' he said to Izzy, as if this was just another day, another crisis, fully expecting her to be there to lend a hand. 'Could you cut off his wetsuit? The pressure of it could be worsening the blood loss. Start with the arms so we can get a drip in. Abby, you set up a cannula as soon as you can.'

They worked in silence except when Mac requested help, stripped the fit young man then laid warmed blankets over his body to help fend off shock. Mac handed tweezers to Izzy.

'Just pick out any neoprene you can see, or anything else that shouldn't be there. Abby, can you flush the wound as Izzy works, flush it hard. I want to X-ray the foot to make sure there are no broken bones, because if there aren't I think we can put him back together again without sending him to Braxton.'

Izzy picked at bits of black material from the tattered skin and flesh and wondered at Mac's confidence.

But he'd no doubt seen worse, the results of bombs or IEDs and had learned to put body parts back together again.

So if anyone could save Ahmed's foot, Mac could.

The X-ray showed no bone damage, and Mac sent for Roger to handle the anaesthesia before giving instructions to the nurses about the instruments and sutures he'd need.

It took three hours, but eventually the young man had what looked like a patchwork but recognisable foot.

'I'd like to keep him here for his parents' sake,' Mac said, turning his attention to Izzy, one professional to another. 'He'll need strong IV antibiotics and at least twenty-four hours of intensive care to monitor him. Can we handle that?'

She knew he'd asked because it was a nursing question and as nurse manager it would be her decision.

'Yes,' she said, no hesitation. 'We'll have to juggle

rosters but we can have someone with him for twenty-four hours, and you can review things after that.'

'Good,' he said, nodding at her, although a little frown that she knew had nothing to do with Ahmed now creased his brow.

'I'll sort out the rosters,' she said. 'Abby, will you take the first shift?'

She left the room, not needing a reply, and not wanting to spend any more time with Mac now the emergency situation was easing and it would be harder to pretend they were nothing more than colleagues.

Though perhaps after her behaviour last night, he'd be pleased to return to just being colleagues, perhaps thinking he'd had a lucky escape...

Izzy covered Abby's shift, knowing it was Sod's Law that they had an unusual number of ED visitors, a small boy with a fish hook in his foot, needing Mac to cut it out and stitch it up; a pregnant woman complaining of feeling sick, her blood pressure far too high, protein in her urine test, all signs of pre-eclampsia.

'Do you usually admit a pre-eclampsia patient for bed rest?' Mac asked Izzy.

'When the blood pressure is this high, we do,' she said. 'We can monitor the baby's well-being as well as hers.'

'I'll give her a series of magnesium sulphate injections—latest studies seem to indicate it can stop it developing to full-blown eclampsia.'

Izzy sent an aide to organise a bed, and prepared the first of the injections Mac wanted while he talked quietly to the patient, explaining what was happening in her body, why it sometimes happened, and how resting and the medication could help her through the pregnancy.

'But the other kids?' she wailed, as Mac gave her the injection.

He looked helplessly at Izzy.

'Three,' she said, 'one at school, two still at home with Mum.'

She turned her attention to their patient.

'Where are the children now?' she asked.

'Their dad's with them but he's back to work tomorrow.'

Izzy touched her lightly on the shoulder.

'Don't worry. I'll talk to Hallie, she'll organise something then go and see your husband and explain it all to him.'

The woman looked relieved, but Mac was obviously puzzled.

'Does Hallie run the entire town?' he asked, and their patient smiled.

'Just about,' she said, 'and if it comes to organising things she's the best so I know whatever she does for the kids, they'll be okay.'

'What *does* she do in cases like this?' Mac asked Izzy as the patient was wheeled away.

Unable to look directly at him, Izzy busied herself cleaning up the room.

'There are a lot of groups—Country Women's Association, church groups, Girl Guides—they all have people who love to volunteer. You'll find she'll soon have a roster of babysitters and probably a cook and a gardener as well, making sure the family is well cared for.'

Mac nodded slowly.

'I suppose to some extent the army is the same, only

there it would be a welfare officer organising it all. And possibly not as efficiently. She'd have made general in the army, your Hallie.'

And Izzy couldn't help but smile at the compliment, but smiling at Mac reminded her of all the reasons she shouldn't, reminded her of all the stuff she had to sort out before she could talk to him—or Nikki for that matter.

Just the thought of it made her feel ill.

'I'd better get on to the general, then,' she said, and slipped away, the ED suddenly quiet, and therefore a dangerous place to be with Mac...

Mac drifted through the hospital, physically there and doing his job, but a part of his mind still struggled with the truly weird experience he'd had the previous evening, when Izzy had gone from a lively and generous lover to a—

Madwoman?

Was she bipolar?

Had some other personality disorder?

But why would his name have triggered such an extreme reaction—so extreme she'd momentarily forgotten they were in her house, not his?

His heart felt heavy with...

What?

Love unspoken?

Despair that whatever it had been between them was now over?

No, there had to be a rational explanation. It was just a matter of getting some time alone with her, and the two of them talking.

Sensibly, rationally.

But he remembered the feel of her skin against his, heard the little noises she'd made as she'd writhed on the bed beneath him.

Could he really be rational about this when just thinking of the previous night had him hard?

At work?

What had happened to common sense?

Professionalism?

He grabbed a roomy white coat from the laundry, although he rarely wore one on the wards, and did a round, not seeing her, but checking all their patients.

He had notes to write up about the district meeting, figures to get ready for the district director, plenty of work to keep him in his office *and* to block a certain red-haired nurse completely from his mind.

Not easy when Hallie arrived, wanting a bit of information about how long he expected the woman with pre-eclampsia to be in hospital.

'Just so I have some idea of how long she'll need help, although she'll still need someone to lend a hand when she gets out, won't she?'

Mac told her what he thought, agreed she'd need help even when he let her go.

'It will depend on whether her blood pressure comes down and stays down,' he explained. 'If not, I'll keep her in until the baby's due. If it goes into full eclampsia—'

'She'll need a Caesar,' Hallie finished for him. 'I started nursing here in the days when the doctors did the lot—well, doctors and nurses—we had a great midwife.'

Mac had to smile. This woman took everything in

her stride—much like Izzy, he supposed, although he didn't really know, Izzy, did he?

Had it all been just too sudden?

Was that what lay behind the panic?

'Are you settling in?' Hallie asked, and he hoped she couldn't read what he'd been thinking on his face.

'Yes, fine, thank you.'

She laughed!

'That's far too polite given you've had one crisis after another from the moment you arrived. I hope Izzy's been some help. She's got a good head on her shoulders, that one. I sometimes think of all the children I've had over the years, she's—well, parents shouldn't have favourites—but Izzy's close. Lila, of course, is Pop's little gift from God. He saved her, you know, from a burning car and she's clung to him ever since.'

And, having delivered these scraps of information, Hallie departed, off to organise her army of volunteers, small-town spirit at its best.

Which was when he realised he *was* settling in, beginning to see how small towns worked...

Feeling at home here?

Well, he *had* been...

Izzy shuffled the nursing rosters, phoned around to see who was available, then drew up a list of those who'd special Ahmed, checking for symptoms of delayed shock or infection, looking after his parents who were taking turns beside his bed.

She put herself down for Ahmed duty for the night shift—doing double shifts had never worried her—but now she'd sneak off home and have a sleep before she began her regular shift at two.

Sneak off?

Well, not exactly, although she crossed her fingers that she wouldn't see Mac as she made her escape.

Crossing fingers—what a childish thing to do—but somehow that was how she felt: as bewildered as she'd sometimes been as a child, having to make a decision that seemed far too complex for her brain.

More than one decision…

Of course she could ignore it—say nothing?

Not to Nikki—

Not to Mac—

And be haunted for the rest of her life?

Once safely home she showered again, feeling new sensitivity in her body, thinking of Mac's hands, his kisses, the joy she'd been feeling.

But she had to sleep, so in the end put all thoughts and memories resolutely from her mind and did sleep, waking just in time to change into a uniform, make a sandwich to eat on the walk down the hill, and arrive at work on time.

She'd just grabbed a sticky bun from the kitchen and was heading for the nurses' station for handover when she ran into Mac.

Inevitably ran into Mac!

'I saw you've put yourself down for the night shift, specialling Ahmed,' he said, very colleague-to-colleague, pure professional.

Well, she could do professional—or would have been able to if she couldn't feel the bit of pink icing from the bun on her cheek.

'I don't mind doing a double shift. And if he's restless, it's better for him to have someone he knows with him rather than one of the agency nurses we have available. He's been trying to teach me to surf—not having much success, but we have a laugh together.'

She wanted to swipe her finger across her cheek, but didn't want to draw attention to the icing.

Some hope! It was Mac's finger that did the swiping, Mac's finger that held up the tell-tale smear before licking it, smiling, and saying, 'Delicious,' in a tone that made her cheeks burn.

Mac saw the colour rise beneath her skin, waited, hoping she'd say something, hoping—

Well, he didn't know what he hoped, except that he'd been keeping an eye on the back entrance to the hospital for the last ten minutes, wanting to catch her, hoping perhaps they could talk.

But when he saw her, iced bun half-eaten in her hand, a smear of pink icing on her cheek, he'd had no words.

He'd lost the questions he wanted to ask—couldn't remember even the basic one—what had happened last night—

Now she whisked away, into the bathroom, no doubt to clean her sticky fingers and check for icing on her face.

How could she think of such mundane things when he burned to know what was going on between them?

When he wanted to know if there *was* anything between them?

Oh, for Pete's sake, what was he doing, maundering around like this?

He didn't do love, he reminded himself, he dallied,

and if the initial meeting in a dalliance didn't work, he moved on.

So move on now!

Right now!

Phone Frances to apologise for leaving the barn dance early, find out whether he was keeping a three-legged goat fed for a year, maybe ask her over to try his Moroccan tagine, which he hadn't actually made just yet, still surviving on toast and packet soup, and a nourishing lunch the kitchen supervisor insisted he eat.

But he didn't phone Frances, instead he checked on Ahmed, talking to his gentle mother, calming down.

Ahmed's condition remained stable through the night, although Izzy was worried about the swelling in his foot. Had they missed a bit of foreign matter, or had infection set in? His temperature was a little raised, but otherwise he seemed to be sleeping peacefully, still dopey from the anaesthetic.

Her relief came in—it would be up to Mac or Roger, whoever was on duty later this morning, to decide if he still needed someone with him.

Weariness descended like a cloud, but aware the arguments going on in her head would keep her from sleep, she changed from her uniform to jogging clothes and set off along the path.

The physical exertion might help her sleep later, but it did little for the muddle in her mind. She tried to narrow it down, to decide what was the worst thing that could possibly happen, and knew the answer—losing Nikki—either Nikki's choice or Mac's, which brought her back to not telling...

Finally realising that after a double shift nothing

was making any sense, she turned her attention to the world around her, seeing what looked like someone sitting by the fresh-water tap.

A walker coming from the other direction?

Another jogger, although now the mornings were getting colder not many were out this early.

By the time she was close enough to realise it was Mac, she was too close to him to suddenly turn tail and run.

Besides which, she had to talk to him sometime, if only to apologise for her behaviour the other night.

'Thought I might see you here,' he said, and she tried desperately to hear something in his voice, or to see a clue as to what he was thinking in his eyes, his face.

'I need to apologise,' she said. 'I behaved stupidly. I'm sorry.'

'More panic than stupidity, I'd have thought.'

Still no hint of thoughts or feelings, while her own body was alive with sensation just being close to him.

Although maybe his coolness made things easier?

Perhaps he'd met to tell her it was all a mistake and they could forget what had happened and just be colleagues.

Except she couldn't forget—couldn't not tell—

'I'm sorry,' she said. 'Really sorry. You must have thought I was mad.'

He didn't answer, studying her instead, then a hint of a smile quirked one corner of his lips and her heart flipped in her chest.

'Not mad but definitely upset about something. Can you talk about it?'

If only he hadn't smiled. She sighed, and shook her head.

'Not just yet,' she said miserably. 'I really want to but I need to think it through, need to get *my* head around it before I can discuss it rationally.'

He reached out and took her hand, drew her closer, almost close enough to kiss, but no kiss, just his hand with a firm grip on hers.

'Maybe I can help,' he said quietly. 'I'm not a total idiot. I knew something I'd said, however inadvertently, had completely thrown you.'

He squeezed her fingers almost as if he didn't mind she'd been so weird.

'It took a while to make sense of it—in fact, it wasn't until last night I had time to actually sit down and go over the conversation we'd been having. And found no clues, until you asked my name.'

'Nicholas!' Izzy breathed the word.

'Nicholas indeed, and that's when I remembered! I'd been telling you about this girl—well, woman— I'd been seeing over in Bali, and when I remembered telling you my first name I also remembered what she used to call me—'

'Nikki Mac?'

Izzy asked it as a question but she already knew the answer.

He nodded, face grave.

'Nikki?'

Izzy shrugged helplessly.

'I don't know—it's what I think. The whole time she was away her texts to me were of no one else—just Nikki Mac. I wanted details. Was it serious? "Not me, not ever!" she replied. It was just a lovely fling with a wonderful, intelligent man, and they both knew that was all it was. She went straight to Sydney to a job Steve had got for her—her dream job, she said.'

'Art,' Mac said, his voice dark, sober...

'She was brilliant,' Izzy remembered, brushing tears from her eyes. 'Drawing, painting, photography, she could make three lines on a piece of paper look like a scene, a few more and it would be a person.'

Mac stood up and drew her close enough to put his arm around her shoulders, holding her, comforting her.

'I saw her work,' he said quietly. 'And she had such plans, such dreams.'

He let her go, turned away, staring out to sea.

'I killed them for her, didn't I? Carelessness on my part, her getting pregnant.'

Now Izzy went to him, touched his shoulder, moved closer.

'We don't know for sure, Mac. Health issues meant she was never regular, so I doubt she knew or even suspected for quite a few months. She knew she'd have support from all of us, but I think the tortured memories of her own childhood came back to haunt her when she realised she was pregnant, and it never took very much to turn Liane back to drugs. It was the only escape she knew and the slightest blip in her life would have her reaching for their oblivion.'

'I had to leave early. I should have found her, I should have checked she was okay.' Mac's own demons were now haunting him. 'She'd talked of Wetherby—that's where I heard the name—but had told me she was going back to Sydney. Told me she was sterile, but still I should have checked. My father was ill, and I'd been posted to Townsville to begin my intern year. I thought about her often, but—'

'You weren't to know. Liane had told the truth as she knew it. She *had* been told she'd never have a child—her body too damaged in childhood, and long-term drug use on top of that.'

Mac knew Izzy's words were meant to comfort him, but the wound went too deep.

How could he not have found her?

How could he not have known he had a child?

How careless he had been back in those joyous holiday days, revelling in the magic that was Bali, and the beautiful woman who called him Nikki Mac?

He took a deep breath and turned back to Izzy.

'Nikki?' he said.

Izzy shook her head.

'I'm not up to that yet. I haven't worked it out. It frightens me, Mac—all the ifs and buts and maybes. I can't talk about it yet.'

She hesitated, then added, 'And in spite of the name and Nikki's blue eyes, she might not be your child. Wouldn't you want to be sure?

Mac knew the words made sense—of course they should make sure—but he also felt as if the night—and all his thinking—had given him something precious. A child...

Did he want to risk losing that?

'I'd be happy to accept her as mine. We could get married,' he said, trying hard to sound sensible and practical when inside he was a gibbering mess. 'Wouldn't that solve all the problems?'

'Get married?'

She almost yelled the words at him. '*You* don't want

to get married, and *I* don't want to marry someone who isn't a for-ever-and-ever person, and how would Nikki feel? She's not stupid. She'd know we were doing it for her and that would be a terrible burden for her to bear.'

'It was just a thought,' Mac said, slightly staggered that she'd been so adamant. He'd thought it quite a good idea. In fact, the more it moved around in his head now, the better it got.

Which just went to show how little he understood women, he supposed, although now the thought was there it wasn't going to go away.

Marrying Izzy had become a very attractive proposition...

All he had to do was work out how to do it—how to persuade her...

Start with a kiss?

CHAPTER ELEVEN

IZZY MOVED AWAY, totally befuddled—by the conversation, by her body's traitorous reaction to Mac's closeness, and by the ridiculous proposal.

Possibly the ridiculous proposal should have come first.

'I'm going back,' she said. 'I need to run, to clear my head.'

And she set off at a brisk jog, pausing only to turn back.

'We should check,' she said. 'Steve had Nikki's DNA taken when she was a baby, wanting to be sure the sleaze bag Liane hooked up with for drugs wasn't the father. If I get a copy to you, can you ask someone to compare them?'

Mac frowned at her.

Had he been serious when he'd said testing didn't matter—that he was happy to accept Nikki as his child?

'Well, could you?' she demanded, as tiredness, confusion and being close to him combined to make standing there any longer almost impossible.

He nodded, nothing more, and she jogged away, turning back a second time.

'You won't say anything to anyone?'

She'd meant to sound firm, in control, but knew it had come out as a wimpy, pathetic plea.

'As if I would,' Mac muttered at her, and she turned back to her run, racing now, as if demons snapped at her heels.

She had to talk it through with someone, try to get her head around it all.

Hallie would be the ideal listener, and would probably offer sage advice, but to tell her about Mac's business—well, about his part in it, if he'd had a part in it—when she'd asked him not to say anything...?

She'd sleep on it, then maybe talk to Mac again, be sensible about the test, so they could decide together how to go forward with it.

But being within a two-metre radius of Mac—forget that, being in the same postcode as him—caused so many physical reactions that battling them left little brain space for common-sense discussions.

Except she'd have to do it.

Maybe after a sleep she'd feel better, think better...

Mac walked slowly back to town, still taking in the fact he was a father, maybe, still obsessing that he should have done something earlier, kept in touch with Liane for all she'd kept reminding him that it would only ever be a holiday fling—a dalliance.

Had she used that word?

Was that where he'd picked it up?

Surely not! He'd moved on, worked, met and married Lauren, been divorced and worked some more.

Then Izzy!

He sighed and walked up to the hospital. Roger was on duty but Mac wanted to see Ahmed, and check on

Rhia, *and* the pregnant woman they'd admitted with pre-eclampsia. For some reason seeing her safely through the rest of her pregnancy was suddenly very important.

Because he was a father?

Might be a father?

Nonsense!

Anyway, being a father was far more than the accident of conception. Being a father was a whole new world of learning.

He stopped at the bottom of the ramp leading into the hospital and turned to look out at the ocean, the revelation so strong it had stolen his breath.

It was what he wanted!

He wanted to be a father, to learn to be a father to Nikki—at least Nikki first. Somehow he and Izzy had to sort this out.

And he and Nikki?

Izzy was right, he had to compare their DNAs, to know for certain, for Nikki's sake as much as his.

He turned back towards the hospital, the exhilaration of his revelation leaving a far more frightening question in his head.

What if Nikki didn't want a father—or want him as a father?

Hell's teeth, no wonder Izzy was in a muddle...

Sleep brought no answers for Izzy, if anything it made her feel more woolly-headed than ever. She made a cup of tea and stared at her much-changed roster on the door of the refrigerator. Next to it was Nikki's monthly calendar of the school and social events.

Rehearsals seemed to figure large in after-school

activities for Nikki and it took a moment for Izzy to recall they must be coming up to the school concert. This was Nikki's first year in the high-school concert, held every second year, the primary school having a similar event in between.

But what was Nikki's group doing? A music video? Well, an onstage performance of a music video, all the year seven students involved either singing and dancing on stage, or making and shifting props around.

Nikki was singing, but then she always did, right from her first year at school.

Could Mac sing?

The thought stopped Izzy dead.

She *had* to do something and do it now!

Not right now as she had to go to work, but today, or tomorrow.

But right now she could contact Steve, get him to email a copy of the DNA results. Until they knew for sure, there was no point in upsetting Nikki with all of this.

But once they knew?

'Oh, help!'

She hadn't realised she'd said the words aloud until Hallie walked in, a tin of freshly baked biscuits in her hands.

'Help what?' Hallie demanded. 'I did knock and when you didn't answer, I thought you'd gone to work.'

'On my way,' Izzy said, grabbing a couple of biscuits.

'And the help?' Hallie asked gently.

'Oh, Hallie, I don't know if anyone can help.'

And with that she departed.

Although maybe Mac and she could talk to Hallie

together. Her mother had seen the best and worst that people could do to each other, and had wisdom that Izzy could never hope to acquire. And Hallie knew children, and relationships, and a lot of psychology…

Fortunately Mac wasn't at the hospital when she arrived, having gone in the ambulance to Braxton with the pre-eclampsia patient whose blood pressure had failed to stabilise and who would probably need a Caesar.

But tomorrow Mac was off, Nikki had early rehearsals, she'd ask Hallie to have a late breakfast with her and Mac in the flat, make pancakes—

She got that far in the planning before panic set in so maybe that was a good thing. The panic usually came much earlier in her plans.

Mac returned as she finished giving out evening medications and the hospital was quietening down for the night.

'We should have DNA results in a couple of days. I forwarded that copy you emailed me of Nikki's along with mine—I had mine done when I joined the army—to a mate who'll fast-track it.'

The couple of days turned into a week, a week of sleepless nights and tortured days as far as Izzy was concerned. Her mind refused to function when it came to anything personal—Nikki, her, Mac—so she changed the hospital rosters yet again, putting herself on night duty to avoid at least one of the problems as much as possible.

But eventually the results came back, positive as she'd been sure they would be, and another weekend lay before them.

'It's Nikki we have to think about,' Mac said, slipping into a chair across the desk where she was writing up the night report, sliding the confirmation email across the desk towards her.

Izzy looked up at the man she'd been avoiding so assiduously, into the clear blue eyes, and felt her heart weep.

'I know,' she whispered. 'And it terrifies me!'

'Should we find someone to talk to first—a child psychologist?' Mac suggested, and Izzy realised he was as anxious about Nikki as she was.

'I was thinking Hallie,' she said. 'If anyone knows children, it's her. And Pop of course, but he's not one for words, but I thought if we talked to Hallie...'

Mac reached out and took her hand, squeezing her fingers gently.

'We'll work it out,' he said.

She gave a little huff that was half despair, half laughter.

'Will we?'

Mac left her to finish her shift, walking downtown to the promenade where he sat, looking out to sea, soothed by the sound of the surf.

And the answer came to him, so suddenly he was suspicious of it. He turned it this way and that, studying it from all directions, from his, Nikki's and Izzy's points of view and decided, yes, he was right.

Excited now, he hurried back to the hospital to catch Izzy as she came off duty.

'Walk you home?' he said, and whether it was the lightness of his words, or the smile that followed them, Izzy stopped dead and stared at him.

'What is it?' she demanded. 'You've won lotto?'

He shook his head and took her hand.

'No, far better. I've thought of how to do it.'

He probably shouldn't have taken her hand as it had set all the nerves in his body atwitch, registering this was Izzy he was touching, reminding him just how attracted to her he was.

But he held tight and they walked together up the hill, bodies touching, hers bombarding his with silent messages that almost made him forget the purpose of the walk.

'You've thought of how to do it?' she finally prompted, no doubt battling her own awareness of him.

Remembering them naked together, as he'd been?

'*I'll* talk to Nikki,' he announced, then wondered why this brilliant solution didn't seem to have affected Izzy as much as he'd thought it would.

'Why? What about?'

He stopped, turned to face her, and took her face between his palms so he could look into her dark eyes, run his thumb across her soft lips.

'I'll talk to her about Liane, about our holiday together, tell her about the Liane I knew, explain why we parted—different life paths for each of us—and how I didn't know about the pregnancy, didn't know I had a child, a daughter.'

He felt the smile as her cheeks moved in his hands.

'And then?'

He dropped his hands and drew her close, slipping his arms around her to hold her loosely in front of him.

'I haven't quite got that far, but she'll have stuff to say, questions, opinions. I thought we'd take a walk, maybe to the lighthouse, and you'd come, too, but be a bit apart, but she'll need you, I know she will.'

He leaned forward and kissed her lightly on the lips.

'What do you think?'

How could she think?

Standing here so close to Mac, his words whirling in her head while emotion whirled in her body.

Instinctively, it felt right what he'd said, or what she'd understood of what he'd said.

And outside, walking, that was good, less formal and more relaxed.

Well, Nikki might be relaxed, at least to start with, but Izzy could feel tension building in her body just thinking about the situation.

She leaned into Mac, and his arms tightened about her.

'We'll work it out, you'll see,' he said, and he sounded so convinced she almost believed him.

Almost because even fuzzy-headed, she could imagine so many scenarios that wouldn't be right—

Or was she over-thinking?

Mac was rubbing his hands up and down her arms, warming and reassuring at once.

'It will be a start,' he finally said. 'We both know this will be a huge emotional mess to dump on Nikki, but together, all three of us, I'm sure we can work through it.'

Izzy nodded, wanting nothing more than to stay there in his arms—for the moment to continue for ever.

'Go get some sleep,' Mac whispered. 'We'll talk later, maybe go out, the three of us, tomorrow afternoon.'

And maybe tomorrow wouldn't come...

But tomorrow did come, and the rush to get Nikki off to another rehearsal with the necessary props meant there was little time for explanations, although Izzy did mention Mac had asked if they'd both like to walk up to the lighthouse with him later in the day.

'Can Shan come?'

Izzy shook her head. She should have expected the question. Since the pair had first met in primary school, Shan had been included in most of their excursions, trips and even holidays.

'Not today.'

Izzy hoped her tone was light enough for Nikki not to ask the inevitable why, but apparently Nikki had already put her own interpretation on the outing.

'Is he going to ask my permission to marry you?' Nikki teased, and Izzy chased her out the door.

But he *had* asked, Izzy remembered, only because of Nikki and family, though, not because he loved her.

Before the thought could settle in her heart, she got busy, doing the spring clean she'd been promising to do, decluttering and cleaning the little flat with ferocious energy.

Anything to stop her thinking about what lay ahead.

About Nikki and how she would take it, what it would mean to her, and the big one—where did they all go from there…?

Mac had arranged to meet them at three, and with no little trepidation Izzy walked with Nikki down to his house.

'I thought we'd drive to the parking area at the bottom of the hill,' he said, stowing a backpack into the boot of the car.

'Is that food?' Nikki asked, and Mac laughed.

'Food and drink—all kinds of stuff that's bad for you, like chips, and cake, and soft drink.'

'So we'll have a picnic, that's great. We haven't been up there for ages, have we, Mum?'

Which was when Izzy realised that her nerves were so taut she was beyond even the simplest conversation. She made a noise she hoped would be taken for agreement and climbed into the car, where Mac's presence was nearly as overwhelming as her tension.

But once walking up through the coastal scrub towards the top of the hill, she relaxed. Mac, with his loaded backpack, was walking with Nikki, asking her about the concert, about her singing, whether she enjoyed it.

Seeing the two of them together, there was no way Izzy couldn't ask herself about what might have been, although she knew it was time to look to the future, not dwell on the past.

But a tear for Liane slid down her cheek.

Finding a sheltered spot where they'd be out of the wind but still able to look out at the ocean, Mac spread the picnic blanket he'd purchased that morning, then brought out his goodies.

As they settled down, drinks in hand, Nikki raised her glass to him, grinned, and said, 'Well, if we're not here so you can ask my permission to marry Mum, why are we here?'

'Nikki!' Izzy protested, but Mac had to laugh. The cheeky question had broken the tension that had been building in him all day.

'No, I've already asked her that and she didn't think it a good idea, but this *is* a family thing, Nikki, and something that's hard for me to tell and maybe going to be even harder for you to hear. I want to talk to you about Liane, your birth mother. You see, I knew her once, a long time ago.'

'You *knew* Liane! But that's amazing, and it's not hard to hear at all. I'm always asking the family about her, poor woman. What chance did she have after such an appalling childhood? And even when she came to live with Hallie she was never happy—running away, getting into trouble, on and off drugs.'

'Exactly,' Mac said, 'but I didn't know about that—she never talked about it—never mentioned the past at all. We were both on holiday, I'd just finished at university and she—well, Izzy tells me Liane had been in detox and the holiday was her reward for being off the drugs.'

'Was this in Bali?'

Mac hesitated. Somehow Nikki was leaping ahead of all his carefully prepared sentences. Had she already guessed where this was going? He looked at Izzy who was looking steadfastly out to sea—no help at all.

'It was,' he told Nikki, and he took her hand. 'And it was magical! The beautiful place, the smiling people, the beaches and the surf, we had such fun. We went up into the mountains, climbing to the very top of a peak that looked out over all the island, we wandered around temples where monkeys played, and bought flowers to weave in Liane's hair—hair like yours, that golden-brown colour.'

He paused, uncertain how this was going, Nikki's eager face suggesting she was taking it all in.

'Go on,' she whispered, so he did.

'She was special, your mother. She laughed and sang—that must be where you get it—and everywhere she went people smiled at her. She was like a beautiful bird or a brilliant butterfly, you had to look at her all the time, to watch her for the extra shine she seemed to bring to everything around her.'

He hesitated, but then added, 'And I loved her.'

Nikki was sitting very still, Izzy apparently turned to stone, but once he'd started, he knew he had to keep going.

'The trouble was it was a holiday—two weeks—and at the end we both knew we'd be parting. I was in the army—they'd trained me as a doctor and I'd been posted to Townsville way up in North Queensland—and she had a fabulous job waiting for her in Sydney. So we'd told ourselves all along it was just for now, and living for the moment, for the day, probably what made it so special.'

He paused, remembering that fateful moment in the hotel.

'As it turned out, we didn't even get two weeks!' he said. 'Two days before our holiday finished I had a message from home. My father was seriously ill and I had to go home. The army gave me leave but it was weeks before he was out of danger, and by then I had to get to Townsville.'

'You didn't keep in touch, didn't email, text, even read each other's social media pages?'

Mac took a deep breath.

'We'd agreed not to, but leaving the way I did, I tried to get in contact with her, but it was as if she'd been nothing but a dream. When she didn't return my calls or emails, I understood she'd meant what she'd said but I cannot tell you how deeply I regret not persevering. I should have contacted her, if only to make sure she'd got to Sydney safely—but we'd promised not to spoil what we'd had by trying to make it last long distance.'

He took Nikki's other hand and waited until she looked up at him.

'I'm sure you've guessed where this is going, and I know this must be terribly hard for you, but I had no idea. Liane said she had been told by doctors that she could never have children. We lived and loved and laughed because we knew our time together was so limited. If I'd known, if I'd even suspected—but I didn't, and what happened happened, and I cannot say how sorry I am.'

The silence was so loud it hammered in Mac's ears as he waited for a reaction.

'So you're my dad?' Nikki said at last, studying his face as if she might recognise it. 'Are you sorry about that?'

'Good grief, no, it's the most amazing thing that's ever happened to me, apart from meeting Liane. Izzy worked it out kind of by accident, but we've checked and it's true. I'm still getting used to it and I don't know if I can be called a dad when you've gone all this time without me to do dad things with you, but I'd like to start, if that's okay with you, and maybe if we start small and get to know each other, eventually it will seem right to both of us.'

'You can walk me down the aisle when I get married!'

The remark was so unexpected that Mac could only gape, but Izzy burst out laughing and reached out to hug her daughter.

'Oh, Nikki, you do bring everything back to basics.'

She pushed the long golden-brown hair off Nikki's face and looked into her eyes.

'I know this is all a huge thing for you to take in. It's been pretty huge for Mac and me as well, but we'll both be there for you, to answer questions or talk about the situation. As Mac said, he can't become an instant father but I think he's a good man and he'll soon learn the job.'

'It's really weird,' Nikki responded, shaking her head as if that might help all the information settle. 'To think I've got a dad. Just wait till I tell Shan and the girls at school.'

And hearing that, Izzy relaxed, smiling at Mac across what was suddenly *their* daughter.

Silence fell between them, punctuated occasionally by a question or remark.

'You really loved her?' Nikki asked.

'I really did,' Mac said, with such conviction Izzy knew it was true.

More silence, then, 'Does this mean we can shift into the doctor's house with Mac? It's a great house, I've always loved it.'

'It does *not*,' Izzy said firmly.

'But you could come for sleepovers,' Mac replied.

'But if we moved in, then you and I would get to know each other better. You said we'd have to do that before we could love each other like a dad and daughter, and if we were living there you and Mum could grow to love each other, too, and then get married and we'd be a family.'

'Pushing things, Nikki!' Izzy warned, well aware of how the girl could tease, and embarrassed that Mac should be put in such a delicate position.

But she'd underestimated Mac.

'It's a great idea, but we needn't rush things,' he told Nikki. 'And I don't need your mother living in my house to fall in love with her because that's already happened.'

Izzy simply stared at him, her lips moving in protest but no sound coming out, and when they did come out they made no sense.

'You can't—you don't—that's silly—'

Nikki, however, was ignoring her, her gaze riveted on Mac.

'You're kidding me, right? You've come down here, found a daughter and fallen in love with her mother— that's fairy-tale stuff, not real life.'

Mac smiled.

'Sounds like it, doesn't it, but it wasn't entirely magical. I had some rough times in the army and needed somewhere peaceful, and I remembered Liane mentioning Wetherby, just once. It was a place, she said, where nothing ever happened. That was exactly what I was looking for so, really, it was your birth mother who brought me here and that's how I found you.'

'Shan will *never* believe this!'

Izzy smiled at Mac and said, 'It's okay, that's a normal reaction from a nearly thirteen-year-old. And I think the days of nothing ever happening in Wetherby are over—if you think Nikki's excited about talking to her friends, wait until the town gossips get hold of this.'

Mac groaned, but he was smiling, and somehow the awkwardness that had stopped the conversation with his love declaration was gone.

Fortunately!

Gone but not forgotten. They lingered on the hill

until the sun began to sink over the rolling hills to the west, then packed up their picnic and walked back to the car.

'Can you drop me at the restaurant so I can tell Shan?' Nikki asked, excitement shimmering in her voice.

Mac looked at Izzy who shrugged, and said, 'Might as well get it over and done with,' she told him. 'The sooner the story starts on the rounds, the sooner it will die. But I need to go home and talk to Hallie and Pop before they hear it from someone else.'

'I'll come with you,' Mac said quietly, and Izzy groaned, but inwardly.

It was the right thing to do, but what she really needed was time away from him.

Not that she believed the love thing he'd said. How could he be in love with her, he who dallied rather than loved?

But having him with her to see Hallie and Pop was a good idea so she'd think about the love business later.

The couple she considered her parents were in the kitchen, sharing a rare bottle of wine.

'Good,' Hallie said, 'you can each have a glass. Pop and I don't ever finish the bottle. It always seems like a nice idea but one glass does us.'

Izzy and Mac joined them at the kitchen table, accepted their wine from Pop, sipped and—

'Something you want to tell us?' Hallie asked.

'Yes, but it's more Nikki than us. Well, us in some ways, or more precisely Mac, but—'

'Perhaps you should let Mac tell us,' Pop said gently,

moving his chair closer to Izzy and putting his arm around her shoulders.

So Mac did, leaving little out, explaining that they'd told Nikki, and she was already spreading the news.

'How did she take it?' Hallie asked, and Mac looked to Izzy to answer.

'Okay so far, but there'll be questions and it will take time for it all to sink in. It's not every day you find your father.'

'Nor every day a father finds his daughter either,' Hallie reminded her, looking at Mac with raised eyebrows.

'In truth, I'm lost,' he said, 'so many conflicting emotions churning inside me. Regret I wasn't there for Liane, that I wasn't there for Nikki when she was born, then worry—or more probably terror—that I might not be any good at this dad business. And now I've found her, what if she decides she doesn't want me? Not immediately—there'll be novelty value for a while, I imagine—but down the track. What if she blames me for her mother going back onto drugs? For her mother's death?'

Hallie smiled and poured him another drink.

'Do you think all parents don't go through that list of doubts and many, many more, every day of their lives? You just hang in there, do your best, be yourself, be as truthful as you can, and hope it all works out.'

'You make it sound so easy,' he said, and Pop shook his head.

'We all know it's not, but worrying about what might be never got anyone anywhere. It's like the holiday you took with Liane, take each day as it comes and get as much joy as you can from it. That's how Hallie

and I always worked. Yes, there'll be tears and probably tantrums and you'll do or say the wrong thing,
but with love, and patience, things usually come right
at the end.'

Having made a speech far longer than she could
remember ever hearing from Pop, Izzy was surprised
when he turned to her.

'Are you all right with all of this, lass?' he asked,
and Izzy felt tears prick at her eyelids.

'Just about,' she admitted. 'Though it will take time
for all of us. I think it's the most wonderful thing for
Nikki and, really, that's all that matters.'

'Humph!' Pop said. 'That's the way you always
think, but it's time you put yourself first, Izzy. Think
of what *you* want and how you would like this to work
for you.'

'Pop's right,' Hallie put in, and Izzy held up her
hands in surrender.

'Okay, but like we've all been saying it'll take time.
It's a big change in all our lives, a huge change for
Nikki and Mac—so we all need time to work out where
we fit.'

And suddenly the energy that expectation and concern had built in her all day drained away, leaving her
in a state of total exhaustion.

'In fact, if you'll all excuse me, I really need to have
a hot shower and a wee rest before I can even begin to
think about the future.'

Mac was on his feet immediately.

'I'll walk you up to the flat,' he said, but Hallie held
up her hand.

'Let her go, Mac,' she said gently. 'It's been a lot for

her to handle as well, and do you think she doesn't have a list of doubts and what-ifs as long as yours?'

Mac subsided into his chair once more, and Izzy beat a hasty retreat.

Her mind was blank—overloaded, she knew—and much as she'd have liked to have Mac's arms around her, she was so emotional she knew where it would lead.

Which was another complication she'd think about later, along with that strange declaration.

How could he love her when he didn't do love?

CHAPTER TWELVE

HE WAS WAITING at the fresh-water tap again the next morning, appearing like a wraith in the light sea mist.

'So, shall we get married?' he said as she bent over to catch her breath.

Catch her breath when he'd just made what sounded very like an extremely casual but probably serious proposal?

She straightened cautiously, and looked into the now-familiar blue eyes.

'Why?' she asked.

He kind of smiled and kind of shrugged, and reached out to touch her cheek.

'It just seems like a good idea,' he finally replied, no smile now, deadly serious.

'For you, for Nikki, or for me?' Izzy asked, the hammering of her heart against her sternum telling her just how important his answer would be.

Wishing...

Hoping...

'For all of us,' he said.

Wrong answer!

Her head dropped, her eyes watered, her body trembled in reaction and he reached out and put his hands on her shoulders, drawing her slightly closer but not close enough for body contact.

Just close!

'And…' he said, and she could read stress in his face, feel tension in his hands.

'And…' she prompted.

Wrong prompt!

'Damn it, Izzy, you know why. I told you yesterday that I love you.'

'You told Nikki that you love me,' Izzy reminded him gently, although her heart had stopped hammering and was doing a little skipping thing in her chest. 'Not the same thing.'

'But you heard me say it,' he protested, and she wondered if she should give him a break.

No way!

'Not to me!'

He drew her close, clasped his arms around her back and rested his chin on her head.

'Oh, Izzy, I have no idea why it's so hard. Perhaps because I've thought for a long time that people say it too readily, too often, and the words lose their meaning. But I've known for days now, probably weeks, yet putting how I feel into words—'

'You're doing okay,' Izzy whispered, feeling the love through the lips in her hair, the hands on her back.

'I love you, Izzy. There, I've said it, but it wasn't just words, it was a pledge of my heart, my life, my love for ever. All for you, my for-ever-and-ever woman!'

She raised her head to his for the kiss to seal the declaration, but put her finger to his lips before they touched hers.

'Isn't it my turn now?' she asked, then had to laugh at the astonished look on his face.

'But of course you love me,' he said. 'You must! We're meant to be together. Even without Nikki it would have been you and me. Besides, you have to marry me, because being with you, loving you has stopped my nightmares.'

'Well, there's a good reason,' Izzy teased.

But Mac was serious again.

'Not as good as love,' he said quietly. 'I think we both knew there was something special between us from our first meeting at the beach that morning. It was as if a whole new world had started—for me anyway.'

'For me, too,' Izzy agreed, and now she did kiss him, revelling in the sense of belonging that filled every cell in her body.

'I love you, Mac,' she whispered as they pulled apart.

'And I you,' he confirmed, and he took her hand to walk back along the track—to a daughter, to marriage, to a family…and to happy ever after.

* * * * *

ONE DAY TO FIND
A HUSBAND

SHIRLEY JUMP

To my husband, who truly is my hero every day of my life. Thank you for blessing me with your love, and with our amazing children

CHAPTER ONE

FINN MCKENNA wanted one thing.

And she was standing fifteen feet away, completely unaware of what he was about to do and definitely not expecting the question he wanted to ask her. He watched the woman—tall, blonde, leggy, the kind any man in his right mind could imagine taking to dinner, twirling around a dance floor, holding close at the end of the night—and hoped like hell his plan worked.

If he was his grandfather, he'd have been toting the McKenna four-leaf clover in his pocket, knocking three times on the banister and whispering a prayer to the Lord above. Finn McKenna's ancestors were nothing if not superstitious. Finn, on the other hand, believed in the kind of luck fostered by good research and hard work. Not the kind brought about by leprechauns and rainbows.

He'd put enough time into this project, that was for sure. Turned the idea left, right and upside down in his head. Done his research, twice over. In short, reassured himself as much as one man could that the lady he was going to talk to would say...

Yes.

"You're insane."

Finn turned and shrugged at his little brother. Riley McKenna had the same dark brown hair and sky-blue eyes as the rest of the McKenna boys, but something about Riley, maybe his grin or his devil-may-care attitude, gave those same features a little spin of dashing. Finn had inherited the serious, hard lines of his workaholic father, where Riley had more of their free-spirited mother's twinkle. "I'm not crazy, Riley. It's business. Risks are part of the job."

"Here." Riley handed him a glass. "I talked the bartender into pouring you and me some good quality Irish ale."

"Thanks." Finn sipped at the dark brew. It slid down his throat with smooth, almost spicy notes. The beer was dry, yet robust, the kind that promised a memorable drink in a single pint. A thick head of foam on top indicated the quality of the ale. Good choice on Riley's part, but Finn wasn't surprised. His little brother knew his brews.

All around him, people mingled and networked over several-hundred-dollar-a-bottle wines and martinis with names so fancy they needed their own dictionary. In this crowd, a beer stuck out like a dandelion in a field of manicured roses, but Finn McKenna had never been one to worry much about breaking the rules or caring what other people thought about him. It was what had fueled his success.

And had also been a part of his recent failure.

A temporary state, he reminded himself. Tonight, he was going to change all of that. He was going to rebuild his business and he was going to use Ellie Winston, interim CEO of WW Architectural Design, to help him do it.

She just didn't know it yet.

Eleanor Winston, known by those close to her as "Ellie," the new boss of WW, her father's company. Henry Winston Sr., one of the two Ws in the company name, had retired suddenly a couple weeks ago. Rumor was he'd had a major heart attack and would probably not return to the chair. The other W, his brother, had walked out in a family dispute eleven years prior, but his name remained on the masthead.

Finn ticked off what he knew about Eleanor Winston in his head. Twenty-nine, with a master's in design from a reputable college, three years working at a firm in Atlanta before moving to Boston shortly after her father's illness. Her design work was primarily in residential housing—the McMansions much maligned by the architectural world—and Finn had heard she was none too pleased to be spending her days designing hospitals and office supertowers. All the more reason for her to accept his offer with gratitude. He'd scoped out his competition for several weeks before deciding WW Architects was the best choice. A fledgling president, overseeing a sprawling company with multiple projects going at any given time—surely she wanted a…helping hand. Yes, that's what he'd call it. A helping hand. A win-win for her and him.

"So this is your grand plan? Talking to Ellie Winston? Here? Now?" Riley asked. "With you dressed like that?"

Finn glanced down at his dark gray pinstripe suit, crisp white shirt and navy blue tie. "What's wrong with the way I'm dressed?"

"Hey, nothing, if you're heading to a funeral." Riley patted his own shirt, as usual unbuttoned at the neck and devoid of a tie. "Make a statement, Finn. Get your sexy on."

Finn shook off that advice. Riley was the more colorful McKenna brother, the one who always stood out in a crowd. Finn preferred his appearance neat, trim and professional—the same way he conducted business. Nothing too flashy, nothing too exciting.

"This is the perfect environment," Finn said, nodding toward the woman. "She's relaxed, maybe had a couple glasses of wine, and best of all—" he turned to his brother "—not expecting the offer I'm about to make."

Riley chuckled. "Oh, I think that's guaranteed."

Finn's gaze centered on Ellie Winston again. She laughed at something the guy beside her said. A full-throated laugh, her head thrown back, her deep green eyes dancing with merriment. Every time he'd seen her, she'd been like that—so open, so exuberant. Something dark and deep stirred in Finn's gut, and for a split second he envied the man at her side. Wondered what it would be like to be caught in that spell. To be the one making her laugh and smile like that.

Damn, she was beautiful. Intriguing.

And a distraction, he told himself. One he couldn't afford. Hadn't he already learned that lesson from one painful mistake after another?

"A woman like that…" Riley shook his head. "I don't think hardball is the right way to play it, Hawk."

"I hate when you call me that."

"Hey, if the nickname fits." Riley grinned. "You, big brother, spy the weak, pluck them up and use them to feather your nest." He put a hand on Finn's shoulder. "But in the nicest way possible. Of course."

"Oh, yeah, of course." A magazine had dubbed Finn "the Hawk" a few years ago when he'd done a surprise buyout of his closest competitor. Then six months later, his next closest competitor. He'd absorbed the other businesses into his own, becoming one of the largest architectural firms in New England. At least for a while. Until his ex-girlfriend's betrayal had reduced his company to half its size, taking his reputation down at the same time.

Now he'd slipped in the rankings, not even powerful enough to make any lists anymore. Or to merit any other nickname other than "Failure."

But not for long.

A waitress came by with a tray of crudités and offered some to Finn and Riley. Finn waved off the food, but Riley picked up a smoked salmon–topped cucumber slice and shot the waitress a grin. "Are these as delicious as you are beautiful?"

A flush filled her face and she smiled. "You'll have to try one to see."

He popped it in his mouth, chewed and swallowed. Then shot her an even bigger grin. "The appetizer is definitely a winner."

The waitress cocked her hip and gave him another, sassier smile. "Perhaps you should try the other, too." Then she turned on her heel and headed for the next group.

"Perhaps I will," Riley said, watching her sashay through the crowd.

Finn rolled his eyes. Keeping Riley focused on the subject at hand sometimes required superhuman abilities. "Do you ever think about anything other than women?"

"Do you ever think about anything other than business?" Riley countered.

"I'm the owner, Riley. I don't have a choice but to keep my eye on the ball and my focus on the company." He'd had a time where he'd focused on a relationship—and that had cost him dearly. Never again.

"There's always a choice, Finn." Riley grinned. "I prefer the ones that end with a woman like that in my bed, and a smile on my face." He arched a brow in the direction of the waitress, who shot him a flirtatious smile back. "A woman like that one."

"You're a dog."

Riley shrugged off the teasing. His playboy tendencies had been well documented by the Boston media. As the youngest McKenna, getting away with murder had been his middle name almost since birth. Funny how stereotypical the three boys had turned out. Finn, the eldest, the responsible one, working since he was thirteen. Brody, the middle brother, the peacemaker, who worked a respectable, steady job as a family physician. And then Riley, the youngest, and thus overindulged by their mother, and later, by their grandmother, who still doted on the "baby" of the family. Riley had turned being a wild child into a sport…and managed to live a life almost entirely devoid of responsibility.

Finn sometimes felt like he'd been responsible from the day he took his first steps. He'd started out as a one-man shop right out of college, and built McKenna Designs into a multioffice corporation designing projects all over the world. His rapid growth, coupled with a recession that fell like an axe on the building industry, and one mistake he wished he could go back in time and undo, had damaged his bottom line. Nearly taken him to bankruptcy.

"Carpe diem, Finn," Riley said. "You should try it sometime. Get out of the office and live a little."

"I do."

Riley laughed. Out loud. *"Right."*

"Running a company is a demanding job," Finn said. Across the room, the woman he wanted to talk to was still making small talk with the other partygoers. To Finn, the room seemed like an endless sea of blue and black, neckties and polished loafers. Only two people stood out in the dark ocean before him—

Riley, who had bucked the trend by wearing a collarless white shirt under a sportscoat trimmed to fit his physique.

And Eleanor Winston, who'd opted for a deep cranberry dress that wrapped around her slender frame, emphasizing her small waist, and hourglass shape. She was the only woman in a colorful dress, the only one who looked like she was truly at a cocktail party, not a funeral, as Riley would say. She had on high heels in a light neutral color, making her legs seem impossibly long. They curved in tight calf muscles, leading up to creamy thighs and—

Concentrate.

He had a job to do and getting distracted would only cost him in the end.

"You seem to make it harder than most, though. For Pete's sake, you have a sofa bed in your office." Riley chuckled and shook his head. "If that doesn't scream lonely bachelor with no life, I don't know what does. Unless Miss Marstein is keeping you warm at night."

Finn choked on the sip of beer in his mouth. His assistant was an efficient, persnickety woman in her early sixties who ran his office and schedule with an iron fist. "Miss Marstein is old enough to be my grandmother."

"And you're celibate enough to be a monk. Get away from the blueprints, Hawk, and live a little."

Finn let out a sigh. Riley didn't get it. He'd always been the younger, irresponsible one, content to live off the inheritance from their parents' death, rather than carry the worries of a job. Riley didn't understand the precarious position McKenna Designs was in right now. How one mistake could cost him all the ground he'd regained, one painful step at a time. People were depending on Finn to succeed. His employees had families, mortgages, car payments. He couldn't let them down. It was about far greater things than Finn's reputation or bottom line.

Finn bristled. "I work long days and yes, sometimes nights. It's more efficient to have a sofa bed—"

"Efficient? Try depressing." Riley tipped his beer toward the woman across from them. "If you were smart, you'd think about getting wild with *her* on that sofa bed. Sleep's overrated. While sex, on the other hand…" He grinned. "Can't rate it highly enough."

"I do not have time for something like that. The company has been damaged by this roller-coaster economy and…" He shook his head. Regret weighed down his shoulders. "I never should have trusted her."

Riley placed a hand on Finn's shoulder. "Stop beating yourself up. Everyone makes mistakes."

"Still, I never should have trusted her," he said again. How many times had he said that to himself? A hundred times? Two hundred? He could say it a thousand and it wouldn't undo the mistake.

"You were in love. All men act like idiots when they're in love." Riley grinned. "Take it from the expert."

"You've been in love? Real, honest-to-goodness love?"

Riley shrugged. "It felt real at the time."

"Well, I won't make that mistake again." Finn took a deep gulp of beer.

"You're hopeless. One bad relationship is no reason to become a hermit."

One bad relationship? Finn had fallen for a woman who had stolen his top clients, smeared his reputation and broken his heart. That wasn't a bad relationship, it was the sinking of the Titanic. He'd watched his parents struggle through a terrible marriage, both of them unhappily mismatched, and didn't want to make the same mistake.

"I'm not having this conversation right now." Finn's gaze went to Ellie Winston again. She had moved on to another group of colleagues. She greeted nearly everyone she saw, with a smile, a few words, a light touch. And they responded in kind. She had socializing down to an art. The North Carolina transplant had made friends quickly. Only a few weeks in the city and she was winning over the crowd of their peers with one hand tied behind her back. Yes, she'd be an asset to his company and his plan. A good one. "I'm focused on work."

"Seems to me you're focused on her." Riley grinned.

"She's a means to an end, nothing more."

"Yeah, well, the only ending I see for you, Finn, is one where you're old and gray, surrounded by paperwork and sleeping alone in that sofa bed."

"You're wrong."

For a while, Finn had thought he could have both the life and the job. He'd even bought the ring, put a down-payment on a house in the suburbs. He'd lost his head for a while, a naive young man who believed love could conquer everything. Until that love had stabbed him in the back.

Apparently true love was a fairy tale reserved for others. Like kissing the Blarney Stone for good luck.

Finn now preferred to have his relationships as dry as his wine. No surprises, no twists and turns. Just a dependable, predictable sameness. Leaving the roller coaster for the corporate world.

He suspected, though, that Eleanor Winston and her standout maroon dress was far from the dry, dependable type. She had a glint in her eye, a devilish twinkle in her smile, a spontaneous air about her that said getting involved with her would leave a man…

Breathless.

Exactly the opposite of what he wanted. He would have to keep a clear head around her.

Ellie drifted away from her companions, heading toward the door. Weaving through the crowd slowed her progress, but it wouldn't be long before she'd finished her goodbyes and left. "She's leaving. Catch up with you later," he said to Riley.

"Take a page from my book, brother, and simply ask her out for a drink," Riley said, then as Finn walked away, added one more bit of advice. "And for God's sake, Finn, don't talk business. At least not until…after." He grinned. "And if you get stumped, think to yourself, 'What would Riley say?' That'll work, I promise."

Finn waved off Riley's advice. Riley's attention had already strayed back to the waitress, who was making her way through the room with another tray—and straight for Riley's charming grin. His brother's eyes were always focused on the next beautiful woman he could take home to his Back Bay townhouse. Finn had much bigger, and more important goals.

Like saving his company. He'd made millions already in architecture, and hopefully would again, if he could make his business profitable again. If not, he could always accept his grandmother's offer and take up the helm at McKenna Media. The family business, started a generation ago by his grandfather, who used to go door-to-door selling radio ad space to local businesses. Finn's father had joined the company after high school and taken it into television, before his death when Finn was eleven. Ever since his grandfather had died three years ago, Finn's grandmother had sat in the top chair, but she'd been making noise lately about wanting to retire and have Finn take over, and keep the company in McKenna hands. Finn's heart, though, lay in architecture. Tonight was all about keeping that heartbeat going.

Finn laid his still-full glass of beer on the tray of a passing waiter, then straightened his tie and worked a smile to his face. Riley, who never tired of telling Finn he was too uptight, too stiff, would say it was more of a grimace. Finn didn't care. He wasn't looking to be a cover model or to make friends.

Then he glanced over at his brother—no longer chatting up the waitress but now flirting with a brunette. For a second, Finn envied Riley's easy way with women. Everything about his little brother screamed relaxed, at home. His stance, his smile, the slight rumple in his shirt.

Finn forced himself to relax, to look somewhat approachable. Then he increased his pace to close the gap between himself and Ellie. He reached her just before she stepped through the glass doors of the lobby.

"Miss Winston."

She stopped, her hand on the metal bar, ready to exit. Then she turned back and faced him. Her long blond hair swung with the movement, settling like a silk curtain around her shoulders. The short-sleeved crimson dress she wore hugged her curves, and dropped into a tantalizing yet modest V at her chest. For a second, her green eyes were blank, then she registered his face and the green went from cold emerald to warm forest. "My goodness. Mr. McKenna," she said. "I recognize you from the article in *Architecture Today*."

"Please, call me Finn." She'd seen the piece about his award for innovative building design? And remembered it? "That was more than a year ago. I'm impressed with your memory."

"Well, like most people in our industry, I have an absolutely ridiculous attention for detail." She smiled then, the kind of smile that no one would ever confuse with a grimace. The kind of smile that hit a man in the gut and made him forget everything around him. The kind of smile that added an extra sparkle to her green eyes, and lit her delicate features with an inner glow.

Intoxicating.

Get a grip, McKenna. This was business, nothing more. Since when did he think of anything other than a bottle of single malt as intoxicating? Business, and business *only.* "If you have a minute, I wanted to talk to you."

"Actually I'm heading out." She gestured toward the door. A continual Morse code of headlights went by on the busy street outside, tires making a constant whoosh-whoosh of music on the dark pavement, even though it was nearing midnight on a Tuesday night. Boston, like most cities, never slept. And neither, most nights, did Finn McKenna.

"Perhaps you could call my assistant," she said, "and set up a meeting for—"

"If you have time tonight, I would appreciate it." He remembered Riley's advice and decided to sweeten the pot a little. Show her he wasn't the cold business-only gargoyle that people rumored him to be. Hawk indeed. Finn could be suave. Debonair even.

His younger brother could charm a free coffee from a barista; talk a traffic cop into forgetting his ticket. Maybe if Finn applied a bit of that, it might loosen her up, and make her more amenable to what he was about to propose. So he worked up another smile-grimace to his face—and tried another tack.

"Why don't we, uh, grab a couple drinks somewhere?" he said, then groaned inwardly. Casual conversation was clearly not his forte. Put him in a board room, and he was fine, but attempting small talk…a disaster.

Damn Riley's advice anyway.

"Thank you, but I don't drink. If you ask me, too many bad decisions have been made with a bottle of wine." Another smile. "I'm sure if you call in the morning—"

"Your schedule is certainly as busy as mine. Why don't we avoid yet another meeting?"

"In other words, get this out of the way and then I can get rid of you?"

He laughed. "Something like that."

"It's really late…"

He could see her hesitation. In a second, she'd say no again, and he'd be forced to delay his plan one more day. He didn't have the luxury of time. He needed to get a meeting with Ellie Winston—a private one—now. In business, he knew when to press, and when to step back. Now was a time to press. A little. "I promise, I don't bite."

"Or pick over the remains of your competitors?"

"That's a rumor. Nothing more. I've only done that… once." He paused a second. "Okay, maybe twice."

She threw back her head and laughed. "Oh my, Mr. McKenna. You are not what I expected."

What had she expected? That he would be the stern predator portrayed in that article? Or that he wouldn't have a sense of humor? "I hope that's a good thing."

"We shall see," she said. Then she reached out and laid a hand on his arm, a quick touch, nothing more, but it was enough to stir a fire inside him. A fire that he knew better than to stoke.

What the hell had been in that beer? Finn McKenna wasn't a man given to spontaneous emotional or physical reactions. Except for one brief window, he'd lived his life as ordered as the buildings he designed. No room for

fluff or silliness. And particularly no room for the foolishness of a tumble in the hay. Yet his mind considered
that very thing when Eleanor Winston touched him.

"I'm sorry, you're absolutely right, it is late and you
must want to get home," he said, taking a step back, feeling…flustered, which was not at all like him. "I'll call
your assistant in the morning."

Riley had said to say what he would say. And Finn
knew damned well Riley wouldn't have said that.

"No, I'm the one who's sorry, Mr. McKenna. I've had
a long, long day and I…" She glanced back in the direction of the closed double doors, but Finn got the sense
she wasn't looking at the black-tie crowd filling the Park
Plaza's ballroom, but at something else, something he
couldn't see. Then she glanced at her watch. "Midnight.
Well, the day *is* over, isn't it?"

"If you want it to be, Cinderella. Or you could continue the ball for a little while longer." The quip came out
without hesitation. A true Riley-ism. He'd been spending
too much time with his brother.

Or maybe not, he thought, when she laughed. He liked
her laugh. It was light, airy, almost musical.

"Cinderella, huh?" she said. "Okay, you convinced
me. It would be nice to end my day with some one-on-
one conversation instead of an endless stream of small
talk." She wagged a finger at him and a tease lit her face,
made her smile quirk higher on one side than the other.
"But I'll have tea, not tequila, while I hear you out on
whatever it is you want to tell me."

"Excellent." He could only hope she was as amenable to his proposal. Surely such an auspicious beginning
boded well for the rest. He pushed on the door and waved
Ellie through with one long sweep of his arm. "After
you…Cinderella."

"My goodness, Finn McKenna. You certainly do know how to make a girl swoon." She flashed him yet another smile and then whooshed past him and out into the night, leaving the faint scent of jasmine and vanilla in her wake.

Get back to the plan, he reminded himself. Focus on getting her to agree. Nothing more. He could do it, he knew he could. Finn wasn't a distracted, spontaneous man. He refused to tangle personal with business ever again. He would get Ellie to agree, and before he could blink, his company would be back on top.

But as he followed one of his biggest competitors into the twinkling, magical world of Boston at night, he had to wonder if he was making the best business decision of his life—or the worst.

CHAPTER TWO

SHE had to be crazy.

What else had made Ellie agree to midnight drinks with Finn McKenna—one of her competitors and a man she barely knew? She'd been ready to go home, get to bed and get some much-needed sleep when Finn had approached her.

There'd been something about his smile, though, something about him charmed her. He wasn't a smooth talker, more a man who had an easy, approachable way about him, one that she suspected rarely showed in his business life. The "Hawk" moniker that magazine—and most of the people in the architecture world—had given him didn't fit the man who had teasingly called her Cinderella. A man with vivid sky-blue eyes and dark chocolate hair.

And that intrigued her. A lot.

So Ellie settled into the red vinyl covered seat across from Finn McKenna, a steaming mug of tea warming her palms. So far they'd done little more than exchange small talk about the weather and the party they'd just left.

She'd never met the fabled architect, the kind of man talked about in hushed tones by others in the industry. She'd read about him, even studied a few of his projects when she was in college, but they'd never crossed paths. If she hadn't been at the helm of WW Architectural Design, she wouldn't even have been at the event tonight, one of those networking things designed to bring together competitors, as if they'd share trade secrets over a few glasses of wine. In reality, everyone was there to try to extract as much information as they could, while revealing none of their own.

"Was that your brother you were talking to in the ballroom?" she asked. Telling herself she wasn't being curious about the contradictory Finn, just conversational.

Finn nodded. "Riley. He's the youngest."

"He looks a lot like you."

Finn chuckled. "Poor guy."

"Is he in the industry, too?"

"Definitely not. He tagged along for the free drinks."

She laughed. "I can appreciate that. Either way, I'm glad that cocktail party is over." She rubbed her neck, loosening some of the tension of the day. "Sometimes it seems those things are never going to end."

"You seemed to fit right in."

"I can talk, believe me." She laughed, then leaned in closer and lowered her voice to a conspiratorial whisper. "But in reality, I hate those kinds of events."

"You and me both. Everyone trying to pretend to be nice, when really they just want to find out what you're up to and how they can steal that business away from you," Finn said. "I think of them as a necessary evil."

She laughed again. "We definitely have that in common." She'd never expected to have anything in common with Finn McKenna, whose reputation had painted him as a ruthless competitor, exactly her opposite. Or to find him attractive. But she did.

"I don't know about you, but I'm much happier behind my desk, sketching out a design. Anything is better than trading the same chatter with the same people in an endless social circle."

"You and I could be twins. I feel exactly the same way. But…" She let out a sigh and spun her teacup gently left and right.

"But what?"

"But I stepped into my father's shoes, and that means doing things as he did." People expected the head of WW to be involved, interactive and most of all, friendly, so Ellie had gone to the event and handled it, she hoped, as her father would have. She had thought taking over her father's position would be a temporary move, but after the news the doctor gave her yesterday…

Ellie bit back a sigh. There were many, many dinners like that in her future. Henry Winston's heart attack had been a bad one, leaving him with greatly diminished cardiac capacity. The doctor had warned her that too much stress and worry could be fatal. A return to work was a distant possibility right now. If ever. It all depended on his recovery. Either way, Ellie was determined to keep WW running, and not worry her father with any of the details. He came first.

"Have you ever met my father?" she asked Finn.

He nodded. "I have. Nice guy. Straight shooter."

"And a talker. I inherited that from him." Ellie smiled, thinking of the father she'd spent so many hours with in the last few years, chatting about design and business and life. Her father had worked constantly when Ellie was young and been gone too much for them to build any kind of relationship. But ever since Ellie went to college, Henry had made a more concerted effort to connect with his daughter. Although she loved her mother dearly, Ellie wasn't as close to Marguerite, who had moved to California shortly after divorcing Henry when Ellie was eighteen. "My father likes to say that he never knows where his next opportunity might come from, so he greets the cashier at a fast food place as heartily as he does the owner of a bank."

"People like that about him. Your father is well respected."

"Thank you." The compliment warmed Ellie. "I hope I can live up to his example."

"I'm sure you will."

The conversation stalled between them. Finn turned his attention to his coffee, but didn't drink, just held the mug. Ellie nursed her tea, then added more sugar to the slightly bitter brew.

She watched Finn, wondering why he had invited her out. If he wanted to talk business, he was taking his time getting to it. What other reason could he have? For all the joking between them earlier, she had a feeling he wasn't here for a date.

Finn McKenna was younger than she'd expected. Surely a man with his reputation had to be ten feet tall, and ten years older than the early thirties she guessed him to be? Heck, he seemed hardly older than her, but his resume stretched a mile longer. What surprised her most was that he had sought her out—her—out of all the other people in that room. Why?

He had opted for coffee, black, but didn't drink from the cup. He crossed his hands on the table before him, in precise, measured moments. He held himself straight— uptight, she would have called it—and kept his features as unreadable as a blank sheet of paper. He wasn't cold, exactly, more...

Impassive. Like the concrete used to construct his buildings. The teasing man she'd met in the lobby had been replaced by someone far more serious. Had that Finn been a fluke? Which was the real Finn McKenna?

And more, why did she care so much?

"I heard WW got the contract on the Piedmont hospital project," he said.

"We haven't even announced that hospital deal yet," she replied, halting her tea halfway to her lips. "How did you know about it?"

"It's my business to know." He smiled. "Congratulations."

"Thank you." She wanted to tell him the thought of such a big project daunted her, particularly without her father's valuable advice. She wanted to tell Finn that she worried the hospital design would be too big, too detailed for her to oversee successfully, and most of all, she wanted to ask him how he had done it for so long single-handedly, but she didn't.

She already knew the answer. She'd read it in the interview in *Architect* magazine. Finn McKenna wasted little time. He had no hobbies, he told the reporter, and organized his workdays in the most efficient way possible, in order to cram twenty hours of work into twelve.

And, she knew better than to trust him. He hadn't earned the nickname Hawk by being nice to his competitors. No matter how they sliced this, she was one of his competitors and needed to be on her guard. For all she knew, Finn was working right this second—and working an angle with her that would benefit his business.

At that moment, as if making her thoughts a reality, Finn's cell phone rang. He let out a sigh, then shot her an apologetic smile. "Sorry. I have to take this. It's a client who's in California right now, while we build his new offices here. I think he forgot about the time change. This should only take a second."

"No problem. I understand." She watched him deal with the call and realized that Finn McKenna had made himself a success by sacrificing a life. That wasn't what Ellie had wanted when she had gone into architectural design, but the more time she spent behind her father's desk, the more it became clear that was where she was heading.

That was the one thing her father didn't want to see. She thought back to the conversation they'd had this morning. *Don't end up like me, Ellie Girl. Get married. Settle down. Have a life instead of just a business, and don't neglect your family to protect the bottom line. Do it before...*

He hadn't had to finish the sentence. She knew the unspoken words—before he was gone. The heart attack had set off a ticking clock inside Henry and nearly every visit he encouraged Ellie to stop putting her life on hold.

The trouble was, she had quickly found that running WW Architectural Design and having a life were mutually exclusive. Now things were more complicated, her time more precious. And having it all seemed to be an impossible idea.

She thought of the picture in her purse, the dozens more on her phone, and the paperwork waiting on her desk. Waiting not for her signature, but for a miracle. One that would keep the promise she had made in China last year.

Nearly three years ago, Ellie had been on the fast track at an architectural firm in North Carolina. Then she'd gone to a conference in China, gotten lost on the way to the hotel and ended up meeting a woman who changed her life.

Ellie never made it to the hotel or the conference. She spent five days helping Sun Yuchin dig a well and repair a neighbor's house in a tiny, cramped town, and fallen in love with the simple village, and bonded with the woman who lived there. Every few months since, Ellie had returned. She'd been there to meet Sun's daughter, Jiao, after she was born, even helped feed the baby, and the following year, helped build an extra room for the child. In the process, Ellie had formed a deep friendship with Sun, a hardworking, single mother who had suffered more tragedies than any person should in a lifetime—her parents dead, then her husband two years later, and near the end of one of Ellie's trips to Sun's town, the woman finally confided the worst news of all.

Sun had cancer. Stage four. After she told Ellie, she asked her an incredible question.

Will you raise Jiao after I'm gone? Take her to America, and be her mother?

Finn ended the call, then put his cell back into his pocket. "The Piedmont hospital will be quite an undertaking for WW," he said, drawing her attention back to the topic.

Was he curious, or jealous? His firm had been one of the few invited to submit a bid. She remembered her father being so sure that McKenna Designs, clearly the leader in experience, would land the job. But in the end, either her father's schmoozing on the golf course or his more competitive bid had won out and McKenna Designs had been left in the dust.

Was this true congratulations or sour grapes?

Ellie gave Finn a nod, then crossed her hands on the table. "I'm sure we're up to the challenge." Did her voice betray the doubts she felt?

"I know a project of that size can seem intimidating," he added, as if he'd read her mind. "Even for someone with your experience."

The dig didn't go unnoticed. She was sure a methodical man like Finn McKenna would already know she'd built her career in residential, not commercial properties. He was expressing his doubts in her ability without coming right out and saying it.

He wasn't the only one with concerns. She'd gone into architecture because she loved the field, and chosen residential work because she loved creating that happy home for her clients, and had been rewarded well for that job. She'd never wanted to be a part of the more impersonal, commercial industry.

But now she was. And that meant she had to deal with everything that came her way, no matter what. And handle it, one way or another, because her father's company needed her to. She couldn't go to her father and risk raising his blood pressure. She'd muddle through this project on her own. No matter what, Ellie would hold on to what Henry had built.

"We have a strong, dedicated team," she said.

"Had."

"Excuse me?"

"You *had* a strong, dedicated team. As I hear it, Farnsworth quit last week."

Damn. Finn really did have his finger on the pulse of WW Architectural Design. Few people knew George Farnsworth, one of the oldest and most experienced architects at the firm, had quit. He'd butted heads with Ellie almost from the day she walked in the door, and eventually said he'd work for her father—or no one at all. Which wasn't quite true, because it turned out Farnsworth had had a lucrative job offer at a competitor waiting in the wings the whole time.

She'd been scrambling ever since to find a worthy replacement. And coming up empty.

"You seem to know quite a bit about my business, Mr. McKenna—"

"Finn, please."

"Finn, then." She pushed the cup of tea to the side and leaned forward. "What I want to know is why."

He gave her a half-nod. "What they say about you is true."

"And what, pray tell, do they say about me?"

"That you're smart and capable. And able to talk your way out of or into just about anything."

She laughed. "The talking part is probably true. My father always said I could talk my way out of a concrete box."

"Refill?" The waitress hovered over their table, coffeepot halfway to Finn's cup. Then she noticed the two still-full cups. "Okay, guess not."

Finn paused long enough for the waitress to leave, then his sky-blue gaze zeroed in on hers. "You asked why I have such an interest in your business, and in you."

She nodded.

"I've done my research on your career, Miss Winston, and on WW Architectural Design because—" he paused a beat "—I have a proposition for you."

"A proposition?" Ellie arched a brow, then flipped on the charm. Two could dance in this conversation. Finn McKenna had yet to tell her anything of substance, and she refused to give away her surprise or her curiosity. He had likely underestimated her as a businesswoman, and after tonight, she doubted he'd do it again. "Why, Finn, that sounds positively scandalous."

He let out a short, dry laugh. "I assure you, Miss Winston—"

"Ellie." She gave him a nod and a slight smile. She had found that a little warmth and charm, accented by the slight Southern accent that she'd picked up in her years in North Carolina, often served her well in business dealings, and she used that tool to her advantage now. No giving Finn McKenna the upperhand. No, she wanted to know what he was after, and more importantly, why. "That's the least you can do, considering I'm calling you by your first name."

"Ellie, then." Her name rolled off his tongue, smooth as caramel. "I...I can assure you—" he paused a second again, seemed to gather his thoughts "—that my proposition is business only."

She waited for him to continue, while her tea cooled in front of her. This was the reason he'd asked her here—not for a date, but for business. A flicker of disappointment ran through her, but she told herself it was for the best. Despite what her father had asked of her, she didn't see how she could possibly fit dating, much less marriage, into her already busy life.

She had her father to worry about and care for, a company to run, and most of all, a home to prepare for the changes coming her way very soon. Getting involved with Finn McKenna didn't even make it on to that list. Heck, it wasn't even in the same galaxy as her other priorities.

"I know that without Farnsworth, you're in a difficult position," Finn continued. "He's the most senior architect on your staff, and you're about to undertake a major hospital project. The kind of thing WW has built its reputation on, and the kind of job that will bring millions into the company coffers."

She nodded. The Piedmont hospital was a huge boon for WW. Her father had worked long and hard to land that project. He was proud as punch to add it on to the company resume, and she was determined not to let her father down. This job would also firmly establish WW's place as a leader in medical facility design—a smart move in an era of increased demand from aging baby boomers.

"As the new CEO," Finn went on in the same precise, no-nonsense manner as before, "you're already at a vulnerable juncture, and losing this project, or screwing it up, could cause WW irreparable damage." He'd clearly studied her, and the company, and was offering an honest, if not a bit too true, perspective. He squared his spoon beside his cup, seeming to gather his thoughts, but she got the feeling he was inserting a measured, calculated pause.

She waited him out. A part of her was glad he'd gotten right to the point, avoiding the male-female flirting dance. She'd met far too many businessmen who thought they could finesse their way through a deal with a few compliments and smiles. Men who saw a woman in charge and took her to be an idiot, or someone they could manipulate over dinner. Finn McKenna, she suspected, was a what-you-see-is-what-you-get man, who saw no need for frills or extra words. Straightforward, to the point, no games. That brief moment in the lobby had been a fluke, she decided. This was the real Finn, aka the Hawk. He wanted something from her and clearly intended to stay until he had it.

"I have two senior architects on my staff who are more than capable of handling the hospital project for you," Finn said. "If you agree to this business proposition, then they would oversee it, sort of as architects on loan. You, Miss Winston—" he paused again, corrected himself "—Ellie, would remain in complete control. And myself and my staff at McKenna Designs would be there as a resource for you, as you navigate the complicated arena of medical facility design, and the troubled waters of the CEO world."

Troubled waters? Did he think she was totally incompetent? She tamped down the rush of anger and feigned flattery.

"That's a mighty nice offer, Finn. Why, a girl would be all aflutter from your generosity…" Then she dropped the Southern Belle accent from her voice, and the smile from her face. He'd made it all sound so smooth, as if the benefit was all to her, not to him. "*If* she hadn't been raised by a father who told her that no one does anything without a payoff. So, I ask you—" she leaned in, her gaze locking on his "—what's in this for you?"

He gave her a short nod, a brief smile, a look that said touché. And something that looked a lot like respect. "My business has struggled as of late. Partly the economy, partly—" the next words seemed to leave his mouth with a sour taste "—because of a project that had some unfortunate results. Although we have a few medical buildings on our resume, our work has primarily been in the retail and corporate world. McKenna Designs would like to move into the medical building field because it's a growing industry that dovetails well with our other corporate work. You would like to strengthen your position as the new head at WW by designing a hospital that puts a really big star in the company constellation, as they say." He spread his hands. "A partnership benefits us both."

"From what *I've* heard, McKenna Designs took a serious blow in credibility and finances over this past year and you've been reeling ever since." They worked in a small industry and people talked. The people who worked for Ellie had been more than happy to fill her in on the local competition when she arrived in Boston. Finn McKenna's name had come up several times.

"We've had our...challenges."

"As have we," she acknowledged.

"Precisely the reason I came to you." Now he leaned back and sipped at his coffee, even though it had surely gone cold long ago. He was waiting for her to make the next move.

As she looked at him, she realized two things. He didn't think she was capable of running the firm without his help and two, he was offering a deal that benefited him far more than her. She could hire another architect— maybe even, with the right incentives, steal Finn's best and brightest right from under his nose—and be just fine. He was just like all the other men she had met, and all the "concerned" colleagues of her father, who saw the little Winston girl as nothing more than a figurehead.

The Hawk was merely swooping in to try to scoop up an opportunity. This meeting had been a waste of time. The one luxury Ellie Winston didn't have.

She rose, grabbing her purse as she did. "I appreciate the offer, I really do, but we're just fine at WW, and we'll be just fine without an alliance with you. So thank you again—" she fished in her purse for a few dollars, and tossed them on the table "—but I must decline. Good evening, Mr. McKenna."

Then she left, hoping that was the last she saw of Finn McKenna.

CHAPTER THREE

ELLIE had vowed not to think about Finn's surprise offer. He was only out for number one, she had decided last night during the cab ride home, and she'd be a fool to even consider it. But as the morning's staff meeting progressed, she found her mind wandering back to that diner conversation.

You're at a vulnerable juncture.

Losing this project could mean irreparable damage.

A partnership benefits us both.

Had he meant what he said? Could it be a genuine offer? And if she accepted, would the benefits outweigh the drawbacks? Or was he trying to get in—and then take over her company? She'd heard how many times he'd done that to other firms.

She had floated Finn's name with a few of her colleagues this morning, trying to get more of a read on the man everyone dubbed "the Hawk." To a person, they'd urged caution, reminding her Finn "preferred to eat the competition for lunch rather than lunch with them."

That meant any sort of alliance with him required serious consideration. Was his proposal all a way for him to take over her father's company? Or would his proposal be a true two-way benefit?

She thought of what lay ahead for her life, about the

child about to become a part of her life, and wondered how she could possibly juggle it all. Was a partnership a good idea?

"I'm worried, Ellie." Larry, the most senior of her remaining architects let out a long breath. "We really need a strong leader on this project. Even though we have a lot of great architects here, without either your dad or Farnsworth to head this, well…"

"We don't have anyone with enough experience and that means we'll be in over our head from day one," Ellie finished for him. She'd known that going in, but had hoped that when she called the staff meeting someone would step up to the plate and produce a resume rife with medical design experience. Hadn't happened. "We have a great team here, I agree. But no one who has direct experience with medical institutions."

Larry nodded. "If we were building a bank, a resort, a hotel, we'd be fine. We could do those in our sleep. And I'm sure we could handle this project, too, but we'd be a whole lot better off with a good senior architect to oversee all those details. As it is, we're stretched thin with the new mall out on Route 1 and the condo project in the Back Bay."

Ellie knew Larry made sense. Between the integrated technology, clean environment requirements and strict government guidelines, a hospital build was so much more complex than an ordinary office building. Farnsworth's specialty had been in that arena, and without him, the team would be on a constant scramble to check regs, meet with contractors and double check every element. "I'll find someone."

"By the end of the week?" Panic raised the pitch in Larry's voice. "Because the initial drawings are due by the fifteenth."

Just a few short days away. "Did Farnsworth get anything done on them?"

Larry shook his head. Ellie's gut clenched. Farnsworth had lied and told her he'd done the initial work, but clearly his disgruntled attitude had been affecting his work for a while. Her father had designed several hospitals and medical buildings over the years, but Ellie certainly couldn't go to him for help, and no one on the current staff at WW had the kind of experience her father and Farnsworth had. She'd just have to hire someone.

But by the end of this week? Someone who could step right in and take the project's reins without a single misstep? And then produce a plan that would meet the critical eye of the hospital owners? She needed someone with years of experience. Someone smart. Someone capable, organized. And ready to become the team leader at a moment's notice.

"I'll find someone," she repeated again. "By the end of the day. I promise."

Ellie gave her team a smile, and waited until everyone had left the room before she let the stress and worry consume her. She doodled across the pad in front of her. It was a good thirty seconds before she realized she hadn't sketched a flower or a box or a stick figure. She'd written a name.

And maybe...an answer. The only problem was right now, this was more of a win for Finn, who would reap the benefits of a partnership, the prestige of the project and a cut of the profits, than for Ellie, who risked looking like a company that couldn't do the job and had to call in outsiders.

She tapped her pencil on the pad. There had to be something Finn could give her that would make a partnership worth the risk of an alliance with the predatory Hawk. It would have to be something big, she mused.

Very big.

Finn sat at his massive mahogany desk, the same one he had bought ten years ago at a garage sale, refinished by hand then installed on his first day at McKenna Designs. Back then, he'd had an office not much bigger than the desk, but as he'd moved up, the desk had moved with him. Now it sat in the center of his office, his headquarters for watching the world go by eleven stories below him. Friday morning had dawned bright and beautiful, with a spring sun determined to coax the flowers from their leaf cocoons. It was the kind of spring day that tempted people to call in sick and spend the day by the Charles River, picnicking and boating and jogging on the Esplanade. The kind of day that drew everyone out of their winter huddles, spilling into the parks and onto the sidewalks, like newly released prisoners.

But not Finn. He had called an early meeting this morning, and had been snowed under with work every second since then. Sometimes he felt like he was just plugging holes in a leaky water bucket. They'd lost another client today, a corporation that said they'd "lost confidence" in McKenna Designs after hearing of the defection of two other major clients. Apparently Lucy's betrayal was still hitting his bottom line, even more than a year later. He sighed.

He'd turn this company around, one way or another. He'd hoped that Ellie Winston would hear his offer and jump at the opportunity for some help. She was out of her league on the Piedmont project, and definitely didn't have anyone on her staff who could handle something of that magnitude. When he'd considered his offer, he'd seen it only as a win-win for her. Yet still she'd said no.

It was a rare defeat to a man who had won nearly everything he put his mind to. The refusal had left him surprised, but not for long. He would regroup, and find another way to convince Ellie that his proposal was in her best interests.

Could she be thinking of hiring someone else? He hadn't heard rumors of anyone considering a job at WW, but that didn't mean there wasn't a prospective candidate. Finn had always prided himself on having an ear to the ground in Boston's busy and competitive architecture world, but that didn't mean he knew everything.

"Knock, knock. Time for lunch."

Finn glanced up and saw his brother standing in the doorway, grinning like a fool. Every time he saw Riley, his brother looked as happy as a loon. Probably because he didn't have a care in the world. Or maybe because things had gone better for Riley with women last night than they had for Finn. "Sorry. Maybe another time. I have a ton of work to do."

"Yeah, yeah." Riley waved that off. "And last I checked you were human…"

Finn dropped his gaze to his hands, his feet, then back up to Riley. "It appears so."

"And that means you need to eat on a regular basis. So come on." Riley waved at him. "Hey, I'll even treat."

Finn chuckled. "Considering that's almost a miracle in the making—"

"Hey." Riley grinned. "I resemble that remark."

"You're the poster child for it." Finn shook his head. Then his stomach rumbled and overruled his work resolve. "All right. You win. But let's make it a quick lunch."

"You know me. I'm always ready to get my nose back to the grindstone. Or rather, ready to get *your* nose back to *your* grindstone, and mine back to lazy living." Riley laughed at his joke, then walked with Finn down the hall to the elevator. "You know it wouldn't hurt you to take a day off once in a while. Maybe even enough time off to have a date or ten."

The doors opened with a soft ding sound and Finn stepped inside, followed by Riley. "We've had this argument before. Last night if I remember right."

"Yep. And we're going to keep having it until you admit I'm right and you're lonely."

"I'm fine." Finn punched the button for the lobby.

"You tell yourself that enough and you might even start to believe it someday, big brother."

Finn ignored the jab. "So how's the waitress?"

"I don't know." Riley shrugged. "I ended up leaving with the brunette."

Finn rolled his eyes.

Riley grinned. "What can I say? The world is filled with beautiful women. Like the one you were supposed to talk to last night. How'd that go?"

"It didn't go quite the way I expected." Had he come on too strong? Too weak? He found himself wondering what she was doing right now. Was Ellie having lunch at her desk? With a friend? Or alone in a restaurant?

She'd been on his mind almost every minute since she'd walked out of the diner. That alone was a clear sign he needed to work more and think less. He wasn't interested in Ellie Winston on a personal basis, even if his hormones were mounting a vocal disagreement.

"What, you struck out? Didn't get her phone number?" Riley asked.

"Her office number is in the yellow pages. I didn't need to ask for that."

Riley shook his head. "And the Hawk strikes again. Always business with you."

The elevator doors shimmied open. Finn and Riley crossed the lobby and exited onto Beacon Street. In the distance, rowers skimmed their sculls down the rippling blue river.

The Hawk strikes again.

Maybe it was the too sunny weather or maybe it was the rejection last night, but Finn found himself bothered by that phrase. He'd never much liked the moniker, but he'd always thought that he, of all people, combined humanity with business. He had never seen himself as quite the cold fish the media depicted.

His brother didn't understand what drove Finn. What kept him at that desk every day. What monumental weights sat on his shoulder, even as he tried to shed them. The one time he'd tried to live a "normal" life, he'd been burned. Badly. More than enough reason not to make that mistake again.

A slight breeze danced across the Charles River, tempering the heat of the day with a touch of cool. They walked for a while, navigating the rush of lunchgoers, heading for the same place they always went, in unspoken agreement. That was one good thing about lunch with Riley—the kind of common mind that came from being siblings. Even though he and Riley were as different as apples and oranges, Finn had always had a closer relationship with him than with Brody. Maybe because Riley was easy to talk to, easy to listen to, and the one who—though he kidded often—understood Finn the best. Even if their minds often moved on opposite tracks.

They reached the shadowed entrance to McGill's. Finn

paused before tugging on the door. "Do you ever wonder…"

Riley glanced at his brother. "Wonder what?"

"Nothing." Finn opened the door and stepped into the air-conditioned interior. The last person he needed to ask for personal—and definitely business—advice was his brother. Riley's standard answer—get a girl, get a room and get busy.

He wanted to ask Riley how his little brother could give his heart so freely. And whether doing so was worth the cost at the end when his heart was broken. He'd seen how much it hurt when the one you were supposed to love no longer felt the same. He had watched that pain erode the happiness in his mother's face day by day. As the youngest, Riley had missed those subtle cues.

Finn shrugged off the thoughts. It had to be the spring weather—and the overabundance of lovey-dovey couples out enjoying the sunshine—that had him feeling so maudlin. He liked his life just the way it was. He didn't need anything more than that.

It took a second for his eyes to adjust to the dim room, and to take in the space. McGill's had a warm interior—dark, rough-hewn plank walls, sturdy, practical tables and chairs and a worn oak floor that had been distressed by thousands of customers' shoes. The food was hearty and good—thick sandwiches, hand-cut fries, stout beer. Finn and Riley came here often, and were waved over to the table area by Steve McGill himself, who was working the bar this afternoon.

Finn waved off the waiter's offer of beer, opting for water instead. "The usual, Marty."

Marty MacDonald had been there for as long as Finn could remember. He had to be nearing seventy, but he moved twice as fast, and had twice the memory of the younger waiters at McGill's. Marty nodded, then turned to Riley. "For you?"

"I'll have my beer, and his. No sense in wasting it." Riley grinned. "And a corned beef sandwich on rye."

Marty chuckled. "In other words, the usual?"

"You know me well, Marty." Riley waited until their server had left, then turned back to Finn. "So what do you think went wrong with the grand plan last night?"

Finn's phone rang. He signaled to Riley to wait a second, then answered the call. "Finn McKenna."

"I wanted to update you on the Langham project," Noel, one of Finn's architects, said. "I heard that Park came in twenty percent lower than us. The client said they're going to go with him instead. Sorry we lost the job, Finn."

Joe Park, a newcomer to Boston's crowded architectural playing field, and someone who often underbid just to get the work. Finn suspected it was the cost savings, and some residual damage to McKenna's reputation that had spurred the client's defection. Finn refused to let another client go.

"No, they won't," he said. "Let me give Langham a call. In five minutes he'll see the wisdom of sticking with us." Finn hung up with Noel, then called the client. In a matter of minutes, he had convinced the penny pinching CEO that working with the established McKenna Designs was a far smarter choice than a rookie newbie. He soothed the worried waters with Langham, and assured him that McKenna Designs would be on top of the project from start to finish. He didn't say anything outright bad about his competitor, but the implication was clear—work with the unproven Park, and the work would be substandard.

After Finn finished the call and put away the phone,

Riley shot him a grin. "I'm glad I'm not one of your competitors."

"It's business, Riley."

"That's not business, that's guerilla warfare." Riley shook his head. "Tell me you didn't treat that gorgeous lady the same way?"

"No, in fact quite the opposite. I think I might have been too nice."

Riley snorted.

"She turned me down. But I'm going to regroup, find another way." Finn reached into the breast pocket of his suit. "I've got a list of pros and cons I'm going to present to her—"

Riley pushed Finn's hand away. "For a smart guy, you can be a complete idiot sometimes."

"This is logical, sound reasoning. Any smart business-person would—"

"I'm sure you're right. And if you have a month or three to go back and forth on pros and cons and hereto-fores and whatevers, I'd agree with you." Riley leaned in closer. "But you don't have that kind of time."

Apparently Riley had been listening to Finn's worries over the past year. Finn was impressed with his little brother's intuitiveness. Maybe he didn't give Riley enough credit. "True."

"So that means you need to change your tactics."

Finn had an argument ready, but he bit it back. Riley had a point. Negotiations took time, and that was pretty much what his list was. He was an expert when it came to the art of the business deal, but this was different— and he'd struck out with Ellie Winston in a big way. He needed a new idea, and right now, he'd take ideas from about anyone and anywhere. "Okay. How?"

Riley grinned and sat back. "Easy. Do what I do."

"I am not sleeping with her just to get what I want." Finn scowled. "You have a one-track mind."

Riley pressed a hand to his heart. "Finn, you wound me. I would never suggest that. Well, I might, but not in your case." Riley paused. "Especially not in your case."

"Hey."

"You are way too uptight and practical to do such a thing."

"For good reason." Nearly every move in his life was well planned, thought out and executed with precision. Even his relationship with his ex had been like that. He'd chosen a partner who was a peer, someone with common interests, in the right age range and with the kind of quiet understated personality that seemed to best suit his own.

It had seemed to be the wisest choice all around. The kind that wouldn't leave him—or her—unhappy in the end. He'd been stunned when she'd broken up with him and worse, maligned his business and revealed she'd only gone out with him to get information.

But had that been real love? If he could so easily be over the relationship, at least emotionally? Was real love methodical, planned?

Or a wild, heady rush?

The image of Ellie in that figure-hugging maroon dress, her head thrown back in laughter, her eyes dancing with merriment, sent a blast of heat through him. He suspected she was the kind of woman who could get a man to forget a lot more than just his business agenda. For just a second, that empty feeling in his chest lifted. Damn, he really needed to eat more or sleep more or something. He was nearly a blubbering emotional idiot today.

Wild heady rushes didn't mix with business. Wild

heady rushes led to heartache down the road. Wild heady rushes were the exact opposite of Finn McKenna.

"The secret to getting what you want, especially from a woman, is very simple," Riley said.

"Flowers and wine?"

Riley laughed. "That always helps, but no, that's not what I meant."

Marty dropped off their drinks, so quietly they barely noticed his presence. Marty knew them well, and knew when he could interrupt and when to just slip in and out like a cat in the night.

"You find out what the other party wants most in the world," Riley said, "then give it to them."

"That's what my list—"

"Oh, for Pete's sake, Finn. Women aren't into lists and pros and cons. Hell, who is?" Then he paused. "Okay, maybe you. But not the rest of the world. Most people are driven by three needs." He flipped out his fingers and ticked them off as he spoke. "Money, love and sex."

Finn chuckled and shook his head. Riley's advice made sense, in a twisted way. Hadn't Finn done the same thing in business a hundred times? Find out what the other party wants and offer it, albeit with conditions that benefited both sides. "Let me guess. You're driven by number three."

"Maybe." Riley grinned. "One of the three is what drives that pretty little blonde you met with last night. Figure out what it is she wants and give it to her."

"Simple as that?"

Riley sat back and took a sip from his beer. "Simple as that."

The room closed in on her, suddenly too hot, too close. Ellie stared at the woman across from her, letting the words echo in her mind. For a long time, they didn't make sense. It was all a muddled hum of sounds, rattling around in her brain. Then the sounds coalesced one syllable at a time, into a painful reality.

"Are you sure?" Ellie asked. She had walked into this office on a bright Monday morning and now it seemed in the space of seconds, the day had gone dark.

Linda Simpson nodded. "I'm so sorry, Ellie."

She'd know Linda for months, and in that time, Linda had become Ellie's biggest supporter as well as a friend. All these weeks, the news had been positive.

Operative words—*had been*.

Ellie pressed a hand to her belly, and thought of all she had given up to be a woman in a male-dominated field. Relationships…children. Children that now she knew would never happen naturally. Adoption, the obstetrical specialist had told her, was the only option.

Maybe it was her father's illness, or the approach of her thirtieth birthday, but lately, she'd been thinking more and more about the…quiet of her life. For years, she'd been happy living alone, making her own hours, traveling where she wanted. But in the last year or two, there'd been no louder, sadder sound than the echo of her footsteps on tile. She had no one but her father, and if the doctors were right, soon she wouldn't even have him.

And what would she have to show for it? A few dozen houses she'd designed? Houses where other people lived and laughed and raised children and shooed dogs out of the kitchen. Houses containing the very dreams Ellie had pushed to the side.

But no more. Jiao was waiting for her, now stuck in a limbo of red tape at an orphanage in China. Jiao, an energetic two-year-old little girl with wide eyes and dark hair, and a toothy smile. Everything Ellie had dreamed of was right there, within her grasp.

Or had been, until now.

Had Ellie heard wrong? But one look at Linda Simpson's face, lined with sympathy and regret, told Ellie this was no joke. The adoption coordinator sat behind her desk, her dark brown hair piled into a messy bun, her eyes brimming with sorrow.

"I need…" Ellie swallowed, tried again. "A husband?"

"That's what they told me this morning. Countries all over the world are tightening their adoption policies. The orphanage is sticking to the government's bottom line. I'm sorry."

A spouse.

Ellie bit back a sigh. Maybe it was time to pursue another adoption, in a more lenient country. But then she thought of Jiao's round, cherubic face, the laughter that had seemed to fill the room whenever Ellie had played with her, and knew there was nothing she wanted more than to bring that little girl home. She had promised Sun, and Jiao.

But how was she going to do that *and* run her father's company? And who on earth could she possibly marry on such short notice? There had to be a way out of this. A workaround of some sort.

"But they told me, *you* told me, I was fine. That because Jiao's mother asked me specifically to raise her daughter and endorsed the adoption before she died, that I wouldn't have to worry about the other requirements."

"The government is the ultimate authority." Linda spread her hands in a helpless gesture. "And they just feel better about a child being placed in a home with two parents."

Ellie tamped down her frustration. Being mad at Linda

didn't help. The coordinator had worked tirelessly to facilitate this adoption, working with both the U.S. and Chinese governments, as well as the orphanage where Jiao was currently living. Ellie had contacted the agency where Linda worked shortly after returning from that fateful China trip. She'd explained the situation to the woman, who had immediately helped set everything up for a later adoption, easing Sun's worries during the last days of her life.

Ellie had expected some delays, particularly dealing with a foreign government, but already three months had passed since Sun had died and Jiao was still in China.

A husband. Where was she going to get one of those? It wasn't like she could just buy one on the drugstore shelf. Getting married took time, forethought. A relationship with someone.

"What happens now?" Ellie asked. "What happens to Jiao?"

"Well, it would be handy if you had a boyfriend who was looking to commit in the very near future. But if not..." Linda put out her hands again. "I'm sorry. Maybe this one isn't meant to be." Linda didn't have to say anything more. Ellie knew, without hearing the words, that her child would go back into the orphanage system and maybe languish there for years.

Ellie couldn't believe that this wasn't meant to be. Not for a second. The entire serendipitous way she had met Sun, the way the two of them had become instant friends, despite the cultural and language barriers.

And Jiao...

She already loved the little girl. Ellie had held Jiao. Laughed with her. Bonded. During her trips to China, Ellie had become a part of Jiao's little family. A second mother, in a way, to Jiao, who had curled into Ellie and clung to her when they had buried Sun. It had broken Ellie's heart to have to go back to the United States without the little girl. She'd only done it because she'd been assured the next few steps of the adoption were merely a formality.

And now Jiao was all alone in the world, living in a crowded, understaffed orphanage, probably scared and lonely and wondering why she had no family anymore. Ellie thought of Jiao's pixie face, her inquisitive eyes and her contagious smile. Desperation clawed at Ellie. *Oh, God, Jiao. What am I going to do?*

Ellie took a deep breath. Another. She needed to be calm. To think.

Damn it. Ellie had made a promise. Jiao deserved to be raised with security and love, and Ellie would find some way to make that happen. "Let me think about this," she said. "Can I call you later?"

Linda nodded, her warm brown eyes pooling with sympathy. "Sure. I have a day or two to get back to the orphanage."

The unspoken message, though, was that after that, Jiao would slip out of Ellie's grasp like wind through the trees. Off to another family or worse, stuck in the system. Ellie needed a miracle.

And she needed it now.

CHAPTER FOUR

FINN McKENNA was not a man easily surprised. He'd heard and seen a great deal in the past ten years of running his own company. But this...offer, if that was what he could call it, from Ellie Winston was a total shock.

"Marriage? As in a church and a minister?" he said. The words choked past his throat.

"Well, I was thinking more like city hall and a judge, but if you insist..." She grinned.

"But...w-we don't even know each other." The words sputtered out of him. He, a man who never sputtered.

Ever since she'd walked into his office five minutes ago and announced she had a counteroffer to his, that was what he had done—sputtered. And stammered. And parroted her words back at her. He couldn't believe what he was hearing. *Shocked* wasn't an adequate adjective.

Marriage?

He had expected her to ask for more autonomy with the project or a larger cut of the fee. Something...practical.

Instead she'd said she would allow him to be an equal partner in the Piedmont hospital project, if he married her.

Marriage.

"I think I need a little more time to...think about this."

Or find a counteroffer that could possibly overrule her insane request. "Perhaps we could table this—"

"I'd rather not." She was perched on the edge of one of the visitor's chairs in his office. The late morning sun danced gold in her hair. She had on another dress, this one in a pale yellow that made him think of daffodils.

For Pete's sake. Every time he got close to Ellie Winston he turned into a damned greeting card.

"If you're free for a little while," she added, "how about we go someplace and talk?"

He considered saying no, but then realized this was his best opportunity to get what he needed from Ellie Winston. In the long run, that would serve him better than staying at his desk. It wasn't the fact that he wanted to see more of her. Not at all. He glanced out his window. "We could do lunch, and be stuck in some restaurant or…the weather is gorgeous. How about a stroll on the Esplanade?"

"Sure. I can't remember the last time I walked along the river." She reached into her purse and pulled out a small bag. "I even have flats with me."

"Practical woman."

She laughed. "Sometimes, not so much, but today, yes." She slipped off her heels, tucked them in her bag, then slid on the other shoes.

Finn told Miss Marstein that he was leaving, then shut down his computer and grabbed his phone. A few minutes later, they were out the door and heading down a side street toward the Esplanade. Finn drew in a deep breath of sweet salty air. "I definitely don't get outside enough."

Ellie sighed. "Me, either. When I was younger, I used to be a real outdoorsy girl. Hiking, canoeing, bike riding. I tried to keep up with that after college, but the job takes up way too much time."

He arched a brow at her dress and the spiky heels poking out of her purse. "You hiked?"

Ellie put a fist on her hip. "Do I look too girly for that?"

His gaze raked over her curves, and his thoughts strayed from business to something far more personal. Damn. "Uh, no. Not at all."

"What about you?" she asked. "Do you hike or bike or anything like that?"

"I used to. I ran track in high school, was on the swim team, you name it. And during college, I biked everywhere. Now I think my bike's tires are flat and there are spiders making webs in the frame."

She laughed. "All the more reason to get it out of storage."

They crossed to the Esplanade, joining the hundreds of other people outside. A few on bikes whizzed past them, as if adding an exclamation point to the conversation. "Maybe someday I will," Finn said, watching a man on a carbon fiber racing bike zip past him. "I do miss it."

"Someday might never come," Ellie said quietly. "It's too easy to let the To Do list get in the way. And then before you know it, another year has passed, and another, and you're still sitting behind the desk instead of doing what you love."

He heard something more in her voice. Some kind of longing. Just for more outdoor time? Or to fill another hole in her life? He wanted to ask, wanted to tell her he knew all about using work to plug those empty spots.

But he didn't.

The bike rider disappeared among a sea of power walkers. Finn returned his attention to Ellie. She looked radiant in the sunshine. Tempting. *Too* tempting. He cleared his throat. "It's hard to keep up with the personal To Do list when the business one is so much longer."

"Isn't part of your business taking care of you? After all, if the CEO ain't happy..." She let the words trail off and shot him a grin.

For a second, Finn wanted to fall into that engaging smile of Ellie Winston's. Every one of her smiles seemed to hit him deep in the gut. They were the kind of smiles that Finn suspected—no, knew—would linger in his mind long after they were done. And her voice... her years of living in the South gave her just enough of a Southern tinge to coat her words with a sweet but sassy spin. It was...intoxicating.

Hell, everything about her was intoxicating. It wasn't just the dress or the smile or the curves. It was everything put together, in one unique, intriguing package.

She had him thinking about what it would be like to take a hike through Blue Hills with her, to crest the mountain and watch the busy world go by far beneath them. He imagined them picnicking on a rock outcropping, while the sun warmed their backs and the breeze danced along their skin.

Damn. What was it about her that kept getting him distracted? He needed to focus on business, and more importantly, on why she had proposed marriage a few minutes ago. No wild, heady anything with her.

Finn cleared his throat. "About your...proposal earlier. No pun intended. Were you serious?"

Her features went from teasing to flat, and he almost regretted steering the conversation back. "Yes. Very." She let out a long breath, and for a while, watched the people sitting on the grass across from them. It was a family of four, with a small dog nipping at the heels of the children as they ran a circle around their parents. "I need something from you and you need something from me. Marriage is the best solution all around."

"We could always do a legal agreement for the businesses. This is just one project, you know."

"For me, it's much more." Her gaze returned to his. "I have to have a husband. Now."

"Why?"

"First, let me lay out the advantages to you." She slowed her pace. "For one, our lack of familiarity with each other is what makes it a perfect idea and a perfect partnership, if you will."

"Partnership, perhaps. Not a marriage."

"I may not know you very well, Mr. McKenna," she went on, "but I know your life. You work sunup to sundown, travel half the year and have all the social life of a barnacle."

She could have opened up his skull and peeked inside his brain. Damn. Was he that transparent? And put that way, well, hell, his life sounded downright pitiful. Riley would have put up two enthusiastic thumbs in agreement.

Perhaps she was joking. He glanced at her face. Saw only serious intent in her features.

"But don't you think it's wiser to work out a business arrangement instead? More money, more prestige, a reciprocal arrangement with my next project?" Something he could quantify, put into those neat little debits and credits columns. Not something like *marriage*, for Pete's sake.

"Perhaps to you it would be. But a business arrangement isn't the number one thing I need right now." She gestured toward a small grassy hill that led to the river, away from the crowds out walking, and the energetic inline skaters rushing past them. He followed her down to the water's edge. In the distance, a rowing team called out a cadence as they skimmed across the glassy blue surface.

Her green eyes met his, and a thrill ran through him. Damn, she had beautiful eyes.

"Not to mention, you're probably as tired of the dating game as am I," she said. "And maybe you've looked ahead to the future, and wondered how on earth you're going to fit the American Dream into your schedule."

He gave her a droll smile. "Actually I had that down for next year, on Tuesday, March 30, at two in the afternoon."

She burst out laughing, which also surprised him and stirred that warmth again in his gut. Those who knew Finn would never have described him as a man with a sense of humor. But apparently Ellie Winston found him funny. That pleased him, and had him wondering what else Ellie thought of him.

Damn. He kept getting off track. It had to be her proposal which had knocked the normally unflappable Finn off balance.

"I was hoping to fit it into my planner a little sooner than that," she said. "Actually a lot sooner."

"Why? Why now? And…why me? I mean, you are a beautiful woman. Smart, charming, sexy. You could have your pick of any man on the planet."

"I…well, thank you." Now it was her turn to sputter. A soft pink blush spread over her cheeks. Then she paused, seeming to weigh her answer for several moments before responding. He got the distinct impression she was holding something back, but what, he didn't know. He thought again about what he knew about her. Nothing pointed to "desperate to get married," no matter how he looked at the details he knew about her. Yet, there was an ulterior motive to her proposal—he'd bet a year's salary on it.

"There's a child in China who needs a mother. I promised her that I would adopt her, and everything was in place for me to do so. Until this morning." She bit her lip and turned to him. "The agency told me I need a husband to complete the adoption."

"Whoa, whoa." He put up his hands. "I'm not interested in becoming an instant father."

"I'm not asking that of you. At all."

"Then what *are* you asking?"

"A marriage based on commonality, not passion or lust or infatuation. We'll stay married for a short time, long enough for me to get the adoption finalized, then get a quiet divorce. Painless and fast."

In other words, no real strings attached and he'd be out of this nearly as fast as he was in it. He should be glad. For some reason, he wasn't. "Sounds so…clinical."

"Mr. McKenna…Finn. We're both detail oriented—clinical in a way—people. I'm not interested in losing my head in a relationship, or wasting a lot of time dating Mr. Wrong, not when I'm concentrating on running my father's company. I need a spouse, in name only, and you need a business partner."

He looked in Ellie Winston's eyes, and saw only sincerity, and a quiet desperation to help a child halfway around the world. He knew she wouldn't have come to him, with this insane offer, if she didn't have to.

Find out what she wants most in the world, Riley had said, and give it to her.

But this?

"I don't know if I agree with this," Finn said. "The child will undoubtedly be hurt when her father disappears after a few weeks."

"You don't have to be a part of Jiao's life at all. Just be there for the home visit and the adoption proceedings. And in return, we can work together on the Piedmont project. That will keep my father's business growing and help yours. It's a win all around."

Pigeons picked at the grass before them, looking for leftover crumbs. In the distance, there was the sound of children's laughter. The swish-swish of rolling cycle tires on the paved walkway. The continual hum of traffic, punctuated by the occasional horn. The world went on as it always did, swimming along beneath a sunny sky.

"It would be a platonic marriage," she said. "Nothing more."

"A purely impersonal alliance?" he asked, still not believing she had suggested this. When he'd made his list of possible ways to convince Ellie a strategic partnership was a good idea, marriage hadn't even come close to being in the mix. "A marriage based solely on like minds and like goals?"

Though when he put the marriage idea like that, it sounded cold. Almost…sad.

He shook off the thoughts. He was a practical man. One whose focus was solely on building his business back to where it had been. He wasn't going to get wrapped up in the foolishness of some romantic ideal—and that wasn't what Ellie was asking for. It was, in fact, the exact kind of relationship he had vowed to pursue. Then why did he feel as empty as a deflated balloon?

She nodded. "Yes."

"And in exchange, our companies partner as well?"

"Yes." She put up a finger. "However, we each retain ownership and leadership of our respective companies, in case…things don't work out." She dug in her purse and pulled out a piece of paper. "I took the liberty of having my attorney draw up a contract."

A contract. For marriage.

Finn skimmed the document and saw that it indeed promised everything she had talked about. The business arrangement, the annulment agreement. All he had to do was sign on the dotted line and he'd be a temporary husband, father in name only.

The businessman in him said it was an opportunity not to be missed. The partnership his business needed, and at the same time, the bonus of companionship. Not sex, clearly, but someone to talk to at the end of the day.

He thought of the nights he'd spent on the rooftop deck of his townhouse. Watching the city lights twinkle in the distance, while he drank a beer, and gathered his thoughts, wondered if he'd made the right choices. Lately those nights hadn't brought the peace they used to. More, a restlessness, a question of "is this all there is?" Except for the times he was with his brothers, his life was staid. Almost dull.

Riley was right. He was lonely, and tired as hell of feeling that way.

At the same time, he didn't want to pursue the empty one-night stands his brother did. He wanted more, something with meaning and depth. Something that was…sensible. Reliable. Practical. Something that wasn't foolish or wild or crazy—not the kind of whirlwind romance his parents had had, that had gone so horribly wrong after the children started coming and they realized that a quick courtship couldn't build a lifetime, not between such badly mismatched people.

Love—or any approximation of it—was a danger-ous thing that left a man vulnerable. Not a position Finn

McKenna relished or welcomed. A marriage of convenience would be void of all those things.

Still, the cynic in him wondered if Ellie was proposing this as a way to knock him off guard, or maybe even an alliance that would allow her to gather facts about him and his business, facts she could use to take over his company later or eliminate him as a competitor. Hadn't Lucy done exactly the same thing?

But the man in him, the one standing beside a very beautiful, very intriguing woman with a smile that stayed with him, hoped like hell it was something more than that.

Was he truly considering this…this marriage of convenience? What choice did he have? He needed to be a part of that hospital project. Making it a joint venture with a company like WW would reestablish his company's reputation, and distract attention from that fiasco last year. And, as calculated as it sounded, a marriage to a charming woman like Ellie would also distract attention from the mess his company had been in lately, give the gossips something else to talk about. He'd be back on top before he knew it, and then he and Eleanor Winston could quietly dissolve the union, as she'd said. She'd have the child, and he'd have his business back. He could feel the old familiar surge of adrenaline that always hit him when he landed a big job, one that he knew could change the future of McKenna Designs.

"This contract looks pretty good," he said.

"I wanted to make it clear this was business only." Her gaze flicked to the water, and she let out a small sigh. Almost like she was disappointed. Which was crazy, because she was the one floating the idea in the first place. "But we don't have a lot of time to waste. Jiao is stuck in that orphanage, farther away from me with every passing day. And you, I suspect, would like to be on board from day one with the hospital project. The initial draw-ings are due the fifteenth so we have very little time to get everyone up to speed."

"The fifteenth? That does put a crunch on our time. By all rights, we should start right away."

"I agree. In the end, Finn, we're both decisive peo-ple, aren't we?" She smiled at him. "I'm not looking for a courtship with flowers and dancing and dinners out. What we are doing is more of a…"

"Partnership. Two like minds coming together."

"Exactly."

A part of him felt a whisper of…loss? Finn wasn't sure that was the right word to describe the yawning empti-ness in his gut. Surely a deal like this—one that would benefit his company and at the same time, fill those quiet, lonely nights with good conversation, was a win-win all around.

Except…

No, he didn't need any more than that. As Ellie had said, a romantic relationship came with complications, emotional drama—all things he didn't have time for, nor wanted in his life. And clearly, not something she wanted, either. She saw him as a means to an end, and he saw her the same way.

Hadn't he learned his lesson with Lucy? A heady re-lationship would do nothing but draw his attention away from the business. In the coming months, the company would need more of his attention than ever, so the kind of relationship Ellie was proposing was perfect. With the addition of the legal contract, the risk to McKenna Designs would be minimal. He saw no downside to this.

Except the fact that it wouldn't be a real marriage. That it would be as faux as the wood paneling that still flanked his grandmother's fireplace, forty years after the house had been built, the same house she lived in because it was the one she'd bought with her late husband, even though she could now afford ten times the house.

A hummingbird flitted by, heading for a bright swath of flowers. Finn watched it for a while, as the world hustled by behind him.

"There's this bird in Africa," Finn said, watching the tiny hummingbird dart from bloom to bloom, "called a honey guide. Its whole job is to find beehives and lead the honey badger to them. When he does, the badger gets in there and gets the honey, clearing the way for the honey guide to eat the bee larvae." He turned to Ellie. "I guess that's sort of what this will be. Us working together to serve a mutually beneficial purpose."

"Not exactly the same as swans mating for life, but yes."

"Definitely not a partnership for life," Finn said. But even as he clarified, he felt a twinge of something like regret. He shrugged it off. Be smart, he reminded himself, like the badger and the bird. In the end, everyone wins.

"I don't want to rush you," she said. "But we need to make a decision. If you don't want to do this...I need to think of something else."

"Fine," he said, turning to her. "Let's go."

She blinked. "What...now?"

"Why wait?" he said, parroting her words back. "I have a friend at the courthouse. He'll take care of it. You can be my wife by the end of the day, Miss Winston."

"Today? Right now?"

"Yes, of course." He watched her closely, and wondered if, despite the contract she'd given him, she was as committed to this partnership as she had sounded. Only

one way to find out, he decided. "You weren't expecting me to get down on one knee with some flowers or a
ring, were you?"

"No, no, of course not." She swallowed. "Business
only."

"My favorite kind of relationship." He gave her a
smile, then turned to go back across the grass. He paused,
turned back, waiting for her to join him. He had called
Ellie Winston's bluff. The only problem...

He wasn't so sure she'd been bluffing.

"Are you ready?"

Was she ready? Ellie had no idea if she was or wasn't.
The events of the last hours seemed surreal, as if it was
some other Ellie Winston who had proposed to Finn
McKenna, then hopped in his Town Car and headed to
Rhode Island in the middle of the day.

Had she really just proposed to him? And had he really
accepted?

She'd gone to his office right after leaving the adoption
agency and then her lawyer's office, her mind filled with
only one thing. She needed a husband and she needed
one now. She'd do whatever it took to get that. She'd seen
Jiao's trusting, hopeful face in her mind and thought of
nothing else. Jiao needed a mother. Needed Ellie.

Linda had made it clear—marriage was the only sure
route to bringing Jiao home. There was no one else that
Ellie knew—not well enough in her short time living here
in Boston—who would marry her on such short notice.
No one who would go along with such a crazy plan, and
not expect a real marriage out of the deal. So she'd gone
to Finn, the only man she knew who needed her as much
as she needed him.

A part of her had never expected him to say yes. But

say yes, he had, and now they were on their way to get married.

Married.

To Finn McKenna.

A man she knew about as well as she knew her dry cleaner.

This was insane. Think of Jiao, she told herself. Just think of Jiao. And as the miles ticked by, that became her mantra.

Massachusetts had a three-day waiting period for a marriage license, Finn had told her, as he got on I-95S and made the hour-long journey to Providence, Rhode Island, where there was no waiting period. The car's smooth, nearly silent ride and comfortable interior made the whole drive seem almost…romantic, even though it was broad daylight and the highway was filled with other cars. It was something about the cozy, dark leather of the car that wrapped around her, insulated them, drew them into a world of just the two of them, like lovers making an afternoon getaway. Which was crazy, because what they were doing was far from romantic. And they were definitely not lovers.

"How did you know there was a three-day waiting period in Massachusetts?" she asked.

"My brother." A grin slid across Finn's face. "Riley is a little…impetuous. We've had to talk him out of more than one crazy decision."

"We?"

"My younger brother Brody and me. We're the ones who received all the common-sense genes."

"Inherited from generations of common-sense McKenna men?"

He chuckled. "Exactly. Though my grandmother might quibble with how much common sense is in our DNA."

"So there are three of you altogether?" Ellie asked.

"Yep. All boys. Made for a busy life. Hell, it still does."

She tried to picture that environment, with three rambunctious, noisy siblings, and couldn't. The camaraderie. The joking. The warmth. "I'm an only child. I can't even imagine what it would be like to grow up with two sisters, or a bunch of brothers."

"It's loud. And sometimes things get broken." Finn put up a hand and pressed three fingers together. "Scouts' Honor, I had nothing to do with that antique vase or the missing coffee table."

Ellie heard the laughter buried in Finn's voice and craved those same kinds of memories for Jiao. She bit back a sigh. Adopting just one child as a single mother was proving to be difficult enough. Adopting multiple children seemed impossible. But maybe someday—

She'd have the warm, crazy, boisterous family Finn was describing.

Except that would mean taking a risk and falling in love. Ellie didn't need to complicate her life with a relationship that could end up hurting her—and in the process her daughter—down the road. This marriage, based on a legal contract and nothing else, was the best choice.

"Remind me to tell you the tree story sometime," Finn said. "And every year at Thanksgiving, we revisit the Ferris wheel one. That one was all Riley's fault. There's always an interesting story where Riley is concerned, and Brody and I try to exploit that at every opportunity."

Her gaze went to the city passing by outside the window, streaks of color in the bright sunshine. Thanksgivings and Christmases with a whole brood of McKenna men sounded like heaven, Ellie thought. Her childhood had been so quiet, so empty, with her mother gone all the time and her father working sunup to sundown. She envied Finn and for a moment, wondered if they would be married long enough for her to sit around the Thanksgiving dinner table with a trio of McKennas, sharing raucous stories and building memories over the turkey.

She pictured that very thing for a moment, then pulled away from the images. They were a bird and a badger, as he'd pointed out, not two swans in love. Besides, she knew better than to pin her hopes on some romantic notion of love. That happened for other people, not her.

"My parents weren't around much when I was a kid. Now my mother lives in California, so it's really just my dad and me." She shifted in her seat to look at him. "I guess you could say my life has always been pretty… quiet and predictable." Now that she said it, she wondered if that was such a good thing. For one, she wanted to add the chaos of a child. Would she be ready for it? She, who had never so much as babysat a neighbor's kid? Save for a few vacations spent in China with Jiao and Sun, she had no experience with children…what made her think she could do this? Heck, Finn, with all those younger brothers, was probably better suited to parenting than she was.

All Ellie had was a deep rooted conviction that she would love her child and be there for her. She wouldn't leave Jiao with an endless stream of babysitters or miss her third-grade recital or pay a tutor to help her with her homework so Ellie could work a few more hours. She would be there.

Somehow, she'd find a way to run WW Designs and be the mother that Jiao needed, the kind of parent Ellie had never had. Even though she knew it would be easier to do that if she had a real husband, one who was a plugged-in father, she vowed to make this work on her own. One attentive, loving parent was better than two inattentive, unavailable parents. And she had no intentions of forcing this marriage to limp along after the adoption was final. The worst thing for Jiao would be to have a distant parent, one who left her wondering if she was truly loved.

Finn turned on his blinker, then exited the highway. "Your life might have been quiet and predictable up until now, but I'd say getting married on the spur of the moment is pretty far from either of those adjectives."

She laughed. "You're right. No one would ever think I'd elope."

"That goes double for me." Finn paused at the end of the off-ramp. He turned to face her, his blue eyes hidden by dark sunglasses. "Still sure you want to do this?"

She thought of what he had just told her. About his brothers and his noisy childhood. Then thought of the quiet, empty life she led. She had her father, yes, but other than that, all she had was work.

"Yes, I'm sure," she said.

"Okay." Then he made the turn, following the signs that led to the downtown area. "Me, too."

He said it so softly, she wondered if there was more behind the words than a simple agreement. Was he missing something in his life, too? Was he looking to fill the empty spaces, add life to those quiet rooms? Or was this solely a business merger for him?

He said nothing more, just drove, and she let the silence fill the space between them in the cavernous Town Car. A little while later, they pulled in front of the courthouse, a massive brick building with dozens of tall windows and a spire reaching toward the clouds. The stately building resembled a church as much as it did a place for justice.

They parked in one of the many parking garages nearby, then walked the short distance to the court. Ellie noticed that Finn opened her car door, opened the garage's door, lightly took her elbow when they crossed a street. Such small gestures, but ones that Ellie appreciated. After all, this was a business deal. He didn't have to play the chivalrous man.

They went up the few stone steps to the entrance, with Finn stepping in front of her to open and hold the heavy courthouse door for her, too. "Thank you."

"It's the least I can do for my future wife."

She faltered at the word. She'd heard it twice already today, and still couldn't believe it was happening. "Are you planning on carrying me over the threshold, too?"

He paused. "We hadn't talked about that detail."

"Which one?"

"Where we're going to live after this."

The mirth left her. Oh, yeah.

She hadn't thought that far ahead. In fact, she'd just gone with this insane plan, clearly not thinking it through. The adoption agency would undoubtedly do its due diligence before signing off on Ellie's adoption. At the very least, they'd want a report from Linda on the living conditions.

It wouldn't take a genius to realize her marriage was a sham if she and new "husband" were living in separate homes. Ellie had never been much of an impetuous woman. Until today and now, she could lose it all by not thinking this through.

"We should live together," she said, all the while watching for his reaction, "or no one will believe it's real. We'll need people to believe we're together for more than just a business deal."

"We'll have to make it seem…real," he said.

"Yeah. We will."

Finn turned to her in the bright, expansive lobby.

People rushed around them, hurrying to courtrooms and offices, their shoes echoing on the marble floors, their voices carrying in the vast space.

But Ellie barely noticed. She stood in a world of only two, herself and the man who had agreed to marry her and in the process, change her life. And Jiao's, too.

"Maybe if people find out I eloped, it'll change their image of me as the Hawk."

She laughed. "And what, turn you into the Dove?"

"I don't think so." He chuckled. "I could get married at a drive-thru chapel in Vegas with Elvis as my best man and that still wouldn't be enough to do that."

"You never know. Marriage changes people. Relationships change them." Her voice was soft, her mind on one person a world away.

"Yes, I think it does. And not always for the better."

She wanted to ask him what he meant by that. Did he mean the ex-fiancée who had ruined his reputation? Or was he talking about something, someone else?

He cleared his throat. "You're right. Our marriage is going to need a measure of verisimilitude, and being in the same residence will do that. In addition, we can work on the hospital project after hours."

Even though Finn's voice was detached, almost clinical, the words *after hours* conjured up thoughts of very different nocturnal activities. Since the first time she'd spotted Finn in the ballroom of the Park Plaza, she'd been intrigued. She'd liked how he bucked convention by having a beer instead of wine, how he'd been so intent yet also charming. From a distance, she'd thought he was handsome. Up close, he was devastating. Her heart skipped a beat every time he smiled. Her traitorous mind flashed to images of Finn touching her, kissing her, making love to her—

Whoa. That was not part of the deal. At all. Keeping this platonic was the only—and best—way to ensure that she could walk away at the end. She didn't want to chance her heart on love, or risk her future with a relationship that could dissolve as easily as sugar in hot tea. Falling for him would only complicate everything.

And marrying him on the spur of the moment wasn't complicated? All of a sudden, a flutter of nerves threatened to choke her. Ellie opened her mouth to tell Finn this was crazy, she couldn't do this, when the door to the courthouse opened behind them and a slim, tall man hurried inside.

"Sorry I'm late. My day has been crazy." He chuckled. "As usual. Story of my life. And yours, too, huh, Finn?"

Finn patted the other man on the back and gave him a grin. "Charlie, how are you?"

"Just fine. Not as good as you, though. Running off to get married. You surprise me, old friend." He grinned, then put out a hand toward Ellie. "Judge Charlie Robinson, at your service."

Ellie gaped. "You said you had a friend in the courthouse. Not a judge."

"Charlie and I have been friends since we were kids. We roomed together at Harvard," Finn said, then shot Charlie a smirk. "To me, he's not a judge. He's the guy who sprayed whipped cream all over my room."

"Hey, I'm still pleading innocent to that one." Charlie raised his hands in a who-me gesture, but there was a twinkle in his eye.

Again, Ellie saw another side of Finn. A side that intrigued her, even as she pushed those thoughts away. She refused to fall for Finn. Now or later. She was here for a practical reason and no other.

Finn chuckled. "Well, we should get to it. I know you have a hectic day."

"No problem. I can always make time for a good friend, especially one who's getting married. So..." Charlie clapped his hands together. "You two kids ready to make this all legal and binding?"

Legal. Binding.

Now.

Ellie glanced at Finn. She could do this. She *had* to. There was no other way. Besides, it was a temporary marriage, nothing more than a piece of paper. But a union that would bring Jiao home and give Ellie the family she had always craved. She could do that, without getting her heart tangled in the process. "Yes," she said.

"Great." Charlie grinned again. "Okay, lovebirds, let's head up to my office and get you two hitched."

Finn turned to Ellie and put out his arm. "Are you ready to become Mrs. McKenna?"

Was she?

She lifted her gaze to Finn's blue eyes. She barely knew this man, but what she knew she liked. Respected. Trusted. Would that be enough?

She thought of Jiao again, and realized it would have to be. In the end, running WW would be fulfilling, but not nearly as fulfilling as coming home to Jiao's contagious smile and wide dark eyes.

"Why, Mr. McKenna, I can't think of another thing I'd rather do in the middle of the day." Then she linked her arm in Finn's and headed toward the judge's chambers.

CHAPTER FIVE

THE whole thing took only a few minutes—including Charlie's beginning jokes and closing quips. They called in his assistant and a court clerk to serve as witnesses, the two of them looking like they'd seen more than one impromptu wedding. Charlie thought they were getting married out of love, and in typical Charlie fashion, strove to make the event fun and memorable. Finn stumbled when Charlie asked him about rings, which Charlie racked up as bridegroom nerves. "I can't believe you, of all people, forgot a major detail like the rings," Charlie said. "No worries, but be sure you make it up to her later with a *lot* of diamonds," he said with a wink, then in the next breath pronounced them man and wife.

Man and wife. The words echoed in Finn's mind, bouncing around like a rubber ball. He'd done it. And no one was more surprised than Finn himself. He, the man who hadn't operated without a plan since he was writing his first research paper in fourth grade, had run off in the middle of the day and—

Eloped.

Holy cow. He'd really done it.

"And now for the best part," Charlie said, closing the book in his hands and laying it on his desk. "You may kiss your bride."

Finn stared at Charlie for a long second. Kiss the bride? He'd forgotten all about that part. He'd simply assumed a quick civil union in a courthouse would be devoid of all the flowers and romance part of a church wedding. "Uh, I don't know if we have to—"

Charlie laughed. "What, are you shy now? Go on, kiss her."

Finn considered refusing, but then thought better of it. Charlie would undoubtedly question a marriage where the groom didn't want to get close with his bride. And if they were going to pull off this fiction in front of their friends and colleagues, they needed to at least look the part. Finn turned to Ellie. Her green eyes were wide, her lips parted slightly. In shock? Anticipation?

She looked beautiful and delicious all at the same time in that simple daffodil-colored dress. In that instant, his reservations disappeared, replaced by a fast, hot surge of want. No, it was more than desire, it was a…craving for whatever inner happiness was lighting Ellie's features.

She stood there, looking as hesitant as he felt. A faint blush colored her cheeks, disappeared beneath her long blond hair. She looked like a bride—pretty, breathless, yet at the same time she possessed a simmering sensuality. He wanted her, even as he reminded himself this was a purely platonic union.

There would be no kisses. No lovemaking. Nothing but this moment. And right now, Finn didn't want to let this moment pass.

Her gaze met his and a curious tease filled the emerald depths. "Well, Mr. McKenna, are you going to do as the nice judge says?"

"I would never disobey a judge," Finn said, his voice low, hoarse. Just between them. Charlie, the witnesses, hell, the entire world ceased to exist.

He closed the gap between them, reached a hand to cup her jaw. Electricity crackled in the air, in the touch. A breath extended between them, another. Ellie's chest rose, fell. Her dark pink lips parted, her deep green eyes widened, and her light floral perfume teased at his senses, luring him closer, closer.

Damn, he wanted her. He'd wanted her from the minute he'd met her.

With one kiss he'd seal this marriage. But was that all this kiss was about? This moment?

No. He knew, deep in his gut, that there was something else happening here, something he wasn't sure he wanted or needed in his life. He could have been standing at the edge of a cliff, ready to plunge—

Into the cushion of water, or the danger of rocks? He didn't know.

All he could feel was this insistent *want*. For her. For just one taste. He lowered his mouth to hers, and at the instant that his lips met hers, he knew.

Knew that kissing Ellie was going to change everything.

Her lips were sweet and soft beneath his, her hair a silky tickle against his fingers. She leaned into him for one long, blissful second, and he inhaled, drawing in the scent of her, memorizing it, capturing the moment in Technicolor in his mind.

Ellie.

Then she drew back and the kiss was over, nearly as quickly as it began. The flush in her cheeks had deepened to a light crimson. Her gaze met his for one hot, electric second, then she looked away, and turned back to Charlie.

Platonic. Business relationship. The heady rush gone.

He told himself he was glad. That it was exactly what he wanted.

"There. It's official now." Charlie grinned, then he reached out and shook hands with both of them. The witnesses murmured their congratulations before slipping out the door. "Congratulations," Charlie said. "May you have an abundance of happiness and children."

Children. Or, rather, a single child. Half the reason they'd embarked on this fake union. Finn glanced over at Ellie, but her gaze was on the window, not on him, hiding whatever she might have thought about Charlie's words.

A few minutes later, they left the courthouse, a newly minted marriage license in hand. The paper weighed nothing, but felt heavier than a concrete block.

Married. To a near stranger.

A stranger whose kiss had awakened a roaring desire inside Finn. He had thought he was doing this just for business reasons, but that kiss was as far from business as the earth was from the moon. And he needed to remember his uppermost goal.

Don't get involved. Don't fall for her. Don't lose track of the priority. Don't get swept up in a tsunami that would leave him worse off in the end.

As they walked down the street toward the parking garage, Finn dug his car keys out of his pocket, then paused. They were married. And that meant the occasion, even if it was merely a professional alliance, deserved some kind of celebration. "How about we get some dinner before we head back to Boston?"

"I should probably get back to work. I left in the middle of my day and have a lot on my To Do list." She stepped to the side to allow a quartet of lunch workers to power past them. "But thanks for the offer."

His To Do list was probably just as long, but for the first time in a long time, Finn didn't want to go back to his office, didn't feel like sitting behind that mahogany desk, even as the sensible side of him mounted a vigorous objection. "It's not every day you get married, you know. We should at least have a glass of wine to celebrate. Or iced tea for you. I'll have the wine."

"Don't you have work to get to, too?"

"Always. But it's waited this long. It can wait a little longer. Regardless of why we got married, this is a big moment for both of us." He grinned. "Don't you agree?"

It was Finn's smile that swayed Ellie. There was something…disarming about the way Finn McKenna smiled. He had a crooked smile, curving up higher on one side of his face than the other. She liked that. Liked the way nothing about him was exactly what you would expect.

Neither was his kiss. She'd thought that he would just give her a perfunctory peck on the lips, a token gesture to seal the deal. But he'd done so much more. Kissed her in a way she hadn't been kissed in forever.

Their kiss had been short, but tender. When he'd touched her jaw, he'd done it almost reverently, his fingers drifting over her cheek, tangling in her hair. He'd leaned in, captured her gaze and waited long enough for her heart to begin to race with anticipation before he'd kissed her. When had a man ever taken such time for something so simple?

It left her wondering what it would be like to really be Finn's wife. Would he kiss her like that at the end of every day? Before he left for work in the morning? For just a moment, she wanted to hold on to that fantasy, to believe that this was real, and not just a means to an end.

Even if it was.

Finn was right—it wasn't every day that she got married, and she wasn't sure she was quite ready to go back to her ordinary world, and all the questions this was bound to raise. They still had to settle on their story, and deal with other practical issues, like where they were going to live afterward.

Whatever little thrill she might have felt faded in the light of reality. This wasn't a date, it wasn't a celebration. It was business, pure and simple.

And nothing more.

"You did what?" The shock in Riley's voice boomed across the phone connection. *"You got married?"*

"Uh, yeah, but it's not…" Finn was about to tell Riley it wasn't a real marriage, then he glanced across the sidewalk at Ellie, standing in the shadowed circle beneath an oak tree. She was talking into her cell phone with someone at her office, her hand moving to punctuate her words. Little bits of sunshine dappled her blond hair, kissed her delicate features and gave her a slight glow.

He had seen hundreds of beautiful women in his lifetime, but none that had that whole package of incredible looks and incredible personality. The kind of woman any man in his right mind would be proud to call his wife.

Except, this was merely a way to resurrect his business. Besides, he didn't need the complication of a relationship, the heady distraction of a romance. He liked his life as straight as a ruler. And he'd continue to keep it that way.

"It's unexpected, is what it is," Riley finished for him. "What were you thinking?"

"I wasn't." That was true. He'd thought he was challenging her offer, then once they were standing in front of Charlie, he'd stopped thinking about the pros and cons of what he was about to do and just…done it. Eloped. He, of all people. He hadn't thought about the incongruity of that when he was in Charlie's office. All he'd seen was Ellie's smile.

"I thought you were all antimarriage. Especially after the Lucy thing."

"I was. I am. This was…" Finn paused. "Different."

"Well, congratulations, brother," Riley said. "You'll be all the talk at the next family reunion."

Finn chuckled. "I'm sure I will be as soon as you get off the phone and call Brody. You spread gossip faster than a church picnic."

Riley laughed with him. "So, where are you guys going on your honeymoon?"

The word *honeymoon* conjured up images of Ellie's lithe, beautiful body beside his. He glanced at her across the way from him, and didn't see the daffodil-yellow dress, but instead saw her on some beach somewhere. Her skin warmed from the sun, all peaches and cream and pressed against him. Taking things far beyond a simple kiss in the judge's chambers.

Damn. That was not productive. At all. He shook his head, but the images stayed, chased by the memory of kissing her. The scent of her perfume. The feel of her in his arms.

Again, he forced them away and tore his gaze away from Ellie.

He'd come close to that kind of craziness when he'd dated Lucy. Granted, most of their relationship had been practical, staid…predictable. Then he'd had that moment of insanity when he'd rushed out to buy a ring, run over to her office to propose—

And found out she was stealing his clients behind his back.

No more of that. He'd gone off the rails for five minutes, and it nearly destroyed his business and his career. A smart man approached marriage like any other business deal—with clarity, sense and caution.

"Uh, we don't really have time for that right now," Finn said, reminding himself that there would be no honeymoon. Not now, not later. "Work schedules, meetings, that kind of thing gets in the way of the best laid plans, you know?" He made light of it because for some reason, he couldn't bring himself to tell Riley the whole thing was a temporary state. That most likely by the time their schedules opened up enough that they could plan a joint vacation, they would be filing for divorce.

"You *are* going to celebrate at least a little, aren't you? I mean, if any occasion screams having a party, this is it." Riley paused a second. "Hmm...I wonder if it's too late to throw you a bachelor party?"

"I don't need one of those, and yes, it is too late." Finn shifted the phone in his grasp. "Actually that's why I called you. I was thinking of taking her out for drinks and dinner. But..."

"You realized that idea sounds about as lame as a picnic in the park?"

"Hey!" Then Finn lowered his voice. "What's lame about a picnic?"

Riley laughed. "Don't tell me. That was your second idea."

Finn didn't want to admit that it had actually been his first idea, but then he'd thought about bugs and sunshine, and proposed a restaurant instead. Damn. He was a hell of a lot rustier at this dating game than he'd thought. Not that this was a date—at all—just his effort to make this business alliance a little more palatable. "It's a nice day. We could grab some sandwiches—"

"Last I checked, you don't get married every day. So

don't do an everyday thing to celebrate it. Here's what I would do," Riley said, then detailed a plan for Finn that far surpassed anything Finn had thought of. A few minutes later, Riley said goodbye and Finn ended the call. At the same time, Ellie tucked her phone away and crossed to Finn.

"Sorry about that," she said. "Duty calls."

Finn chuckled. "Believe me, I understand. It calls me all the time, day and night." At the same moment, Finn's phone began to ring. He fished it out of his pocket, about to answer, when Ellie laid a hand on top of his.

"Don't." Her fingers danced lightly across his, an easy, delicate touch, but one that sent a shock wave running down his arm. "Let's put our phones away. I don't want to deal with work for now."

"Me, either." He pressed the power button, turned the phone off, then slipped it into his jacket pocket. "Besides, I have plans for you, Mrs. McKenna."

Her eyes widened at the use of her married name. "Plans? What kind of plans?"

"You'll see," he said, then said a little prayer that he could execute Riley's plans as well as his brother would have. Because just for today, Finn wanted to woo the woman who was now his wife.

Tomorrow was soon enough to get back to business— and stay there. For as long as this practical, contracted arrangement lasted.

How he'd done it, Ellie didn't know. She stared in wonder at the tableau laid out before her. Chubby terra cotta pots held thick, lush flowering shrubs, lit from above by soft torch lights on bronze poles. A pair of squat white wicker chairs with fluffy striped cushions flanked either side of a matching table, already set for dinner with floral plates and crystal wine goblets. Candles flickered in the soft breeze, dropping a blanket of golden light over everything.

The sun had started setting, casting Boston's skyline in a soft purple glow. Lights twinkled in the distance, while the red and green bow lights of passing boats dotted the harbor.

She'd had no idea that Finn had been planning this while they were riding back from Providence. Or how. They had kept their phones off, as agreed, and spent the hour of travel talking about everything and nothing—from growing up in the city to the challenges of architectural design in a world going green.

She'd learned that Finn hated spinach but loved the Red Sox, that he had his one and only B in seventh grade Science and that his first job had been delivering newspapers. She'd told him that her favorite food was cake, and that she'd been the last on her block to learn to ride a bike. She told him about the time she'd gotten lost in the train station and the day she got her braces.

It was the most she'd shared with anyone in a long, long time, and it had felt nice. Then the car pulled up in front of Finn's building and Finn had turned to her and said, "All those details should really help when we meet with the adoption people," and Ellie had been reminded that her marriage was nothing more than a sham.

If that was so, why had Finn gone to all this trouble to set up such a romantic tableau?

"How…when…" She let out a breath. "This is incredible, Finn."

He grinned. "Thank you."

"How did you do it?"

"Remember that rest stop we went to on the way back from Rhode Island?"

She nodded.

"I made a few phone calls while you were…indisposed."

"A few fast phone calls. And clearly productive."

"I'm a man who likes to get things done." He reached for her hand, and she let that happen, wondering when touching Finn had become so easy or if she was just telling herself it was to preserve the mood, and then they walked forward onto the private terrace of his building, temporarily transformed into an outdoor dining room.

Just as Finn pulled out her chair, music began, a soft jazz floating from an unseen sound system. A waiter emerged from a door at the side, bearing a tray with water glasses and a carafe filled with two bottles—one a chilled white wine, the other a sparkling grape juice. He placed the water glasses on the table with merely a nod toward Ellie, then uncorked the wine and juice, pouring Ellie's nonalcoholic version first, then Finn's wine, before disappearing back through the door again. Finn had remembered she didn't drink, and had clearly put a lot of time and thought into the entire evening. Why?

He raised his glass and tilted it toward her. "To… partnership."

"Partnership," she echoed, and ignored the flutter of disappointment in her gut. In the end, they would go their separate ways, and for that, Ellie was glad. She didn't need the complication of dating Finn, of a relationship. Just enough information and time with him to effectively pretend…

Pretend they were in love. "And to business," she added, for herself as much as him. "Only."

CHAPTER SIX

The glint of gold caught Finn's eye before he was fully awake. It took a second before he remembered why he had a ring on his left hand. And why he was waking up in a room he didn't recognize.

Last night. Marrying Ellie Winston. The rooftop dinner. The rings he'd given them—purchased earlier that evening by his assistant and delivered to the terrace before they arrived—so the two of them had the outward evidence of a marriage.

Then, after a dinner that alternated between tense and friendly, bringing her to her townhouse, and by mutual agreement, he'd spent the night. In the guest room.

Of his *wife's* home.

From outside the room, he heard the sound of music. Something upbeat…a current pop hit. He got out of bed, pulled on a pair of sweatpants from the bag he'd brought with him and padded out to the kitchen. Everything about Ellie's townhome was like her—clean, neat, bright. Lots of whites and yellows with accents of blue. It was the complete opposite of his heavy oak, dark carpet apartment. Softer, more feminine. Nice.

Ellie was standing at the kitchen sink, her hips swaying in time to the music as she filled a carafe with water. She was already dressed for work in a pale blue skirt and a short-sleeved white sweater. Her hair was curled, the tendrils curving over her shoulders and down her back in tantalizing spirals. Her feet were bare, and for some reason, that made him feel like he was intruding. It was such an unguarded, at-home kind of thing.

And oh, so intimate.

In the light of day, the reality of moving in with Ellie presented a bit of a dilemma. Like how he was going to resist her when she was right there every day, in bare feet, humming along to the radio. How was he going to pretend he hadn't felt anything with that kiss in the courthouse?

Because he did. He'd thought about it all last night, tossing and turning, a thousand percent aware she was also in bed, and mere feet down the hall. He'd made a concerted effort to keep their celebratory dinner more like a board meeting than a date, but still, a part of him had kept replaying that kiss. And had been craving another.

Hadn't he learned his lesson already? Getting distracted by a relationship left him vulnerable. Made him make mistakes, like nearly marrying someone who wanted only to destroy him. He saw where that kind of foolishness got a person—and it wasn't a path he wanted to travel.

So he forced his gaze away from her bare feet and her tantalizing curves, and cleared his throat. "Good morning."

She spun around, and nearly dropped the carafe. "Finn. Oh, hi. I almost forgot…" A flush filled her face. "Good morning. Do you want some coffee?"

"Yes. Please."

She busied herself with setting up the pot, then turning it on. When she was done, she pivoted back to him.

"I'm sorry I don't have much for breakfast. I'm usually running out the door with a muffin in my hand."

"A muffin's fine. Really. This whole…thing was unexpected." His gaze kept straying back to the ring on her hand. He was now the husband of Ellie Winston. No… Ellie McKenna.

Just a few days ago he'd been thinking how he wanted a relationship without any drama. One based solely on common interests, none of that silly romantic stuff that clouded his brain and muddled his thinking. Now, he had that—

And for some reason, it disappointed him like hell.

What was he thinking? He didn't need the crazy romantic notion of love. He needed something steady, dependable, as predictable as the columns in his general ledger. The problem was, there was a part of Ellie that Finn suspected, no, knew, was far from predictable. And that was dangerous.

The song shifted from pop to a ballad. The love song filled the room, stringing tension between them.

"I have, uh, blueberry and banana nut." She waved toward the breadbox. "Muffins, I mean."

He took a step farther into the kitchen. The walls were a butter-yellow, the cabinets a soft white. No clutter that he could see, merely a few things that added personality—a hand-painted ceramic bowl teeming with fruit, a deep green vase filled with fresh daisies, and a jade sculpture of a dragon, probably picked up in China. It seemed to suit her, this eclectic, homey mix.

Beside him, the coffeepot percolated with a steady drip-drip. The sun streamed in through the windows, showering those curls, those tantalizing curls, with gold. He wanted to reach up, capture one of those curls in his palm. "I'd love one."

"Which?"

It took him a second to realize she meant which flavor, not which he wanted—her or the muffins. "Blueberry, please."

"Sure." She pivoted away, fast. The breadbox door raised with a rattle. Ellie tugged out the plastic container holding the muffins, then spun back. The package tumbled out of her grasp and dropped to the floor. Muffins tumbled end over end and spun away, spinning a trail of crumbs. Ellie cursed.

Finn bent down, at the same time Ellie did, to reach for the runaway muffins. They knocked shoulders and Finn drew back. When had he become so clumsy? This wasn't his usual self. "Sorry."

"It's okay, it's my fault." She reached for the muffin closest to them, at the same time he did. Their hands brushed. She staggered to her feet, nearly toppling, and reached out a hand to steady herself. It connected with his bare chest, just a brief second, before she yanked her palm away.

A jolt of electricity ran through Finn. His gaze jerked to her face. Ellie's eyes were wide, her lips parted. "Sorry," he said again.

"No, I am." She looked away from him, back at the floor. "I can make toast, if you prefer."

Toast? Muffins? Had she been affected at all by that accidental touch? "I'm not hungry. I should get to work."

Yes, get to work, get to the office and get on with his day. Rather than indulge in any more of this craziness. Get his head clear—and back on straight.

"I'll clean this up," she said, gesturing to the mess on the floor. "If you want to hop in the shower and get ready."

"Sure, sure." He dumped the crumbs in his hand into the trash, then turned to go.

"Finn?"

His name rolled off her tongue, soft, easy. For a second, he wondered what it would be like to hear her say his name every day. Every morning. Every night. He turned back to face her, taking in those wide green eyes, the sweet smile that curved across her face, and yes, those bare feet. "Yeah?"

She shot him a grin. "Coffee's ready."

Coffee's ready.

A heavy blanket of disappointment hung over Finn while he got ready. Hell, what had he expected her to say? Stay? Kiss me? Take me back to the bedroom?

No, he didn't want that. He wanted exactly what he had—a platonic relationship that let him focus on work and didn't send his head, or his world, into a tailspin.

Except the image of Ellie in her kitchen, swaying to the music and doing something so mundane as making coffee, kept coming back to his mind. He had lived alone for too long, that was all. That was why the sight of her affected him so much.

He got ready, then headed out the door, leaving Ellie a note that he had to stop by his office and would meet her at WW later. He knew it was the coward's way out, but he'd been thrown by waking up in her place. It was all moving so fast, and he told himself he just needed some time to adjust.

Later that morning, he was heading up to the tenth floor of the building housing WW Architects, flanked by Noel and Barry, two of his best architects, who'd met him in the lobby. The team Finn brought in had been part of the bidding process, and was already familiar with the Piedmont hospital project, so the trio exchanged small talk until they reached Ellie's floor. A few minutes later, an assistant led them to a conference room where the WW staff had already assembled. Ellie stood at the head of the table. Her curly blond hair was now tucked into a tight bun, the bare feet were clad in sensible black pumps, and her curvy figure hidden beneath a jacket that turned the blue skirt into a suit.

She was all business now. Exactly what he wanted.

Then why did he feel a sense of loss?

"Thank you for coming today, gentlemen." Ellie made the introductions between her team and Finn's. Finn headed to the front of the room to stand beside Ellie. "Before we get started, we...I mean, Finn and I, have an announcement."

She exchanged a look with Finn. He nodded. They had talked about this last night, and decided the best way to spread the news was fast and first. "We...Ellie and I... we got *married*."

Jaws dropped. People stared.

"You got married?" Larry asked. "As in...married?"

"Last night." Ellie nodded and smiled, the kind of smile that reached deep into her eyes, lit up her features. Just like the smile of a happy new bride. "It was an impromptu thing."

"You married her?" Noel scowled at Finn. "Is *that* why we're working together?"

Finn wasn't about to tell their employees the real reason he had married Ellie. If he did, it would taint the project. No, let them all think it was some act of passion. Cover up the truth with a lie.

A lie that a part of Finn wished was true. The part that was still thinking about coffee with Ellie and seeing her in the kitchen. "Not at all. Working together is just a...

fringe benefit," Finn said. "Ellie and I agreed to merge our companies for this project. After that, we go back to being separate entities."

Ellie leaned in and grabbed his arm. That same jolt of electricity rushed through his veins. "Separate business entities at least." She grinned up at him and for a half a second, he could almost believe she loved him. Damn, she was good at this.

"*You* eloped last night?" Noel let out a little a laugh. "I don't believe it. I'm sorry, Finn, but I just don't see you as the eloping kind."

Explaining that the practical, methodical Finn they all knew had done just that was suddenly much harder than he'd expected. "Well, I...I..."

"Blame it on me," Ellie said, pressing her head to his arm. "I didn't want the fanfare of a big event, and so I told Finn, let's just run to the courthouse and get it done. Then we can all get back to work." She peered up at him, her eyes soft and warm. "We'll take that honeymoon a little later."

"Uh...yeah," he said, his thoughts running rampant down the path of what a honeymoon with Ellie would be like. When she was looking at him like that, he could almost believe this was real. That at the end of the day, they were heading back to a little house in the suburbs with a fence and a dog and a dinner on the stove. And more—much, much more—after the dishes were done and the lights were dimmed. "We're, uh, planning on leaving as soon as this project is done."

"Well, then congratulations are in order," John said. He shook with Finn, then Ellie. "Best of luck to both of you." The rest of the group echoed John's sentiments. They congratulated, they shook and they beamed. And Ellie pulled the whole thing off with nary a blink.

"Okay, back to work. We have a major project ahead of us, and not a lot of time," Ellie said. "So as much as we'd love to take time for a celebration, we need to dive in and work until we have the particulars hammered out."

Larry, one of Ellie's architects, grumbled under his breath, but didn't voice any objections. The rest of the team seemed to be giving Finn's people the benefit of the doubt. "I appreciate you bringing us in on this project, Ellie," Finn said, rising to address the group. "I'm confident that by combining the experience of both McKenna Designs and WW Architectural Design, we can create a hospital that will outshine all others in the New England area."

Ellie shot him a smile. "That's our goal, too." She opened the folder before her. "Okay, let's get to work. Piedmont wants this design to be groundbreaking. One of the key elements that sold them on WW as the architects was our innovative approach. Rather than basing the design on existing models, WW talked about approaching the design process from the patient's perspective, from admission through discharge. The challenge is to create an environment that creates a healing atmosphere, one that offers warmth with minimal noise, while also keeping patient safety as the top priority."

"Excellent ideas," Finn said, nodding to Ellie.

"Thank you. Although I have to admit that one of the challenges we are having is creating that warm, healing atmosphere. WW specializes in corporate buildings, which aren't usually described as cozy." Ellie gestured toward Finn and his team. "I think if we combine our expertise in the safety arena, with yours in environment, we'll have a winner."

"I agree." Finn sketched out a drawing on the pad before him, then turned it toward Ellie and the others.

"We'll design standardized rooms, where every medical element is in the same place, no matter what floor or wing, yet also give each room its own flair. Install ambient lighting in addition to the harsher lighting needed for procedures, and soundproof the space so patients aren't bothered by constant pages and hallway traffic. Studies have shown that a warmer, quieter space speeds patient healing." Finn filled in another section of the drawing, sketching in fast movements, limited in details, focused on getting the bare bones on the page first. "We should also provide a small visiting area in each room for family members. Nothing huge, but something far superior in comfort and flexibility to the current models in today's hospitals."

"What about pricing? That kind of thing is going to raise the costs." Larry scowled. "Piedmont will not be happy."

"Easy," Finn said. "We call the vendors and tell them that they're going to be part of a groundbreaking new hospital. One that will have plenty of media coverage. They'll be jumping at the opportunity to be a part of that, and be very amenable to lowering their pricing."

"In other words, beat them up until they cave?" Larry said.

"I think it's a good strategy," Ellie said. "Thanks, Finn." She clapped her hands together and faced the room. "Okay, what else?"

As if a wall had been dismantled, the room erupted with ideas, people from both teams exchanging and brainstorming, no longer separated into an "us" and "them," but becoming one cohesive unit, brimming with creativity. Ellie got to her feet and jotted the ideas on the whiteboard behind her, quickly covering the wall-length space. Finn pulled out his computer to take notes, his fingers moving rapidly over the keys of his laptop. It occurred to him somewhere into the first hour that he and Ellie made a good team. Neither tried to outtalk the other or prove their idea the best. Their thoughts seemed to merge, with her suggesting one thought, and him finishing it. He was so used to being the one in charge, the one who had to pull the team together and take the lead, that suddenly sharing the job was...nice. When the group broke for lunch, Finn stayed behind in the room.

"We work well together," he said, rising and crossing to Ellie. He picked up a second eraser and helped her clean off the whiteboard.

She smiled. "We do indeed."

Out in the hall, the team was whispering and exchanging glances in the direction of the conference room. "Seems we've got people talking," Finn said.

"It was bound to happen. Though I thought we'd have a little more time to..."

"Work out our story?"

"Yeah. We should have talked about it more last night. I really didn't think that part through."

"Me, either. I was too focused on work."

She laughed. "I know what you mean. That's how my days have been, too." She moved away from him, then stretched, working out the kinks in her back. He was tempted to offer her a massage, but instead he kept his hands at his side. A massage was definitely not part of this...partnership.

"You pulled it off well," Finn said. "Hell, even I believed..."

She cocked her head. "Believed what?"

"That you were wildly in love with me."

She laughed, and that told him that there was no doubt she'd been acting earlier. Finn told himself he was glad.

"Well, I'm glad it worked. Anyway, I guess I'll see you back here in a little while."

"Wait. Do you have lunch plans?" he asked, then wondered what he was doing. Was he asking her on a date—a date with his wife—or a simple lunch meeting to discuss the project? He told himself it was just because people would expect them to eat together. He was keeping up the facade, nothing more.

"I have one of those frozen dinners in the office refrigerator." She gave him an apologetic smile. "I usually eat at my desk."

"So do I." Outside the sun shone bright and hazy, a warm day with the promising scent of spring in the air. Inside, all they had was climate controlled air and a sterile office environment. The same kind of place where he spent five, sometimes six, days a week. He thought of the calls waiting to be returned, the emails waiting to be answered, the projects waiting to be completed. Then he looked at Ellie, and wanted only a few minutes with her, just long enough to hear her laugh again, see her smile. Then he'd be ready to go back to the To Do lists and other people's expectations. "Let's go have lunch on the plaza. Get out of here for a while. I think both of us have spent far too many afternoons at our desks."

"Two days in a row, taking time off? My, my, Finn, whatever will people say?"

Damn. He was really starting to like the way she said his name. "Oh, I think we've already given them plenty to talk about, don't you?"

She looked up at him, and a smile burst across her face. It sent a rush through Finn, and he decided that if he did nothing else, he would make Ellie smile again. And again.

"Oh my, yes, I do believe we've done that in spades,

Mr. McKenna." Then her green eyes lit with a tease and she put her hand in his. "What's a little more?"

As time ticked by and the afternoon sun made a slow march across the sky, Ellie was less and less able to concentrate on her sandwich or anything Finn was saying. On her way into work that morning, Ellie had called Linda and left her a message telling her that she had gotten married, and now the wait for Linda's return call seemed agonizing. Thank God for the meeting, which had taken her mind off the wait, and for Finn, who had convinced her to leave the office and get some fresh air. Still, she had checked her cell at least a dozen times.

Finn had taken two calls, and she'd been impressed with the way he handled business. Efficiently, with barely a wasted word. He argued with a contractor who wanted to make a change that Finn felt would compromise the building's structure, and negotiated a lower price on materials for another project.

"I can see where you got the nickname," Ellie said when Finn hung up. "You're relentless."

"I just like to get the job done."

"Yeah, but negotiating a discount, while at the same time moving up the deadline, I'd say you pulled off a miracle."

"Just doing my job." He seemed embarrassed by her attention.

"You do it well. Does that come from being the oldest?"

"I don't know. I guess I never thought about that. Maybe it does."

"Well, it seems to be working for you." She felt her phone buzz and checked the screen, then tucked it away.

"Waiting on a call yourself?"

She nodded. "From the agency. I told my adoption co-ordinator that we got married. I'm just waiting to hear back."

He unwrapped the sandwich they had bought from a street vendor, but didn't take a bite. "How are you planning on doing this?"

"Doing what? The interview? It should be relatively straightforward."

"No, not that. This whole—" he made a circle with the sandwich "—raising a child alone thing."

"People do it every day."

"Not people who also happen to be CEOs of busy, growing companies."

"True." She glanced at the park across the street. It bustled with activity. Children ran to and fro, filling the small park with the sound of laughter. Dogs chased Frisbees and couples picnicked on the grass. "I'm sure it's going to be hard." That was an understatement. She'd worried constantly that she wouldn't be able to juggle it all. "But I'll figure it out somehow."

"Would it have been better if you had waited to marry someone who could...well, create a real family with you?" Finn asked.

Ellie watched a family of three pass by them, mother and father on either side of a toddler, who held both his parent's hands and danced between them. "Maybe. But honestly, I never intended to get married."

"Ever?"

"I guess I was always afraid to get married," Ellie said softly.

"Afraid? Of what?"

"Of being a disappointment and of getting my children caught in an endless limbo of...dissatisfaction." Ellie sighed. "I looked at my parents, and they were more roommates than spouses. They came and went on their own schedules, and we very rarely did anything as a family. I guess I never felt like I knew how to do it better."

"I think a lot of people feel that way," Finn said after a moment.

"Do you?"

He let out a short laugh. "When did this become about me?"

"I'm just curious. You seem the kind of man who would want to settle down. Complete that life list or whatever."

"Yeah, well, I'm not." He got to his feet and tossed the remains of his sandwich in the trash.

He had shut the door between them. She had opened herself to him, and he had refused to do the same. The distance stung.

Ellie glanced at the family across the park. They had stopped walking and were sitting on the grass, sharing a package of cookies. The mother teased the son with a cookie that she placed in his palm, then yanked back, making him giggle. Over and over again they played that game, and the little boy's laughter rang like church bells.

A bone-deep ache ran through her. Deep down inside, yes, she did want that, did crave those moments, that togetherness. She'd always thought she didn't, but she'd been lying to herself.

She watched Finn return to the bench and realized she wasn't going to find that fairy tale with the Hawk. He was going about their marriage like he did any other business deal—with no emotion and no personal ties.

It was what she had wanted. But now that she had it, victory tasted stale.

Because a part of her had already started to get very, very used to him being her husband.

CHAPTER SEVEN

An hour on the treadmill. A half hour with the weight machines. And a hell of a sweat.

But it wasn't enough. No matter how much time Finn spent in the gym, tension still knotted his shoulders, frustration still held tight to his chest. He'd been unable to forget Ellie—or bring himself to go home to her.

Home. To his wife.

Already he was getting far too wrapped up in her, he'd realized. They'd had that conversation at lunch about marriage, and he had found himself wanting to tell her that he felt the same way. That he had never imagined himself getting married, either.

Then he had come to his senses before he laid his heart bare again, and made the same mistakes he'd made before. He'd watched his parents locked in an emotional roller coaster of love and hate, then repeated those mistakes at the end of his relationship with Lucy. No way was he going to risk that again with Ellie. She saw him as a means to an end—a father on paper for her child—and nothing more.

He pulled on the lat bar, leaning back slightly on the padded bench, hauling the weights down. His shoulders protested, his biceps screamed, but Finn did another rep. Another. Over and over, he tugged the heavy weight down.

It wasn't just the distraction of getting close to Ellie that had him sweating it out in the gym. It was the growing reality of the child she was about to adopt.

No, that *they* were about to adopt. He'd promised Ellie that he would go along with her plan, but now he was wondering if that was the right thing to do.

How could he be a temporary husband, temporary dad, and then, at the end of the hospital project, just pack up his things and go? If anyone knew firsthand what losing a parent suddenly could do to a child, it was Finn. He'd gone through it himself, and watched the impact on his younger brothers. They'd been cast adrift, emotional wrecks who took years to heal, even with the loving arms of their grandparents. How could he knowingly do that to a child?

He gave the lat bar another pull, his muscles groaning in protest, then lowered the weight back to the base. He was finished with his workout, but no closer to any of the answers he needed.

He showered, got dressed in jeans and a T-shirt, then hailed a cab and headed across town toward Ellie's townhouse. Night had begun to fall, draping purple light over the city of Boston. It was beautiful, the kind of clear, slightly warm night that would be perfect for a walk. Except Finn never took time to do that. He wondered for a moment what his life would be like if he was the kind of man who did.

If he was the kind of man who had a real marriage, and spent his life with someone who wanted to stroll down the city streets as dusk was falling and appreciate the twinkling magic. But he wasn't. And he was foolish to believe in a fantasy life. His mother had been like that—full of romantic notions that burned out when she saw the reality of her unhappy marriage. Finn was going to be clearheaded about his relationships. No banking on superfluous things like starry skies and red roses.

He paid the cabbie, then headed up the stairs to Ellie's building. He paused at the door and caught her name on the intercom box. Ellie Winston.

His wife.

Already, he knew they had a connection. It wasn't friendship, but something more, something indefinable. A hundred times during the meeting today, he found his mind wandering, his gaze drifting to her. He wondered a hundred things about her—what her favorite color was, if she preferred spring or fall, if she slept on the left side of the bed or the right. Even as he told himself to pull back, to not get any deeper connected to this woman than he already was. This was a business arrangement.

Nothing more.

As he headed inside, he marveled again at the building she had chosen—the complete opposite to the modern glass high-rise that housed his apartment. Ellie lived in one of Boston's many converted brownstones. Ellie's building sported a neat brick facade and window boxes filled with pansies doing a tentative wave to spring adorned every window. The building's lobby featured a white tile floor and thick, dark woodwork. The staircase was flanked by a curved banister on one side, a white plaster wall on the other. A bank of mailboxes were stationed against one wall, lit from above by a black wrought-iron light fixture that looked older than Finn's grandmother, but had a certain Old World charm.

He liked this place. A lot. It had a...homey feeling. At the same time, he cautioned himself not to get too comfortable. They weren't making this a permanent thing, and letting himself feel at home would be a mistake. He'd get used to it, and begin to believe this was something that it wasn't. He'd fooled himself like that once before.

Never again.

He found Ellie in the kitchen again, rinsing some dishes and loading them into the dishwasher. "Hi."

Kind of a lame opening but what did one say to a wife who wasn't a real wife?

She turned around. "Hi yourself. I'm sorry, I ate without you. I wasn't sure what your plan…" She put up her hands. "Well, you certainly don't have to answer to me. It's not like we're really married or anything."

There. The truth of it.

"I grabbed a bite to eat after the gym." He dropped his gym bag on the floor, then hung his dry cleaning over the chair. "Did you find out when the interview would be?"

"In a couple days. Linda's trying to coordinate all the schedules."

"Okay. Good." The sooner the interview was over, the sooner they could go their separate ways. And that was what he wanted, wasn't it?

"After this morning, I think we should work on our story," she said. "You know, in case they ask us a lot of questions. I don't want it to seem like…"

"We barely know each other."

She nodded. "Yes." She gestured toward a door at the back. "We can sit on the balcony out back if you want. It's not a rooftop terrace, but we'll be able to enjoy the evening a little."

They got drinks—red wine for him, iced tea for her— and Ellie assembled a little platter of cheese and crackers. Finn would have never thought of a snack, or if he had, it probably would have been something salty, served straight from the bag. But Ellie laid everything out on a long red platter, and even included napkins. The night air drifted over them, lazy and warm. "You thought of everything,"

She shrugged. "Nothing special. And it's not quite the evening you planned."

"No, it's not." He picked up a cracker and a piece of cheese, and devoured them in one bite. "It's better."

She laughed. "How is that? There's no musicians, no twinkling lights, no five-course meal. It's just crackers and cheese on the balcony."

"Done by you. Not by others. I don't have that home-making touch. At all."

"I'm not exactly Betty Crocker myself. But I can assemble a hell of a crudités platter." She laughed again. "So I take it you can't cook?"

"Not so much as a scrambled egg. But I can order takeout like a pro. My grandmother is the real chef in the family. She doesn't cook much now, but when I was a kid, she did everything from scratch."

Ellie picked up her glass and took a sip of tea. "Where are you parents? Do they live in Boston?"

The question was an easy one, the kind people asked each other all the time. But for some reason, this time, it hit Finn hard and he had to take a minute to compose the answer.

"No. They don't. Not anymore." Finn was quiet for a moment. "My parents…died in a car accident, when I was eleven. Brody was eight, Riley was just six."

"Oh, Finn, I'm so sorry." She reached for him, and laid a soft hand on top of his arm. It was a simple, comforting touch, but it seemed to warm Finn to his core. He wanted to lean into that touch, to let it warm the icy spots in his heart.

But he didn't.

"We went and lived with my grandparents," he continued. "I think us three boys drove my grandmother nuts with all our noise and fighting."

"I bet you three were a handful."

He chuckled. "She called us a basketful of trouble, but she loved us. My grandmother was a stern, strict parent, but one who would surprise us at the oddest times with a new toy or a bunch of cookies."

Ellie smiled. "She sounds wonderful."

"She is. I think every kid needs a grandmother like that. One time, Brody and I were arguing over a toy. I can't remember what toy it was or why. So my grandmother made us rake two ends of the yard, working toward each other. By the time we met in the middle, we had this massive pile of leaves. So we jumped in them. And the fight was forgotten."

Ellie laughed. "Sounds like you learned some of your art of compromise from her."

"Yeah, I guess I did. She taught me a lot." He hadn't shared that much of his personal life with anyone in a long, long time. Even Lucy hadn't known much about him. They'd mainly talked about work when they were together.

Was that because she didn't care, or because it was easier? Or was it because Finn had always reserved a corner of himself from Lucy, with some instinctual self-preservation because he knew there was something amiss in their relationship?

Was Ellie's interest real, or was she just gathering facts for the interview? And why did he care? On his way here from the gym, he had vowed to keep this impersonal, business only. Why did he keep treading into personal waters? He knew better, damn it.

"I think every person needs someone like your grandmother in their lives," Ellie said softly.

"Yeah," he said. "They do."

Damn, it was getting warm out here. He glanced over at Ellie to find her watching him. She opened her mouth, as if she was going to ask another question, to get him to open up more, but he cut her off by reaching into his pocket for a sheet of paper. He handed it to her. "I, uh, thought you'd want to know some things about me for the interview. So I wrote them down."

She read over the sheet. "Shoe size. Suit jacket size. Car model." Then she looked up at him. "This doesn't tell me anything about you, except maybe what to get you for Christmas."

"That's all the particulars you would need right there."

She dropped the sheet of paper onto a nearby table, then drew her knees up to her chest and wrapped her arms around her legs. She'd changed into sweatpants and a soft pink T-shirt after work, and she looked as comfortable as a pile of pillows. "What a wife should know about a husband isn't on that list, Finn."

"Well, of course it is. A wife would know my shoe size and my car—"

"No, no. A wife would know your heart. She'd know what made you who you are. What your dreams are, your fears, your pet peeves. She'd be able to answer any question about you because she knows you as well as she knows herself."

He shifted in his chair. The cracker felt heavy in his stomach. "No one knows me like that."

"Why?"

It was such a simple question, just one word, but that didn't mean Finn had an answer. "I don't know."

"Well, surely the woman you were engaged to got

to know you like that. Like the story about your grandmother. That's what I want to hear more of. Or tell me about your fiancée. Why did you two not work out?"

"I don't want to talk about Lucy."

Ellie let out a gust. "Finn, you have to talk about something. We're supposed to know each other inside and out."

"That's why I gave you the list—"

"The list doesn't tell me anything more about you than I already knew from reading the magazine article." She let out a gust and got to her feet. For a while she stood at the railing, looking out over the darkened homes. Then she turned back to face him. "Why won't you get close to me?" Her voice was soft and hesitant. It was the kind of sound that Finn wished he could curl into. "You take two steps forward, then three back. Why?"

"I don't do that." He rose and turned to the other end of the balcony, watching a neighbor taking his trash to the curb. It was all so mundane, so much of what a home should be like. Between the crackers and the cheese and the sweatpants—

Damn, it was like a real marriage.

"What are we doing here, Finn?" Ellie asked, coming around to stand beside him.

When she did, he caught the scent of her perfume. The same dark jasmine, with vanilla tones dancing just beneath the floral fragrance. It was a scent he'd already memorized, and every time he caught a whiff of those tantalizing notes, he remembered the first time he'd been close enough to smell her perfume.

He'd been kissing her. Sealing their marriage vows in Charlie's office. And right now, all he could think about was kissing her again. And more, much more.

Damn.

"We're pretending to be married," he said.

"Are we?" He didn't respond. She lifted her gaze to his. "Can I ask you something?"

"Sure."

She let a beat pass. Another. Still her emerald gaze held his. "Why did you agree to marry me?"

"Because you said that's what it would take. To get on board with the hospital project."

"You are 'the Hawk,' Finn McKenna," she said, putting air quotes around his nickname. "You could negotiate your way out of an underground prison. But when I proposed this…marriage, you didn't try to negotiate at all. You agreed. What I want to know is why."

The night air seemed to still. Even the whoosh-whoosh of traffic seemed to stop. Nothing seemed to move or breathe in the space of time that Ellie waited for his answer. He inhaled, and that damned jasmine perfume teased at his senses, reawakened his desire.

Why had he married her? She was right—he could have offered something else in return for her cooperation on the hospital project. Or he could have just said no. "I guess I just really needed that project to help my business get back on track."

She took a step closer, and lifted her chin. "I don't believe you."

"Truly, it was all about business for me."

"And that was all?"

She was mere inches away from him. A half step, no more, and she'd be against him. Desire pulsed in his veins, thundered in his head. His gaze dropped from her eyes to her lips, to her curves. "No," he said, with a ragged breath, cursing the truth that slipped through his lips. "It's not."

Then he closed that gap, and reached up to capture one of those tendrils of her hair. All day, he'd wanted to do this, to let one silky strand slip through his grasp. "Is it for you?" he asked.

She swallowed, then shook her head. "No. It's not." She bit her lip, let it go. "It's becoming more for me. A lot more."

Finn watched her lips form the words, felt the whisper of her breath against his mouth. And he stopped listening to his common sense.

He leaned in, and kissed Ellie. She seemed to melt into him, her body curving against his, fitting perfectly against his chest, in his arms. She was soft where he was hard, sweet where he was sour, and the opposite of him in every way. Finn kissed her slow at first, then harder, faster, letting the raging need sweep over him and guide his mouth, his hands. She pressed into him, and he groaned, in agony for more of her, of this.

His cell phone began to ring, its insistent trill ripping through the fog in Finn's brain. He jerked away from Ellie, then stepped away. "I'm sorry." He flipped out the phone, but the call had already gone to voice mail. The interruption had served its purpose.

Finn had regained his senses.

Ellie stepped toward him, a smile on her lips, and everything in Finn wanted to take her in his arms and pick up where they left off. But doing so would only do the one thing he was trying to avoid—

Plunge him headlong down that path of wild and crazy. The kind of roller-coaster romance that led to bad decisions, bad matches, and in the end, unhappiness and broken hearts.

"We can't do this." He put some distance between them and picked up his glass, just to have something to do with his hands—something other than touch Ellie again.

"Can't do what?" A smile curved across her face. "Let this lead to something more than a contract?"

"Especially not that. We can't treat this like…like a real marriage. It's a business partnership. And that's all." He shook his head and put the glass back on the tray. The remains of their snack sat there, mocking him. Tempting him to go back to pretending this was something that it wasn't.

But Ellie wasn't so easily dissuaded. She stood before him, hands on her hips. "What are you so afraid of?"

"I'm not afraid of anything. I just think it's best if we keep this business only."

"So that's what that kiss was, business only?"

"No, that was a mistake. One I won't make again."

"And the rooftop dinner? The kiss in the courthouse? Also mistakes?"

He sighed. This was why he hadn't wanted to go down this path. He could already see hurt brimming in Ellie's eyes. He'd done this—he'd made her believe their fake marriage might be leading to something more—and he'd been wrong.

Was any project worth hurting Ellie? Seeing her crying, just like he had seen his mother crying so many times?

He exhaled, then pushed the words out. The words he should have said long ago. "After the interview, I don't think we should wait to annul this marriage." There. He'd said it. Fast, like ripping off a bandage.

Didn't stop it from hurting, though.

Her green eyes filled with disbelief. A ripple of shock filled her features. "What?"

"The business deal can be maintained if you want," he said. He kept his voice neutral, his stance professional. If he treated this like business as usual, perhaps she would, too. But the notes of her perfume kept teasing at his senses while the tears in her green eyes begged him to reconsider. Finn struggled to stick to his resolve. This was the best thing, all around. "Uh, if you like, I'll keep my team in place at WW, and help you through the project. It seems like they're working well together. No reason to break that up."

"That wasn't the deal. You were supposed to help me adopt Jiao."

"I'll do my part. When the interview is set up, just let me know and I'll be here for that."

"Pretending to be my husband."

"Wasn't that the arrangement?"

She didn't say anything for a while. Outside her building, a car honked, and a dog barked. Night birds twittered at each other, and the breeze whispered over them all.

"Was that all you were doing a minute ago? Sealing a business deal?"

She made him sound so cold, calculated. So like the Hawk nickname he hated. "You think that's the only reason I kissed you?"

"Isn't it? You wanted an alliance that would help your company. I wanted a child. We each get what we want out of this marriage. It's as simple as that. That's all this marriage is about. A simple business transaction." She took a step closer, her gaze locked on his. "Isn't it? Or did it start to become something more for you, too?"

She was asking him for the truth. Why had he married her if it wasn't about the business?

He couldn't tell her it was because he was tired of sleeping on that sofa bed. That he was tired of hearing nothing other than his own breath in his apartment. Tired of spending his days working and his nights wondering why he was working so hard. And that when he had met

Ellie he had started to wonder what it would be like to have more.

But he didn't.

Because doing that would open a window into his heart, and if he did that, he'd never be able to walk away from Ellie Winston. He'd get tangled up in the kind of heated love story that he had always done his best to avoid. No, better to keep this cold, impersonal. Let her think the worst of him.

He let out a gust. "This is anything but simple."

"Why? What is so bad about getting involved with someone, Finn? What makes you so afraid of doing that?"

"I'm not afraid of getting involved. We got married, remember?"

"In name only. That's not a relationship. It's a contract. And I know that's what I said I wanted when we started this thing, but…" She let out a long breath and shook her head. "You know, a few times, I've thought I've seen a different side of you, a side that is downright human. And that made me wonder what it would be like to take a chance with you. I'm not a woman who takes chances easily, especially with my heart. But in the end, you keep coming back to being the Hawk."

He scowled. "That's not true."

"You're a coward, Finn." She turned away. "I don't know why I thought…why I thought anything at all."

Why couldn't she understand that he was trying to be smart, to put reality ahead of a fantasy they would never have? Acting without thinking and living in a dream bubble got people hurt. Ellie needed to understand that.

"You think we can turn this fantasy into a real marriage?" he asked. "Tell me the truth, Ellie. Was a part of you hoping that maybe, just maybe, we'd work out and make a happy little family with two-point-five kids and a dog?"

"No." She shook her head, and tears brimmed in her eyes. Above them, a light rain began to fall, but they both ignored it. "Not anymore."

His gaze went to the glass balcony door. The reflection of the neighborhood lights shimmered on the glass like mischievous eyes. Droplets of rain slid slowly down the glass, and Finn thought how like tears the rain could appear. "I'm sorry," he said. "But I have to be clear. I can't give you any more than what the contract stipulated."

Ellie didn't see the ramifications that he could. He had been through this already, seen his parents suffer every day they lived together. Sure, he and Ellie could have some hot, fiery romance, but in the end, they'd crash and burn, and the child would be the one who suffered the most. She was already starting to head down that road, and if he didn't detour them now, it would go nowhere good.

Tears began to slide down Ellie's cheeks, and for a moment, Finn's determination faltered. "That's all I am? A contract?"

"That's what you wanted, Ellie. And it's what's best for all of us." Then he turned on his heel and headed out into the rain.

Before the tears in her eyes undid all his resolve.

CHAPTER EIGHT

HE WAS having a good day. The smile on Henry Winston's face told Ellie that, along with the doctor's tentatively positive report. They were on an upswing right now, and her father was gaining ground. For the first time, the doctor had used the words "when he goes home."

Gratitude flooded Ellie, and she scooted the vinyl armchair closer to her father's bedside. Happy sunlight streamed through the windows of his room at Brigham and Women's Hospital. Her father had more color in his face today. The tray of food beside him was nearly empty. All good signs. Very good.

After last night's bitter disappointment with Finn, Ellie could use some good news. She'd tossed and turned all night, trying to think of a way to convince Finn to help her with Jiao. If he didn't, how would she make this work? He hadn't said for sure he'd get an annulment, but she hadn't heard from him since the conversation on the balcony. She could pick up the phone and call him herself, but she didn't. Because she didn't want to hear him say he'd ended their marriage. And ended Ellie's hopes for adopting Jiao.

Maybe Linda could try appealing to the Chinese again. Perhaps if they saw how committed Ellie was to adopting Jiao, they'd relent on the marriage rule.

Ellie bit back a sigh. From all Linda had told her, that was highly unlikely. Ellie was back at square one, with Jiao stuck in the same spot. Finn had let her down. He'd accused her of wanting this to be a real marriage.

Was he right? Did a part of her hope, after those kisses and that dinner, and all the jokes and smiles, that maybe this was turning into something more than just a platonic partnership?

She glanced out the window, at the city that held them both, and at the same time separated them, and realized yes, she had. She'd let herself believe in the fairy tale. She'd started to fall for him, to let down her guard, to do the one thing she'd vowed she wouldn't do—entangle her heart.

Time to get real, she told herself, and stop seeing happy endings where there weren't any.

For now, Ellie focused on her father instead. One thing at a time. "How are you doing, Dad?"

"Much better now that you're here." He gave her a smile, one that was weaker than Henry's usual hearty grin. But beneath the thick white hair, the same green eyes as always lit with happiness at her presence. "They've got me on a new med. So far, it seems to be working pretty well." He lifted an arm, did a weak flex. "I'll be ready to run the Boston marathon before you know it."

She laughed. "And the Ironman after that?"

"Of course." He grinned, then flicked off his bedside television. His roommate had gone home yesterday, so the hospital room was quiet—or as quiet as a room in one of Boston's busiest medical facilities could be. "How are you doing, Ellie girl?"

"I'm fine, Dad. You don't need to worry about me."

"Ah, but I do. There's some things that don't stop just because your kids grow up."

She gave her father's hand a tight squeeze. She wasn't about to unload her problems on his shoulders. He had much more important things to worry about. "You just concentrate on getting better."

"How are things going with the adoption? I'd sure love to meet my granddaughter."

Ellie sighed. "I've run into a bit of a snag." Then she forced a smile to her face. Worrying her father—about anything—was not what she wanted. Henry didn't need to know about her marriage or her new husband's refusal to help. Chances were, Finn had already filed the annulment and Ellie's marriage was over before it began. For the hundredth time, she was glad she'd kept the elopement a secret from her father. "It'll be fine. It'll just take a little bit longer to bring Jiao home."

"You sure? Do you want me to call someone? Hire a lawyer?" Her father started to reach for the bedside phone, but Ellie stopped him.

"It'll be fine. I swear. Don't worry about it at all." She didn't know any of that for sure, particularly after Finn had told her he wanted nothing to do with the adoption, but she wasn't about to involve her poor sick father. "Just a tiny delay. Nothing more."

"Well, good. I can't wait to meet her. I've seen enough pictures and heard enough about her that I feel like I know her already." Her father settled back against the pillows on his bed, his face wan and drawn. "Hand me that water, will you, honey?"

"Sure, sure, Dad." She got her father's water container, and spun the straw until it faced Henry. She helped him take it, and bring it to his mouth, then sat back. "You sure you're up to a visit?"

He put down the water, then gave her a smile. "Seeing my little girl always makes me feel better. Now, talk to me about something besides doctors and medications. Tell me how things are at the company."

"Good." She hadn't told her father about any of the problems she'd encountered with Farnsworth quitting and the rush to get the Piedmont project underway. She wasn't about to start now. Maybe down the road when he was stronger and feeling better.

He tsk-tsked her. "You always tell me that things are good. I know you're lying." He covered her hand with his own. "I know you have the best of intentions, but really, you can talk to me. Use me as a sounding board."

Oh, how she wished she could. But the doctor had been firm—no unnecessary stress or worries. Her father, who had worked all his adult life, had a lot of trouble distancing himself from the job, and right now, that was what he needed most to do. Whatever she wanted—or needed—could wait. "You need to concentrate on getting better, Dad, not on what is happening at work."

"All I do is lie here and concentrate on getting better." He let out a sigh. Frustration filled his green eyes, and knitted his brows. "This place is like prison. Complete with the crappy food. I need more to do. Something to challenge me."

"I brought you a lot of books. And there are magazines on the counter. A TV right here. If you want something else to read—"

He waved all of that off. "Talk to me about work."

"Dad—"

He leaned forward. The strong, determined Henry Winston she knew lit his features. "I love you, Ellie, and I love you for being so protective of me. But talking about work *keeps* me from worrying about work. I'm not worried about you being in charge—you're capable and smart, and I know you want that business to succeed as much as I do—but I miss being plugged in, connected. That company is as much a part of me as my right arm."

She sighed. She knew her father. He had the tenacity of a bulldog, and now that he was feeling better, she doubted she could put him off much longer about WW Architectural Design. Maybe she could set his mind at ease by sharing a small amount of information, and that would satisfy his workaholic tendencies. "Okay, but if your blood pressure so much as blips, we're talking only about gardening the rest of the day."

He grimaced at his least favorite topic, then crossed his heart. "I promise."

"Okay." She sat back and filled him in, starting with a brief recap of Farnsworth's defection, followed by glossing over most of the setbacks on the Piedmont project, and finally, touting the positive aspects of her temporary alliance with Finn. She kept the news mostly upbeat, and left out all mentions of her elopement.

"You are working with Finn McKenna," Henry said. It was a statement, not a question.

She nodded. "He has the experience we need. I could hire a new architect but we don't have enough time to do another candidate search and then bring that person up to speed. The prelims are due the fifteenth."

"Finn McKenna, though? That man is not one you should easily trust. He's made an art form out of taking over small companies like ours. You know he's our competition, right?"

"Yes, and we have worked out an amicable and fair arrangement. His business got into a little trouble—"

"Do you know what that trouble was? Did he tell you?"

"He didn't give me specifics." Dread sank in Ellie's

gut. She could hear the message in her father's tone. There was something she had missed, something she had overlooked. Damn. She had been too distracted to probe Finn, to push him to tell her more.

She knew better. She'd rushed headlong into an alliance because her mind was on saving Jiao and nothing else.

"He got involved with the daughter of a competitor. In fact, I think he was engaged to her," Henry said. "And when things went south in the relationship, several of his clients defected to the other firm, taking all their business with them. I heard Finn raised a ruckus over at his office, but it was too late. A lot of people said he only proposed to her so he could take over her company and when it ended badly, she stole his clients instead."

Daughter of a competitor. Wasn't that what she was, too? Had Finn married her for control of the company?

Oh, God, had she made a deal with the devil? Her gut told her no, that Finn was not the cutthroat businessman depicted by the media. But how well did she really know him? Every time she tried to get close to him, he shut the door.

Wasn't this exactly why she had stayed away from marriage all these years? She'd seen how her parents had been virtual strangers, roommates sharing a roof. She didn't want to end up the same way, married to someone she hardly knew because she mistook infatuation for something real.

Ironic how that had turned out. Well, either way, the marriage would be over soon. She told herself it was better that way for all of them.

"Just be cautious, honey," Henry said. "I've heard Finn is ruthless. You know they call him—"

"The Hawk." The nickname had seemed like a joke

before, but now it struck a chord. Had she missed the point? Was this entire marriage a plan by Finn to get his company back—

By taking over WW Architectural Design?

Maybe his "help" was all about helping his own bottom line. "I'm sure Finn will be fine," she said, more to allay her own fears than her father's. Because all of a sudden she wasn't so sure anything was going to be fine. "He's really smart and has been a great asset on this project."

"I'd just be very cautious about an alliance with him," her father said. "He's one of those guys who's always out to win. No matter the cost."

"He's been very up-front with me, Dad. I don't think he has a hidden agenda." Though could she say that for a hundred percent? Just because she'd married Finn and kissed him didn't mean she knew much more than she had two days ago. Every time she tried to get close to him, he pushed her away.

"Don't trust him, that's all I'm saying. He's backed into a corner, and a dog that's in a corner will do anything to get out."

Anything. Like marry a total stranger.

And try to steal her father's legacy right out from under her.

CHAPTER NINE

RILEY and Brody dragged Finn out for breakfast. The two brothers showed up at Finn's office, and refused to take no for an answer.

"Why are you stuck in this stuffy office, instead of spending time with your hot new wife?" Riley said. "You've been married for almost a week now, and I swear, you spend even more time here than you did before you got married."

Brody gave Riley's words a hearty hear-hear. "Jeez, Finn. You'd think being married would change you."

He didn't want his brothers reminding him about his marriage—or lack of one. Or the fact that he hadn't seen Ellie in a couple of days. He'd gone home after that night on the balcony, and had yet to return to her apartment, or her office.

He'd sent his senior architects to most of the meetings at WW, and only gone to one when Ellie wasn't scheduled to be there. He conferred with his team back here at his office, and in general, avoided Ellie. Entirely. He used the excuse that the drawings were due in a few days, but really, he knew that was all it was—an excuse. An excuse to keep his distance. Because every time he was with her, he considered the kind of heady relationship he'd spent a lifetime avoiding. "I am changed."

Riley arched a brow. Brody outright laughed. "Sure you are. Prove it and leave the shackles behind for a little while."

Finn scowled. "I have work to do."

"Come on, let's get something to eat," Brody said. Like the other McKenna boys, Brody had dark brown hair, blue eyes and a contagious smile. As the middle brother, he had a mix of both their personalities—a little serious and at the same time a little mischievous.

Riley turned to Brody. "What do you say we kidnap him?"

Brody put a finger on his chin and feigned deep thought. "I don't know. He's pretty stubborn."

"We'll just tie him up." Riley grinned. "So there's your choice, Finn. Either come with us or we're going to haul you out of here like an Oriental rug."

Finn chuckled. "Okay. I can see when I've been beaten." He wagged a finger at them. "But I only have time for a cup of coffee, no more."

The three of them headed out of the office, and instead of going down Beacon to their usual haunt, Riley took a right and led them toward a small corner diner on a busy street. The sign over the bright white and yellow awning read Morning Glory Diner. It looked cheery, homey. The opposite of the kind of place the McKenna boys usually frequented. "Hey, I really don't have room in my schedule to go all over the city for some coffee," Finn said. "My day is very—"

Riley put a hand on his arm. "You gotta ask yourself, what do you have room for?"

"Because it's sure not sex." Brody laughed. "I can't believe you've been at work bright and early every morning. Haven't you heard of a honeymoon period?"

Finn wasn't about to tell his brothers that his was far

from a conventional marriage. A honeymoon was not part of the deal. Nor was he even living with his "wife." "Take advice on marriage from you? The eternal bachelor twins?"

"Hey, I may not be interested in getting married—ever." Riley chuckled. "But even I know a newly married man should be spending all his time with his new bride."

"Yeah, and in bed," Brody added.

Damn. Just the words *bed* and *wife* had Finn's mind rocketing down a path that pictured Ellie's luscious curves beneath him, her smile welcoming him into her heart, her bed, and then tasting her skin. Taking his time to linger in all the hills and valleys, tasting every inch of her before making slow, hot love to her. Again and again.

He'd had that dream a hundred times in the days since he'd met her. He found himself thinking of her at the end of his day, the beginning of his day, and nearly every damned minute in between.

And that alone was reason enough to end this. He was a practical man, one who made sensible decisions. The sensible side of him said keeping his distance from Ellie was the wisest course. The one that would head off the disaster he'd created before. A part of him was relieved.

Another part was disappointed.

The part that dreamed about Ellie Winston and wondered what it would be like to consummate their temporary marital union.

Finn cleared his throat and refocused. He was in a platonic marriage, and there was no definition of that word that included having sex. "I'm not taking relationship advice from you two."

"Maybe you should, brother." Riley quirked a brow at him, as they entered the diner and sidled up to the counter. The diner's namesake of bright blue flowers decorated the border of the room, and offset the bright yellow and white color scheme. "So, besides the fact that you aren't in bed with her right now, how is it going with the new missus?"

"Do you want to talk about anything else this morning?"

Riley glanced at Brody. "Not me. You?"

"Nope. Finn's life is my number-one topic of conversation."

He loved his brothers but sometimes they took well-meaning just a step—or ten—too far. "Well then, you two will be talking to yourselves." Finn ordered a black coffee, then gestured toward Riley and Brody. "What do you guys want?"

"Oh, you're paying?" Riley grinned. He turned to the waitress, a slim woman with a nametag that read Stace. "Three bagels, a large coffee and throw in some extra butter and cream cheese. Can you pack it in to-go bags, too? Thanks."

"Two blueberry muffins and a large coffee for me," Brody said.

"You're guys aren't seriously going to eat all that, are you?" Finn fished out his wallet and paid the bill.

"Hell no. I'm getting breakfast for the next three days." Riley grinned again.

"Yeah, and considering how often you offer to pay, maybe I should have ordered a year's supply." Brody chuckled.

Finn rolled his eyes. "You two are a pain in the butt, you know that?"

"Hey, we all have our special skills," Riley said. "Except for you, because you're the oldest. You get the extra job of taking care of us."

"Last I checked you were grown adults."

"Hey, we may be grown, but some us aren't adults." Riley chuckled.

"Speak for yourself." Brody gave Riley a gentle punch in the shoulder.

Finn pocketed his change and followed his brothers over to a corner table. Since it was after nine, the breakfast crowd was beginning to peter out, leaving the diner almost empty. The smell of freshly roasted coffee and fresh baked bread filled the space.

"You know, I was just kidding," Riley said. "You don't have to take care of us. Or buy us breakfast."

"I didn't see your wallet out."

Riley grinned. "You were quicker on the draw." Then he sobered. "Seriously, sometimes you gotta take care of you."

"Yeah, you do," Brody said.

Finn looked at his brothers. "What is this? An intervention?"

Riley and Brody both grinned. "Now why would you think that?" Brody said, affecting innocence that Finn wasn't buying. His brothers clearly thought he was working too much and living too little. "This is just coffee, isn't it Riley?"

Their youngest brother nodded. A little too vigorously. "Coffee and bagels." Riley held out the bag. "Want one?"

Finn waved off the food. He glanced around the diner. Filled with booths and tables, the diner had a cozy feel. Seventies tunes played on the sound system, while Stace, apparently the lone waitress, bustled from table to table and called out orders to the short-order cook in the back. "What made you pick this place?" Finn asked. "I didn't even know you came here."

"Oh, I don't know. We thought it'd be nice to have

a change of scenery." Riley's head was down, while he fished in the bag.

"Change of scenery?" Finn tried to get Riley's attention, but his brother seemed to be avoiding him. "What is this really about?"

The bell over the door rang and Riley jerked his head up, then started smiling like a fool. He elbowed Brody. "Well, there's our cue to leave."

"What? We just got here."

Riley rose. Brody popped up right beside him, guilty grins on both McKenna faces. "Yeah, but someone much better company than us just showed up." Riley dropped the bag of food onto the table. "I'll leave these. Be nice and share."

"What? Wait!" But his brothers were already heading for the door. Finn pivoted in his seat to call after them. And stopped breathing for a second.

Ellie stood in the doorway, framed by the sun, which had touched her hair with glints of gold. She had on a dark blue dress today that skimmed her knees and flared out like a small bell. It nipped in at her waist, and dropped to a modest V in the front. She wore navy kitten heels today, but still her legs, her curves, everything about her looked amazing.

Finn swallowed. Hard.

Riley and Brody greeted Ellie, then Riley pointed across the room at Finn. Riley leaned in and whispered something to Ellie, and her face broadened into a smile. It hit Finn straight in the gut, and made his heart stop. Then Ellie crossed the room, and Finn forgot to breathe.

Her smile died on her lips when she reached him. "I didn't know you'd be here this morning."

"I didn't know, either." Finn gestured toward the door. "I suspect my brother is at work here."

"I think you're right. I've seen him in here a couple times. I recognized him from the cocktail party and we got to talking one day. I told him I'm here pretty often for my caffeine fix. I guess he figured he'd get us both in the same place."

"That's Riley." Finn shook his head. "My little brother, the eternal optimist and part-time matchmaker."

"He means well. And he thinks the world of you." She cocked her head and studied him. "Wow. You three do look a lot alike."

"Blame it on our genes." Finn wanted to leave, but at the same time, wanted to stay. But his feet didn't move, and he stayed where he was. He gestured toward the bag on the table. "Bagel? Or do you want me to get you a coffee?"

She glanced at her watch. "I have about fifteen minutes before I have to get to a meeting. I really should—" Her stomach growled, and she blushed, then pressed a hand to her gut, then glanced at the growing line at the counter. Despite the light banter, the mood between them remained tense, nearly as tough as the bagel's exterior. "Okay, maybe I have enough time for just half a bagel."

Finn opened the bag and peered inside. "Multigrain, cheese or plain?"

"Cheese, of course. If I'm going to have some carbs, I'm going all out."

"A woman after my own heart." Finn reached in the bag, pulled out a cheese-covered bagel and handed it to her, followed by a plastic knife and some butter. She laid it out on a napkin, slathered on some butter, then took a bite. When the high calorie treat hit her palate, she smiled, and Finn's heart stuttered again.

"Oh, my." Ellie's smile widened. "Delicious."

He watched her lips move, watched the joy that lit her features. "Yes. I agree."

"Oh, I'm sorry, do you want some?"

"Yes," he said. Then jerked to attention when he realized she meant the bagel. And not her. "Uh, no, I already ate this morning."

"Let me guess." She popped a finger in her mouth and sucked off a smidgen of butter. Finn bit back a groan. Damn. He wanted her. Every time he saw her, desire rushed through him.

"You had plain oatmeal," Ellie went on. "Nothing fancy, nothing sugary."

"No. Muffins."

Her brows lifted and a smile toyed with the edge of her mouth. "Not ones from the floor, I hope?"

The words brought the memory of that day in her kitchen rocketing back. Their first day as a married couple. The sexual tension sparking in the air. The desire that had pulsed in him like an extra heartbeat.

He cleared his throat. "Freshly baked and boxed," he said. "From a bakery down the street from my apartment. I rarely eat at home and usually grab something on the way to work."

"This bagel is delicious." She took another bite. Butter glistened on her upper lip, and Finn had to tell himself—twice—that it wasn't his job to lick it off.

Except she was his wife. And that was the kind of thing husbands did with wives.

Unless they were in a platonic relationship.

But were they? Really? How many times had he kissed her, touched her, desired her? Had he really thought he could have a friends-only relationship with a woman this beautiful? This intriguing? A woman who made him forget his own name half the time?

And that was the problem. If he let himself get distracted by Ellie, he'd make a foolish decision. Finn was done making those.

"Why not?" Ellie asked.

"Uh…why not what?" His attention had wandered back to the bedroom, and he forced it to the present.

"Why not eat at home?"

It was a simple question. Demanded nothing more than a simple answer, and Finn readied one, something about hating to cook and clean. But that wasn't what came out. "It's too quiet there."

Her features softened, and she lowered the bagel to the napkin. The room around them swelled with people, but in that moment, it felt like they were on an island of just two. "I know what you mean. I feel the same way about where I live. The floors echo when I walk on them. It's so…lonely."

Lonely. The exact word he would have used to describe his life, too.

A thread of connection knitted between them. Finn could feel it closing a gap, even though neither of them moved. "Have you always lived alone?"

"Pretty much. Even when I was younger, my parents were never there. My dad worked all the time and my mom…" Ellie sighed and pushed the rest of her breakfast to the side. "She had her own life. In college I did the dorm thing, but after that, I had an apartment on my own. I used to love it in my twenties, you know, no one to answer to, no one to worry about, but as I've gotten older…"

"It's not all it's cracked up to be." He wondered what had made him admit all this in a coffee shop on a bright spring day. He'd never considered himself to be a sharing kind of man. Yet with Ellie, it seemed only natural to open up. "Though it was nice to share your space for a couple of days."

Her face brightened. "Was it? Really?"

"Yeah. Really." The kind of nice he could get used to.

He ignored the warning bells ringing in his head, the alarms reminding him that the last time he'd allowed a woman to get this close, it had cost him dearly. He couldn't live the rest of his life worried that someone was going to steal his business. Riley and Brody were right. It was time for him to stop taking care of everyone else and focus on himself for a little while. Just for today.

"I agree." She toyed with the bagel. "I guess my priorities have shifted, too. I built all these houses for other people and after a while, I realized I wanted that, too."

"What?"

"You were right the other day." She lifted her gaze to his and in her eyes, he saw a craving for those intangible things other people had. "As scared as I am of falling in love, of having the kind of bad marriage my parents had, I really do want the two-point-five kids. The block parties. The fenced-in yard. Even the dog."

His coffee grew cold beside him. He didn't care. People came and went in the busy coffee shop. He didn't care. Time ticked by on his watch. He didn't care. All he cared about was the next thing Ellie Winston was going to say. "What…what kind of dog?"

"This is going to sound silly and so clichéd." She dipped her head and that blush he'd come to love filled her cheeks again.

"Let me guess. A Golden retriever?"

She gave him an embarrassed nod. "Yeah."

He shook his head and chuckled.

"What?"

"When I was a kid, I asked Santa for a dog. My mother

was allergic, so it was never going to happen, but I kept asking. Every Christmas. Every birthday. And the answer was always the same. No." He shrugged. "They got me a goldfish. But it wasn't the same."

"What kind of dog did you want?" Then her eyes met his and she smiled. "Oh, let me guess. A Golden retriever."

The thread between them tied another knot. What was it Ellie had said about a real marriage? That it was one where the two people knew each other so well, they could name their dreams and desires?

Were they turning into that?

Finn brushed the thought away. It was a coincidence, nothing more. "Billy Daniels had a Golden," he said. "It was the biggest, goofiest dog you ever saw, but it was loyal as hell to him. Every day when we got out of school, that dog would be waiting on the playground for Billy and walk home with him. Maybe because Billy always saved a little something from his lunch for a treat. He loved that dog. Heck, we all did."

"Sounds like the perfect dog."

"It seemed like it to me. Though, as my mother reminded me all the time, I wasn't the one dealing with pet hair on the sofa or dog messes in the backyard."

"True." She laughed. "So why didn't you get a dog when you grew up?"

"They're a lot of responsibility. And I work a lot. It just didn't seem fair to the dog."

"But every boy should get his dream sometime, shouldn't he?"

She'd said it so softly, her green eyes shimmering in sympathy, that he could do nothing but nod. A lump sprang in his throat. He chastised himself—they were talking about a dog, for Pete's sake. A gift he'd asked for when he was a kid. He was a grown man now, and he didn't believe in Santa anymore. Nor did he have room in his life for a dog.

What do you have room for? Riley had asked. And right now, Finn didn't know. He'd thought he had it all ordered out in neat little columns, but every time he was near Ellie, those columns got blurred.

"You know what I do sometimes?" Ellie said, leaning in so close he could catch the enticing notes of her perfume. "I go to the pet store and I just look. It gives me that dog fix for a little while."

"Maybe if I'd done that more often when I was a kid, I wouldn't have kept bothering Santa."

She got to her feet and put out her hand. "Come on, Finn. Let's go see what Santa's got in the workshop."

"What? Now? I thought you had a meeting to get to."

"It can wait a bit." To prove it, she pulled her cell phone out of her purse and sent a quick email. "There. I have an hour until they start sending out the search party."

He had a pile of work on his desk that would rival Mount Everest. Calls to return, emails to answer, bills to pay. He should get back to work and stop living in this fantasy world with Ellie. Instead he took out his phone and shot an email to his assistant. "There. I have an hour, too," he said.

"Good." She smiled. "Really good."

Finn took Ellie's hand, and decided that for sixty minutes, he could believe in the impossible.

CHAPTER TEN

ELLIE had been prepared to walk out of the diner the second she saw Finn this morning. To refuse the bagel, the offer of coffee, to just ignore him as he'd done to her for the last few days. Then Riley had leaned over and whispered, "Give him a chance. He's more of a softie than you know."

And so she'd sat down at the table, and wondered what Riley had meant. Was Finn the competitor her father had cautioned her against, or was he the man she had seen in snippets over the past days?

Today, he'd been the man she'd met in the lobby—complex and nuanced and a little bit sentimental. And she found herself liking that side of him.

Very much. Falling for it, all over again, even as her head screamed caution.

Then he'd gone and surprised her with their destination and she realized she didn't just like him a little. She liked him a lot. Finn McKenna, with his gruff exterior, was winning her over. Maybe doing a lot more than that. Even as she told herself to pull back, not to get her heart involved, she knew one thing—

Her heart was already involved with him. Ellie was falling for her husband.

The problem was, she wasn't sure he wanted to be her

husband anymore, nor was she positive she could trust him. Her father's words kept ringing in her head. *He's backed into a corner, and a dog that's in a corner will do anything to get out.*

Did Finn have a secret agenda to take over her company? Was that why he kept retreating to the impersonal? Or was he struggling like she was, with the concept of a marriage that wasn't really a marriage?

A contract, he had called it. The word still stung.

If that was all he wanted, then why was he here? What did he truly want?

"Are you two looking to add a dog to your family?"

The woman's question drew Ellie out of her thoughts. "No. Not yet. We're just looking."

Beside her, Finn concurred. He had a brochure from the animal shelter in his hand, and had deposited a generous check into the donation jar on the counter. The director of the shelter, a man named Walter, had come out to thank Finn, and engaged him in a fifteen-minute conversation about the shelter's mission. When Ellie had asked him to go to the pet store, she'd been sure he'd drive to one of the chain stores in the city. But instead he'd pulled into the parking lot of the animal shelter, and her heart had melted. Finn McKenna. A softie indeed.

Every time she told herself not to get close to him, not to take a risk on a relationship that could be over before it began, he did something like that.

"Well, we have plenty of wonderful dogs here to look at." The woman opened a steel door and waved them inside. "Take your time. I'll be right back. We're a little short-staffed today, so I need to get someone to man the phones, then I'll join you." She left the room, and as soon as the door clicked shut, the dogs took that as their cue.

A cacophony of barking erupted like a long-overdue

volcano. Down the long corridor of kennels, Ellie could see dogs of every size and breed. They pressed themselves to the kennel gates, tails wagging, tongues lolling, hope in their big brown eyes.

"Everyone wants to go home with us," Finn said as they started to walk down the row and the barking got louder. "We could be the people in *101 Dalmatians*."

We. Had that been a slip of the tongue? Or was she reading too much into a simple pronoun?

"I don't think so." Ellie laughed. "One dog would be plenty."

Finn bent down, wiggled a couple fingers into the hole of the fenced entrance and stroked a dachshund under the chin. The dog's long brown body squirmed and wriggled with joy. "Hey there, buddy."

Ellie lowered herself beside Finn and gave the little dog a scratch behind the ears. "He's a cutie."

"He is. Though…not exactly a manly dog."

"You never know. He could be a tiger at the front door."

Finn chuckled, then rose. They headed down the hall, passing a Doberman, some Chow mixes and a shaggy white dog that could have been a mix of almost every breed. Finn gave nearly every one of them a pat on the head and the dogs responded with enthusiastic instant love. Ellie's heart softened a little more. She kept trying to remind herself that she didn't want to fall for this man, didn't want to end up unhappy and lonely, trapped in a loveless marriage, but it didn't seem to work.

Finn walked on, then stopped at a cage halfway down on the right side. A middle-aged Golden retriever got to her feet and came to the door, her tail wagging, her eyes bright and interested. "Aw, poor thing," he said softly. "I bet you hate being here." The dog wagged in response. "She's a beautiful dog."

Ellie wiggled two fingers past the wire cage door and stroked the dog's ear. The Golden let out a little groan and leaned into the touch. Finn gave her snout a pat, then did the same to the other ear. The dog looked about ready to burst with happiness. Ellie reached up and retrieved the clipboard attached to the outside of the cage. "It says her name is Heidi."

"Nice name for a dog. Wonder why she's here?"

Ellie flipped the informational sheet over. It sported bright, happy decorations with lots of "Adopt Me" messages, along with a quick history of Heidi. "The paper says her owner got too old to take care of her." Ellie put the clipboard back. "That's so sad."

"Yeah. Poor thing probably doesn't understand why she's here." He gave Heidi another scratch and she pressed harder against the cage.

"Stuck in limbo, waiting for someone to bring her home." Ellie sighed. She grasped the wire bars of the cage, the metal cold and hard against her palm. The dogs in the kennel began to calm a little, their barks dropping to a dull roar, but Ellie didn't hear them. She looked into Heidi's sad brown eyes and saw another pair of sad eyes, on the other side of the world. "So tragic."

"You're not talking about the dog, are you?"

Ellie bit her lip and shook her head. "No."

Finn shifted to scratch Heidi's neck. The dog's tail went into overdrive. "Tell me about her."

Ellie glanced up at the clipboard again, scanning the information on the top sheet. "She's six years old, a female, spayed—"

"Not the dog. The little girl in China."

"You mean Jiao?" Ellie said, her heart catching in her

throat. Finn had never asked about Jiao, not once since the moment she had proposed the marriage of convenience. "You really want to know about her?"

Finn nodded. He kept on giving Heidi attention, but his gaze was entirely on Ellie. "Yeah, I do."

She wanted to smile, but held that in check. Just because Finn asked about Jiao didn't mean he wanted to be part of Jiao's life. He could be making conversation. "She's two. But really bright for her age. She loves to read books, although her version of reading is flipping the pages and making up words for what she sees." Ellie let out a laugh. "Her favorite animal is a duck, and she has this silly stuffed duck she carries with her everywhere. She's got the most incredible eyes and—" Ellie cut the sentence off. "I'm rambling. I'm sorry."

"No, please, tell me more." He got to his feet. "She's important to you and I want to know why. How did you meet her?"

Ellie searched Finn's blue eyes. She saw nothing deceitful there, only genuine interest. Hope took flight in her chest, but she held a tight leash on it. "I went to China for a conference a few years ago. But on the way to the hotel, my cabdriver took a wrong turn, and I ended up in a little village. His car overheated, and while we were waiting for it to cool down, I got out and went into this little café type place. The woman who served me was named Sun, and since I was pretty much the only customer, we got to talking. I ended up spending the entire week in that village."

"Is Sun Jiao's mother?"

Ellie nodded. Her gaze went to the window, to the bright sun that shone over the entire world. In China, it was dark right now, but in the morning, Jiao's world would be brightened by the same sun that had greeted Ellie's morning. "She was."

"Was?"

"Sun...died. Three months ago." Just saying the words brought a rush of grief to her eyes. Such a beautiful, wonderful woman, who had deserved a long and happy life. Fate, however, had other plans and now the world was without one amazing human being.

Finn put a hand on her shoulder. "Aw, Ellie, I'm so sorry. That's terrible."

She bit her lip, and forced the tears back. "That's why Jiao needs me. Over the years, I made several trips back to China and became close friends with Sun. On my last trip, Sun told me about her cancer. Because we were so close, she and I worked out an arrangement for me to adopt Jiao. And I've been trying ever since to bring Jiao home."

He turned back to the dog, and she couldn't read his face anymore. "That's really good of you."

"It's a risk. I don't know if Jiao will be happier here with me, or in China with another couple. I don't know if I'll be a good mother. I just...don't know." She wove her fingers into the fence again, and Heidi rubbed up against her knuckles.

Finn placed his hand beside hers. Not touching, but close enough that she could feel the heat from his body. "I'm sure you'll be fine. You have a certain quality about you, Ellie, that makes people feel...at home."

She met his gaze and saw only sincerity there. "Even when I drop muffins on the floor?"

"Even then." He looked at Heidi again, and gave the dog some more attention. "That's a valuable quality to have for raising a kid, you know. When your home is uncertain, it makes it hard to just be a kid."

She sensed that this was coming from someplace deep in Finn. They kept their attention on the dog, as the conversation unwound like thread from a spool. "Did you have a hard time just being a kid, Finn?"

He swallowed hard. "Yeah." He paused a moment, then went on. "I was the oldest, so I saw the most. My parents loved us, of course, but they should have never married each other. They knew each other for maybe a month before they eloped in Vegas. My mother was pregnant before they came home. My father always said he would have left if not for the kids."

"Oh, Finn, that had to be so hard on you."

"I wasn't bothered so much by that." Finn turned to Ellie, his blue eyes full of years of hard lessons. "It was that my father had fallen out of love with my mother, long, long ago, but my mother kept on holding on to this silly romantic notion that if she just tried hard enough, he'd love her again like he used to. If he ever did. So they fought, and fought, and fought, because she wanted the one thing he couldn't give her."

"His heart."

Finn nodded. "He provided money and clothes and shoes, but not the love my mother craved. I watched her cry herself to sleep so many nights. I've often wondered if…"

When he didn't go on, Ellie prodded gently. "If what?"

"If they got into an accident that night because they were fighting again." He let out a long breath. "I'll never know."

She understood so much more now about Finn. No wonder he shied away from relationships. No wonder he kept his emotions in check, and pulled himself back every time they got close. Was that why he buried himself in work? Instead of giving his heart to someone else? "You can't let that stop you from living, too."

"It doesn't."

"Are you sure about that?" she asked. He held her gaze for a moment, then broke away.

"Did you get a date for the home visit yet?"

He had changed the subject once again, pushing her away whenever she got close. Why? "Yes. I was going to call you today. Friday at eleven."

He nodded. "I'll be there."

"You will? I wasn't sure…" She bit her lip. "I didn't think you would. After what you said the other day."

"I'll be there. Because—" his fingers slipped into the thick fur on Heidi's neck again, scratching that one spot that made her groan "—no one should have to be in a place like this. No dog. No person."

She wanted to kiss him, wanted to grab him right then and there and explode with joy. But she held back, not sure where they stood on their relationship, if they even had one. Doors had been opened between them today, and Ellie was hesitant to do anything that might shut them again. "Thank you."

"You're welcome." His gaze met hers, and for a long heartbeat, it held. Then Heidi pressed against the cage, wanting more attention, and Finn returned to the dog. "You're a good girl, aren't you?"

If anyone had asked her if she had thought Finn "the Hawk" McKenna would be a dog lover who would be easily brought to his knees by a mutt in an animal shelter, she would have told them they were crazy. But in the last few days, she had seen sides of Finn she suspected few people did. And she liked what she saw. More every minute. "You really like dogs, huh?"

"Yeah." He turned to her and grinned. "Don't tell Billy

Daniels, but sometimes I snuck his dog a little of my left-over lunch, too."

She laughed and got to her feet again. "My, my, Finn. You do surprise me."

He rose and cast her a curious glance. "I do? I don't think I surprise anyone."

"You're not what I thought. Or expected."

He took a step closer, and the noise in the room seemed to drop. The dogs' barking became background sounds. "What did you expect?"

"Well, everything I heard about you said you were business only. The magazine articles, the way the other architects talked about you." What her father had said about him. Right now, she had trouble remembering any of those words. "Everything you said, too."

"My reputation precedes me," he said, his voice droll.

"But when I first met you, well, not when I *first* met you, but that day in the office, you were like that. A cool cucumber, as my grandmother would say. You didn't seem like the kind of man who would have dramatic outbursts or irrational thoughts. And from what I've seen, you're smart and good at your job."

He snorted. "That sounds boring."

"And then I see this other side of you," she went on. "This guy who makes corny jokes about Cinderella, and eats at fast food restaurants so he doesn't have to stay in an empty house, and has a soft spot in his heart for a dog he never even owned. A guy who takes a girl to an animal shelter instead of a pet store."

"I just thought, there are tons of unwanted dogs and why buy a puppy when…" He shrugged, clearly uncomfortable with the praise. "Well, it just made more sense."

"It did." She smiled, and leaned ever so slightly toward him. She wanted more of this side of Finn, more of him in general. Every moment she spent with him showed her another dimension of this man who was her husband, yet at the same time, still a stranger. A man who had been wounded by his childhood, and yet, seemed to still believe in happy endings.

The Finn she saw today—the one who pitied a dog in a shelter and realized how like Jiao's life the dog's was—that Finn was the man she was...

Well, starting to fall for. And fall hard. Damn. Every time she tried not to—

She did.

The thought caused a slight panic in her chest, but that disappeared, chased by a sweet lightness. Could she really be falling in love with her husband?

"You're a good man." Ellie smiled.

"Thank you," he said, his voice gruff, dark. He reached up a hand and cupped her jaw, and Ellie thought she might melt right then and there. God, she loved it when he touched her like that. She saw something in his eyes—something that said maybe this wasn't just a contract to him, either, despite what he'd said.

Ever so slowly, Finn closed the gap between them, winnowing it to two inches, one. His breath dusted across her lips and his sky-blue eyes held hers. Anticipation fluttered in her chest. The dogs, apparently realizing no one was interested in them right now, quieted. But Ellie's heart slammed in her chest, so fast and loud she was sure Finn could hear it.

"You are surprising, too," he said. "In a hundred ways."

"Really?"

"Really." Then he kissed her.

He took his time, his lips drifting across hers at first, tasting and tempting. Then his hand came up to cup the back of her head, tangle in her hair, and with a groan, his kiss deepened. His mouth captured hers, made it one with his, and Ellie curved into him. Finn's body pressed to hers, tight and hard, and their kiss turned breathless, hurried. Each of them tasting the other with little nips, shifting position left, right, his tongue plundering her mouth and sending a dizzying spiral of desire through her body.

This was what she had dreamed of in those nights since Finn had slipped a wedding ring on her finger. What she'd had a taste of at the courthouse, and then later on her balcony. This was what she had imagined, if the two of them had a real marriage. The heat nearly exploded inside of Ellie and she knew that if they hadn't been standing in the middle of an animal shelter, they would have been doing a lot more than just kissing.

Behind them, the dogs began barking again and Ellie drew back, the spell broken. "I can't do this."

"Why not?"

She looked into his eyes and saw the same hesitation as before. She wondered if it was true emotional fear on his part, or if her father's cautions were right. Or because she knew she was risking her heart, and he was keeping his to himself. When would she learn? "Because every time I kiss you, I only get half of you, Finn. You keep the rest of yourself locked away."

"I'm not—"

"You are. You told me yourself that you watched your parents suffer through a miserable marriage. I know that has you scared, because I saw the same thing when I was a kid, and I've done my best to avoid getting close to anyone ever since. But you know what I learned in China? What Sun taught me just before she died? That it's okay to love with your whole heart. It's okay to take that risk, even if it costs you everything. Because in the end, the people you love will be better off for having you in their hearts."

He shook his head and turned away. "Sometimes all you end up with is a broken heart."

"Just like in business, huh? Sometimes you win, and everything works out perfectly. And sometimes you lose and take a dent to the bottom line. But you can't do either if you don't take a risk."

She waited a long time for Finn to respond. But he didn't.

Because the truth hurt or because he was keeping his distance, and stringing her along just to grab the business out from under her later? The part of her that had seen Finn take pity on a shelter dog wanted to believe otherwise, but the part that had read the news reports and heard about how he nearly married another competitor's daughter, wondered.

Was she letting herself get blinded by her emotions? The very thing she'd vowed not to do?

Behind them, the door opened and the woman from the shelter stepped inside. "Did you two find anything you wanted?"

Ellie glanced back at Finn one more time. His features had returned to stoic and cold. The man she thought she'd seen earlier today was gone. If he'd ever really been there at all.

"No," she said. "There's nothing I want here. I'm sorry for wasting your time."

CHAPTER ELEVEN

FINN drove back to his office alone. By the time he reached the sidewalk—after being detoured by Walter, who stopped a second time to thank Finn for his donation—Ellie was gone. She'd either walked or taken a cab. It didn't matter. The message was clear.

She was done with him.

He should be glad. For a minute there in the shelter he had lost his head, and let his hormones dictate his decisions. He'd kissed her, allowed himself to start falling for her, and stop thinking about the smart decision. The one that would leave everyone intact at the end.

Ellie had accused him of being afraid of repeating his parent's mistakes. Hell, yes, he was afraid of that, and afraid of doing it with Jiao caught in the crossfire. The already orphaned girl had been through enough. She didn't need to watch the marriage of her new parents fall apart.

He thought of the orphaned dogs he'd seen earlier. They were all so sad, yet at the same time so hopeful. Their tails wagged, tongues lolled and their barks said they were sure these two visitors would be their new saviors.

All it required was saying yes, and opening his heart and home.

Then why had he never done that? Never adopted a dog. Never settled down, never had children. Ellie was right. He'd taken risks in everything but his personal life. And where had it gotten him?

He stepped into his office and looked at the towering stacks of work sitting in his IN box. Everything was in its place, labeled and ordered, easy to organize and dispense. This was where he felt comfortable, because here he could control the outcome.

With a marriage or with a child...there were so many opportunities to make a mess of things. Finn excelled here, in the office, and even that had turned into a disaster in the past year. What made him think he could handle a dog, or a child? Heck, except for that goldfish, he'd never even had a pet.

And even the goldfish had gone belly up within a week.

He dropped into his desk chair, and let out a sigh. He dove into the piles of papers stacked beside him and spent a solid two hours whittling it down from a mountain to a molehill but work didn't offer the usual solace. If anything, the need to be in the office grated on him, and made him feel like he was missing out on something important.

"Hey, Finn, how's married life?"

Finn looked up and grinned at Charlie, then waved his friend into his office. "What are you doing here?"

"Had some business to take care of in Boston." He thumbed toward the street. "Remember my aunt Julia, who lived here?" Finn nodded. "Well, she died last month, and her will's just been a mess over at probate."

"I'm sorry to hear that."

"It's no big deal. It gives me a chance to come back and see some of the guys from the old neighborhood."

Charlie settled into one of the visitor's chairs and propped his ankle on his knee. "I miss having you guys around. The four of us got into a lot of trouble."

Finn chuckled. The McKenna boys and Charlie had been the neighborhood wild children, whooping it up until their mothers called them in for supper. "We did indeed."

"Then we all grew up and got serious. Well, all of us except for Riley."

"I don't think Riley's ever going to grow up. He's the perpetual kid."

"Sometimes that's good for us." Charlie gestured toward Finn. "Besides, who are you to talk? You *eloped*, my man. If I didn't marry you myself, I never would have believed it."

Finn waved it off. "Temporary moment of insanity."

"I met your wife, remember? I gotta say, I think that was the smartest decision you ever made in your life."

"Smartest, huh?" It hadn't felt so smart lately. He had married a woman, thinking he could keep it all about business. Considering how many times he'd kissed her, he'd done a bad job of business only. It was as if he was drawn to the very thing that scared him the most—an unpredictable, heady relationship fueled by passion, not common-sense conclusions.

"She's perfect for you, Finn. Intelligent, beautiful, funny. And willing to marry *you*."

"Hey. I'm not that bad."

"No, not *that* bad." Charlie grinned. "But, I've known you all your life and you can be a bit…difficult."

"Difficult?"

"Yeah, as in a mule in the mud. In business, that's served you well. You put your head down, plow through any obstacles and don't take no for an answer. And look where you are today." Charlie waved at Finn's office. "Up on top of the world, overlooking the city of Boston. Doesn't get much better than that."

"I don't know. I had a bad year last year."

Charlie waved it off. "Lucy did her damage, yes, but in the end, it toughened you up, made you a better businessman. If you never had any failures to knock you down, you'd never be able to appreciate the successes that bring you back up."

Finn took in the city below him, then thought of the company he had built from the ground up. Sure, he'd suffered a pretty bad setback last year, but overall, he was still in business and still doing what he loved. "True."

"And really, you didn't fail. You just met someone who is exactly like you." Charlie chuckled. "A Hawkette."

Finn thought about that for a second. Was that where all his careful planning, detailed lists and sensible dating got him? He'd tried so hard to find someone who was similar to him in personality, career and goals, and it had backfired. He'd tried to mitigate the risk by being smart—

And in the process, made an even bigger mistake. "I did, didn't I?"

"Yep. That's why I think this Ellie is good for you. She's sunshine to your storm clouds."

"I'm not that bad. Am I?"

"Nah. But you could use someone who rounds you out, Finn. You've always been a practical guy and when you're running a business based on straight lines, that's important. But when it comes to the heart, man—" Charlie thumped his own chest for emphasis "—you gotta follow the curves."

"Maybe you're right."

"Hey, I'm a judge. I'm always right." Charlie grinned.

"So, how are the kids?" Finn asked, just to change the subject.

"Perfect, as always." Charlie beamed. "But then again, I'm a little biased."

Finn could see the joy and pride in Charlie's face. He'd known Charlie since elementary school, and had never seen his friend this happy. He seemed to have it all—a great career, a wonderful wife, incredible kids. He and Finn had started in the same place, grown up side by side, followed similar paths—college, then starting at the bottom and working their way up—that it made Finn wonder if maybe there was some secret to having it all that he was missing. "Don't you worry about messing it up?"

"Of course I do. Being a husband and a father is the biggest risk of all because you have other people's lives in your hands. But in the end, it's so worth it." Charlie had pulled out his wallet and was flipping proudly through the pictures of his kids. "This is what it's all about, my friend. Sophie just lost her two front teeth, and she goes around whistling everywhere. Max signed up for T-ball…"

Finn wasn't listening. He was looking at the clear love in Charlie's face, the determination to do right by his kids, and realized where he had seen that look before.

On Ellie's face. When she talked about Jiao.

She was scared to take the risk of being Jiao's parent, but she was doing it anyway. Clearly Ellie loved this little girl. Finn had no doubt she'd be a good mother. For a second, he envied her that love, that clear conviction that she could raise a child she barely knew. He was sure she would be a terrific mother. Any child would be blessed to be raised by a woman as amazing as Ellie Winston.

As Finn watched one of his oldest and best friends talk about the wondrous joy a family could bring to a man's life, he felt a stab of envy. Ellie was his temporary wife, and after all this was over, there would be no pictures or bragging or stories to tell.

He glanced at the clock and realized there was one thing he could do before they got divorced. He could help her bring that child home.

And make sure Ellie's floors would no longer echo.

CHAPTER TWELVE

ELLIE had spent the better part of Friday morning scrubbing her house from top to bottom. Cleaning helped distract her, helped take her mind off the worries about work, the home visit today, and the worries about Jiao. She had called the orphanage earlier and been assured that Jiao was fine and healthy, but that didn't help set Ellie's mind at ease when it came to her daughter's future. Every hour that ticked by with Jiao stuck in adoption limbo was undoubtedly hurting her emotionally.

When she wasn't worrying about the adoption, her mind was on Finn. For a while there, she'd thought they were building something. She'd thought...

Well, it didn't matter what she'd thought. Finn had made it clear over and over again that he wasn't interested in a relationship with her. There was the home visit today, and then the hospital plans were due to be delivered to the client on Tuesday, and after that, she was sure their alliance would end. Probably a good thing, she told herself.

Tears rushed to her eyes but she willed them back. Finn was the one losing out, not her. She told herself that a hundred times as she scoured the shower walls. But the tears still lingered.

A little after ten-thirty that morning, her doorbell rang.

Ellie peeled off her rubber gloves, dropped them into a nearby bucket, then ran downstairs to answer it. Finn stood on the other side.

"You came."

"I promised you I would." He was wearing a light blue golf shirt and a pair of jeans that outlined his lean, defined legs. The pale color of his shirt offset his eyes, and made them seem even bluer. Her body reacted the same as always to seeing him—a nervous, heated rush pumping in her veins—even as her head yelled caution.

"Thank you."

"No need to thank me." He gave her a grin, that lopsided smile that made her heart flip. "I'm here to help you get ready. Not that I'm a whole lot of help in the home department, but I figured you'd be a wreck, and need a hand getting things done."

He could have been reading her mind. Joy bubbled inside her, but she held it back, still cautious and reserved. This was everything she'd ever wanted. Finn would be a temporary husband, just as she'd planned, he'd do the home visit with her, then go back to living his own life, leaving her and Jiao alone, to form their own little family of two. She should have been happy.

Then why did she feel so…empty? *Focus on Jiao. On bringing her home. Not on what will never be with Finn.*

"That sounds good," she said. "Thank you."

"We don't have much time before they arrive," Finn said. "And a lot to do. So let's get to work." Finn grabbed a box that she hadn't noticed beside his feet. "I brought a few more of my things to put around the house, so it looks more like I'm living here. I didn't bring enough before."

"Good idea."

"I was just trying to think through all possible angles.

People will expect us to have commingled belongings. I brought some clothing, the two photographs I have of myself, and a six-pack of beer."

She laughed at the beer. "That sounds like a typical male."

"That was my intent. I want to make sure we have maximum plausibility."

Disappointment drowned out her hope. This whole thing wasn't about Finn being thoughtful, it was about him being methodical and thorough, covering all his bases. Just when she thought the Hawk had disappeared…he came to the forefront again. She wondered again if this was true help, or a calculated move to help his business.

She'd focus on the adoption, and worry about the rest later. Linda would be here soon and Ellie only had this one shot to convince her and the social worker that Jiao would be happy here.

"You should probably put your things in my bedroom," she said.

"Yeah." His gaze met hers in one long, heated moment. She turned away first, sure that if she looked at him for one more second, she'd forget all the reasons she had for not getting involved with him.

"Why don't I help you?" She turned on her heel and led Finn up the stairs, trying not to think about how surreal this all was. She was taking her husband to her bedroom, for the sole purpose of pretending she shared the room with him. In the end, he'd pack up his things and be out of her life. Forever.

"I already moved the things you left behind in the guest room into here," she said. "I didn't know if you'd be here today and I guess I wanted to set up maximum plausibility, too."

"We think alike." He grinned. "Maybe that's a good thing."

"Maybe." She opened the door to the master bedroom, then followed Finn inside. Then she turned back and laid a light hand on his arm. "If I don't get a chance to tell you later, thank you."

He shrugged, like it was no big deal. "You're welcome."

"No, I mean it, Finn. This is huge for me, and I really, really appreciate you helping with this."

His eyes meet hers, and she felt the familiar flutter in her chest whenever he looked at her. "You're very welcome, Ellie."

The moment extended between them. Her heart skipped a beat. Another.

Behind her, Ellie was painfully aware of the bed. The wedding rings on their hands. If this had been any other marriage, would be in that bed together, every night, making love. If this had been any other marriage, she would have stepped into Finn's arms, lifted her face to his and welcomed another of his earth-shattering kisses.

If this had been any other marriage…

But it wasn't. And she needed to stop acting like it was.

She spun around and crossed to the closet. "Uh, let me shift some of my clothes over, and we can fit yours in there." She opened one of the double doors and pushed several dresses aside, the hangers rattling in protest, then she turned back to Finn. He was smiling. "What?"

"Hootie & the Blowfish." He pointed at her closet.

She turned back and saw the concert T-shirt hanging in her closet. It had faded over the years, but still featured the band's name in big letters on the front. "Oh my. I forgot that was in there. That was oh, almost fifteen years ago." She pulled out the hanger and fingered the soft cotton shirt. "I don't know why I hung on to it for so long."

"Did you hear them in concert?"

"Yep. Me and two of friends went. We were both hoping to marry Darius Rucker. They were my favorite band, and I figured I could hear Hootie songs every day if I married the lead singer."

He chuckled. "I guess that didn't work out."

"Kinda hard to catch his eye when we're in the fortieth row." She laughed, then clutched the shirt to her chest. "Do you like Hootie & the Blowfish?"

He nodded. "I went to a concert, too, one of their last ones before Rucker branched out on his own."

She propped a fist on her hip. "Yes, but do you have the T-shirt to prove it?"

He dug in the box and pulled out a threadbare brown T. Laughter exploded from Ellie when she read the familiar name on the front.

"I saw them at the Boston Garden," he said.

"Providence for me." She flipped over her shirt to show the concert information. "We could go out as twins."

"Uh, yeah…no." He laughed. "I think that would be more damaging than anything. People would think we're crazy."

"Oh, it might be fun. And get people talking."

She remembered the first time she'd said that. It had been back in the office, on their first day as a married couple. They'd shared lunch in the outdoor courtyard, and for a little while, it had felt so real, as if they were any other couple sneaking in an afternoon date. And the time they had spent in her house, had seemed real, too. Had they been pretending? Or had a part of it been

a true marriage? And why did she keep hoping for the
very thing she told herself she didn't want?

Finn moved closer to her, and the distance between
them went from a foot to mere inches. Ellie's heart began
to race. Damn, this man was handsome.

"They already are talking," he said.

"Really? And what do you think they're saying?"

His gaze locked on hers. Ellie's pulse thundered in her
head and anticipation sent a fierce rush through her veins.
She held her breath, waiting on his words, his touch.

A slight smile curved across his lips. "I think they're
saying that they can't believe I married you."

"Because I'm such a bad match for you?"

"No. Because you are such an amazing woman." He
reached up and drifted his fingers along her jawline, sliding across her lips. She nearly melted under that touch,
because it was so tender, so sensual. "Smart and funny
and sexy and a hundred other adjectives."

"Finn…" She drew in a breath, fought for clarity.
Every time she thought she understood Finn and his
motives, he threw a curveball at her. Was he here for
business, or something more? Was there anything between them besides an architectural alliance? A *contract*?
Because right now, it sure as hell felt like something
more. A lot more. And oh, how she wanted that more.
She was tired of being afraid of falling in love, afraid of
risking her heart. She did want the whole Cinderella fantasy, damn it, and she wanted it with Finn. The trouble
was, she didn't know what he wanted.

"Every time I see you, I stop thinking—" he leaned
in closer, and her heart began to race "—about anything
but how much I want to kiss you again."

"Really?" The hope blossomed again inside her. Lord,
she was in deep.

His fingers did a slow dance down her neck. Her nerves tingled, chasing shivers along her veins. "Really." Then finally, when she thought she could stand the wait no longer, he kissed her.

This kiss started out slow, easy, sexy, like waltzing across the floor. Then the tempo increased, and the spark between them became an inferno, pushing Ellie into Finn, searching, craving, more of him. She curved her body into his and the inferno roared down every part of them that connected. His hands roamed her back, sliding along the soft cotton of her T-shirt, then slipped over the denim of her jeans, sending a rush of fire along her back, her butt. Oh, God, she wanted him. She arched into him, opening her mouth wider, her tongue tangoing with his. Insistent, pounding desire roared through her veins. *More, more, more,* she thought. *More of everything.*

"Oh, God, Ellie," he said, his voice a harsh, low groan. Then, one, or maybe both of them began to move and in tandem, they stepped back, two steps, three, four, until Ellie's knees bumped up against the bed and they fell onto it in a tangle of arms and legs.

Finn covered her legs with one of his, never breaking the kiss. His mouth had gone from easy waltz to hot salsa, and Ellie thought she might spontaneously combust right then and there if she didn't have more of Finn. Of his kiss, his touch, his body. Damn, his body was hard in all the right places, and on top of hers, and sending her mind down the path of making love. His hand slid under her T-shirt, igniting her bare skin. She moaned, rose up to his touch, then gasped when his fingers brushed against her nipple. She gasped, arched again, and his fingers did it again. Oh, God. Even through the lacy fabric of her bra, she could feel every touch, every movement.

She murmured his name, then wrapped a leg around

his hips, pressing her pelvis to his hard length. God, it had been so long since she had been with a man, so long since she had been kissed. She wanted Finn's clothes off. Wanted his naked body against hers. Wanted him inside her.

Finn seemed to know everything about her. Every touch stoked the fire inside her, every kiss added to the desire coursing through her veins, clouding her every thought. Then as she shifted to allow him more access, the clock downstairs began to chime the hour.

Ellie jerked back to the present. What was she doing? Where was she going to go with this? Was she letting her hormones overrule her brain again? She shifted away from him and scrambled to her feet. "Why are you doing this?" she asked.

"Because I want you. Because you're the most beautiful woman I've ever met. Because—"

"No. Why are you helping me? Why are you here today for the home visit?" The clock downstairs chimed ten, then eleven times, and fell silent.

"Because I made you a promise." His sky-blue eyes met hers and when he spoke his voice was quiet, tender. "And because when you were telling me about Jiao at the animal shelter, I saw how much you loved her. Every child should have a parent who loves them like that. Who would move heaven and earth to provide them with a safe and loving environment."

"Is that all there is? No hidden agenda to steal WW out from under me?"

He looked surprised. No, he looked hurt, and she wanted to take the words back. "You think that's why I did all this? Really? After everything?"

"You told me yourself that your company has had a bad year and that you were desperate to recoup the business you had lost. Desperate enough to marry the daughter of your competitor?" She bit her lip, and pushed the rest out. She didn't want him here if in the end he was going to take away the very thing her father treasured. Nothing was worth that price. "Like you almost did before?"

"Is that what you think? That I go around town marrying the competition to try to build my business up? That the Hawk swoops in and drops engagement rings to lure them in?"

She crossed her arms over her chest. "I don't know, Finn. You tell me."

"I don't. The fact that you and Lucy both work in the industry is a coincidence."

"Is it? Because it seems to me that marrying me has given your business an advantage and I want to be sure my father's company is protected."

He cursed. "Ellie, I didn't marry you for your father's company. And I have no intentions of stealing it."

"Is that what you told Lucy, too?"

The doorbell began to ring. Linda was here. Ellie cursed the timing. "We'll have to finish this later."

"Okay." He turned to the box and quickly stowed the rest of his clothes in her closet. Finn finished hanging up his clothes, then turned to the dresser and nightstand to put out a few of his personal items. Ellie crossed to the door of the bedroom and took one last look at the closet that held the incongruity of her life. Finn McKenna's dress shirts and pants hung beside her dresses, making it look like her husband was truly a part of her life.

When that was as far from the truth as could be.

Two hours later, Linda and the social worker finished their visit at Ellie's house. As they were heading out the door, Linda leaned her head back in and shot Ellie a smile. "This went great. Thanks to both of you for being available on such short notice."

"You're welcome. It was our pleasure," Finn said. He shook hands again with Linda, then took his place beside Ellie, slipping an arm around her waist. Still playing the happy couple, and after a couple hours of it, it was beginning to feel natural. Hell, it had felt natural from the minute he'd said "I do."

"We'll get the report off to the orphanage in China and from there it should only be a few days." Linda beamed. "I'm so excited for the two of you. I'm sure Jiao will be very, very happy in her new home."

Ellie thanked Linda again, then said goodbye. After the two women were gone, she closed the door and leaned against it. Finn stepped back, putting distance between them again. The charade, after all, was over. He should have been relieved.

He wasn't.

He realized that this was it. They had finished the preliminary drawings for the hospital project and save for one more meeting to go over a few details, the business side of their alliance was done. And now, with the social worker gone and the home visit over, the personal side of their partnership was over, too. He had no other reason to see Ellie again.

And that disappointed him more than he had expected.

"Thank you again," Ellie said. "You were fabulous. Really believable."

"You're welcome."

"I loved how you managed to slip in that thing about us sharing the same favorite band, and the stories about how we both saw them in concert. I think it's the details that really make a difference."

"Yeah, they do." That damned disappointment kept returning. Was it just because they'd shared an amazingly hot kiss—and a little more—back in the bedroom? Or was it because they'd been pretending so well, it had begun to feel real, and now he was mourning the loss of a relationship that had never really existed? One that he had been doing his best to avoid? "I, uh, should get going."

Her smile slipped a little. "Okay. I'll, uh, see you Monday. At the meeting."

"Sure, sounds good." He picked his keys up from the dish by the front door—another realistic touch that he had added—and pressed the remote start for his car.

"Do you want to take your stuff now?"

"Maybe I should leave it. In case they come back."

"Oh, yeah, sure. Good idea." She paused. "Are you sure there isn't anything you need?"

"No, I'm good. Oh, wait. I left my wallet on the nightstand." He thumbed toward the stairs. "Is it okay if I go up and get it?"

"Sure. This is your house, too. At least for show."

He chuckled, but the sound was empty, the laughter feigned. This wasn't his house and even though he'd pretended to for a little while, he wasn't living here anymore. He headed up the stairs and into her room.

He paused inside the doorway and took in the room one last time. A fluffy white comforter dominated her king-sized bed. Thick, comfortable pillows marched down the center of the bed, ending with a round decorative pillow in a chocolate-brown. Sheer white curtains hung at her windows, dancing a little in the slight breeze. In one corner a threadbare tan armchair sat beside a table with a lamp. Close to a dozen books stood in a towering stack on the table. Finn crossed to them, smiling at the architectural design books, then noting the mysteries and thrillers that filled out the pile. Two of them were on his own nightstand.

They listened to the same music. Read the same books. Worked in the same field. Everything pointed to them being perfect for each other.

Except...

His gaze skipped to the bed. There was a fire between them, one he couldn't ignore. It made him crazy, turned his thoughts inside out and made him do things he had never done before—like elope.

Risk.

That's what marrying Ellie had been. A huge risk. And Finn, the man who never made a move that wasn't well thought out and planned, had taken that risk with both eyes wide-open. He glanced at a picture of Ellie posing with a smiling, gap-toothed two-year-old girl with dark almond eyes and short black hair. Jiao. The two of them looked happy together, already resembling the family they would soon become.

A part of him craved to be in that circle, with Ellie and Jiao. Wanted to form a little family of three. That was the biggest risk of all, wasn't it?

He'd taken it in the last few days and realized that every time he was with Ellie, he felt a happiness he'd never known before. A lightness that buoyed his days. Was he...falling for her?

And was he doing it too late?

Finn grabbed his wallet and turned to leave. Ellie stood in the doorway, watching him. "You never answered my question."

He sighed and dropped onto the bed. Did she really think the worst of him? That he was the Hawk, through and through? "I didn't propose to Lucy with the intention of stealing her company. I proposed to her because I thought she was the right one to settle down with."

Ellie hung back by the door. "The love of your life?"

He snorted. "Far from it. She was the one who met all the mental pros and cons I had listed in my head for a relationship. She fit my little checklist, so I told myself we'd be happy. And you know what?" He shook his head, and finally admitted the truth to himself. "I was never happy with her. I was content."

"Is that so bad?"

"It's horrible. Because you never have that rush of joy hit your heart when you see the person you love." His gaze met hers, and a whoosh ran through him. "You never hurry home because you can't wait to see her smile. You never catch yourself doodling her name instead of writing a contract. You never feel regret for leaving her instead of staying to the very end." He rose and crossed to Ellie. "The most impetuous thing I did was propose to Lucy—I rushed out and bought the ring at the end of the day. After I'd compiled a list of pros and cons." He shook his head and let out a breath. "Who does that? Pros and cons?"

"Some people. I guess."

"She didn't expect me to show up at her office, and definitely didn't expect me to propose. When I got there, I walked in on a meeting with her and my biggest client. In that instant, I knew that the whole thing had been a fraud. My gut had been warning me, but I'd been too busy being practical and sensible to listen."

"What was your gut saying?"

"That she didn't love me and I didn't love her, and that I was making the biggest mistake of my life. After I broke it off, she smeared my name all over town. Made it her personal mission to steal the rest of my clients." He looked deep into her green eyes. "You were right. I am afraid of risking my heart. But then again, so are you."

"Me? I'm not afraid." But her eyes were wide and her breath was quickened. He had hit a nerve, clearly.

"Really? Then why did you do your best to push me away?"

"This isn't going anywhere. You said so yourself."

He reached up as if he was going to touch her cheek, but his hand fell away. "And you accused me of being here to steal the company."

"Are you?"

"You know that answer already. Quit trying to put up walls that don't exist."

"I didn't…" She bit her lip.

"You did and so did I. It was all so easy, because we both kept saying this marriage had an end date. You did the same thing as me, Ellie. You got close, you backed away. Got close, backed away. I think you're just as scared as I am."

"I'm not."

"Really?" He leaned in closer. "Then what would you say if I said let's not end this?"

"Didn't…end the marriage? But that was the deal."

"I realized something today when I was here, in your house, pretending to be your husband for the last time." He caressed her cheek with his thumb. "The whole time I was wishing it was real. Because the time I've spent with you has been the best damned time of my life."

Fear shimmered in her eyes. Fear of being hurt, of letting go. Of trusting. When it came right down to it, Ellie was just as scared as he was of opening her heart. "Oh, Finn. I don't know what you want me to say."

"That you're ready to take that risk, too. That you want more than just the fiction."

She just shook her head. Finn released Ellie, then walked out the door, finally leaving behind a fairy tale that wasn't going to end with happily ever after.

CHAPTER THIRTEEN

ELLIE's heart sang with the words the doctor had just said. *Great recovery. Going home soon. Should be okay to resume limited activities.* Her father had surpassed medical expectations and was going to be all right. He'd be on a limited schedule, of course, but he would be alive, and that was all Ellie cared about.

"You're doing fabulous, Dad," Ellie said. "The doctor is thrilled with your recovery." Henry was sitting up today, looking much heartier than last time. The color had returned to his face, and he appeared to have put back on some of the weight he had lost while he was sick. In the next bed, his new roommate was watching a reality show about wild animals.

"I'm just trying to do what I'm told," Henry said.

She laughed. "For the first time in your life?"

He chuckled. "Yeah." He patted the space beside him on the bed. "Come. Sit down and tell me how things are going for you."

"Good. Well, great." Except for the fact that she hadn't talked to Finn since that day at her house, things were great. She should have been relieved that the marriage was over, but she wasn't. A part of her wondered if maybe Finn was right—if she had let him walk away because it was easier than taking the risk of asking him to stay.

"The McKenna team worked with us to draw up the plans for the Piedmont hospital project. We submitted them to the client on time, and the initial review was really positive. But that's not the really good news…"

"What?"

"Well, you're about to be a grandfather." She smiled. "Jiao will be here in a few days."

A smile burst across his face. "Honey, that's wonderful! And while I'm excited to hear such good news about the business, I'm more excited about your addition to the family." He reached for the sheet of doctor's recommendations sitting on his end table and showed them to his daughter. "You can bet I'll be sticking to every one of these rules because I want to take my new granddaughter to the zoo and the park and wherever else she wants to go."

Ellie sat back, surprised at this change in her father, a man who'd never had time for those things before, a man who had stubbornly lived by his own rules—which was part of what had made him so unhealthy. "Wow. Really?"

"Really." His face softened, and he took her hand. "I missed all that with you, because all I ever did was work. Lying here in this bed has given me a lot of time to think, to regret—"

"Dad, I grew up just fine. You don't need to have regrets."

"I do. And I will. I want you to know how sorry I am that I missed out on your soccer games and band performances and prom nights." His face crumpled and tears glistened in his eyes. "Aw, Ellie, I should have been there more, and I…I wasn't."

She gave his fingers a squeeze and sent God a silent prayer of gratitude for this second chance with her father. "It's okay. We're building a great relationship now, and that's all that matters."

"No, it isn't." He let out a long sigh. "Once I'm out of this hospital, I have a lot to make up for with you, starting with asking you to move up here and take over the business. I never should have done that."

"Dad, I love architecture. I love this industry."

"But you don't love commercial buildings. I knew that, and still I asked you to take over my business." His green eyes met hers. So like her own, and filled with decades more of wisdom and experience. "You were happy designing houses."

She was, but she wasn't about to tell her dad that. She would never complain about stepping in for him at WW. It was a family business, and when your family needed you, you went. Simple as that. "You're my father. You were sick. You needed me. I didn't mind."

"I know you didn't, and that's the problem. You are too good of a daughter, Ellie girl." He sighed. "That's why I want you to quit."

"Quit? What? Dad, you're in no condition to run the company yourself. Not now." She didn't add the words *maybe never*. Because there was hope, and she wanted her father to hold on to that. "I'll stay until you come back and—"

"No." His voice was firm, filled with the strident tones people usually associated with Henry Winston. His heart might be weak but his personality and resolve remained as strong as ever. "You have a daughter to raise. You go do that."

She laughed. "Dad, I still need to pay my bills. I'll keep working and we'll work it out."

"No. I want you to quit WW Architectural Design…. and start your own division. A residential division. Bring those beautiful houses you designed in the South to the Boston area. And hire lots of great people to work under you so that you don't have to put in the kind of hours I did."

"A residential division?" A thrill ran through her at the thought of getting back to designing houses again, to return to the work that had given her so much reward. "But who will run the commercial side?"

"Larry and...Finn McKenna."

Had she heard him wrong? When had Finn come into the mix? "Finn McKenna? Why? I thought you didn't trust him."

"You told me he was smart, and capable. So I gave him a call this morning," Henry said. "He told me all about how you two collaborated on the hospital project and how well it went for everyone. I never really got to know Finn before, only knew him by reputation, but now I realize I was wrong about him. He may be a tough businessman, but he's also a nice guy. Cares a lot about you."

She let out a gust at that. "He cares about his business."

"He cares about a lot more than that, but I'll let you find that out for yourself."

Was the Finn she had started to fall for the real man? Or was he the Hawk that had pushed her away a hundred times? She couldn't think about that now, she decided, not with her father to worry about, and Jiao arriving any day.

Her father shifted in the bed, and Ellie realized Henry looked a hundred times better now than he had when he'd first been admitted. It was as if having this taste of something to do had given him a new energy and it showed in his face.

"Are you sure about wanting me to quit?" she asked.

Working in residential design again, particularly if she didn't have to be there full-time, would give her the flexibility she needed to raise Jiao. She'd be able to have time with her daughter, something the little girl was going to need after such a traumatic year. It was a gift beyond measure, and she couldn't begin to thank her father enough.

He reached out and drew his daughter into a warm hug. "I don't want to see you make the same mistakes I did. I want you to watch your daughter grow up. And I want to have the time to watch her grow up, too. I didn't build this business just to watch you repeat my mistakes."

Ellie tightened her grip on her father. Tears slid down her cheeks, moistened the sleeve of his hospital gown. "You didn't make any mistakes, Dad. Not a single one."

Finn had stayed away for weeks. He'd told himself it was easier this way, that he could wean himself off Ellie Winston, and forget all about her. If that was the case, then why had he gone to see her father? Agreed to the idea of joining their companies? And heading up the new venture?

Because he was crazy. Doing that would put him in the same building as Ellie every day, and he'd known that going into this deal. He just hadn't been able to let go, even as every day he looked at his To Do list and saw "call lawyer" at the top. Procrastination had become his middle name.

Either way, it didn't matter. By the time he had the particulars in place and had set up a space in the more spacious offices of WW Architectural Design, Ellie was gone. On maternal leave, he'd been told. Her assistant went on for a good ten minutes about Ellie's trip to China, and her new daughter. Every day he heard another tidbit about Ellie and Jiao.

And every day it felt like someone had cut out his heart and put it on a shelf.

Now he stood at the entrance to a small playground carved out of the limited green space near Ellie's neighborhood. Bright red, yellow and blue playground equipment dominated the center of the space, flanked by matching picnic tables and chairs. Green trees stood like sentries inside the wrought-iron fence. The musical sound of children laughing and playing carried on the air.

Finn's gaze skipped over the mothers sitting in clusters, chatting while their children played. Past the kids playing tag in the courtyard. Past the tennis players working up a sweat on the court next door. Then he stopped, his breath caught in his throat, when he saw her.

Ellie, sitting on a blanket, with Jiao beside her, and Jiao's stuffed duck flopped against the young girl's leg. They were having a picnic lunch, the little dark-haired girl giggling as Ellie danced animal crackers against her palm. The two of them formed a perfect circle of just them. Beside her, Linda stood and watched, a happy smile on her face. The two women chatted for a moment longer and then Linda left.

As she headed for the exit, she saw Finn and stepped over to him. "Why hello, Finn."

He gave the dark-haired woman a smile. "Hi, Linda. Nice to see you again."

"How have you been?"

"Good." Finn's gaze kept darting toward Ellie and Jiao. He'd missed Ellie's smile. A hell of a lot.

Linda thumbed toward Ellie. "You know, you really should go over there and meet Jiao. She's a wonderful little girl."

Finn opened his mouth, shut it again. He wasn't sure what to say. If he admitted he'd never seen Jiao before, then Linda would know the marriage had been a farce and maybe that would cost Ellie. Maybe even undo the adoption Ellie had worked so hard to bring to fruition.

Linda put a hand on Finn's arm. "Don't worry. I already figured it out."

"You did? How? Was it because I didn't go to China with Ellie?"

Linda laughed. "No, it was something much more simple. Your shoes."

"My shoes?"

"When we came by the house, you had clothes in the closet and a wallet on the bedside table, but not a single pair of shoes anywhere. I had had my suspicions about Ellie's fast marriage, but I didn't say anything."

Damn. He couldn't believe he'd missed such a simple detail. He'd thought he'd covered everything. He'd almost ruined the most important thing in Ellie's life. "Why? I thought Ellie had to be married to adopt Jiao."

"She did. And she was. I told the Chinese orphanage that her husband had to stay in America for a family emergency, so they didn't wonder why you didn't come to China to pick up Jiao. Either way, I knew that with or without a spouse on paper, Ellie was going to be a fabulous mother." Linda glanced over her shoulder at Ellie and her daughter. "She loves that little girl more than life itself. That's a blessing."

"I agree." The two of them seemed to go together like peas and carrots. Envy stirred in Finn's gut. He had never felt more on the outside than he did right now. Ellie had everything she'd ever wanted, and it hurt to realize that didn't include him. Perhaps if he had handled things differently, they wouldn't be here right now.

Maybe he shouldn't have married her at all. If they'd kept things entirely on a business level, then he wouldn't have this deepening ache in his chest for a life he never really lived. This stabbing regret for a relationship that had slipped away.

"You know, it's a scary thing," Linda said.

"What is?"

"Giving your heart away. Ellie did that, not knowing if she was going to be able to bring Jiao home. But she took that risk, and put everything on the line, because she loved that little girl." Linda's gaze met his. "And I think you took a big risk, too."

"Me?" He snorted. "I didn't do anything."

"You married her and stood up as her husband when she needed you most. That's a risk. And you gotta ask yourself why you did it."

"Because she needed me." He watched Ellie with Jiao, their faces close together as they laughed over something. It was the perfect picture of maternal love. Yes, he'd done the right thing in helping Ellie. In that, he took comfort.

"Maybe," Linda said. "And maybe you did it for more than just that. Maybe if she believes that, she'll take that risk, too." Then she patted him on the shoulder. "I've got to get back to work. Enjoy your family."

Linda was gone before Finn could tell her that this wasn't his family. Not at all. And no amount of wishing would make it so.

He was about to turn away when a dozen kids from a daycare center came bursting into the playground, and Finn stepped aside to let them through. Ellie looked up at the sudden noise of the newcomers. Her eyes widened when she saw him. She'd seen him, and leaving was out of the question.

He crossed the park to Ellie. "Hi."

There couldn't possibly be a lamer opening than that. All these weeks, he'd thought of what he'd say when he saw her again. "Hi" wasn't on the list at all.

She looked up at him, sunglasses covering those green eyes he loved so much. "What are you doing here?"

"I'm…" He hadn't played that out in his head, either. "Looking for you."

Better to start with the truth than to make up something. Besides, his lying skills were pretty awful. And where had lying gotten him so far anyway? Still stuck in his empty apartment, staring at the wedding band sitting on his nightstand, wondering if he'd made a huge mistake by letting her go.

Beside Ellie, Jiao bounced up and down, saying something that sounded sort of like "cracker." Ellie smiled, then placed another animal cracker in Jiao's palm, keeping an eye on her daughter while the toddler ate the treat. "How did you know where I'd be?"

"The women at the office are always talking about you and your daughter. They fell in love with her, I think."

Ellie grinned and chucked Jiao gently under the chin. "That's easy to do."

"Anyway, they said you come here almost every day."

"Jiao loves to be outside. I think it's because she was inside for so many months at the orphanage. So we try to make it here every morning." Ellie gave her daughter a tender glance, then turned back to Finn. "Why were you looking for me? Is there something going on at the office we need to talk about? Because really, Larry is your go-to guy on the commercial side, now that I'm handling residential."

It stung that she thought the only reason he would seek her out was because of work. But then again, when had he ever made it about the personal? He'd always retreated behind the facade of the job. "I wanted to see how you were doing."

"We're fine. I should be back at work next week, but just part-time. Heading up the new division."

He'd heard all about Ellie's move into the housing sector from her father. He'd spent a lot of time talking to Henry Winston in the last few weeks, and found he liked Ellie's father a lot. He was becoming not just a friend to Finn, but also a sort of surrogate father. "I know."

"How are things going with the merger?"

"Pretty smooth. Your father had a phone conference meeting with all the employees to explain the changes. I think that helped set some minds at ease." They were still talking about business, and Finn knew he should reroute the conversation, but as always, he stayed in his comfort zone.

"How's the Piedmont project going?" Jiao, content with her cookie, climbed into Ellie's lap and laid her head on Ellie's shoulder. Ellie rubbed a circle of comfort onto Jiao's back. Finn watched, seeing the obvious love Ellie had for her new daughter. Jiao was clearly comfortable with Ellie, too, and snuggled against her adoptive mother as if they'd always been a family.

He started relating the details of the hospital project, all the while thinking that this was what they had become. Colleagues who worked at the same company. There was no hint of the woman he had been married to in her voice, no flirtation in her smile. It was just two co-workers having an ordinary conversation.

That was what Finn had said he wanted from the very beginning. How he had imagined things ending between them. They'd ally for the deal, work on the project, then split amicably and remain friends. But what he hadn't expected was how much that would hurt. He almost couldn't stand there and get the words out. Because he had fallen in love with her, and as much as he told himself he could be her colleague—

He couldn't. He wanted to be her husband, damn it.

He stopped midsentence and let out a sigh. "I can't do this."

"What?" Jiao had fallen asleep, and Ellie shifted to accommodate the additional weight.

"Stand here and talk about blueprints and city regulations as if there was never anything between us. As if we're practically strangers." Finn bent down, and searched for the woman he knew, but she was hidden behind those damnable sunglasses. "You took the coward's way out, Ellie."

"Me? How did I do that?"

"You didn't file for the annulment. Didn't call a lawyer. You just let us…dissolve."

"Finn, I have a child to raise. I can't be spending my time chasing—" She shook her head and looked away.

"Chasing what?"

She turned back to face him. The noise of the playground dropped away, and the world seemed to close in until it was just them. "Chasing something that will never be." Her voice shook a little. "We pretended really well for a while there, but both of us are too committed to other things to be committed to each other."

"Are you sure about that? Or is that just an excuse because you're just as afraid as I am of screwing this up?" Because he was afraid, scared as hell, to be honest. But the part of Finn that had been awakened by meeting Ellie refused to go away. And kept asking for more.

"I'm…" She let out a breath. "Okay, I am. But that's only because I have so much more at stake here." She nuzzled a kiss into Jiao's ebony hair. It fluttered like down against Ellie's cheek. "I can't take a chance that Jiao will be hurt again. She's already been through so much."

He'd said all this himself, hadn't he? Finn wanted to take the words back, to tell Ellie he was wrong. He understood Ellie's fear, because he'd felt it himself a hundred times before.

Was it fear, or was he trying to push for feelings she would never reciprocate? Was he repeating his past? "If you and I didn't work out—"

"You were right." She shrugged, but the movement was far from nonchalant. "She would be damaged. And I can't do that to her."

"But what about you, Ellie?"

"I'll be fine." But her voice shook again. "I am fine."

"Are you really?" He tried to search her gaze, but couldn't see past the dark lenses. What was going on inside her?

"Of course I'm fine." She cleared her throat, then got to her feet, hoisting Jiao onto her hip to free a hand to stuff their picnic things into the basket underneath.

She was leaving and he hadn't found the magic words to make her stay. "Ellie—"

"You know, Finn, you were right. I was afraid to fall in love. And so were you. It's a risk, maybe the biggest risk of all. But if you don't jump in with both feet, you'll never know what you were missing." She nuzzled her daughter's hair, and he saw the love bloom in Ellie's eyes. Then she bent down and buckled Jiao into the stroller. When she was done, she straightened and faced Finn with an impartial smile. "Anyway, I wanted to thank you for taking over the corporate side of WW. My father speaks highly of you."

"Is that what we're back to? Business only?"

She lifted her gaze to his and this time he could see the shimmer of tears behind her sunglasses. "When did we ever leave that, Finn?" Then she said goodbye to him, and left the park.

CHAPTER FOURTEEN

ELLIE told herself a hundred times that she had done the right thing by letting Finn go. That falling for him would only complicate things. Maybe he was right, maybe she was taking the coward's way out.

Okay, not maybe. Definitely.

She'd done one more cowardly thing after seeing him that day at the park—she'd contacted a lawyer of her own and put the annulment into motion. By now, Finn undoubtedly had received the legal papers from his lawyer. He hadn't called, hadn't stopped by, and her heart broke one last time. He hadn't been serious about them staying together—if he had, he would have fought the annulment. She'd been right not to risk her heart on him.

She dressed Jiao in a bright yellow sundress then strapped her into the stroller and set off down the sidewalk toward the park. The whole way, Jiao let out a steady stream of happy chatter, babbling in a jumbled mix of baby talk, Chinese and English. It was like music to Ellie's ears and she laughed along with her daughter. Jiao had adjusted pretty well to the changes in her life, and Ellie had great hopes for the future. Henry had been spoiling his new granddaughter mercilessly, with clothes and toys and visits.

"You wanna go to the park?" Ellie said, bending down to talk to Jiao.

Her daughter kicked her legs and waved her hands. "Yes, Momma. Yes!" Her English was improving every day. The little girl was bright and was picking up the second language quickly.

"Okay, let's go then." She pushed the stroller and increased her pace a little. "How about today I take you down the slide, and later we can go on the swings and—"

"Gou!" Jiao shouted, bouncing up and down. "Gou, Momma! Gou!"

Ellie's Chinese was minimal at best, and it took her a second to connect Jiao's enthusiastic words with the object of her attention. Across the street, a man was walking a little white poodle. Jiao kept pointing at it and shouting *"Gou!"* Ellie laughed. "That's a dog, honey. Dog."

"Dog," Jiao repeated. "Jiao dog?"

"No," Ellie said softly. "Not Jiao's dog."

"Jiao dog," her daughter repeated, reaching her fingers toward the white pooch, and Ellie pushed forward, putting more distance between them and the poodle. Jiao's voice trailed off in disappointment.

As Ellie walked, her mind went back to the day at the animal shelter with Finn. How he had opened up his heart, and let her see inside for just a little while. Every boy should have his dream, she had said. And so, too, should every girl.

Her dream had been the family in the two-story house. With all the laughter and the Thanksgiving dinners and the messes, and everything that came with that. She loved her daughter, loved her little home in the Back Bay, but a part of her still wondered—

What would it be like to have the kids and the house and the yard and the dog?

Had she made a mistake letting Finn go? Had she let her fears ruin her future happiness?

He had never left her mind, not really, though she had worked hard to forget him. She had come across the concert T-shirt the other day, and put it on, just because it reminded her of Finn. Then after a few minutes, she took it off and tucked it away in the back of her closet. Where she stored all the things that were memories now, not realities.

She'd buy a house in the suburbs and a dog, and have that dream herself. But the thought filled her with sadness.

If she did that, she'd be *content*. Maybe not ever truly happy.

Finn was right. She hadn't been brave enough to really push forward with this relationship when he'd offered her the chance. She'd backed off, so afraid of getting hurt again. She'd preached about risk, and not taken one herself.

She and Jiao rounded the corner and entered the park. Her daughter was practically bounding out of the stroller by the time Ellie stopped and unbuckled her. Jiao dashed over to the toddler-sized play area, complete with a rubber ground cover and a half dozen pint-sized puzzles and mazes for the little ones to play with. Jiao had already made friends at the park, and she toddled off with two other little girls she saw nearly every day. Ellie settled back on a bench and raised her face to the sun.

Something wet nuzzled her leg. Ellie jumped, let out a shriek, then looked down.

At the dark, moist snout of a Golden retriever. "Hey, you. What are you doing here?"

"Looking for you."

Finn's voice jerked Ellie's head up. "Finn." Then she

looked down at the dog again, and realized the retriever's leash was in Finn's hand. Her heart leaped at the sight of him and she knew that no piece of paper would ever make that stop. Damn. He still affected her. Maybe he always would. "Is this your dog?"

"Yup. Meet Heidi." Finn chuckled. "Wait. You already did."

She looked down again and realized it was, indeed, the dog from the shelter. "You...you adopted her?"

He nodded. "I did."

"Why? I mean, it's awesome, but I thought..."

"That I was the last person who would take on a dog?" He shrugged. "I am. Or I guess, I was. But something changed me recently."

She still couldn't believe she was seeing the shelter dog with Finn. He had gone back there, and given this puppy a home. It was one of the sweetest things she'd ever seen, and her heart melted all over again. "What changed you?"

He reached into his back pocket and pulled out a piece of paper. When he unfolded it, Ellie recognized it as the annulment agreement. Her heart sank. Had he signed it? Was it over?

"This came to my office the other day, and when I got it, it was like a slap across the face."

"Finn, I'm sorry, but we—"

"Let me finish. It hit me hard because I realized if I signed this, it was all over. I had lost you. Forever."

"You were right, though. I let this drag on, and I shouldn't have. Someone needed to pull the plug."

Finn bent down to her, his face level with hers, those blue eyes she loved so much capturing hers. Her heartbeat tripled, and she caught her breath. "Is this what you really want, Ellie?" His voice was low and quiet.

How she wanted to lie, wanted to just keep up the facade. All along, she'd been telling Finn to take a risk when she'd been the one too scared to do the same. She thought of the future that lay ahead. One where she was content, and never happy, and decided she didn't want that. Not anymore. "No." She shook her head and tears brimmed in her eyes. "I don't."

Finn reached up and cupped her jaw. Ellie leaned into that touch, craving it like oxygen. "Neither do I. Not one damned bit. You were so right about me. I picked Lucy because it was the practical decision, and told myself when it didn't work out, it was because love was too risky. But I was wrong. I never took that risk, Ellie. I never opened my heart. I made up this little list and tried to fit a relationship into a column, and then was surprised when it didn't work out." He ran a thumb along the line of her jaw, and caught her gaze. Held it. "Falling in love is risky. Riskier than anything I've ever done. So I came over here today because I couldn't let the most amazing woman I've ever met walk out of my life. Not without telling her one thing first."

"Tell her what?" It was the only word she could get out. Her breath caught in her throat, held, while she waited for his answer. Damn, this man had her heart. Maybe he always had.

Finn's smile curved across his face, higher on one side than the other, and filling her with a tentative joy. "I love you, Ellie. I fell in love with you the first time I saw you, but I didn't know it. I love the way you talk, I love the way you work, I love the way you smile. Every time I see you, I feel…happy."

Happy. Not content. "Oh, Finn—"

"Let me finish." He let out a long breath, and his gaze softened. "I've never been very good at relationships.

Give me a drafting board and a pencil and I can handle anything you throw my way. But when it comes to telling people how I feel…not exactly my strong suit. I guess it was because after my parents died, my little brothers looked to me for comfort. For answers. I couldn't break down and sob on their shoulders. I had to let them sob on mine. And as they got older, I kept on being the rock they stood on."

"They do. I can tell by the way they talk about you. They respect and admire you a lot."

He grinned a little at that, clearly surprised to hear his brothers speak so well of him. "Being a rock came with a price, though. I never wanted to rely on anyone, to be vulnerable to anyone, and most of all, I didn't want to let anyone down. Or take that risk you kept asking me to take." His fingers tangled in her hair and Ellie let out a little sigh. "I told myself I'd keep my heart out of it and then we could walk away and no one would be hurt. But that plan failed."

Across from Ellie, Jiao was standing at the edge of the toddler playground, watching them. Ellie sent her daughter a little wave. "How did your plan fail?"

"My heart got involved the very first day, even if I didn't want to admit it to myself or to you. And still, I wouldn't take that risk." His smile widened. "But then when I got the papers dissolving our marriage, I realized all I want to do is stay married to you, Ellie. Forever. I want to open my heart. I want to jump off that marriage cliff with you and trust that it's all going to work out for the next fifty, hell, hundred years. I want—" his gaze went to Jiao, and the smile grew a little more "—us to be a family. The question is whether you do, too. You took a risk adopting a little girl from halfway around the world. I'm asking you to take a risk and fall in love with me."

She looked into his eyes, and felt the fear that she had clutched so tightly for so long begin to dissolve. Right here was everything she'd ever wanted. All she had to do was reach out and take it. She could tell him no now and watch him walk away.

And regret it forever. She'd been given a second chance. She'd be a fool to throw it away.

So she took a deep breath, then tugged the annulment papers out of his hand and ripped them in two. "I don't want an annulment, Finn. Not now, not later."

She caught the glint of a gold band on his left hand. He'd never taken it off. And her cautious heart finally let go of the last guardrails and trusted. Her husband. The man she loved.

"I don't, either," Finn said then he drew her into his arms and kissed her, a tender, sweet kiss, the kind that would stay in her memory forever. She felt treasured and loved and...like a wife. "I love you, Ellie."

"I love you, too, Finn." She ran a hand through his hair and stared deep into his sky-blue eyes. How she knew those eyes, knew every inch of his face, every line in his brow. "I love you *because* you are the Hawk."

"The man who swoops in and buys up the competition?" He scowled.

She shook her head. "No. That's not what I mean. I looked up hawks one day when I took Jiao to the library. And yes, they're fierce predators, but they're also fiercely loyal and protective. They pick a mate and a nest and they stay there for life." She looked at Finn McKenna and saw the hawk inside of him, a man who would do anything for those he loved—he'd been doing it with his brothers ever since he was a child and he had done it for her simply because she had asked. He was a hawk—a man she could depend upon forever.

"So I should start to like the Hawk nickname, huh?" He grinned.

"Maybe you should." She smiled, then pressed a kiss to his lips. She thought of how close she had come to ending their relationship with a piece of paper. "I was so afraid to believe that you could be the kind of man I could depend on, count on to be there when I needed you. I never realized that the very traits I admired about you were the same ones that make you the perfect man for me. The perfect husband, and perfect father, if you want to be."

His gaze traveled to Jiao, and she saw his features soften as a smile curved across his face. "I want to be the kind of dad who pulls out pictures of my kid's band performance at a meeting and who hangs up their artwork in my office. I don't want to be content, Ellie." He swiveled back to face her. "Not anymore."

"Neither do I, Finn. Neither do I." She held his gaze for a long moment, then put out an arm, and waved over Jiao. "Then let me introduce you to your daughter."

Jiao hurried across the playground to Ellie's side. But when she saw the stranger, she hung back, biting her bottom lip, and giving Finn tentative, shy glances. "Jiao, I want you to meet Finn," Ellie said. "And Heidi the dog."

Jiao wiggled two fingers at Finn, then dropped back a little more. Her head popped up when she noticed the dog. Jiao looked at Ellie with a question in her eyes. "Dog?"

Ellie nodded. "Jiao's dog."

The little girl's eyes widened. She pointed at Heidi, then back at herself. "Jiao dog?"

"Yes," Finn said. He gave the leash a light tug, and Heidi scrambled to her feet, then pushed her furry head against Jiao's shoulder. The little girl laughed, exuberance bursting on Jiao's face. Heidi licked her face, tail wagging like a flag in the wind.

"Heidi, Jiao dog," the little girl said softly, happily. "Jiao dog!"

Then Jiao paused and took a step back, looking up at the man who was, essentially a stranger to her. "Momma?"

Ellie bent to her daughter's level, and waited until Finn did the same. "This is Finn," she said to Jiao. "He's your dad."

Jiao plopped a thumb into her mouth and hung back, studying Finn from under the veil of her lashes.

Finn put out his hand. "Hello, Jiao. It's nice to meet you."

Jiao paused a long moment, looking up at Ellie, then over at Finn. Her eyes were wide, wondering about this new development in her life. The little girl who had left China with nothing suddenly had a mother, a father, a dog. Ellie nodded. "It's okay," Ellie said.

Still, Jiao hesitated. The thumb wavered in her mouth.

"How about we start with Jiao dog?" Finn asked the little girl. "Would you like that?"

After a moment, Jiao nodded and gave Finn a shy smile. "Okay."

Finn ran his hand over Heidi's neck, and Jiao's smaller hand joined his. The two of them petted the patient dog for a long time, not saying a word, just bonding one second at a time while Heidi panted softly. Then Jiao shifted and stood closer to Finn. She looked up into his face. "Jiao…dad?"

"Yes." Finn nodded then met Ellie's gaze. Tears of joy glimmered in his eyes. "Yes, I'm Jiao's dad. And Ellie's husband."

"You are indeed," Ellie whispered, thanking the stars above for this amazing gift. "For real."

Then Finn reached out both his arms and drew all his girls into one great big hug. And on a sunny playground in the middle of Boston, a family was born. They laughed, and the dog barked, and the sounds of their happiness rang in the air, telling Finn and Ellie that from now on, the floors of their home would never echo again.

* * * * *